An Absence of Faith

A Tale of Afghanistan

Craig Trebilcock

BookLocker
Trenton, Georgia

Copyright © 2024 Craig Trebilcock

Print ISBN: 978-1-958892-43-5
Ebook ISBN: 979-8-88531-710-8

All rights reserved. No part of this publication may be reproduced, stored in a retrieval system, or transmitted in any form or by any means, electronic, mechanical, recording or otherwise, without the prior written permission of the author.

Published by BookLocker.com, Inc., Trenton, Georgia.

This is a novel, inspired by real world events. Characters, conversations, and incidents presented are either the product of the author's imagination or are used fictitiously. If the name of a public figure or event is mentioned to provide historical context for the Afghanistan War, any dialogue or actions are purely fictional. Historical events that did occur during the Afghanistan War, such as the bombing of the Doctors Without Borders Hospital in Kunduz, are taken out of their historical timeline, for purposes of illustrating the story. The issues of widespread corruption during the Afghanistan War are well-documented, but the characters created to illustrate those issues here are fictional. Any resemblance to actual persons, living or dead, or their actions, is entirely coincidental.

Library of Congress Cataloging in Publication Data
Trebilcock, Craig
An Absence of Faith: A Tale of Afghanistan by Craig Trebilcock
Library of Congress Control Number: 2024908145

Incoming Writers, LLC
2024

Dedication

For those who dreamed of a better future.

OTHER BOOKS BY THE AUTHOR

One Weekend A Month

No Time for Ribbons

For more information on the author and his books, visit www.soldierauthor.com

Acknowledgments

Many thanks to those inspirational individuals without whom this story would never have been told: the staffs of EF3 and EF2 of Headquarters, Resolute Support, who faced danger in Afghanistan every day to combat corruption with a selfless commitment to duty and a not misplaced sense of gallows humor.

Special thanks to Ms. Josie Stewart; Lieutenant Colonel Chad Brooks, USMC; Mr. Charles Hyacinthe; Michael Hartmann, Esq., and Hamid. Each of whom, through their service, gave hope to a people denied it by their own government.

I am very grateful to those who gave their time to help proofread and edit this work. These include Lieutenant Colonel Mark Kimmey, USA (Retired); Terrie Trebilcock; Ms. Josie Stewart; Ms. Nancy Stewart; and Mr. John Hargreaves. It is always humbling to see how others can make one's own scribbling so much cleaner and dynamic, helping a collection of interesting but disparate ideas evolve into a book that one hopes is worth reading. Thank you.

Finally, special recognition to my wife, Terrie Trebilcock, who has been my rock during numerous overseas deployments and provided the same unwavering support as I attempted to translate the insanity of war onto paper. I couldn't have done any of it without you.

Introduction

Why did Afghanistan fall so quickly in August 2021? How did a bitter twenty-year internal war in which the United States and its NATO[1] allies committed to defeating a terrorist insurgency, come to a sudden, muted end in a matter of weeks? These are questions that have been skirted by Western government leaders as either an unanswerable mystery or dismissed as a historical inevitability not warranting closer scrutiny. They are neither.

The seeds of defeat were planted soon after America and its allies removed the Taliban from power in late 2001 and gave the new Afghan government unfettered rein. As this tale begins, it is helpful to know, "who were these players?" The Taliban is a militant organization founded on pro-Pashtun[2] nationalist and Islamic fundamentalist principles. Their roots are in Pakistan and the southern Afghan Province of Kandahar. They ruled Afghanistan from 1996 through 2001, until forcibly removed for their complicity in hosting Al Qaeda during the September 11, 2001, attacks on the United States. Prior to Taliban rule, Afghanistan had been torn apart by the Soviet invasion of 1979 and an ongoing civil war that left the country politically, economically, and militarily broken. The defeat of the Soviet military put dynamics into action that ultimately brought the Taliban to power.

Whether one measures the misery of life for the average Afghan against conditions before or after the Soviet invasion in 1979, the landlocked country had become a failed state by 2001. There was little economic growth, and even less opportunity. Public floggings,

---

[1] NATO – North Atlantic Treaty Organization. The U.S. military mission in Afghanistan was a NATO mission pursuant to the collective defense provision of Article 5 of the NATO Treaty, which provides an attack upon any member State is an attack upon all members. Article 5 was invoked for the first time in the treaty organization's history following the attacks on the U.S. by Al Qaeda on September 11, 2001, bringing many European and Canadian troops, among others, to fight in the war.

[2] The Pashtun are one of the major tribes of Afghanistan, located in the south of the country.

amputations, and executions were carried out by the Taliban for perceived moral offenses and minor crimes, reminiscent of medieval justice. Women were property. Crucifixion was an option for serious offenses.

Post-9/11 Western aid was intended to help the Afghan people lift themselves above a life where they did not have access to sufficient food or medicine, where half the nation's population was not allowed education, and "justice" was merely a tool wielded by the strong to impose their will upon the weak. In 2001, Afghanistan was one of two nations where polio and the plague still existed. Its history of instability and lack of meaningful governance made it a perfect haven for destabilizing groups such as Al Qaeda to plan and execute operations against the West.

The policy vision adopted by the intervening Western powers after September 11, 2001, was based on the belief that by providing funding to the fledgling, post-Taliban government—the Government of the Islamic Republic of Afghanistan (GIRoA)—it would gain legitimacy in the eyes of the Afghan people. The theory was that a well-resourced government would work to revitalize the economy and address equitable and quality of life issues across the board. These achievements would stabilize the region, extremist elements would retreat, and U.S. and NATO troops could withdraw.

Between the Taliban's incompetent rule and the destruction wrought by Afghanistan's chronic internal wars, there were few functioning services or government offices operating when the NATO allies intervened militarily in 2001. In this near-vacuum, hopes grew that by rebuilding a government with Western guidance and investment, Afghanistan would no longer be a viable haven from which terrorists could attack America. Unfortunately, the Western nations had little understanding of the culture or traditions of the country that they sought to protect and mentor.

NATO allies poured billions in poorly-monitored funds and military aid into the hands of Afghanistan's politicians who had strong traditions of buying loyalty—*patronage networks*—and little interest in the concept of rule of law. Instead of promoting stability, Western money super-charged what became an Afghan government kleptocracy, as a society with little prior ability to sustain itself was suddenly awash with billions in unregulated cash and materiel.

Afghanistan cannot be solely blamed for the corruption that flourished. Basic accountability principles were often secondary to the West's geopolitical imperative of exacting retribution on Osama bin Laden and his Al Qaeda operatives for the harm caused to the American people. By the time bin Laden was killed in a 2011 U.S. raid in Pakistan, Afghan government malfeasance was solidly entrenched, including the inflation of military payrolls with "ghost soldiers," whose salaries were paid for by the U.S., but who did not exist. These surplus salaries padded Afghan generals' and politicians' personal accounts. Yet, the West continued to push more money into the Afghan government every year, paying 80% of the nation's annual budget without linkage to any required reform. Diversion of NATO military equipment and supplies for personal use and sale, accompanied by *de facto* immunity from stealing, became standard conduct by Afghan officials in positions of power, not an exception.

Initially, NATO took the lead in conducting combat operations against the Taliban. By 2011, there were over 100,000 American troops on the ground, many engaged in direct combat. After the death of bin Laden, U.S. political interest in the war waned, and responsibility for fighting the Taliban was transitioned to Afghan government security forces in 2014. By 2015-16, the time of this story, American troop presence was down to 8,500 personnel, primarily engaged in training, advising, and assisting (supplying) the Afghan military.

There is no spoiler-alert needed here about the Afghanistan War's end. The defeat was trumpeted across the headlines of international newspapers, as Afghan soldiers chose not to defend a government they did not believe in, and the Taliban walked back into Kabul, virtually unopposed. But the story of *why* that happened and how it happened has not been given adequate attention. Nor have the behind-the-scenes efforts that came close to saving Afghanistan yet been told. The courage and selflessness of Afghans who did not give up their fight for dignity and justice still needs to be preserved and recognized. For it is likely that the final chapter in Afghanistan's long and painful political evolution has yet to be written.

The Afghanistan War is presented in this tale through the eyes of two protagonists, an Afghan army private and a U.S. Army colonel. Their experiences reveal how the war described by Western political leaders, and the war experienced by Afghan and NATO soldiers, were terribly different. So different, that U.S. forces considered their Afghan army allies to be a greater threat than the Taliban by the time the war staggered to a close, and Afghan soldiers despised their own superiors more than the enemy forces.

One can reasonably ask, how does an uncoordinated force of insurgents stroll back into power in Kabul when the world's strongest superpower has spent over a trillion dollars, thousands of lives, and two decades to defeat them? Surprisingly, military might isn't required.

All it takes is an absence of faith.

Conventions

There are several conventions applied throughout this book that may be new to the reader. Some reflect the peculiarities of Afghanistan and military culture, for which the following explanations may be useful.

A person from Afghanistan is referred to as an Afghan. An Afghani (abbr. Af or Afs) is the unit of currency used in the country, not a person. Afghans are often given one name at birth, such as "Azir," as opposed to the Western tradition of a given and a family name, such as "Azir Smith." This can and does vary, of course, but many of the characters in this book simply have one name in keeping with this cultural practice.

Afghanistan is a country defined by tribal divisions and loyalties, as well as corresponding language differences. The national language is Dari, a close relative of Iranian Farsi. But simply because Dari is the official language does not mean everyone speaks it. The farther one gets from Kabul, the more dominant are tribal and regional languages such as Pashto, Turkmen, and Urdu. There are at least twelve languages spoken, and using one immediately labels you with positive or negative attributes in the mind of the listener.

Regarding spoken language, U.S. soldiers in a combat zone are a salty-tongued bunch. About every fifth word is some colorful profanity. While using such language in a book might be historically accurate, it can get in the way of telling a story. So, in this story there is profanity, in keeping with the tone of a military environment, but it is greatly toned down for readability's sake.

This is a book about soldiers, so there are many ranks and titles used. For those interested, a chart of U.S. and Afghan military ranks is provided in an Appendix at the back.

References are made throughout the book to "GIRoA," which is the formal name of the Afghan government in existence between 2004 until its collapse in August 2021: the *Government of the Islamic Republic of Afghanistan*. The Afghanistan War was essentially a civil war between two groups claiming to be the legitimate leaders of the country. The side supported by the U.S. and NATO was GIRoA, first led by President Hamid Karzai and then in 2014 by President Ashraf Ghani. The opposing side was the Taliban. After 2001, the Taliban dispersed into Pakistan and the mountains of Afghanistan where they maintained a shadow government of governors, judges, and officials who awaited their return to power for twenty years. As using nebulous terms such as *Afghan leaders* might cause confusion as to which side is being discussed, depending on one's perspective, the U.S. backed Afghan government is referred to throughout the book as "GIRoA" or "Afghan politicians," while the Taliban is called "Taliban," or "the insurgents."

Different U.S. federal agencies often pursued independent policies from each other in Afghanistan. What the White House and Congress wanted to occur in Afghanistan was frequently nebulous and shifted repeatedly over twenty years. During times when these political branches were silent, the war continued, and officials at the Departments of Defense (DOD) and State (DOS) were still busy with daily military and political initiatives that couldn't wait for Washington's reticence. In the absence of coherent direction from the top, decisions by these agencies often conflicted. Such discord was tolerated, as part of an ongoing political calculation that not taking a strong position on major policy issues, such as rampant GIRoA corruption, gave Washington politicians the best chance to avoid ownership of potentially negative political consequences. As such, this story will posit that some of the greatest battles in Afghanistan were not with the Taliban, but rather between DOD and DOS. Against such a background, meaningless terms such as "U.S. policy" will be avoided.

Finally, this book does not present the role of those mission-essential personnel who made interaction with the Afghan government possible–the Afghan translators. For the sake of readability and story flow, the fact that most communications with Afghan officials were done through Afghan translators contracted by the U.S. Government is omitted. That was a literary necessity, only, for if conversations in this story were said by one character and then repeated through a translator character, the text would become laborious. But in the theater of operations, translators were critical to clear and effective communications. These cultural and language experts shared all the dangers of NATO and U.S. troops, and when

Afghanistan fell, they and their families suffered reprisals from the Taliban. Many were abandoned during the hasty U.S. withdrawal. The United States and the people of Afghanistan owe them a great debt.

We hang the petty thieves and appoint the great ones to public office.

– Aesop

The events we're seeing now are sadly proof that no amount of military force would ever deliver a stable, united, and secure Afghanistan—as known in history as the "graveyard of empires."

– Statement of President Biden, August 16, 2021, as Kabul fell.

Map of Afghanistan

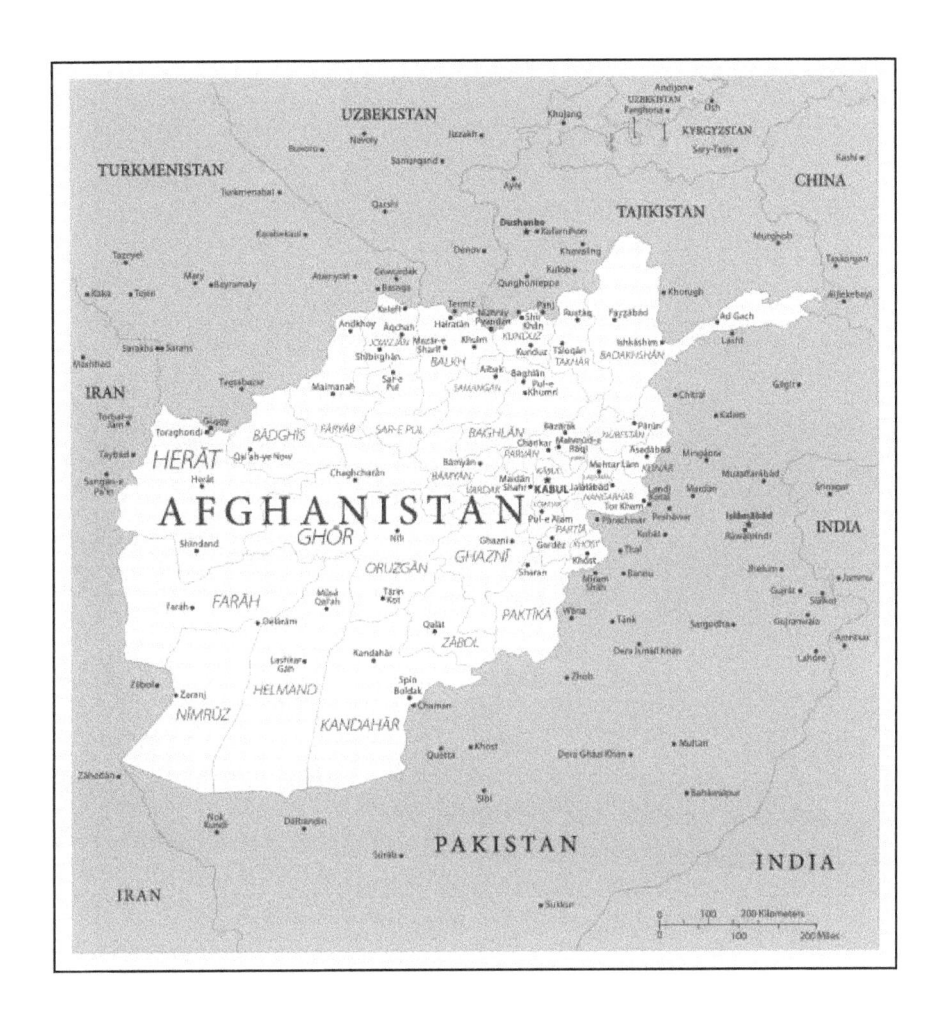

Chapter 1

Kabul, Afghanistan, August 2021

"Why are they leaving?" asked the boy.

No answer.

The wind swirled across the mountain face, mimicking the helicopters below. Dawn had come to Kabul, but the sun had yet to climb above the peaks surrounding the city. The capital lay shadowed in the bottom of a granite bowl, embraced by the arms of the Hindu Kush. The mountains had many times witnessed the world's greatest armies broken and retreating through their merciless passes. The chaos at the airport this morning was another fleeting moment in their history.

The boy repeated, "Why..."

Below him, the man sheltering behind the boulder sighed. He didn't look up from the weapon he was cleaning. "They have forgotten why they came, so now they leave," he answered wearily. His one good eye peered from a weathered face, scanning to ensure all the small pieces from the rifle still lay on the rock. His aging legs were stiff from their climb last night and he was in no mood for idle talk. This new weapon, an American rifle, which Hajji Khan had given him, was unfamiliar. A puzzle. As such, it was worthy of his complete attention. It would not do to lose a piece in the rocks of their hiding place. He preferred his old Kalashnikov—its few, well-worn parts, the smooth feel of its wooden stock against his cheek—but there was now unending American ammunition from the collapse of the army, so he had accepted the new weapon with gratitude. *So many pieces,* he mused. *The infidels like to make things complicated.*

"Why did they come?" the boy asked, looking down from his perch atop the boulder to watch the man in the black eye patch push a tiny pin into a shiny metal tube.

"We have forgotten too," the man replied, gratified when the pin clicked into place, despite his lack of depth perception. The morning was already warm. A trickle of sweat ran between his shoulders. "Watch your position, donkey," he snapped, noting the boy's concentration wandering from the military airfield below. "We are to count aircraft and soldiers, not to chatter like women."

The two had spent several hours the night before scrambling across the broken hillside to gain this position above the airport. From below their hideout was invisible. On neighboring hills, the Afghan National Army had abandoned its outposts the week before. Should a helicopter come near, a hollow at the base of the large boulder provided concealment. *This is a good position,* he convinced himself. *Unless we're spotted,* he allowed his soldier's fatalism to creep in, *in which case we're dead.*

The boy shrugged, turning back to his task. He was careful to adjust the dark cloth atop his head, concealing his outline from enemies below who might be scanning the rocks. *It is impossible to count all of the small aircraft with the whirling blades,* he thought. *They come and go so quickly.* He was sure he had counted several of them twice already, as they buzzed angrily in circles about the airfield's walls, trying to keep the desperate civilians back. The big gray planes were easy. They were slow and when they took off the earth shook.

Despite his admonishment to the boy, the man let his own thoughts drift, as he continued to reassemble the weapon. Why did they come? It was a good question. Why do they all come when the treasures of this land are blood and rock? The Americans came because those fools from Saudi Arabia destroyed their buildings. But the others from the north came in my father's time as well, with their tanks and killer helicopters. Their armored vehicles still lay rusting at the end of the runway below, he observed. The remnants had been dumped there when the Shuravi[3] had declared victory before fleeing north.

The red jackets came in my father's grandfather's time, he recalled. Through Khyber. Then, it was horses, cannons, and swords. They thought we were weak. Savages. They learned this is death's

---

[3] Dari for Soviets or Soviet soldiers.

garden. The outcome is always the same—broken armies praying to escape—only the uniforms change. These latest ones from America came first with bombs and then tried sweet words. They would teach us how to live better. How to be like them. They shook the earth and blackened the sky with their kindness. Not like the ones when my father was young. There were no sweet words then. Obey or die. Perhaps they were more honest, he considered. They told you they were going to kill you and did it. These, these new ones, promise you peace, then they kill you anyway.

His memories carried him back to his home—the last place he had been truly happy. He remembered his mother making their evening meal over the fire. When he pestered her about when the food would be done, she would smack him lightly with her wooden spoon. "Get out of my kitchen, Muhammad," she teased with a twinkle in her eye, as she squatted by the fire in their back yard. She had seen a picture of a kitchen in a magazine once and had adopted the strange word. There was the joyful face of his younger brother, Tamir, the last time he had seen him. The night before the wedding. His brother had been so happy and nervous—his entire life still before him. "What do I do with a woman as beautiful as Hadiya?" he had asked his older brother, as they climbed the rocky slope outside their village in Ghazni province.

"If you do not know yet, I have failed as a brother," Muhammad laughed, as they approached a grove of gnarled apricot trees clinging to the hillside. *These trees were old when my father was a boy,* the older brother reflected, *and soon my brother's sons will play beneath them.*

Their gathering was a modest one. The evening cooled as several other pairs of young men climbed the worn path to the orchard. Their village was a collection of several dozen mud homes scattered along a now abandoned trade route. It had once held importance as a caravan resting place, but now, if a truck came through once a week, it was big news. Muhammad, the bridegroom Tamir, and six of their childhood friends, were joining together one last time before the wedding to choose a sheep for the feast, and to sneak a drink of fermented peach juice away from the eyes of their village elders.

Each of them had spent many hours of their childhood in the shade beneath these trees, watching the animals of the village, serving as guardians against wild dogs and thieves from other villages. Now they were men, about to take their place as leaders in the community. Only their friend, Khalid, still lacked facial hair, a fact about which the others mercilessly taunted him. "Perhaps we can trim some wool from the ass of this sheep," Muhammad teased him, "to glue to your face with honey." Khalid replied with the obligatory obscene gesture that inspired laughter amongst the group who had spent their youth listening to Khalid and Muhammed bicker.

The distant buzz of a passing aircraft did not even cause them to raise their eyes. Theirs was an area over which the Afghan air force's new A-29 Tocano aircraft frequently passed en route to Taliban targets further south. It was mere background noise to their daily lives, unimportant to those carving out a subsistence life in the rocky foothills. The active fighting was currently many days away. The war had left them alone thus far to eke out an existence not different from generations past. *Insh'allah.*

Above their gathering, the Afghan air force pilot, Major Tamaki, was having a bad day. Assigned to respond to an enemy ground attack upon a "critical supply intersection," he had found the position deserted. He surveyed the area, circling ever lower in the propeller driven aircraft. The Tocano was designed for operations in the thin air of the mountains and was a symbol of growing military credibility to Afghanistan's enemies, both internal and external.

Today's mission was not going well, however. There was no enemy. No friendly forces. A wall of sandbags sat along a dirt road cutting through an empty patch of desert scrub. The road was controlled by a boom barrier, next to an empty flagpole. A makeshift wood hut completed the outpost. Abandoned. *I'm burning hundreds of liters in fuel, for what?* the major asked himself. He gestured to his wingman flying in a second Tocano that their mission was a bust.

The major knew what had happened without having seen it. It was now a weekly occurrence. Two or three Taliban likely fired on the government checkpoint from the relative safety of the rocks. The outpost was probably manned by a half-dozen paramilitary police. The police transmitted to their higher headquarters that they were fighting against overwhelming odds and then ran... or drove if there was an officer present... down the road, abandoning their post and its contents. Within minutes, the building had been picked clean of food, water, weapons, medical supplies, and anything else valuable to the insurgents. *To cover their cowardice, it's then relayed to my operations center that this junction is under a major enemy attack, and here I am, flying above...nothing.*

The Interior Ministry's paramilitary forces claimed to operate checkpoints on highly trafficked routes to interdict Taliban supplies, but in fact did so as a vast extortion network, demanding bribes from passing civilians. Despite receiving hundreds of millions in aid dollars from the United States, the paramilitary forces had little interest in becoming effective regional militias, actively combatting the Taliban. Theirs was a money-making operation, and revenue did not improve through firefights with the Taliban. Any local unwise enough to travel along a road controlled by the Ministry of Interior could expect to be detained and threatened until they paid a "toll" that went directly into the pockets of the police. To avoid such expensive humiliation, the locals preferred side routes through rougher terrain controlled by the Taliban, which was both safer and cheaper.

Major Tamaki knew this history and was not surprised to find a peaceful scene upon arrival over the target area. He radioed negative enemy contact to the air operations center located at Hamid Karzai International Airport in Kabul. As often occurred when one mission aborted, Major Tamaki was diverted to a secondary target—suspected enemy caves near the Pakistani border. The fledgling Afghan air force had four Tocano aircraft to cover a territory roughly the size of the East Coast of the U.S., so every flight hour was precious.

The top priority for the Afghan Ministry of Defense was to convince their American sponsors to provide more planes, so returning from any mission without positive results was not an option. *"Metrics"—that was the funny word that the Americans loved so much,* Tamaki recalled. *As long as numbers on a page claimed that something was true, the Americans believed it. Afghans know all numbers lie—only that which you can see and touch and taste is real. The Americans are so naïve in that way,* Tamaki marveled, *it is remarkable they are so powerful.*

The operations officer transmitted a set of target coordinates the major instantly knew made no sense, as they identified a valley several dozen kilometers inside Pakistan. *They'd blame me for that mistake, and later deny giving the bad coordinates.* Tamaki responded to operations, "Karzai Three, perhaps we should refrain from bombing Pakistan today? Over." There was radio silence, as he imagined the operations team scrambling to re-check their coordinates under the watchful eye of an American advisor.

A different voice soon came on the frequency to transmit new coordinates to Tamaki and his wingman. *That is Captain Noyan*, the pilot recognized. *He is Hazara[4]—a reliable man—not like those Tajiks[5] running the squadron.* "Acknowledged. Will comply, over." Tamaki responded. The new target was ten kilometers inside the Afghanistan border, along a smuggling route frequently used by the Taliban. *Near*, but not in Pakistan. He would have to fly a tight pattern to not violate the border and excite the Mirage fighters flown by their despised neighbor.

After several minutes at maximum air speed, Major Tamaki approached the new coordinates. At twelve hundred meters over an austere land of sharp ridge lines and plunging desert valleys, barren to the eye except for wild goats and scrub brush, Tamaki saw no caves. He had known he would not. If they existed, they would be well camouflaged. Faint foot trails, mere scratches on the earth, were the only evidence of human presence. The major knew the enemy was likely watching him from below, but the war had not dragged on for fifteen years by the Taliban being foolish enough to reveal themselves to overhead aircraft.

Standing orders from his squadron commander were for pilots to drop their bomb load before returning to base, even when they did not see enemy activity. Dropping bombs ensured positive reports back to Washington and kept the flow of money and supplies open: the Americans assumed a dropped bomb reflected success against the enemy. Enemy casualty figures were always suspect, if not

---

[4] The Hazara are a major tribe of central Afghanistan who are frequently a target of ethnic discrimination.

[5] Tajiks are the second largest ethnic tribal group in Afghanistan, after the Pashtuns. Tribal favoritism and prejudice played a significant role in personnel advancement and inefficiency in the Afghan security forces.

outright fiction, but the dropping of a bomb was a quantifiable event the Americans could add to the situation reports as evidence of operational success. *Metrics.*

But the major had grown weary of such games. *Too many years and too much death have haunted my country to play these paper games,* he had decided. "We will not bring peace to our people by moving some rocks," he had argued to his commander when told of the new order.

"You will do as ordered, major," the commander hissed, "or I will find someone whose loyalty is not in question.*" The man's smugness was all the more galling,* Tamaki thought, *as he gained his command only by being a cousin of the defense minister.*

Shaking off the memory, the major ground his teeth, as he scanned the empty terrain. It's impossible to make out any trace of a cave in this area. This is all a game because the Americans are watching today. I'm through killing goats, he resolved, before radioing "negative contact," a second time to the operations center. There was no response for several moments. "Return to base," came the clipped response. With the American Air Force officer present in the tower, operations could not order him to dump his bomb load.

"Returning to base," Tamaki radioed his reply.

*"*The Shah won't like it," warned his wing man, invoking the derogatory name they used for the squadron leader over their private channel. Tamaki ignored the comment and increased speed to gain altitude, his aircraft carving a broad arc back toward Kabul. *He's right. The colonel will no doubt call my dedication into question again,* he thought bitterly. *He hates me because my family is Hazara.* Tamaki felt anger building in his gut. *He doesn't think I deserve to fly in his squadron. Let that fat fool fly these missions. He wouldn't last a day.* Minutes blurred as Tamaki stewed in the unfairness of his situation. He was cornered into either being a liar or sacked for being disloyal. His mood sank as he pondered, *what will my family do if I lose my flight slot? We need the money.*

The clouds were turning orange and purple as the sun dipped toward the horizon. Nearby peaks were casting long shadows across the terrain as the countryside embraced the coming evening. The drone of his engine lulled the major into a trance, as he had little to do until he neared Kabul.

Tracer fire on a hill to his left, barely visible below his wing, brought Tamaki out of his reverie. Bright sparks stuttered across the blue-gray shadows of the ravines. *Had he imagined it? No.* A second weapon joined—no mistake—a reddish flash distinct near a small cluster of buildings stretching along a roadside.

In the ancient apricot grove below, Muhammad admonished his companions. "Do not waste your ammunition in celebratory fire yet, my friends. He has to bag his prey before the hunt is over, and he is so ugly that she may well come to her senses before the deed is done." The group cackled in appreciation at the insult, the skin of forbidden alcohol passing quickly between the men. Muhammad sat down at the base of his favorite tree. "Maybe she…" Muhammed began another joke, choking on the rough liquor, as Khalid let loose another burst of fire into the air.

The evening erupted into searing light and shattering blast as a high explosive bomb struck ten meters up the slope from the young men. Death was immediate, as brains liquified and steel splinters twisted joints apart, sculpting the remnants into unnatural heaps of burnt flesh. Only Muhammad, who fortune had placed against the far side of the ancient tree, was the unfortunate survivor. His tortured screams eventually brought the villagers out of the holes into which they fled when the bomb struck. His uncle found Muhammad pinned under a large branch with both arms and legs broken, his crushed left eye dangling from its socket. Burns, already swollen, covered his face and hands. A village elder stuffed a dirty rag into Muhammad's mouth to muffle his screams, as several older men worked to lift the branch. Tamir and his friends were a dark smear across the face of the slope, indistinguishable one from another.

"Karzai Three" the Major transmitted, working to keep his voice devoid of emotion, "Tocano One reporting enemy contact." He paused to slow his breathing from the adrenalin. "Direct hit on enemy ground formation seeking to infiltrate critical village intersection. Estimate twelve enemy KIA. Grid to follow…" *There will be no lecture from the colonel tonight,* Tamaki smiled to himself, *and the Americans will be pleased.*

◇ ◇ ◇

"Look!" the boy's excited voice snapped him out of his memories. The horror of the grove receded. Muhammad was back above the airfield. Somehow the American rifle had reassembled itself. "One of their helicopters has crashed at the edge of the airfield," the boy exclaimed. "It's on fire." The faint sound of sirens echoed in confirmation.

"Good," Muhammad whispered, quickly wiping his one good eye with a shaking hand before the boy could notice. "Let them all die."

Chapter 2

Lashkar Gah, Helmand Province, August 2015

Azir staggered back from the pit toilet behind the outpost. The desert heat made his knees liquid. He was barely able to hold his thin frame upright. A groan escaped his lips as he dropped into the hole he shared with his friend Daniyal along the airfield's perimeter. A thin strip of camouflage netting, supported by four rusty poles, was their only protection from the hammering southern Afghanistan sun.

"You look like death," Daniyal commented soberly, as Azir pressed back against the cool dirt sides of their outpost. There was no color in his friend's face. Azir's eyes were closed above sharp cheekbones accenting hollow cheeks.

"I can't keep anything down," Azir said, licking his dry lips. "And anything I do keep down goes right through me."

"You should go on sick call," Daniyal offered.

Azir snorted. "You know how that goes. You wait three or four hours to see a pretend doctor who accuses you of malingering."

"And if you convince him that you are sick, he tells you there is no medicine because the convoys can't get through," Daniyal continued, regretting he had even suggested the idea.

"And, when you return to duty, the sergeant gives you extra duties for setting a bad example," Azir continued in a sing-song monotone, as if reciting an overread script.

Daniyal stared over the small pile of sandbags surrounding the hole they occupied. Their position was thirty meters inside the perimeter of the army camp occupied by the 225th Corps headquarters, the backbone of operations against the Taliban in Helmand Province. This area had been the focus of the war since 2002, as first the U.S. Marines, then the British, and more recently a rotating dance card of NATO countries had tried to eliminate the Taliban. Yet their efforts were like trying to squeeze a balloon.

Pressure at one point made enemy activity increase elsewhere. The Afghan army had taken over the southern campaign from the Americans in 2014. Now the Afghan soldiers were to lead the fight against the insurgents, supported by money and supplies from a much-reduced NATO headquarters in Kabul.

A haphazard collection of crumbling walls, razor wire, and rusted chicken wire comprised the perimeter this far out along the runway. In some places the barrier was defined more by its holes than its fence. The barrier was supplemented in this area guarded by Azir and Daniyal by the crumbling walls of a long unused building. Romanian troops, who had temporarily occupied this same post a decade ago, had found it easier to simply build the decrepit structure into their defensive scheme than to tear it down.

Daniyal spotted a black and white bird sitting on the wall of the ruin looking at him. It cocked its head, as if trying to see him better.

"Azir, look: a magpie. On the wall."

"Ah, that means you will be getting a message soon," assured Azir.

"You don't believe such superstition, do you?"

"I believe that magpie has better sense than us, because he can fly away," said Azir.

The job for Privates Azir and Daniyal this week was to guard this remote part of the flight line against Taliban infiltrators who might seek to penetrate the base. Daniyal's lips tightened to a grim smile. *Who would try to break into hell?* he pondered.

Both soldiers were armed with AK-47 rifles and had 6 rounds apiece. Ammunition rationing was needed due to supply convoys being ambushed on the long road from Kabul—so they were told. An old flare gun lay on the sandbags before them. Half a dozen illumination flares lay in a metal box near their feet. They were issued one red star cluster shell to fire only if enemy contact was confirmed. Firing the red flare would trigger the post's quick reaction force to respond to repel the attack. "So be certain it's not just a wild dog sniffing around," warned their staff sergeant. Daniyal knew from prior experience that only about half the illumination rounds ever worked. Thankfully, he had not yet had to fire the red star cluster.

A portable radio in a worn, green canvas bag completed their equipment. Ideally, the radio was to transmit any suspicious activity to the operations section in the headquarters building. However, the radio's battery was depleted two months ago and had not yet been replaced. Each team assigned to guard the perimeter was still issued the dead radio each day by a bored supply sergeant, who threatened to beat the cost of the device out of them if it wasn't returned "in the same good condition."

"I have not tasted meat in over six months," Azir broke the silence. "Every day it is the same shit. Flavorless gruel. It is like they are *trying* to starve us."

Daniyal had heard his friend's complaints many times before but knew that venting them might raise his spirits, so he joined in. "I know. I used to buy meat from the corps commander's store until they raised the prices too high. The last time I bought their meat, there were maggots in it."

"I heard from the corporal it is from animals killed on the road," added Azir.

"I wouldn't doubt it. When I was new to the unit, I used to believe their lies about the supply lines," Daniyal said, "until one day I was the company runner and took a message to the captain during the mid-day meal. They made me wait outside the officer's mess, but when he came out, I could see inside. There were plates of kebab, piles of fresh bread, and fruit. They had *fresh* fruit," he emphasized. "When the captain saw me looking in the door at the food, he cuffed me and told me to return to duty."

Azir had also heard the story many times before. There were few stories they had not exchanged during their long, boring hours of guard duty together. But he dutifully reacted with fresh outrage to the injustice. "If I were in charge, things would be different," Azir added, in the familiar lament of enlisted soldiers across history.

There was a short lull in their conversation. "My mother makes the best kabob in our village," Azir announced, imagining the small, crooked table in their house laden with food on Eid. "The secret is the onion. She only uses red onions." He smiled and closed his eyes.

"Drink some water," Daniyal suggested, watching the heat waves ripple across the sand.

"If I drink more water, I'll shit more," Azir protested.

"If you don't drink, you're going to die."

"And that's bad why?" replied Azir, licking his cracked lips, and smiling weakly.

"It would be a tragedy for me to be denied your brilliant conversation while sitting in this hole twelve hours a day," countered his friend.

"Well, we can't have you bored," Azir obliged, raising his canteen for a swallow of stale water.

"Why don't you close your eyes for a while?" Daniyal offered. "I'll keep watch. Get some rest. It's the best thing for your body. I'll wake you when it gets dark and cooler."

"And if the sergeant comes?"

Daniyal laughed. "I can hear that donkey huffing and puffing a mile away. If I hear his braying, I'll wake you before he's within two hundred meters."

Azir relaxed. "You're a good friend Daniyal. Tell me one of your stories and I will try to fall asleep."

"What kind of story?"

"You know the ones I like. The funny ones."

Daniyal wrinkled his brow. "Okay, I don't think I've told you this one. It is about Mullah Nasruddin."

Azir chuckled. "Those are the best." He settled into the corner of their hole.

"Okay, it goes like this…," Daniyal began. "Mullah Nasruddin was very excited to be going on his first pilgrimage in many years. He looked forward to traveling to distant lands and took his favorite book to help pass the time. Unfortunately, when he returned home, he accidentally left the precious book behind. "Oh no," he lamented. "The book was a gift from my daughter and now I have lost it forever." A week later, he was walking through his village when he spotted a goat walking up the path with a book in its mouth. The animal walked up to the Mullah and stared at him. *Could it be?* he wondered and pulled the book from the animal's mouth. It was his special book! "It's a miracle!" he declared, extending his arms toward heaven. "Not really," replied the goat. "You wrote your name inside the cover."[6]

Daniyal waited for a laugh, but Azir was already snoring. "I guess I'll tell it again when you wake up," he shrugged.

Daniyal squinted at the barren desert terrain about him. *I should have brought my notebook*, he chastised himself. *I could have written my mother.* The wind whipped dust into his open mouth before he could cover his face. He spat the bitter taste over the pile of sandbags in front of him. As with guard duty throughout history, their assignment along the flight line was mind-numbing and physically miserable. Daniyal glanced at Azir with envy. *Unconscious—that's the best way to survive guard duty.*

Daniyal's stomach rumbled, but he knew they had a single piece of bread each to get them through the night before being relieved at dawn. That, and a liter and a half of warm water. *I guess I'll walk around the area until it gets dark,* he decided. *Once the sun goes down, we're stuck in this hole.*

◊ ◊ ◊

"*Wake up,*" a voice whispered through unsettled dreams.

"Mmph?"

"Azir, wake up," Daniyal hissed into his ear. "Someone is moving out there."

Azir opened his eyes and was momentarily disoriented. He was staring into the rear wall of their trench. It was well past sunset.

"Shh..." Daniyal directed quietly, as Azir struggled to turn over and regain his feet.

"Over there, by the wall," Daniyal gestured toward the half-crumbled ruins in front of their position. His body was taut. The

---

[6] The tales of Mullah Nasruddin are folk tales that are hundreds of years old and known throughout Asia and the Middle East.

stupidity of leaving a crumbling building along the perimeter screamed at him now that his life was in jeopardy.

Azir crawled up next to his friend, slowly inching his face over the sandbags. "I don't see anything," he said in a hushed voice, staring at the ruin they had often pelted with rocks during periods of boredom.

"There's nothing now. Wait for it," Daniyal whispered. The airfield approach lights cast a dim orangish light against the crumbling stone wall. "I think they threw something over," Daniyal advised, bringing Azir up to date on his observations. "Now, there's nothing."

"How many?" asked Azir, groping into the trench's darkness to find his rifle.

"I don't know. I thought I saw a head above the wall, and then something dropped over."

"I thought there were mines out there?" Azir questioned.

"There's a sign for mines. That's not the same thing."

"There!" Daniyal whispered fiercely. "Above that small tree. A face."

Azir followed Daniyal's gaze to the small pomegranate tree that grew at the base of the wall. Directly above the tree, perched, as if a decoration on top of the crumbling wall, was a man's face, flashing darkly orange against the rotating field lights. "You have good eyes my friend. I would never have seen that."

"What is he doing?" Azir continued in a hushed voice.

"Watching. He knows there's an outpost here somewhere. He's looking for movement."

"What do we do?"

"Wait."

"For what?"

"I don't know."

"Should we shoot the flare?"

"I don't know," Daniyal whispered. "If we do, it will show them exactly where we are." He hesitated, trying to think of the best plan, but doing nothing was all he kept coming up with. "Make sure your barrel is clear," he advised Azir. "If you got dirt in it when you were sleeping, the barrel will explode when you fire."

Azir touched the tip of his rifle barrel. "It's clear."

"Hsst," Daniyal signaled, nodding his head toward the wall. A figure wriggled down the ten-foot wall, legs kicking, then crouched behind the small pomegranate tree.

"Fire the flare," Daniyal decided, changing his mind. "We don't want an entire platoon in our lap before help can reach us."

"I can't tell one type from the other in the dark," Azir replied fumbling through the box of flares. He could feel fear and fatigue starting to cloud his thoughts. Everything seemed to be moving in slow motion.

"The shells in the box are illumination rounds. The red star shell was laying on the sandbags to the left of where you are," replied Daniyal calmly. "That's the one we want."

"It's not there now," Azir responded, groping about in the darkness.

"Are you sure?"

"Yes, I've looked everywhere. No wait—I can see it. It's in front of our position—on the ground. It must have gotten knocked off." The dull green casing of the flare lay in the dirt before their fighting position.

"Well, I'm not going out to get it," replied Daniyal. "Fire an illumination round instead. Maybe that will catch someone's attention back at operations."

Azir's hands shook uncontrollably as he reached into the box of flares. He found one and opened the gun to insert it.

"Hurry," Daniyal urged.

A stabbing deep in his bowels sent an uncompromising message to Azir. "I have to shit," he groaned.

"Not now," Daniyal cut him off. "Fire the flare or we're dead."

Azir snapped the gun shut, leaned across the sandbags, and pointed the barrel upwards. As he pulled the trigger, there was a hiss and sputter. The illumination round discharged from the barrel with a *POP*, as Azir discharged into his ragged uniform pants with a groan. The flare clipped the forward edge of the camo netting, sputtered a mere twenty feet above their position, and exploded, showering Azir and Daniyal with burning chemicals. Curses escaped Daniyal's lips, as his left forearm arm was singed.

Azir caught the worst of it: his thin shirt caught fire. He leapt from the trench to roll in the dirt behind their position, crying aloud as he tried to smother the flames. In the chaos, Daniyal saw the infiltrator rise from behind the small tree, making a throwing motion in their direction. *Grenade,* he thought. Daniyal raised his rifle to his shoulder and let loose with a short burst at the tree before diving to the bottom of the trench.

He held his breath and waited, but there was no explosion.

No explosion?

The time between when a grenade is thrown and when it explodes is an infinite period for the one on the receiving end. Daniyal was certain a grenade should have exploded by now. He carefully rose and peeked above the sandbags. Behind him Azir was still writhing on the ground, kicking his legs, and moaning from his burns. In front of them there was no sign of their interloper.

"Azir…Azir, how badly are you hurt?" Daniyal called from the trench, afraid to expose himself to gunfire.

"My back is cooked," Azir whimpered through gritted teeth. "Bring the kit. Hurry."

"Maybe they've gone," Daniyal suggested hopefully, as he fumbled to find their medical kit in the darkness of the trench. "But stay low, in case it's a trick." Azir did not reply.

"Got it," Daniyal announced, as he laid his hand on the medical bag. He low-crawled over the rear sandbags to reach the suffering Azir. Azir remained on his back, pressing his seared flesh into the cool dirt, fists clenching and unclenching. "Roll on your stomach so I can treat the wound," Daniyal directed, while continuing to cast fearful looks toward the crumbling building. Azir slowly rolled over, liberating the sickening sweet stench of burnt flesh and shit into Daniyal's nostrils. Daniyal retched, as he saw the back of Azir's shirt was burnt away, leaving a canvas of charred, twisted flesh. Edges of the shirt were now melted into Azir's flesh.

Daniyal spat bile from the back of his throat. "You're going to be okay, Azir. It doesn't look bad," Daniyal lied. Despite his shaking hands, he managed to unseal the medical kit. *I need to get those wounds covered. All that dirt ground into the wound is going to cause infection. Some morphine to prevent shock, as well.* In his anxious state, Daniyal was holding the medical kit upside down as he opened it, causing its contents to spill onto the dirt. Three safety pins, a shoelace, and three long strips of cloth from an old military uniform fell to the ground.

There was no burn salve, morphine, antibiotics, or sterile bandages—the expected contents of a combat medical kit. "Son of a whore!" he declared. *There is nothing here to help Azir.* He quickly transitioned from fear to anger. *They put us on the perimeter to fight with safety pins and shoelaces?*

"I'm cold, Daniyal," Azir's voice trailed away. He was shaking.

"It's okay, Azir, help is on the way," he lied again.

How do I get help? The radio is broken. Daniyal looked for any sign of the quick reaction force approaching in response to the shots fired. *Nothing.* Nor was there any movement from the direction of the crumbling building. *They must have left, or we'd be dead by now,* he reasoned. *These sandbags don't provide much cover.* Daniyal could feel his frustration growing. *The fools in the operations center probably think my firing was an accidental discharge. They're not going to come out of their comfort to investigate.*

The star cluster, he remembered. *Although the illumination round had failed, the star shell might still work and bring help.* Daniyal crab-crawled to the front of their fighting position, expecting a burst of gunfire to drop him at any moment. *No choice—Azir is going into shock.*

The star shell still lay in front of the sandbags. A small pomegranate also lay nearby, which did not register at the moment.

He scooped up the precious shell and rolled back into the trench. The flare gun was still warm, as he put the star shell into the chamber. Not risking further interference from their camouflage netting, he climbed out of the trench and kneeled next to Azir, pointing the barrel toward the sky. *Please Allah, let this one work,* he prayed.

With a large *POP*, the red streamer arced into the sky and burst at a great height, visible to everyone on the flat desert base. *Thanks be to Allah. Finally, help will come,* he breathed in relief.

A moan caught his attention. It was Azir. No, it's coming from the direction of the wall. Daniyal froze. *I am a fool, remaining in the open.*

"Mama," a weak voice cried in the local Pashto language. "Mama, help me."

Daniyal dropped flat to the ground. *This is a trick.*

"Please...."

Daniyal noticed a small bundle of rags moving slightly at the base of the wall, partially obscured by the stunted pomegranate tree.

Does this nightmare never end? Daniyal thought. *I will wait until help arrives,* he resolved. *I will not be killed by some enemy trick.*

Daniyal crawled back into the trench to find Azir's weapon. His own was empty. There was nothing he could do for Azir with safety pins and strips of cloth. He could see truck headlights far down the airfield and other lights coming on in the cluster of buildings near the operations center. *They are coming at last.* "Azir, help is coming," he called out the rear of the trench. A moan responded to his news.

The arrival of the first mortar rounds on their position was presaged only momentarily by their shrill whistle. The red star cluster had indeed been seen by the operations officer, who reported it to the corps commander. "Saturate the perimeter with high explosive," the general ordered, returning to his dinner of lamb and saffron rice. "Sweep up the scraps with the reaction force," he burped.

An Absence of Faith

Azir was killed in the first salvo, which fell short of the perimeter. The twelve-year-old boy at the base of the pomegranate tree, who was sneaking into the camp to find food for his family, was a pile of bloody rags when the barrage lifted. In tomorrow's intelligence summary, he would be labelled a Taliban infiltrator. No one questioned why the terrorist had only a small bag of pomegranates and no weapon. The attack had been heroically stopped by the vigilance of the 225th Corps, the morning situation report to Kabul bleated. Daniyal was found half buried, yet alive, in the trench, with a serious concussion and both ear drums ruptured. The military doctor ordered his return to full duty two days later to avoid encouraging malingering among the enlisted troops.

The corps commander, Major General Rahman, received a commendation from the Minister of Defense for his decisive response to the attack. The incident was reported through channels to the NATO[7] Resolute Support Headquarters in Kabul as "Enemy recon of unknown strength interdicted at Lashkar Gah HQ airfield perimeter, Red KIA-6, Green KIA-1, WIA-1, Blue KIA/WIA 0."[8]

The war continued to go well.

---

[7] NATO – North Atlantic Treaty Organization

[8] In U.S. military reports and briefings, enemy forces are referenced as "red forces." Allied military forces, such as those of a host nation are referred to as "green forces." During Operation Resolute Support, all NATO forces, including U.S. forces, under the command of a U.S. four-star general, were referenced as "blue forces." Thus, a report mentioning a green-on-blue attack was instantly recognizable as an Afghan government soldier changing allegiance and attacking NATO personnel. To many NATO personnel this was a greater threat than the Taliban. KIA=Killed in Action. WIA=Wounded in Action.

Chapter 3

Lashkar Gah, Helmand Province, September 2015

    Daniyal pulled back the rusty door to his barracks. It was late afternoon, and the sun was still strong. The familiar army smells of body odor, canvas, and mildew filled his nostrils. The long room that occupied the ground floor consisted of twelve double bunks along each wall, with a wooden box at the end of each bed for soldiers' personal items. A half dozen windows, minus glass, punctuated the concrete walls. No one was present. *Must still be on duty,* Daniyal concluded, or the room would be packed with soldiers lying about, cleaning equipment, writing letters, and engaging in the routine tasks that young men away from home use to endure the boredom of military service.

    Daniyal was relieved to be back. His head still pounded from the barrage, and his vision was blurry. But he knew he stood a better chance of recovery outside the hospital. More soldiers on the base died of secondary infections or diseases caught while in the army clinic than of their original injuries. He had watched the same IV drip shared between two different patients that morning, without any attempt to sterilize it. The hospital had been opened with much fanfare as a state-of-the-art facility financed by the Americans. Several years passed, though, and the high-end equipment broke, supplies disappeared, and training lapsed. Today it was a place all soldiers feared.

    He had dreaded one aspect of his return to the barracks, however. He knew Azir would not be here. Daniyal glanced down to the far-left end of the room, where Azir's thin sleeping mat was rolled up on an empty bed frame. The top of his barracks box was open. The scene lent a sense of finality to what he already knew. Four days ago, this had been Azir's place in the world. Now, his life and death were memorialized by a rolled-up mat and an empty box.

    Daniyal let his eyes drift to the barracks' far right corner, his own assigned sleeping area. A jolt went through him. His sleeping mat was also rolled up and his box was similarly thrown open. He walked quickly to the far end. The locking hardware was missing, and the cover was broken off. *Where are my letters? My pictures? My clothes?* he asked himself.

As if in answer, the outer door behind him creaked and his platoon members noisily flooded into the room. Amir, the schemer, was first, followed quickly by Hassan from Herat, and Ali, the unit bully. The rest followed. The cacophony of sound grew, as soldiers dumped their weapons and equipment on the floor, talking over each other. Amir was the first to notice Daniyal standing silent at the far end of the room. "Look who is back from the dead," Amir taunted in his nasal voice. When Daniyal did not respond, he continued, "We were told you were dying in the hospital."

"Better if he had," the large Ali grunted, dumping his pack onto his bed halfway down the room.

"Good to see you, Daniyal," Hassan added quickly, avoiding eye contact.

"Are you certain?" Daniyal asked. "Because it seems you're enjoying the shirt my mother sent me." The telltale orange trim on the collar was poking out from the neck of Hassan's uniform. The room became quiet, as embarrassed glances were exchanged. "What about the rest of you? How many of you went shopping in my box when you heard I was hurt?"

Hassan stammered, "Daniyal, we thought you were…"

Ali cut him off. "Do not explain to this son of a whore. If you want to know the truth, Daniyal, there was a party when we heard you weren't coming back. Everyone liked Azir. It's a shame he died. But you are *beghairat*[9] and no one trusts you anymore. We heard you ran away and let him die alone defending his outpost. This barracks is cleaner with you gone."

Danial could feel the rage rising in himself. "Azir died because no one came to help us," he spat between gritted teeth. "I fired the alert flare, but the corps hit us with artillery instead of sending reinforcements. Were you all warm here in your beds while we were being blown apart?"

---

[9] Urdu insult for a person without shame, or who is not respected.

Hassan kept his eyes averted, staring at his bed. Amir stared at the tips of his well-worn boots. Ali slowly removed his belt, holding Daniyal with his glare. Ali slowly wrapped the canvas strap about his hand, and advanced on Daniyal. "He just left the hospital," a nameless voice in the back of the barracks pleaded. "Shut up," Ali directed, continuing forward. "He called every man in this unit a coward. Let him defend that."

Daniyal's rage was so strong that Ali's outweighing him by 20 kilos did not check his anger. He threw the broken barracks box lid at Ali, then rushed him. His anger in seeing Azir die a senseless death poured forth in a howl of rage. Unfortunately, Daniyal's fighting skills did not match his passion. Ali knocked the lid aside and easily sidestepped the charging Daniyal, who was still unsteady from his concussion. Daniyal's fists struck air, while Ali smashed his belt covered fist into Daniyal's left temple. The effect was immediate, with Daniyal crumpling insensible to the ground.

The fight had ended, but the punishment had not. Ali kicked Daniyal viciously in the abdomen, knocking the air out of him. He then delivered a series of kicks to Daniyal's already bruised ribs, which the absence of consciousness mercifully spared him from feeling.

"I liked your pictures, *Gho kor*[10]," Ali mocked to the still body. "Especially of your sister."

Hassan looked on in horror. "He's unconscious. That's enough." But the fever of cruelty had taken over. "It's over when I say," Ali declared, stomping on Daniyal's left forearm, with an audible crack of bones.

Amir, horrified by the abuse, took a different approach. "Ali, the sergeant won't like it."

Ali delivered another kick, stubbing his foot on Daniyal's knee bone. "He won't care. He knows he's a worthless soldier—I heard him say so to the captain. He thinks he's better than us because he went to university."

"He will care about having to fill out more paperwork to explain why Daniyal is still not available for duty," Amir persisted.

---

[10] Afghan insult: "shit eater"

This argument broke through Ali's rage. He knew the sergeant cared primarily about one thing—doing as little work as possible. If Ali created work for the sergeant, his life would become difficult.

"Hmph," Ali responded. "Then get him out of here." He thought for a moment. "We'll put him by the stairs behind the motor pool. It will look like he fell." Ali delivered another vicious kick to the side of Daniyal's head. "Maybe that will keep him from remembering."

Ali wrinkled his nose in disgust. "And make it quick. This fool has soiled himself. I don't need him stinking up my barracks." Ali already planned for the day when he would be the sergeant, with his word law. Giving orders to the others felt good.

Hassan, Amir, and several others placed a rubber rain poncho next to Daniyal and gingerly lifted him onto it. "He weighs nothing. Maybe we should take him back to the hospital," suggested Hassan. Blood trickled from the corner of Daniyal's slack mouth. "He might die."

"Maybe you should stop thinking and do as you're told," snarled Ali. "Whoever finds him will take him there and it will be fewer questions for us."

Four men lifted the corners of the poncho and shuffled to the door. They used the advancing darkness to conceal their movement to the motor pool, where they left Daniyal broken and alone at the bottom of the rusty metal staircase.

Hassan looked back, as they skulked away. The still pile of clothes did not even resemble a man. It looked like an animal that had been hit by the roadside. *He's going to die, and we could have stopped it,* he chastised himself.

Chapter 4

Lashkar Gah. Helmand Province, September 2015

Command Sergeant Major Mahmood of the 225th Corps was a mountain of humanity. In a country where marginal nutrition resulted in most adult men topping out at slightly above five feet in height, he was six feet four inches, weighing in at 280 pounds. A former university wrestler in France, where his father had been a diplomat for the old government, he was an intimidating presence who wore a perpetual scowl on swarthy, heavily-lined features. An ethnic Pashtun, he had risen to the highest noncommissioned rank in the nation's most combat-ready corps by being stronger, more ambitious, and far more ruthless than his competition.

A command sergeant major's responsibility was wide. He was the senior enlisted advisor to the corps commander, Major General Rahman. He was responsible for the combat readiness, training, and condition of all enlisted personnel who served in Helmand Province. He was also unofficially tasked with managing the corps commander's private accounts—for property skimmed from supplies and fiscal resources issued to the corps. This alone was a full-time job, as it meant nearly a third of the corps' assets had to be separately managed, maintained, and invested, but not be accounted for in official records. The entire private portfolio totaled nearly sixteen million U.S. dollars annually.

Under this latter mantle, the sergeant major was also the manager of the corps' soldiers' store, where the enlisted troops could purchase personal comfort items, such as extra food rations and clothing. Meat, fruit, fresh vegetables—they were all available, for a price. The soldiers were not allowed off the base, which meant the store could set its prices without competition. *It was a genius concept,* he had to admit. *We issue their pay with one hand and take it back with the other.* Rather than provide cheap cuts of meat to the soldiers in the mess hall for free, as planned for in the defense ministry budget from NATO funding, the food was instead diverted to the corps store. The soldiers then had to use their meager monthly paychecks to pay for enough nutrition to survive. *Otherwise, their rations in the mess hall were basically watery gruel, not fit for dogs*, the sergeant major smirked.

Everyone benefited, he rationalized, *which is why the idea was so remarkable. The soldiers still receive meat, and don't waste their pay on distractions such as gambling.* As a former private himself, he knew how soldiers would squander a month's pay in one night on games of chance. While this justification ignored that soldiers were then also unable to send money home to their families, such concerns fell under the label of "personal problems" about which the sergeant major did not concern himself. *I get my share*, the sergeant major smugly pondered. *The corps commander gets his, the corps inspector general gets a little taste to keep him on the leash, while the General Staff Quartermaster in Kabul gets a quarterly "gift" that keeps him from looking too closely at complaints about soldier's poor living conditions.*

Today's duties, however, did not involve the corps store. He was to visit the post hospital and congratulate the wounded for their loyal service—a morale building exercise the corps commander had assigned him. As he climbed the metal stairs in front of the two-story building, they groaned beneath his weight. An orderly pulled open the door to the lobby and greeted him in a quavering voice, "Good morning, Sergeant Major, we are honored you are visiting us this morning."

"I'm sure you are," Mahmood replied flatly, giving the man no more than a glance as he brushed past. Broken and yellowed linoleum tiles echoed with his footsteps, as he made his way from the lobby to the first-floor trauma ward. He had spent time in this same ward himself as a young sergeant when a truck he was riding in had hit an old Russian landmine. He remembered shrapnel being pulled from him without anesthetic in this same building. He had not given them the satisfaction of seeing his pain. A familiar sour chemical smell now filled his nostrils. *Hospitals always smell the same,* he thought—*a combination of piss, disinfectant, and despair.*

A doctor waited for him at the door to the main ward, a stained surgical coat hanging loosely over his uniform. "Good morning,

Sergeant Major, I am Major Nooristani, Chief of Internal Medicine. I will be your guide today."

"*Command* Sergeant Major," Mahmood instructed, asserting his authority. He did not usually bother with the trivialities of titles, but he enjoyed correcting officers. "Shall we begin? My schedule is very full."

"Of course. This way please, Command Sergeant Major." The doctor gestured down the hallway. "As you know, ours is one of the most sophisticated hospitals in Afghanistan, recognized by the President himself..."

A look from the sergeant major cut the doctor off in mid-sentence. He was in no mood for a canned promotional speech.

"Here we are, Command Sergeant Major. This is our critical care unit—this ward contains many of our more serious cases," the doctor explained. "Many of them are from the tent fire last week." The doctor pushed the swinging door into the ward open. The sweet, rotten smell of dying flesh flooded out, invading the sergeant major's nostrils. He swallowed hard, seeking not to show his revulsion. *Even breathing through my mouth, I can taste it,* he thought. *This will indeed be a quick visit.*

The sergeant major entered the room. It was a typical military hospital ward, comprised of two rows of metal framed beds along two long walls, with a single aisle down the middle. Twenty beds in all. The first ten were occupied by the burn victims. Their flesh was swollen and tortured, varying in shades from dark pink to purple. Audible moaning came from several of the beds. Only two had IV units dripping some clear substance into blackened, scabbed arms.

"I thought there were more in the tent," noted the sergeant major, coldly taking in the horror.

"There were, but we are now a week after the event and secondary infections and pneumonia have taken many. We are losing several every day," the doctor said.

"What are you giving them?" he gestured to one of the IV bottles.

"Mostly saline, to aid tissue regeneration. They take turns with the bottles due to shortages. It has a nice placebo effect as well...for some."

"And for pain?"

"We have nothing for chronic pain. The small amount of morphine we have is only for acute injury—bullet wounds or punctures—to avoid shock. We can't spare it for comfort."

"Hmph," the sergeant major cleared his throat. "Good morning, heroes of the Corps," he projected, his deep voice rumbling the length of the ward. "I'm Command Sergeant Major Mahmood, your corps sergeant major. On behalf of Major General Rahman, commander of this historic corps, I have come to thank you for your service."

"*Home*," one of the men to his left responded in a weak voice. "Send me home. *Please*. I want to die at home."

Ignoring the interruption, the sergeant major continued, as if addressing a parade ground of new recruits. "The commander admires you for your brave service. Your family is proud of you. The President is proud of you. I am proud of you."

"Send me home. Allahh-h-h..." the same man responded, his high-pitched wail trailing off into sobs.

"Who else is here?" the sergeant major snapped at the doctor, anxious to escape this hell.

"We have two cases of self-inflicted wounds, several malnutrition cases, and one man who fell down a stairwell while fighting an infiltrator."

"Let me meet him—the one who actually fought."

"He is in radiology at the moment. We can go see him there," the doctor offered, extending his arm to guide the sergeant major back to the hallway.

Outside the ward, the sergeant major paused, taking a deep breath to clear the stench of fetid wounds out of his nose. "I will send the military police to arrest the two malingerers this afternoon. Have them ready. We will waste no medical resources treating cowards."

"Yes, Command Sergeant Major." Although the doctor was an officer and outranked the sergeant major, there was no doubt where the power lay between them. Proximity to the corps commander carried its own distinct authority that no number of rank pips or professional credentials could outweigh.

"This way, please, Command Sergeant Major," the doctor invited, gesturing toward another set of double doors at the opposite end of the lobby. Even as he did so, the doors swung open, revealing an orderly pushing a frail figure in a wheelchair. "Aah, here's our hero, now..." the doctor stated with too much enthusiasm, his nervousness over the sergeant major's continued presence showing.

Daniyal eyed the doctor warily from his wheelchair, wondering who the massive hulk with him was. *Eyed* was the correct term, as only one of his eyes was uncovered, the other bearing a heavily taped foil patch to reduce movement while his shattered eye socket healed from the stomping Ali had delivered. Both arms were immobile as well, secured in plaster casts connected behind his back.

The sergeant major observed the green and black bruises of Daniyal's face, along with his gaunt condition. "You must be a tough one to survive such a fight. How many were there?"

Daniyal remained silent.

In the uncomfortable silence, the doctor interjected, "Private, this is Command Sergeant Major Mahmood, the corps sergeant major. He has come to visit you."

Daniyal stared at the sergeant major, without emotion.

"Is there anything you need?" the sergeant major suggested. Again, there was no answer nor movement from the wounded man.

Command Sergeant Major Mahmood turned to the doctor. "Is he brain damaged?" he asked, his brow furrowed in confusion.

Daniyal laughed lightly, the first sign that he understood his surroundings. "No more than the rest of us, Sergeant Major. Thank you for visiting me. I hope it wasn't the lie that I am a war hero that brought you here."

"Private..." hissed the doctor.

"Let the man speak," ordered the sergeant major. Something in the direct way that this private spoke interested him. It reminded him how his opponents used to try to get inside his head prior to the start of their wrestling bouts.

"You ask what I need? If you are serious, then I need to have my bandages changed more than once per week so I do not get the stinking infections that kill every other man on my ward, Sergeant Major. I need to have some meat and vegetables so my body can heal, and not pretend that eating the watery slops we are served here are going to make my bones knit. I need antibiotics so my wounds do not fester. But I expect I will get another beating, or perhaps you will shoot me for insubordination? Maybe I could have a medal first, since everyone is lying that I stopped an infiltrator, instead of being stomped by my own platoon. It's all the same to me at this point."

"I a-apologize, Command Sergeant Major...," the doctor stuttered.

Ignoring him, the sergeant major asked, "Your speech—you sound as if you've had some education. True?"

"Yes, Sergeant Major," Daniyal replied flatly. "Kabul University. I finished three years before I was volunteered into the back of an army truck by a gang of thugs. I was snatched off the sidewalk outside campus a year ago and haven't seen my family since."

"What was your course of instruction?"

"Business and accounting."

"And what are your duties here?"

Daniyal smirked. "They vary from getting shelled by my own artillery to having the shit kicked out of me by my own platoon, Sergeant Major." Daniyal looked unblinking into the giant man's dark eyes.

"Private!" the doctor snapped, seeking to stop the insolence.

The sergeant major ignored the nervous officer, soberly assessing Daniyal. The injured man did not look away. *Whatever fear this one had, is gone. A man with nothing to lose can be very valuable*, he concluded.

The sergeant major turned to the doctor, whose bulging eyes regarded the massive NCO[11] with fear. "You will find this man his own room, doctor. He works for me now. I will send over food and

---

[11] NCO. Noncommissioned Officer. Collective title for corporals and sergeants, the mid-level managers who make the Army work.

An Absence of Faith

medicine for him from a supply shipment we received yesterday. It goes to him—no one else. Are we clear?"

"Yes, Command Sergeant Major."

"If you need anything else to heal him, let me know. If he does not recover, I will be very unhappy. The corps commander will be unhappy as well. Are we clear?"

"Yes, Command Sergeant Major," the doctor squeaked.

"I need him in thirty days, as healthy as you can make him, do you understand?"

"He has serious injuries..." the doctor cautioned, before the sergeant major's glare stopped him. "Yes, Command Sergeant Major," he concluded.

Turning back to Daniyal, the sergeant major looked into his lone unblinking eye. "You belong to me now. You have thirty days to regain your strength. Then, you will report to me at the Corps headquarters. Are we clear?" Clear or not, the sergeant major did not wait for a reply, marching out of the hospital to free himself from the stink of suffering.

Daniyal regarded the departing man. He had expected to be beaten or maybe even shot for his insolence. Another beating would not have mattered and being shot would have been a relief. *What just happened?* he asked himself. There was something in the sergeant major's gaze that reminded him of a man who has found a gold coin in the sand.

"Put him in the VIP suite," the doctor directed the orderly, who had stood mutely by during the extraordinary exchange. "And give him my tray from the officer's mess." To Daniyal he merely commented, "You are the luckiest fool on earth. That man could have ended your life with a wave of his hand."

Chapter 5

Lashkar Gah, Helmand Province, November 2015

"Daniyal, come into my office," Sergeant Major Mahmood called from his desk. Two months had passed since Daniyal's initial encounter with the sergeant major in the hospital.

"Yes, Sergeant Major," Daniyal responded, jumping to his feet from behind the cheap metal desk sitting outside the sergeant major's door. He grabbed a notepad and pencil to record any directions he was given, as the sergeant major's orderly.

"Leave the pad," the sergeant major added, before Daniyal cleared the threshold.

Daniyal paused to comply with his orders, and then entered the sergeant major's spacious office, which occupied the end suite on the second floor of the corps headquarters. It was a good location. Close to the Corps Commander's suite, halfway down the hall, but isolated enough to dissuade casual visitors. Fine dark wood furniture sat tastefully spaced around a dark red Persian rug. The windows were hung with heavy green cloth drapes to keep out the strong desert sun. An air conditioning unit hummed on the wall above the sergeant major's chair, a luxury that soldiers in the barracks could only imagine. Daniyal would sometimes sneak into the office for moments at a time when he knew the sergeant major was away to experience the cold air, a welcome break from the relentless pounding heat of a Helmand summer.

"Sit." The sergeant major gestured to one of the upholstered chairs opposite his desk.

What is going on? Daniyal wondered. He was not often invited to sit in the sergeant major's presence. His role in life was to carry out the sergeant major's wishes as quickly and efficiently as possible. Run here, fetch that, deliver this immediately. *Not* to sit.

The sergeant major eyed him, without speaking. Daniyal waited as the tension grew, but he maintained eye contact with his boss.

"You were one of the two soldiers caught in the artillery barrage on the perimeter in August, correct?"

"Yes, Sergeant Major," Daniyal replied. *Sacrificed would be more accurate*, he thought.

"You stayed at your post."

"Yes, Sergeant Major."

"Hmmm," the sergeant major mused, continuing to examine Daniyal through narrowed eyes below thick eyebrows. "And this was because of your love for country?" he asked neutrally.

Daniyal hesitated, sensing the trap. He knew the sergeant major had a talent for detecting deception and he didn't want to forfeit the trust of the man who had rescued him from the barracks. "No, Sergeant Major. The other soldier I was with—Private Azir—wa, was...my friend. I would not leave him."

"Hmm, so it was personal loyalty that caused you to risk your life?"

"Yes, Sergeant Major."

"Why did you not say it was love of country?" he pressed. "That would make you a patriot. A hero. I could give you a medal." The sergeant major nearly sneered as he asked the question.

Daniyal could feel heat in his cheeks as he replied. "My *country*. My *country* kidnapped me and threw me in the back of a truck with a stinking potato sack over my head. When I was a boy my *country* let my father die in a hospital waiting room after he had a stroke, because he wasn't important enough or rich enough to receive medicine they had sitting on their shelves. Every day, on my way to campus, I dodged *my country's* police to avoid paying the bribes they demanded, while they pretended my identity papers were not in order." Daniyal paused, feeling he had said too much.

"Go on," the sergeant major allowed, revealing nothing.

Daniyal felt his face growing hot again. "When my mother naively went to the police station to report a young man who stole a bag of food from her in the market, the police seized the other bag *as evidence,* leaving her with nothing. So, I have learned the danger of selling one's heart to something as fickle as one's *country.*"

"Your words are dangerous...anywhere outside this room. I respect your honesty, but you must never repeat these thoughts to others while you work for me. Do you understand?"

"Yes, Sergeant Major."

"One's country is a wonderful thing, in the right context. It has made me powerful. It is also a wonderful tool—especially when dealing with the Americans. They get teary-eyed every time their flag goes up. Like children. They assume others are also children, fawning over a piece of cloth instead of protecting one's family, one's tribe. That is where strength is. That is where *power* lies. *Country* provides useful theater."

Daniyal said nothing, watching the sergeant major's fists clench as he spoke these words through gritted teeth.

"My father was a great man," the sergeant major continued. "A diplomat. Respected for his service to his country. Do you know where he is today?"

"No Sergeant Major."

"In a pauper's grave in Paris. When the Taliban seized control, he was left without a home, a government, or any resources. He was shunned by former colleagues and left to fend for himself. He became *inconvenient.* He even tried to run a small Tabak shop as a political refugee but was denied the necessary licenses by the French government, as there was a warrant for his arrest from the new Taliban government. He believed in his country and died penniless. So, I too have a healthy distrust of countries and governments and will fight to see my family is never left destitute by loving one too much."

"Yes, Sergeant Major," replied Daniyal, wondering why this very personal information was being shared with him. The answer came soon enough.

The grim man leaned forward across his desk. "I have a mission. A special mission that requires a man of your talents and...philosophy."

Daniyal waited.

"There is a delivery of supplies—authorized by the corps commander—that needs to be handled with extreme delicacy due to...political considerations. There are too many eyes and spies on this base to conduct this delivery through the normal channels. So, I will need your assistance. Can you drive a two-and-a-half-ton truck?"

"I've never done so, Sergeant Major."

"Learn."

"Yes, Sergeant Major," Daniyal gulped. He had never driven *any* vehicle but did not believe the sergeant major cared to hear those details.

"You have one week. I will tell the motor sergeant to instruct you. Show me my faith in you is not misplaced."

"I will do as you say, Sergeant Major."

"Good. Now get out."

Chapter 6

Lashkar Gah, Helmand Province, December 2015

Daniyal heard nothing more regarding the special mission, and ten days later assumed the entire thing had blown over. He learned how to drive the Romanian cargo truck, an old supply vehicle left behind from a prior NATO rotation. It was not difficult once Daniyal learned the gear configuration, which the motor sergeant reinforced by smacking his right hand with a heavy wood stick whenever he made an error.

After an absence of several days, Sergeant Major Mahmood returned to the headquarters, wearing his usual scowl. "We go tonight," he quietly announced, barely pausing by Daniyal's desk. "Be at the motor pool at 1800 hours. No weapon. No equipment. Leave your ID behind."

Daniyal had no chance to ask questions before the sergeant major's door closed in his face. *What kind of special mission involves no equipment or weapon? And why no ID? Unless it is a one-way trip,* he fretted. The rest of the workday blurred past, as Daniyal found it difficult to concentrate on anything other than the looming mission.

Daniyal walked toward the motor pool as darkness embraced the base, planning to arrive ten minutes early to avoid the sergeant major's well-known wrath for tardiness. Daniyal had spent the afternoon writing a letter to his mother, which he had left in his middle desk drawer. He had no idea what his mission was, but he had been in the army long enough to know that when the word *special* was attached to any mission it often meant that privates ended up dead and officers ended up with medals.

As he approached the motor pool, he saw members of the headquarters security detail spread in a loose cordon about the building. They were instantly recognizable due to their size, newly pressed uniforms, and American M4 rifles. Daniyal approached a dark-skinned sergeant he had seen in the headquarters. Expecting to be rebuffed, he stammered, "I...I was told..."

"I know who you are," the sergeant cut him off, jerking his head toward the open bay doors. "Go ahead."

He knows who I am, Daniyal wondered, slipping past before his luck changed. The entrance to the motor pool was through two oversized garage doors. The sharp smell of acetone and lubricants greeted him. The interior was dimly lit by a half-dozen flickering fluorescent lights that had not yet burned out. The work bay was large—big enough for a dozen vehicles to be worked upon at the same time, although that was rarely the case.

The Afghan National Army had long ago learned it was easier to ask the Americans for a new vehicle, rather than routinely repairing what they had. The Americans were always accommodating. If a vehicle needed repairs, it was written off the books as a combat loss—hit by rocket, struck a mine—ensuring a constant influx of new equipment and the existence of a secret fleet of trucks that were available for off-the-books uses, such as tonight's mission. The number of "dead trucks" continuing to move about Afghan roads would have impressed Lazarus.

The truck on which Daniyal had trained sat at the far end of the large bay, with its motor idling. The sergeant major was in the cab, checking on something Daniyal could not see.

"Good evening, Sergeant Major," Daniyal called to get his attention.

The sergeant major glanced at him, irritated as usual. "Wait," he snapped.

Daniyal waited.

Five minutes passed. The sergeant major finally dismounted and checked the tires and the rear gate of the truck, never speaking to Daniyal. Finally satisfied, he turned to the private. "The commander will be here soon. You do not speak to him unless he speaks to you." The sergeant major pressed close to Daniyal so that his nose was inches from his own. "If he asks you a question, your answers are 'yes' or 'no.' If you don't know the answer, don't guess. Do you understand?"

Daniyal's head swan. *Commander? Which one? This base has dozens of commanders.* He had many questions, but also knew the sergeant major would tolerate none of them. "Yes, Sergeant Major," he said.

The garage doors behind Daniyal squealed an unlubricated protest as they came down to seal the bay closed.

"Come to attention," the sergeant major hissed. Daniyal complied.

The sound of footfalls grew louder behind him, echoing off the cement walls. They stopped behind him. Daniyal could hear wheezing.

"Is this the man?" a voice rasped behind him.

"Yes, Major General," the sergeant major barked in his deepest command voice.

"Keep your voice down, you idiot," the voice hissed. "We are not on the parade ground."

Streams of sweat ran down Daniyal's sides. *Major General? This was the corps commander? It had to be—no one else would dare speak to the sergeant major so.* Daniyal could feel the man's eyes boring through him, as he passed closely to his left.

"He doesn't look like much," the general said, still breathing heavily.

"He's loyal," the sergeant major replied. "He's what we need for such a...sensitive mission."

"*I* will decide what we need, sergeant major," the general sneered. Despite working on the same floor of the headquarters, Daniyal had never seen the corps commander up close before. He was a ghost, an ever-present force of mythological prominence, but not a corporeal being. Stories of his temper were legend within the corps. He had once shot a member of his own security detail who had fallen asleep behind the wheel of his vehicle outside a meeting with the Governor of Kandahar. Rather than discipline the man, he simply unholstered his sidearm and blew the man's brains out as the Governor was bidding him farewell.

Daniyal was surprised to see that the corps commander was a rather short, fat man with lank, thinning hair combed over a bald head. A protruding gut challenged the buttons of his green fatigue blouse, which he was wearing without rank. Daniyal had always envisioned another behemoth, like the sergeant major, due to his fearsome reputation. The corps commander was known to use techniques in questioning prisoners that had led to protests from human rights groups and even half-hearted expressions of concern from the Americans. But, because he kept the Taliban largely in check in Helmand, his "eccentricities" were tolerated by the Ministry of Defense.

Daniyal was snapped out of his thoughts by a question directed at him. "Do you know how to keep your mouth shut, private?" the corps commander asked him in Pashto, while still looking at the sergeant major.

"Yes, sir," Daniyal replied.

Major General Rahman turned his face to Daniyal, without turning his body. *He has no neck,* Daniyal realized.

"This is a special mission," the corps commander continued. Your role is to be a delivery boy. Do you know of General Raziq?"

"Yes, Major General."

"Who is he?" the officer insisted.

Daniyal glanced at the sergeant major, who nodded. "He is the chief of police for Kandahar, Major General."

"Correct. He is also my most important ally in the fight against the filthy enemy. He kills as many of the Taliban as this entire corps." Daniyal noted that the general's breathing was becoming more labored. His face was red and his eyes bulging.

"And yet," he continued, "our American friends have directed that none of the military supplies they've provided can be shared with General Raziq, because they find his methods too…difficult to digest." He snorted. "We have to kill the enemy with an appropriate level of kindness and consideration that will keep the American politicians happy and the dollars flowing."

The general paused, eyeing Daniyal closely, watching a trickle of sweat run down his face.

"We are correcting that disequilibrium this evening," the commander continued. "You will take this truck of supplies to Raziq's people to help his continued battle against the enemy. You will follow the sergeant major's HMMWV[12] to a rendezvous point he will show you on the map. Your job is simple. Drive the truck to the handoff point. Do not talk to anyone. Do not let anyone talk to you. Leave the truck there and return to the sergeant major who will be waiting in a nearby compound."

He paused. "And then forget you ever were there."

"Yes, Major General."

"You do this job well and you will be rewarded. If you do not follow my directions completely, I will cut off your balls."

Daniyal stared into the cold eyes of General Rahman, having no doubt he would personally wield the knife.

◊ ◊ ◊

Two hours later, the sergeant major slowed his HMMWV to a crawl near a group of small, mud brick huts. Daniyal was completely lost but sensed that they had been heading in a southeast direction for much of their trip. The buildings sat at the intersection of two one-lane roads in a narrow valley overshadowed by low hills. A large, walled residential compound, encircled by eight-foot mud walls, sat to the left of the road, past the huts. A blue metal gate bisected the wall. The gate swung partially open as the sergeant major approached. A hand waved a white rag through the opening. The sergeant major signaled Daniyal to stop his truck on the road, before pulling his HMMWV through the gate into the compound. It was now fully dark and only the orange running lights of the truck provided any illumination.

It's strange that the sergeant major has not brought any of his security, thought Daniyal. I suppose General Raziq has this area well secured.

The sergeant major was at his window, startling Daniyal.

---

[12] HMMWV. High Mobility Multipurpose Wheeled Vehicle, colloquially referred to as a HUMVEE. The Army's all-purpose modular tactical vehicle.

"This is where we part," the sergeant major instructed. "You continue straight ahead for 300 meters. This road is straight," he repeated. "At three hundred meters there will be an intersecting road to the right. It is little more than a path. There will be a bicycle lying by the side of the road. If the bicycle is not there, do not go down the road. Turn around and come back. If the bicycle is there, take the right-hand road." Daniyal noted sweat pouring down the sergeant major's face. "Now, repeat what you are to do."

"Drive straight ahead for three hundred meters," repeated Daniyal. "Look for a bicycle. If it is not there, come back." Daniyal prayed silently that the bike would not be there. He also wondered to himself how he could ever turn this large truck around on this narrow road but continued. "If the bicycle is there, take the right turn."

"Good," said the sergeant major. "Once you take that right turn, keep driving for slightly more than half a kilometer. It becomes narrower—it is rough, but wide enough for the truck, if you are *careful*. Drive until the road ends at a rocky overhang. You will be met there by a man. Give him the keys and walk back here. Do *not* talk to him, do you understand?"

"Yes, Sergeant Major."

"The less you know, the better. The commander was a fool to run his mouth in front of you. Forget everything he said. Do you understand?"

"Yes, Sergeant Major." Daniyal felt that he understood little but knew that he was expected to comply.

"Any questions?"

Daniyal was sufficiently nervous by all of the intrigue that his normal reserve was overcome in the moment. He had spent the past two hours imagining everything that could possibly go wrong. Breakdowns. Enemies. Every pothole he hit on the shabby roads made him wince that his truckload, of what? —ammunition? explosives? — would go up in a bright flash. "What if something goes wrong?" he half whispered. "What if the man is not there? Or I run into the enemy? I have no weapon," he half pleaded.

An Absence of Faith

The sergeant major regarded him with steely eyes. "If something goes wrong, you'll be dead and having a weapon will make no difference. Why do you think I'm staying here? Now go." The sergeant major was gone.

Daniyal felt his guts turn to liquid. There was no choice but to put the truck into gear and slowly move into the darkness. His hand shook as he shifted into drive. Nothing was visible to his side, as he slowly moved forward. The tactical running lights created a half-moon of visibility ten meters in front of the truck that helped him stay on the road. The rest of the world existed under a dark blanket on either side. He felt he had been driving for kilometers when his silent prayers went unanswered, for the bicycle was exactly where promised, leaning against a large boulder on the right side of the road. *Someone is waiting ahead*, he realized without comfort.

Daniyal turned onto the narrow two-track road, wincing as the truck lurched across a small drainage ditch. He wiped his hands on his trousers, while peering into the murk. Mist was rising from the ground. *I'm a lamb to slaughter*, he realized. *Anyone within a kilometer can hear this truck grinding along this road and see my running lights, but I'm blind.* Due to the poor condition of the side road, Daniyal kept the truck under ten kilometers per hour. He imagined boxes of grenades and rockets in the back of the truck teetering precariously as the tires seemed to find every hole and bump along the path.

No sense worrying, he assured himself. *It is all in Allah's hands. If I am meant to live, I will live. If not...* A rabbit broke from the brush next to the path and cut in front of his path, jarring him from his thoughts. Sweat ran down the inside of his blouse. *I am truly a great warrior*, he mused bitterly, *now I am even scared of rabbits.* At this slow pace the road seemed to go much further than the half kilometer that had been described. *Maybe I missed something—a turn? No, there was to be no turn.* He could feel anxiety...doubt building. *I will soon be joining Azir,* he resolved, taking small comfort. And, then there was a pale wall of granite before him. The rocky overhang.

This is a road to nowhere, he thought. *What is its purpose...* Before he could finish his thought, he saw the man, sitting on a shallow ledge two meters above the ground. He wore the traditional dress of the local Pashtun tribes, with a dark vest and a flat Pakul hat. An old rifle lay across his lap. A dark beard with streaks of gray covered his jaw. He waved his hand slowly in front of his eyes. His lips were moving, but Daniyal could not hear him over the grinding of the engine.

This is not who Daniyal had expected to meet. He was not sure what he had expected, but General Raziq was the all-powerful chief of police in Kandahar, and this man looked like a goat herder. Daniyal turned off the engine.

The man's voice now reached him. "Brother, can you turn off your lights? You are showing our position to everyone within 20 kilometers." The man spoke in Pashto, the local dialect, not in Dari, the national language. Daniyal killed the lights, leaving himself temporarily blind, as his eyes adjusted.

"Thank you, brother," the voice was now immediately below him next to the truck. *How had the man moved so quietly?* Daniyal marveled.

"What is your name?" the man asked. Daniyal did not answer, fumbling nervously for the door handle. He opened the door and climbed down to ground level.

"Do you not speak Pashto?" the man asked patiently.

"No...yes, I do. Some." stammered Daniyal. "My orders are to not speak to anyone."

The man chuckled. "You soldiers are always filled with orders. I am not *anyone*. I am Doctor Baseer. I merely want to thank you for this important gift you bring. Who may I have the pleasure of thanking?"

Daniyal struggled. His orders were not to speak, but to ignore this man's polite question would be a gross insult that could trigger a bad reaction.

"My name is Daniyal," he replied, then instantly realized he should have lied. *I am a fool. This man's manner is very disarming.*

"Thank you, Daniyal, for bringing these important supplies to my people. They will save many lives. The Hajji will be pleased."

An Absence of Faith

Daniyal froze. His heart was a stone in his chest. *Hajji?* He couldn't breathe.

Baseer moved to the rear of the truck. "They must think highly of you to give you such an important job," he continued. "These supplies are priceless." Baseer unhooked the latch on the tailgate and lowered it carefully. As Daniyal moved his leaden feet to the back of the truck, Baseer produced a small flashlight and shone it into the dark interior.

The boxes were neatly stacked and tightly bound together. "U.S. Army trauma pack—24 Count," read the stencil on the nearest box. Red Cross coolers lined the passenger wall of the truck. "Whole blood, Caution—thermal insulation inserts in use. Keep refrigerated." "Bundeswehr—Morphium" was on another box next to Baseer, sitting next to other German hospital supplies marked, "Infusionsbetel—18." The front of the cargo bay was packed with cots, litters, and mosquito netting, the very makings of a rudimentary field hospital.

The strength left Daniyal's knees. He was lightheaded. *This is not a transfer of weapons to General Raziq, but the delivery of medical supplies to the Taliban,* he realized. *Supplies that were intended for 225th Corps soldiers. To treat the burned men in his ward. For Azir, who had died in pain, with shoelaces and cloth strips mocking his service. This is treason.*

Baseer looked at Daniyal out the corner of his eye. "Did you not know, my friend? You look pale. Perhaps you could use a blood transfusion?" He chuckled. "We have the ability now."

"You…you're not working for Raziq," Daniyal croaked out the obvious.

Baseer smiled. "We do have a relationship. He puts bullets into my patients, and I take them out. Fighters, women, children, old people…they are all the same to a man like Raziq. A great leader. He is committed to killing his way to a more peaceful Afghanistan."

Bile rose in Daniyal's throat.

"Sit down, sit down my friend," Baseer encouraged, slowly lowering Daniyal onto a flat rock beside the truck. "Here, take some water." Baseer produced a skin from beneath his vest. He sprayed the warm, leathery water into Daniyal's mouth, who spat to cleanse his mouth.

Baseer patted Daniyal's shoulder. "The truth can be very disorienting," he offered. "When we learn that up is really down, it is hard to keep one's balance."

Does the sergeant major know? Of course, he knows. What a fool I am, Daniyal thought.

"I felt much the same way after my village was destroyed in 2008," Baseer continued. "I was teaching medicine at Kabul University. I was told the Taliban had destroyed my village." He paused, remembering. "I was angry and rushed home. I wanted to help the army make them pay. I found death, but no Taliban. The truth was the army had misfired their artillery and destroyed our homes. An army major came and blamed the Taliban, even though we found unexploded American shells amidst the rubble. He said they could not send help, and I would have to do my best to help the wounded. I realized everything I had been told was a lie. Days later the Taliban did come and took away our surviving young men, who wanted revenge. I decided to go where the medical need was greatest, so I followed."

"But you are the enemy," Daniyal choked, still trying to wrap his thoughts around what was occurring with the truck.

Baseer laughed. "The enemy of who? I take shrapnel out of old men, women, and children. I patch up people who never wanted to fight anyone until the fight came and killed their families. I have given you water and comfort. Am I your enemy?"

"But the sergeant major...the corps commander...how?"

"I do not claim to understand the chaos in your army. I am a doctor. I was sent here to get medical supplies, and now we have had a nice conversation. Those are the facts I know."

"I need to go," Daniyal choked out, while struggling to his feet. "The sergeant major will expect me back soon."

"It was good to meet you, Brother Daniyal. Duty is an admirable thing, but remember, putting too much trust in governments—or their armies—will get you killed. Take care and blessings upon your family. *Salaam.*"

"Peace also be with you," Daniyal murmured mechanically, as he stumbled up the road into the night. He had already decided that Dr. Baseer was right about one thing. If he told the sergeant major of this conversation, his life expectancy would be short indeed.

Chapter 7

Approaching Bagram Air Force Base, Afghanistan, November 2015

Colonel William Trevanathan awoke in the front row of the C-17 cargo plane, high over the southern Afghan desert. *These planes are always cold,* was his first waking thought. *Gotta' take a leak,* was his inevitable second. Returning to his seat after taking care of business, he looked out over the passenger module occupying the front third of the massive plane. Sleeping troops, using their gear and jackets for pillows, were strewn across the seats. Some were replacements, like himself; others were returning from leave.

The fifty-five-year-old colonel regarded the young faces. A stiff neck and the slight limp from a recent hernia operation reminded him that he could be the grandfather to most of these soldiers. *Lovely.* Trevanathan had entered the Army when Europe was still divided by the Iron Curtain, with the Soviets menacing on one side and NATO dug in on the other to repel them. He had been stationed fifteen kilometers from The Fence—what the troops called the Iron Curtain—when it came down in 1989. *None of these troops were even born then,* he realized. Now he was going to join a new iteration of NATO, in its efforts to prop up Afghanistan.

An airman from the crew paused as he passed the colonel, who was the ranking officer on board. "We're about 45 mikes[13] out from Bagram, sir. Lights will be coming up in a minute."

"Thanks, I appreciate it," the colonel replied. He then gingerly lowered himself into his seat, trying to not further aggravate the stitches from his recent procedure. The civilian doctor's orders had been to not lift more than 40 pounds for the next six weeks to let everything heal properly. Army regulations mandated that a soldier could not deploy for six weeks after any type of operation—no exceptions. So, four weeks after being sliced and diced, Trevanathan

---

[13] Mikes – Military term for minutes.

had *motivationally explained*, that is, lied his way through the pre-deployment medical screening at Fort Bliss, Texas, and was now flying to Afghanistan with 180 pounds of equipment in three duffel bags.

The erosion of political and military conditions in Afghanistan was driving his sense of urgency. A new general was due to take over the training command under which Trevanathan would serve, and that general would soon make the decision whether the Rule of Law office Trevanathan was slated to lead was going to continue or be dismembered so its staff positions could be distributed among other staff sections in the headquarters. His predecessor warned that the buzzards were already circling, anxious to scoop up the valuable personnel slots for their respective departments.

Colonel Trevanathan was part of the U.S. Army Reserve, not a full-time soldier. Army Reservists were the guys on the television commercials, along with the National Guard, who were referred to as serving one weekend a month. That used to be true, before the Pentagon started shipping their "citizen soldiers" off to fill most of the personnel demands in Iraq and Afghanistan over the past twenty years. Yet, it was his part-time status that made Trevanathan valuable for the current mission.

In civilian life, Trevanathan was a criminal court judge in rural Pennsylvania. He ran a courtroom, hammered drug dealers, coordinated with prosecutors and defense attorneys, and had launched two community programs to reform the justice system to focus on mental health and drug rehab issues, rather than a tunnel-visioned default to incarceration. In short, he knew how civilian legal systems should work, where their weaknesses were, and how to shepherd limited resources to best influence the civilian community. Active-duty legal officers did not have the benefit of such civilian court experience.

In the weeks before his deployment, Trevanathan reviewed several years of reports from his predecessors in Afghanistan to prepare himself. He paid particular attention to the most recent assessments by his old friend, Brigadier General Doug Maywood, who he was replacing. Maywood wrote that the average Afghan citizen was a daily victim of the Afghan government, which used its authority to pocket foreign aid and strip its citizens of their meager wealth. Afghans did not look to the government for protection; they sought any way to avoid contact with officials, as all such contact inevitably led to a demand for bribes. Only the well-connected or those willing to pay for justice could expect favorable treatment. The prevalence of corruption, combined with compulsory military service in a never-ending war, led most Afghans to look at the central government with increasing antipathy. There was little love for the government or the Taliban, as both sides made everyday life a miserable slog for survival.

But a man can never be too prepared. When the interior lights of the plane came on, Trevanathan began reviewing the latest briefing notes, received just prior to his departure. Unsurprising, the continuing erosion of confidence in the Afghan government was not only an Afghan domestic issue, it created a growing problem for the NATO countries supporting the Government of the Islamic Republic of Afghanistan[14]. They were tired of financing someone else's civil war, where their investment was regularly skimmed off into the pockets of Afghan officials. As Trevanathan's plane descended into Bagram Air Base, he re-read the last message he had received from Maywood, warning Trevanathan that his tour might be a short one if NATO allies voted to stop funding their joint mission at an upcoming NATO conference, scheduled to occur in Poland in July 2016.

The truth was that fifteen years after the 9/11 attacks, everyone was sick of the Afghanistan war—the longest armed conflict in U.S. and NATO history. Osama Bin Laden was dead at the hands of U.S. Special Ops forces, so the original reason for putting ground troops there no longer existed. Successive White House administrations sought to escape the conflict without facing political hellfire for appearing to forget the victims who died in those airliner attacks. Their European allies were increasingly sensitive to domestic pressure to reduce their overseas military commitment, which had become too expensive and too open-ended when European

---

[14] "Government of the Islamic Republic of Afghanistan" was the formal name of the Afghan government created and supported by NATO after the Taliban were driven from power following the attacks of September 11, 2001, and usually abbreviated as "GIRoA." Pronounced "Ji-Ro-a," it was the everyday shorthand reference for the Afghan government amongst Western troops and diplomats serving there.

economies were faltering. It was a Catch-22. No one wanted to stay, and no one could politically afford to allow defeat of a dysfunctional Afghan military.

Many Western generals had begun their careers as captains in Afghanistan, returned as battalion and brigade commanders, and now wore general's stars in the same fight. They had lost troops in the Afghan dirt over two decades with marginal military and political progress to show for it. Yet despite the legitimacy of the Afghan government declining, a path that would allow the U.S. and NATO to withdraw in a palatable manner seemed further away than ever.

Trevanathan knew that even the United States, which had directly suffered the terrorist attacks of September 11th, had grown weary of the conflict. As a reservist, who lived a life in both the civilian and military worlds, he knew that his Army friends were regularly rotated through Afghanistan, while his civilian friends and relatives were not even aware the war was still grinding on. In 2011, while the memories of September 11th were still somewhat fresh, the United States had one hundred thousand troops fighting an Asian land war in Afghanistan. Yet, unless a family member was in that hundred thousand, few members of the public were paying any attention, Trevanathan recalled. "Sex and the City," the "Twilight" series, and the engagement of Prince William and Kate Middleton captured the public's attention instead.

Now, as Trevanathan approached Bagram Air Base, a cap of eighty-five hundred troops had been imposed by the White House, which was concerned with the bad optics of more U.S. casualties. "The war is like a bad relationship that no one knows how to break off simply because the couple had been together so long," General Maywood had written him.

This doesn't sound very optimistic, Trevanathan pondered as he read page after page of analysis that seemed to admire the problems but provided little insight on a path forward. The U.S. was looking for a way to hand the war off to the Afghan National Army[15] to fight the remaining Taliban elements in country, which were described as "roughly thirty thousand insurgent forces on the decline." The new plan was to provide the three hundred thousand Afghan security

---

[15] Commonly referred to as the ANA in conversation.

forces with the necessary tools and training so they could fight the war against the Taliban insurgents themselves. This was now a civil war, and the Afghans should take the lead to defend their own country, ran the theme in his briefing notes. *That's convenient*, thought Trevanathan, *unless you're an Afghan caught in the middle.*

Train, Advise, and Assist was the catch phrase for the recently renamed Operation Resolute Support mission. In short, U.S. soldiers and marines were no longer going to go up the goat trail into the wilds after the Taliban. The U.S. would train the ANA to go up the goat trail instead, using U.S. weapons, ammunition, and technology. Afghan soldiers would be driving American HMMWVs and firing American weapons, supported by American artillery, aircraft, and intelligence.

It all looks so clean on paper, Trevanathan thought, shaking his head as he read. *It's like a rerun from Iraq*, he recalled from his service there as a major, a dozen years before. The bias in U.S. military planning is always that any problem can be solved if enough money and firepower is thrown at it. Trevanathan had just completed his graduate course at the U.S. Army War College, where he read the fallacy of such an approach had supposedly been learned in Vietnam. *I guess some people skipped the reading*, Trevanathan mused.

His briefing documents spent at most a paragraph describing the domestic political situation in the country, concluding that ethnic tribes continued to play a major political role in supporting the central government's authority. *Not that helpful,* Trevanathan thought. *Where does the loyalty of the people lie, is the question? In Iraq it was to their family and tribe first. Religion was next. The government was an afterthought. Is it the same here?*

The gravelly voice of the plane's crew chief came over the cargo bay speaker. "We are on final approach to Bagram Air base. If Bagram is not your final destination, you have seriously fucked up." Trevanathan smiled. *This guy is a frustrated comedian.*

The crew chief continued, "Weather conditions are clear. Remain in your seats until the aircraft comes to a complete stop. Then immediately follow the ground crew to the terminal. Take your weapon and body armor, but do not wait for your other gear. As soon as this plane stops it's a magnet for indirect fire, so un-ass the plane ASAP. Bunkers are in front of the terminal for your use and enjoyment. I hope you've enjoyed flying the friendly skies."

Trevanathan shook his head and smiled. *The vets always like to put a scare into the newbies*, he understood, before continuing his reading.

The battlefield situation was essentially a stalemate, the Pentagon assessments related. The Taliban lacked the ability and manpower to hold terrain, including major urban centers. Opposing them, the ANA was used to defending objectives taken by U.S., British, and other NATO forces, and not conducting offensive operations. But they did what the Afghans do best when they don't intend to follow through on an idea–they agreed to it. They accepted the U.S. plan for the ANA to take over offensive operations and then promptly ignored it. Except for a few special operations units, offensive operations against the Taliban largely ceased with the 2014 transition to Operation Resolute Support.

Trevanathan heard the landing gear descending. *This briefing is too generic. Time to get on the ground and see what the real play is.*

Trevanathan was not a big fan of flying, but at least the landing of the massive aircraft was smooth. As he touched down at Bagram on November 23, 2015, to take charge of NATO's Director of Rule of Law operations, he knew he had to learn quickly, or he'd soon be irrelevant. In the alphanumeric jumble of military life on the NATO wire diagram, his staff section was titled EF3 for *Essential Function 3*[16], with a mission to deter corruption within the Afghan government. While Trevanathan could have been flattered that he was being sent as a colonel to fill the job of a one-star general, he was realistic enough to know it more likely meant that no one-star officer wanted the job, as thirteen predecessors had been unsuccessful in deterring the rampant bribery and theft within the Afghan halls of power. But for the moment, his thoughts were more mundane. *I would give a hundred bucks for a cup of coffee, an ibuprofen, and an ice pack*, he considered, as his hernia incision talked to him once again.

---

[16] Another Section titled EF2 existed to prevent corruption through education and training. EF3 was the enforcement arm.

Chapter 8

Camp Resolute Support, Kabul, November 2015

"ARRHHOOO," the siren wailed through the fog of Trevanathan's sleep-deprived mind. The colonel was still sleeping off his jetlag in the visiting officer's quarters of Camp Resolute Support in central Kabul when the alarm for incoming fire sounded. It had been eleven years since his last deployment, but his combat reflexes remained largely intact. He rolled off the mattress and hit the floor, hard, scrambling into the flak jacket he had positioned there. Before he had the chance to pull on his helmet, two explosions shook the room. It was hard to tell their exact distance or even if they were within the camp. *If you can feel it through the ground though, it's not that far away.*

The colonel belatedly put on his helmet and secured the chin strap, while still lying on the floor. *I could use some light but can't stand up and make myself a bigger target for any metal flying around. So what do I do?* He fumbled around in the dark and found his pistol. *I must still be sleep deprived,* he chastised himself. *A pistol isn't going to help me. I just need to sit tight until they sound the "all clear." If I go out to find a bunker, some excited guard will probably shoot me.*

He crawled to his window and briefly raised himself to peek out between the blinds. A large metal condenser and the wall of another building several feet away were all he could see. *I guess that neighboring building gives me some cover*, he hoped, returning to the floor.

While he was considering his next move through the grogginess of traveling eleven time zones, the "all clear'" announcement sounded. The colonel could feel his heart beating against the inside of his flak jacket. *Well, that was quick. But I'm not getting back to sleep now. What time is it?* He checked his watch to see that it was just 0400, local time. *Shower, chow. Take baby steps*, he decided.

A bang on his door spiked his adrenalin again. *I'm going to have words with management,* the colonel thought, as he stumbled across the room to find the light switch. A second round of banging thundered on his door as he found the switch. "Just a fucking minute," the colonel mumbled, as he undid the latch and opened the door. Outside was a wide-eyed, sandy-haired Navy lieutenant[17], who he had met briefly at the helicopter field when he had arrived the day before.

"General Maywood asked me to check on you if we had any incoming overnight, sir…" His voice trailed off as he looked Trevanathan up and down. The colonel stood in the doorway in his boxer shorts, wearing a flak jacket, a helmet, and holding his 9mm pistol in his right hand.

Trevanathan noted the look and then slowly regarded his own attire. He sighed. "Transom, right? This is not a good moment for either of us, Lieutenant," the colonel replied. "I'm jet-lagged and firing on one brain cell. So, you're going away, and coming back in a half hour to take me to breakfast. If you mention this get-up to anyone"—he gestured to himself—"You'll be reassigned to a mine sweeping detail in Kandahar." He laughed to cut the tension. "Clear?"

"Roger, sir. Breakfast in 30 mikes. No mine sweeping."

"Thank you."

Exactly thirty minutes later, Lieutenant Transom was back at his door and Trevanathan had pulled himself together with a quick shower. He was dressed in his battle dress uniform, the camouflage pattern of which was affectionately known among the troops as, *vomit splatter pattern number one.* "I feel like a hundred bucks," he joked to the naval officer, who still did not know how to take his new boss.

"Yes, sir," Transom replied, deferentially.

The two officers made their way through the pre-dawn murk to the dining facility, which was open twenty-four hours to sustain the various shifts necessary to keep the war running. Trevanathan

---

[17] A Navy Lieutenant is in the grade of 03 and equivalent in rank to an Army Captain.

coughed deeply and noted Lieutenant Transom held a bandana over his mouth.

"What's with the air?" the colonel asked. "It's almost rust colored. I can taste it."

"Yessir. In winter, the locals burn kerosene, coal, and shit to stay warm. The smoke is trapped in the bottom of this valley until spring by the cold weather. Called an 'inversion.' It's worse at night. During the day it's almost breathable. You're basically breathing burnt shit."

"Nice. And the incoming fire? What's the frequency of that?"

"Depends, sir. Runs hot and cold. It's almost always at night, because they set up their rockets on the outskirts of town and that's easier to do when the local cops can't see them. I'd say we get a visit two or three nights a week, but we can go a week with nothing and then have an entire week of excitement the next. No rhyme or reason. Probably depends on their supplies. They like to hit us on holidays, too, so Thanksgiving and Christmas will probably be a hoot."

Trevanathan stepped around a large pothole in the road. "What are the other threats?"

"Well, there's the car bombs. They cruise the streets outside the Green Zone looking for our convoys to ram. They're bad news. Six hundred pounds of HE[18] packed into a sedan will do a world of hurt to anything we have. That's why we have these very attractive 'T-walls[19]' all around." He gestured toward a gate they were passing that was lined with tall concrete barriers.

"Anything else?"

"The main threat to our EF3 personnel is the ANA and MOI guards."

---

[18] High Explosive

[19] T-Walls are twenty-feet high concrete walls that come in portable segments that can be placed side by side to create a walled perimeter. They have a wider base and a narrower vertical wall section, so they look like inverted letters T when in place. The Kabul Green Zone was a rat's maze of T-walls lining all streets and multiple compounds, creating a fortified hub in the center of the capital for many GIRoA ministries, the Presidential Palace, Camp Resolute Support, and Western embassies.

"In what way?"

"Green-on-blue attacks, sir. Doesn't get much press back home, but we're much more likely to get shot by an Afghan cop or soldier than by the Taliban, and we have to interact with them every day to do our job."

"You're right, it doesn't get coverage."

"Well, the American public isn't going to be too thrilled about sending billions of dollars to a country where the hometown troops like to shoot us in the back, so that info is pretty tightly controlled."

"And this is happening, why? The old 'Death to infidels' bit?"

"Depends on who you ask, sir. Lots of guesswork, because the shooter often ends up dead. Sometimes the shooter is a Taliban or ISIS plant who got into the army to carry out insider attacks. Sometimes it's a guy who got radicalized by internet videos or his mosque. Too often it's some dupe who had one of his children kidnapped by the bad guys and told the kid will be tortured to death unless he whacks an American. We had another guy last year who shot a British army captain because the Brit talked to him too harshly and he felt dishonored."

"And this happens how often?"

"Again, hard to quantify. They come in bunches. Once there is one attack, then there tends to be more copycat attempts shortly thereafter. I'd say there's probably an attempt every four to six weeks and we lose maybe four or five people a year. It varies, ya' know? Luckily, the Afghans can't shoot very well, but an AK-47 makes up a lot in volume for lack of accuracy. Especially at close range."

The two officers entered the one-story dining facility[20] and signed the obligatory meal sheet for officers. It was a standard Army mess hall, and it was excellent. *This is a pleasant surprise*, thought Trevanathan, remembering the invasion of Iraq, where for three weeks he had eaten unheated spaghetti out of a green plastic bin that had sat in an Army warehouse for God knows how many years, before supplies had caught up to his unit.

---

[20] Often referred to by soldiers as the DFAC (D-fak) in speech.

An Absence of Faith

At this hour, the chow hall was largely empty, but hot food was waiting. The colonel worked his way down the serving line, staffed by contractors from Bangladesh, loading his plate with scrambled eggs, bacon, and fried potatoes. He felt like he had maybe overdone it, until he saw a short, overweight troop ahead of him in line who had double the amount of food on his tray. *Well now I don't feel so bad,* he thought. He did a double-take as the portly soldier turned and walked away, revealing two stars on his collar. *Guess there's no PT[21] test over here*, Trevanathan thought.

The colonel went in search of a table but stopped in front of a display rack next to a cooler full of individual milk cartons—skim, whole, and chocolate, as well as a half dozen flavors of yogurt. *Holy shit, they have Fruit Loops and Cocoa Puffs*, he marveled. *This place is amazing. Car bombs and Cocoa Puffs—this is going to take some getting used to. Can't believe they use space on aircraft to ship kid's cereal here.*

"Hey sir, over here," beckoned Transom, who had seated himself across from a broad-shouldered, black-haired soldier in well-used sweats. Trevanathan went to join them. "Sir, this is Major Chuck Brandt, your deputy."

"Good to meet you, sir," Major Brandt announced, extending his hand with a grin. "I apologize for the appearance; I just came from the gym."

"In the gym at 0400; that's admirable," commented Trevanathan.

"I like to get in there and lift before the Nancy boys show up and start clogging the place."

"Speaking of that, who is the two-star over there with the cardiac special breakfast?"

"That's Major General Porcher, sir. An Advisor to the Ministry of Defense. He just got in a couple weeks ago. Don't know much about him except he's one of the vultures circling around hoping to grab our staff positions if EF3 is shut down. He was going to be the next III Corps commander, but got sent here instead, because he's a fat boy."

---

[21] PT. Physical Training – a mandatory physical fitness test of running, push-ups, and sit-ups all soldiers were required to pass.

"And where does that process stand right now, the staff issue, I mean?" the colonel asked.

"It's up to the COM[22] and Major General Crist, the new CSTC-A[23] commander, to work out. Above my pay grade, sir," Brandt replied. "Hopefully, you can influence it," he added, sizing up his new boss.

Trevanathan nodded. "So, where did you come in from?" he asked Brandt.

"D.C. area, sir."

"Belvoir?"

"Fuck no, sir. Quantico."

"Ah, Marine."

"Oorah, Sir."

"Great. So what can you tell me about our section?"

"Overall, a good group. But like any group, you have some who are stronger than others. Right now, we have twelve people on Camp RS, who are responsible for coordinating with their legal counterparts in the Ministry of Defense and Ministry of Interior, plus our translators. We have another half-dozen police advisors up at the airport, who are supposed to be doing training with the Afghan cops but are currently underemployed through no fault of their own. Money has dried up for training and no one seems to care because the Afghan cops are so dirty."

"What's our breakdown of military versus civilian personnel?"

"All the cops are civilians. NYPD, Chicago homicide—all on leave of absence to us under contract. The EF3 staff on RS is 50/50—half in uniform and the other half are DOD[24] civilians. The translators are Afghan nationals. The best one, Ahmed, is a U.S. citizen who is on his fourth tour."

"What do the civilians do?"

---

[22] COM – The shorthand nickname for the Commander of U.S. and NATO forces in Afghanistan. A four-star U.S. Army General.
[23] Combined Security Transition Command - Afghanistan
[24] U.S. Department of Defense civilian employees.

"Liaison with MOD[25] and MOI[26], mostly. Smile, collect info, try to keep a finger on what is going on. One or two are war tourists. Just here to burnish their resume so they can make GS-*something* when they get home. Hardly go off post but spend a lot of time with tasks that don't really matter."

"Explain that."

"Well, sir, Camp RS is a weird place. It's like Disneyland in a war zone. There are some people here who are never going to interact with an Afghan outside the walls of this base. They spend all day creating briefings that superficially sound good and reinforce *groupthink*, but don't say anything important. If you want to be well-regarded around here, just try to figure out new ways to say we're doing everything right here and GIRoA is winning the war. Nobody shoots a messenger with good news. Those types then spend their off-duty hours hitting the Thai restaurant, going to the hair salon, and watching movies while cashing in on their tax-free pay."

"Hair salon?"

"Yes sir. Staffed by some chicas from Uzbekistan. You can get a hair styling and a massage if you want. Go buy a pint of Haagen Dazs at the Italian PX and spend the evening in your hooch watching one of five thousand movies from the post server. Used to be a lot of porn on there until some Bible thumper wrote their congressman. You can shovel about six thousand calories of food into your piehole three times per day, go home fat, and declare yourself a war hero. It's like not even being in a war zone, 'cept for the pesky rocket attacks."

"Not what I expected."

"Well, there's another real war going on side by side with that one that's no joke. The war tourists are focused on buying Afghan jewelry, sending stray cats home, and getting awards for not upsetting the status quo. Group two is those working with the Afghans to try to unfuck this place: get an honest government, or something close to it that the people can believe in; trying to turn the ANA and the cops into a real fighting force; and dodging suicide bombers and green-on-blue shootings to meet with Afghan officials,

---

[25] MOD – Ministry of Defense
[26] MOI – Ministry of Interior

who themselves might be dead tomorrow. There's a daily urban guerilla war outside these walls. All of these people—the tourists and the no-shit players—eat in this room together each morning, but they're each living a different war."

A high-pitched giggle broke through the nearly empty room to punctuate Major Brandt's point. Trevanathan looked over his shoulder at a table behind himself where a young air force captain was smiling too broadly at a laughing blonde in a tight teal jump suit. The colonel cocked his head back toward Brandt.

"Miami Dolphins cheerleaders, sir. Arrived last night to do an MWR[27] show for the troops. We had WWE wrestlers last week. That captain's main job in life is escorting VIPs and then writing up their visits for the command website. He'll go home with a Bronze Star and ruck full of lies about his wartime service."

"Surreal," said Trevanathan.

"It's the nature of Camp RS, sir," said Brandt. "Part wartime operational base, part war movie set for visiting politicos from D.C. It's a build-your-own-war workshop. You can be a Fobbit[28], play a role in the war movie, or do a no-shit mission that might make a difference to the future of the millions of Afghans who don't want to live under a fucked-up, medieval horror show again. Everyone gets a shiny new medal regardless of what they do or don't do, and everyone is a true patriot, even if their contribution was eating ice cream and watching movies."

Trevanathan shook his head. "My last deployment was OIF1[29]. I'm JAG[30], not infantry, so I don't want to overstate this. But that war was getting eaten alive by sand fleas, 130-degree days, moldy food, and a lot of death. So, this war of hot showers, restaurants, cheerleaders, and warm chow is hard for me to get my head around."

---

[27] Morale, Welfare, Recreation

[28] Mil. Slang derogatory term for a person who never leaves the safety of the base. A play on words that combines FOB (forward operating base) with the Hobbit characters from J.R.R. Tolkien's books, who traditionally valued comfort and an absence of adventure above all else.

[29] Operation Iraqi Freedom – 1st rotation of troops, i.e., the initial invasion of Iraq in 2003.

[30] Judge Advocate General Corps– Uniformed Army lawyers.

"Still plenty of death to go around here, sir. You're just closer to the flagpole now, so there's some benefits here the grunts out in the boonies never see. You had a bucket in Iraq? You must've been a field grade officer[31]," teased Major Brandt.

Trevanathan laughed. "Yeah, it was fur lined too."

Brandt looked serious for a moment. "Word is you caught some metal in that last tour, if you don't mind me asking."

"Yes, I had some bad luck at the end of my tour. IED. But they stuffed my guts back in and after about thirty-units of blood and five surgeries I was good as new," Trevanathan grinned, but remembered it wasn't so humorous at the time.

"And you still decided to volunteer for this adventure?"

The colonel shrugged. "You know how it is. I have the experience for the job. I've started and reformed courts in Iraq and in the States. It's not about what I want. If it was, I'd be drinking rum out of a coconut somewhere."

"Got it, sir. Just wanted to confirm you were as crazy as I had heard from General Maywood."

"Doug…, that is, the General's known me for over twenty-five years, so you can be sure that at least half of what he says isn't complete bullshit. When is he heading out, by the way?"

"He's already at Bagram, sir. You probably passed him on your way in. His orders were running out, so he had to catch today's flight to Kuwait. He left a note for you in your office. If you give me twenty minutes to throw on my uniform, I'll meet you in front of the HQ and give you a quick orientation to the place," Brandt offered.

"Perfect. I need to get my bearings."

---

[31] Major rank or above.

Chapter 9

Camp Resolute Support, Kabul, November 2015

Trevanathan took the next few minutes to indulge in a second cup of coffee and began to feel life returning to his body. He asked Transom the next thing on his mind, which had been bothering him since the rocket attack. "LT[32], I don't see any bunkers on post. Am I missing something?"

"There aren't any, sir. I've never heard why exactly. Maybe it's a space thing. Things are pretty cramped on the post and with rocket fire being not all that accurate, I dunno…"

"We have pizza shops and a beauty salon, but no bunkers to protect troops from indirect fire? The priorities seem kind of messed up. It only takes one lucky shot to ruin your day."

"That's pretty much it, sir."

"So when rockets come in, we…?"

"We put on our flak jackets and get low."

"Really? And what if the outer wall gets breached? Are there assigned fighting positions?"

"Umm, no one's ever talked about that, sir. I'll have to ask. The guidance is just to get off the streets and let the Georgians[33] do their thing."

"Get off the streets where? The temporary quarters I'm in right now has thin prefab walls that aren't going to stop any rifle rounds if the Georgians or bad guys start mixing it up. The only building on post with walls that look thick enough to stop gunfire is maybe the

---

[32] A common military reference for anyone in the rank of Lieutenant is LT, pronounced "EL TEE."

[33] Troops from the former Soviet Republic of Georgia were the security force at Camp Resolute Support, aka Camp RS, along with Macedonian soldiers.

headquarters. You're as likely to get killed by a stray round inside as outside."

"I wish I had the answer, sir."

"So our section doesn't have a plan in case of a ground attack?"

"Not as such, sir..." Transom's voice trailed off. "There's a big blimp over the camp so we can see trouble coming from any direction," he added hopefully.

"Really? A blimp?"

"Yessir, it's on a cable and mounted with all sorts of surveillance cameras to see all over Kabul."

"Did that blimp stop the car bomb that cooked off about a block from here last year?"

"No sir. That killed a bunch of civilians just up the street from the main gate here. A couple of our gate guards were wounded."

"And if they had rammed that car bomb up against the wall of this base before cooking it off?"

"Probably a big hole." Transom paused, looking uncomfortable. "I get it, sir. Seems like maybe we need a plan."

"I'll look forward to your first draft of it on Monday."

"Sir?"

"Congratulations. Add unit security officer to your list of additional duties."

"I've never done anything like that before, sir. Sure, you don't want someone else...?"

"Consider it an opportunity to excel. Don't worry, our lives only depend on you doing a good job." Trevanathan smiled inwardly as he kept a straight face and watched the color drain from Transom's face. "All right, I need to meet the major," he concluded.

"I'm heading that way too, sir."

The two officers exited the DFAC and started up the one-lane road that was the main east-west pedestrian route across the base.

They passed a makeshift cross with a pile of dried out flowers on the curb to their right.

"What's that?" the colonel inquired.

"Remember the blimp? A new pilot—British, I think—hit the cable with his tail rotor on his first approach to our landing zone last month. Didn't see it until too late. Crashed right here in the middle of camp. Killed four people in the bird, including him. It was a miracle the fuel didn't catch fire or this entire part of the base would be gone."

Trevanathan looked about at several two-story office structures in their immediate area, as well as the small PX[34] and laundry drop-off window to his left.

"Hard to believe only four people were killed. This looks like a high traffic area."

"Everyone's got a story 'bout it, sir. I was heading down here to drop off my laundry when General Maywood called and asked me for a copy of an article I had written. I went back to get it for him—probably saved my life. I've heard a dozen stories just like that since then. One thing I've learned from this deployment is the number of ways you can get killed that have nothing to do with the enemy. Helo crashes, earthquakes, rabies, green-on-blue, accidental discharges. Seen it all."

"Rabies? Really?"

"Yes sir, we have cats on base to keep the rat population down. The authorized have their ears notched and are taken care of by the post vet. But this is a big city and strays climb in over the wall all the time because they smell food. We had some do-gooder DOD civilian who was feeding the cats instead of letting them catch the vermin. She got bit by one of the feral cats and didn't tell anyone, because she didn't want to get in trouble. By the time she got sick and they med-evac'd her it was too late."

"Damn, I've never heard of anyone dying from rabies in this day and age."

---

[34] Post Exchange – Store run by the military for soldiers where they can buy personal supplies, cigarettes, toiletries, and snacks.

"You're in a time machine, sir. This is one of the few countries on earth where they still have leprosy and polio. Very unforgiving environment. I use hand sanitizer a dozen times a day."

"Thanks for the tip."

"Roger, sir. Well, here's the major, so I'll hand you off to him. I'll see you later at the office."

Brandt was waiting in front of the headquarters in his desert Marine fatigues. He snapped a salute to the colonel as he walked up.

"We do that here too, huh?" commented the colonel, returning the courtesy. "No one is worried about snipers?"

"If you look up around the wall top, sir, they have sniper screens around most of the perimeter to block the view from taller buildings. It's not one hundred percent, but there's never been an incident."

"Well, that's good. God forbid some general didn't get his quota of salutes each day."

"Damn sir, you're a bit of a rebel, aren't you?" laughed Brandt. "I was worried they'd send some tight assed by-the-book pogue[35] to terrorize us."

"I just focus on results, Chuck. The military fluff and ribbons are all really neat, and I love tradition as much as the next guy, but if something doesn't help get the mission accomplished—or worse, gets in the way—I don't have much patience for it. I've seen too many mediocre officers cling to form over substance and get people hurt. Any dumb shit can mindlessly follow a rule. Understanding why the rule exists and if it makes sense in any given context takes a brain."

"Oorah, sir."

"OK, what else do I need to know about my new home?"

"Well, sir, let's start with this street. The camp is basically a big square, with four main streets. You came up from the DFAC past the PX and the laundry drop-off on the southern-most street. On the other side of the DFAC is the Italian PX, which is better and has more inventory because they'll pay bribes to the Afghan border

---

[35] Pogue – Mil. slang for a person who is not on the front lines of combat.

guards to get it through from Pakistan. Our PX won't pay bribes, so the Afghans sometimes make our trucks sit in Pakistan for several weeks, claiming the papers aren't in order," Brandt stated matter-of-factly.

"So, we fight for them, supply them, and give them a few billion in cash each year, but they don't let our trucks in without a bribe? Awesome."

"You got it, sir. When you turned onto this northbound street you passed the pizza parlor on the corner, which isn't half-bad. It's closed this time of day but is a nice break if you get tired of the DFAC. We take our Afghan contacts there sometimes—they seem to like it."

"Contacts?"

"Well, we have insiders who keep us informed about what's going on in the Afghan government ministries. The ground truth. Not the BS the Afghan officials tell us in formal meetings, none of which is true."

"*Afghan* insiders?"

Brandt shrugged without replying aloud.

"We're not doing intel work, are we?" asked Trevanathan, lowering his voice.

"Oh no sir, we never want to call it that. We just call it conversations with our allies." Brandt grinned mischievously.

"This is getting more interesting. OK, what else?"

"You passed by both haircut shops down there on the right. There's the cheaper one that charges about three dollars and usually has the longer line, and then there's the one with the Uzbek girls, who do a better job and charges ten."

"What's this green area?" the colonel asked, pointing through an open pedestrian arch across from the headquarters, into a half-block sized, grassy square punctuated with walking paths, picnic tables, and several gazebos.

"It's a park, of sorts, sir. This base used to be a school campus of some type. The current landing zone was its soccer field. This park was here when we moved in, so people just kinda' hang out there when off duty. One of the few green spaces in central Kabul, since the locals cut down most of the trees for firewood during the Taliban years. There are two or three groundskeepers who hang out in the back in a shack, probably cooking heroin and gathering intel for the Taliban."

"Very nice."

"Yessir. Our office is across the street next to the headquarters on the left through that metal gate. We share a small compound with some special ops guys. No idea what they do. They keep to themselves. We're up on the second deck."

"Other than the headquarters and the dining hall, it looks like a lot of the buildings on the post are temporary. Am I right?"

"Pretty much, sir. A few original buildings have been adapted, but overall Camp RS is a hodgepodge of beat-up trailers and modular office units connected by catwalks and metal stairwells. Our office is basically a double-wide trailer stacked on another double wide that would be at home in any trailer park in America. When it rains the entire post turns to mud, so having the catwalks is nice. Most people live in CONEX shipping containers around the DFAC area, that've been converted into quarters. You'll probably get one for yourself since you're an 06[36]. Otherwise, its three to six men to a CONEX, depending on rank."

"If it's got a roof and no camel spiders, I'll be happy," the colonel said.

"The other nice thing about the CONEX units is you won't get buried during the earthquakes."

"You're a fountain of joy. Anyone ever tell you?"

"Better to know ahead of time, right, sir? We get a couple each month. The small ones feel like a train going by. With big ones you sometimes ride your bed across the room. Don't store anything heavy high on a shelf you don't want to land on your head."

---

[36] 06 is the pay grade for a full colonel. Military personnel often interchange using formal rank titles and equivalent pay grades when engaged in casual conversation. A second lieutenant is an 01, a captain is an 03, and so on. See rank chart in the Appendix.

An explosion echoed in the distance. Trevanathan turned to look in its direction. Brandt didn't break cadence in his conversation. "One advantage of the shoddy construction is everything just kinda sways when the earth moves, rather than collapsing," he continued. "There's lots of give."

"That reminds me," the colonel resumed. "I mentioned to the LT about coming up with a plan in case the outer perimeter was ever breached. But you've been here awhile. What do you think?"

"Not the worst idea, sir, because we'd be among the first to know. The closest street that the bad guys could access is that wall right there on the far side of the park." Brandt gestured to a thirty feet high masonry wall that ran the length of the far boundary of the park. "There's a public street on the far side, even though it's within the Green Zone. If I was Joe Shit the Taliban Man, I'd blow a hole in that wall and pour a half dozen guys with AKs and suicide vests through. You notice no one on base carries anything except pistols, other than the gate guards. There'd be a shit-ton of casualties before the mess got sorted out."

"Well, I'm not in charge of post security, but I think we need a plan for our section, so people know where they need to be and how to act if things go south. Especially with all the civilians in our section," said Trevanathan.

"Yes sir, the greatest danger is probably them shooting themselves or each other if the crap really hits the fan." said Brandt.

"Well, they don't have weapons, right?"

"They *all* have weapons, sir. Every GS-13 through 15 they ship over here to do accounting or office work is issued a weapon. Most of them carry the 9mm pistol, but a few have qualified with the M4 rifle during their two weeks' weapons' training stateside and are eligible to carry those, if need be."

"Are you shitting me? They're giving military assault rifles to civilians in a combat zone who have had two weeks' target practice?"

"Didn't say it was a good idea, sir. Just the way it is. Last rotation we had a civilian come in from the Air Force. Claimed she was in their reserves. I don't fuckin' know. She pulled out her pistol to show it to one of her office mates and, I kid you not, a four-inch-long dust bunny fell out of the grip. I asked her the last time she had shot a weapon before her two-week combat killer course, and she said they don't do that in the Air Force, so it had probably been a decade. So yeah, if the bad guys ever show up here, we're gonna' have all sorts of people blowing their toes off and putting one into the back of their neighbor, due to poor weapons discipline as the adrenaline kicks in."

"OK, I'm going to need your help on a few things. First, I need a new section policy written up that no one pulls an M4 for a mission unless you or I approve it in writing. Unless they're prior service, I don't care how well they can hit a paper target, they have no business carrying an assault rifle in an urban combat zone. That will keep some Barney Fife from killing an Afghan general or one of us by mistake."

"Roger, sir."

"Next, I want your assessment of who among the civilians seems comfortable with their weapon and who seems out of their depth. Do it quietly so we don't embarrass anyone. Maybe we can get them some additional training – if there is such a thing in this place," said Trevanathan.

"I can do that."

"Last, help the LT out with the section emergency response plan."

"Roger, sir, part of that plan should account for people when the shooting stops, because most days we have people all over Kabul and all over the post. Chances are we won't be together when the shit hits the fan. I'll work with the LT on it. He's a smart guy, but being Navy, his plan will probably be to call in the Marines anyway," Brandt laughed at his own joke.

"I'd appreciate it. Anything else I need to see?"

"Only if you want to go to the Hajji market."

"And that is?"

"Locals have a space about a hundred meters north of here to sell rugs, souvenirs, fake lapis bowls. You can even get a suit made."

"Outside the wire?"

"No, sir. They're on the camp."

"They're inside the camp?" the colonel repeated in disbelief.

"Yes sir. They've been vetted, and some have been here a decade or more."

"That's a decade where the enemy can use them to gather intel on us?"

"Damn, you are a suspicious one," Brandt laughed. "Well, good, that'll keep you alive."

"I learned in my last adventure that the enemy exploits our best impulses against us. They know we like kids, so they use kids to gather intel. Our male soldiers won't search women out of respect for their culture, so they smuggle RPGs under their chador[37]. As soon as something is routine, that is where they bite us. But I think I've had all the tour I can take for today. I need to get my head around what I've seen so far."

"Roger, sir. It takes some getting used to. Let me show you your office."

Trevanathan and Brandt entered the small compound that was home to the EF3 section and climbed metal stairs to the second floor. Trevanathan found his new office just inside the door. It was a six by eight feet broom closet of a room, with unpainted plywood walls, bare two-by-four studs, and a poster of a 747 flying in through a fake window. A government issue metal desk and a rusty filing cabinet were his furniture, along with a bent office chair on wheels and a single metal folding chair placed across from the desk. A three-foot high wooden cross mounted on a wooden base behind the door baffled him for a moment until he realized it was a stand for his flak jacket and helmet. In the middle of the desk lay an envelope with his name handwritten across the front. *Must be Doug's guidance,* he realized. *Too bad we didn't have time to talk but can't blame him for beaming out since I was delayed by this hernia.*

Trevanathan tore open the envelope, anxious to gain any parting words of wisdom from his old friend and predecessor. The note was reassuring:

---

[37] A piece of clothing worn by Muslim women that is wrapped around the head and body leaving only the face exposed.

"Don't fuck it up. Don't die. Hugs, Doug"

Chapter 10

Camp Resolute Support, Kabul, December 2015

"Sir, the boss wants to see you."

Trevanathan looked up from the papers on his desk. His new aide, First Lieutenant Ripple, stood in the door.

"Which one?"

"CSTC-A[38], sir: General Crist."

The full title was unnecessary. Major General Crist was the new commanding general of the Combined Security Transition Command—Afghanistan, the hybrid organization responsible for training and supplying the Afghan National Army, as well as doing the same for the paramilitary police from the Ministry of Interior. When the U.S. and NATO handed off the ground combat role to the Afghan army in 2014, the mission of CSTC-A became critical to the Afghan's future success. CSTC-A was the engine that worked to ensure the Afghan security forces had the supplies, weapons, and know-how to take the fight to the Taliban.

Whenever "The COM," as General Peterson, the four-star NATO commander of the Resolute Support mission in Afghanistan was known, or his staff, or even his wife, had a new idea on how to transform Afghanistan from a war torn, corruption-ridden weeping sore into a stable democracy, it typically became Crist's job to make it happen. Crist was a rising star in the Army—a mentally-sharp West Point grad who had held all the important command and senior staff jobs needed to climb to the highest levels of the Army. His energy level was inexhaustible, and he was often seen in the post gym after midnight lifting weights and running treadmills into the ground after completing his duty day. His staff joked that if you were a bad person in life you weren't sent to hell, you were assigned to be Crist's aide, as there would be eternal toil without rest.

---

[38] Pronounced "C-stick-ah."

Crist could size up a situation—or person—in seconds. Despite a lifetime in an organization whose primary mission was destroying the nation's enemies through firepower, Crist understood the strength of soft power—strategic communications, economics, and politics—the intangibles that often decide whether radical armed militias or democratically-elected policy makers control a country. He appreciated on an instinctive level that if the Afghan people did not believe in their government—that if they weren't willing to send their sons to fight for its survival— all the bombs and bullets in the American arsenal would not make a difference in the end.

Crist's office was shoehorned into a rabbit's warren of temporary trailers and metal catwalks behind the COM's headquarters. Entering the trailer door marked "CSTC-A Commander," Trevanathan encountered three soldiers squeezed behind desks in a space the size of many small bathrooms back in the States. The General's aide, First Lieutenant Mann, he already knew. The Public Affairs Officer, who had been shmoozing the Dolphins cheerleader earlier in the week, was typing away on a laptop on an Army field desk in the far corner. A master sergeant named Fields occupied the largest piece of real estate, a gray government desk two feet inside the door. "Sir," Fields nodded, barely raising his eyes from his work.

"Let me check that the boss is ready for you, sir," said Lieutenant Mann, knocking lightly on an interior door to Trevanathan's right before slipping inside.

Trevanathan looked around the room, the usual forward deployed headquarters. The walls were papered with maps and Equal Opportunity, Inspector General, and command culture policy memos from Central Command[39] mandating how to be kind to each other in a war zone.

The door to the inner office threw open and a blue-eyed whirlwind emerged, smiling, with hand extended. "William

---

[39] Central Command, also known as CENTCOM, is the Pentagon's combatant command in charge of all military operations in the Middle East and Afghanistan. The U.S. Commander in Afghanistan (The COM), who also wears the dual hat as NATO commander in Afghanistan, answers to his U.S. chain of command through the CENTCOM commander. This is all very clear to military personnel and is mind-numbing torture to non-government civilians.

Trevanathan! Or is it 'Bill?' You are the man I've been waiting for. Welcome aboard." Major General "Skip" Crist had the grip of a longshoreman. Bright eyed, medium height, with short-cropped salt and pepper hair, his energy was infectious. "Come in, come in," he declared, disappearing back into his office before Trevanathan could even open his mouth.

"Good luck," said Master Sergeant Fields under his breath, again not looking up from his work. To him, the colonel's visit meant twenty to thirty minutes of quiet before the general came up with another new idea that created more work for him.

"Have a seat," the general gestured to a wooden dining room chair across from his desk, as he practically sprinted back behind his desk. "So, I looked at your record. Very impressive. Bad stuff what happened to you in Iraq. Are you OK, now? Good!" the general declared without waiting for an answer. "Some craziness in D.C. too, huh? But you came out of that clean. You're obviously not afraid to stick to your guns, are you?"

"Yes, sir," was all Trevanathan got out.

"Bill, I've a helluva' problem and you're going to fix it. It's December. In six months, July 6, 2016, to be exact, the NATO donor's conference meets in Warsaw. That's where the money comes from to run this war. Or doesn't if things don't improve. The U.S. foots a huge part of the bill, but Congress only agrees to that because our NATO allies are also pitching in. No money, no war, and the bad guys win.

"Three months later—October in Brussels—is the European Union donors' conference—that's where money for everything else here that's not warfighting comes from—government salaries, airports, schools, sewer, water, health—you get it. The donors, mostly the same NATO countries, plus Japan, Korea and a handful of others thrown in, will be asked to commit to paying for 80 percent of this country's gross budget for the next five years. That money provides Ghani's government the financial stability it needs to even exist—and for Afghanistan to not become the next Somalia.

"This country can't support itself. Most folks don't know that. Hell, we might as well make Afghanistan the 51st state, because Congress pays more of the Afghan national budget than they do for any state back home. Don't tell the taxpayers back home though." Crist laughed, kicking his feet up on his desk.

Suddenly, he brought his feet back down. "Damn, forgot I can't do that here—the whole bottom-of-the-shoes being an insult thing."

"No problem, sir," laughed Trevanathan.

"No, it is. How you train is how you fight, and if we aren't disciplined in here, then we'll mess up in an engagement with the locals," he admonished himself.

"Roger, sir."

"Want a candy bar?"

"Sir?" replied Trevanathan, taken off guard.

"Local school back home sent over a ton of candy for Christmas. I can't stand the stuff. Take this back to your folks." The general reached under his desk and came up with two handfuls of brightly wrapped Hershey's kisses, candy canes, and small holiday-wrapped chocolate bars that he dumped on his desk.

"Umm, thanks sir, I'm sure they'll appreciate it." Trevanathan quickly scraped the bounty into his pants' cargo pocket.

Not hesitating, Crist went back into his riff. "So, both the NATO countries and other donor countries are tired of their money being ripped off and turned into private yachts in Dubai and villas on the Riviera by Afghan officials. There's substantial political pressure by voters in Europe to cut their commitment here when they have their own economic challenges."

"That's understandable," Trevanathan said.

Crist continued. "There's a serious risk that if one or two donor nations vote against more aid at either Warsaw or Brussels, it will trigger a domino effect and a stampede to the exits."

Trevanathan nodded. "And no money means either we're holding the bag alone, or worse case, it gives Congress cover to cut our commitment here, as well."

"Bingo. Americans are very generous people, but they have no long-term memory. Nine out of ten people couldn't even tell you why we're in Afghanistan, and they sure couldn't find it on a map."

"Yessir. They love to sing Lee Greenwood. But don't bother them with the messy details."

Crist cocked his head and gave an impish grin. "A cynic, Colonel?"

"No sir. At least not as a steady diet. Like you, this isn't my first rodeo, and I'm simply aware who pays the price when chest-thumping politicians and civilian wannabes declare '*we* need to go to war.' Never seems to be much *me* in *we*."

Crist threw his head back, cutting loose a throaty laugh. "Not much *me* in *we*," he repeated, as if filing it away for later use.

"So, what do you want me to do, sir? My first question coming in here was if you were going to stick a fork in our section. Word on the street was EF3 was on the chopping block."

Crist furrowed his brow. "That was someone else's vision. Not mine. Short-sighted, too. It doesn't matter what the other staff sections do or plan to do if the international aid money dries up. This entire mission hinges on getting the Afghans to understand they are about to kill their golden goose by bad behavior. So, no, you aren't going away. In fact, you're going to grow if I have my way."

"Roger, sir." Trevanathan felt great relief. *I still have a job,* he realized. "What's next?"

"First, *think* before we do anything. Everyone comes to Kabul full of piss and vinegar, sure they know how to bomb or quick-fix our way out of this war. That hasn't worked for fifteen years. I need a thinker, not a chest-pounder. I looked at your personality profile from the War College—top percentile in creative problem solving. I need that skill set here."

Trevanathan nodded. *Hmm, this guy does his research.*

"Second, advise me what you think needs to be done. Don't tell me—*ever*—what you think I want to hear. I don't need an echo chamber. There's too much of that around here."

"Got it, sir," replied the colonel.

"Third, time is not our friend. I'll take a good idea in two weeks over a perfect idea two months from now. Wish it weren't that way, but July is a hard deadline with Warsaw on the horizon, and we have until then to build consensus to keep our allies bankrolling this fight for another five years."

"OK, sir."

"Last..." at this point, the general's tone became serious as he leaned across his desk, looking intently into Trevanathan's eyes. "Don't get killed."

Trevanathan started to nervously laugh, having heard similar advice in Doug's note, before he saw the general was not reciprocating in the humor.

"I can't go into any detail," Crist continued soberly, "but one of your predecessors is in Arlington right now, because he was too effective in fighting corruption. He got whacked as a message to us to back off. No one is going to officially acknowledge that, but it's the reality. That unfortunate incident led to some...lack of resolve, including discussion about possibly closing down EF3. The truth is you'll either make enemies here or you'll not make a difference. There're billions in skimmed funds at stake and the pigs at the trough are not going to let their food supply be taken away easily. Some of the Afghans who promise to be your best friend will be doing it to get close enough to set you up. You need to be aware of that and not trust anyone in GIRoA with your life."

Trevanathan's stomach fell. *Well, this is wonderful news. Go make a difference, but the people you're trying to help will be trying to kill you.*

"You got hit in Iraq, correct?"

"Yes. IED, sir."

"Plenty of those here." Crist examined Trevanathan's face for any sign of hesitancy.

"Comes with the job, sir. Don't plan on lightning striking twice." He returned Crist's stare with a confidence he did not completely feel.

Crist shifted back into his buoyant self. "OK, then. Well, if there wasn't some risk, it wouldn't be interesting, right?" he beamed. "How much time do you need to come up with your plan?"

"Sounds like you gave me two weeks, sir."

"I did. Ten days would be even better."

"Roger, sir."

Crist rose, signaling the end of their meeting, and Trevanathan also stood. He was about to render a salute, but Crist bounded around the corner of his desk, another two handfuls of candy cupped before him. The colonel awkwardly received the parting gift and edged to the door.

"I'll have my aide set up a follow-up in ten days, then," Crist said. He ushered Trevanathan into the outer office before closing his door.

Lieutenant Mann looked up from his tiny desk. "How'd it go, sir?" he asked expectantly.

"Great," Trevanathan muttered, a little stunned. "I got a bunch of candy and ten days to fix the country's corruption problem." Sergeant Fields snickered without looking up from his computer.

Chapter 11

Camp Resolute Support, Kabul, December 2015

Trevanathan was sitting in his plywood office, staring at the 747 coming through the window poster on his wall. That seems appropriate, he smirked. *How the hell am I going to come up with a plan to counter corruption in another country's government, when I can barely find my way around post yet?*

As if in answer to his thoughts, Major Brandt appeared in his door. "Sir? Someone I'd like you to meet if you have a minute?"

"Sure, come in," Trevanathan replied.

Brandt entered the office, followed closely by a thirtyish, blonde woman wearing gym gear. "Sir, this is Jodie Upton, from Her Majesty's Foreign Office, an old friend of mine."

"DFID[40], actually. Very nice to meet you colonel," offered Upton, extending a firm handshake.

Trevanathan had no idea what DFID was, but he was grateful for the interruption, as he was getting nowhere on a plan for Crist.

"Nice to meet you as well," replied the colonel. "What's your role at the embassy?"

"A number of things, but right now my main portfolio is coordinating counter-corruption issues, as our Afghan friends have an unfortunate tendency to pilfer whatever we send them."

"Hmm, small world. Please have a seat," Trevanathan gestured to the metal folding chair across from his desk. Upton took the chair, leaving Brandt leaning in the doorway.

---

[40] DFID – Department for International Development, a branch of the UK government that oversees the distribution and expenditure of foreign aid.

"I mentioned to Jodie that you're working on a counter-corruption plan for RS, so she wanted to meet you," Brandt volunteered.

"*Working*, is too generous of a word," Trevanathan responded. "I don't have much of a feel for who the players are yet and now I have a ten-day deadline from my boss to come up with a plan for how to turn decades of corruption around—doing so within six months by the way."

"Why six months?" asked Upton.

"That's the countdown to the Warsaw funding conference, at which time everyone paying the bills for this war will decide whether to stay or go. Word on the street is some are already getting a bit weak-kneed about it."

"Hmm, I have definitely heard concern from the Italians and the Dutch," said Upton. "The Japanese are very dodgy on continuing as well, even though they are not NATO. The Germans are the ones to watch. If they go, there will be a flood of other countries in their wake," Upton observed.

"And your government?" the colonel asked.

"It depends on the day of the week. The Prime Minister is under pressure. Next to the U.S., our country has deployed the most troops and suffered the most casualties here. Our citizens are questioning the ongoing cost when there doesn't appear to be a return on investment in either reducing corruption or ending hostilities, and the MPs[41] are paying attention. There's still a strong core group in the government who think fighting corruption here is an opportunity—a chance to build a model that could be replicated elsewhere—but they can be drowned out by the growing impatience."

Trevanathan nodded.

"Jodie has been working these issues for some time, sir. She has pretty good insight on what motivates the key players – both in GIRoA and in the donor community," Brandt offered by way of endorsement.

"So, how do you two know each other?" Trevanathan asked.

---

[41] Members of Parliament

Upton laughed lightly. "I use your gym here on post quite often. I met the major in one of the spin classes run by your Marines. He was on a bike in front of me wearing a T shirt that said 'I kill bad people so good people can sleep at night'. So, I asked him how many bad people he had killed that week." Upton's bright blue eyes danced with mischief.

"I told her it was only Wednesday, so I didn't have a full tally yet," grinned Brandt. "Then our talk turned to work, and we found out we were both working the same issues."

Trevanathan nodded. "So, in a perfect world what would you do?" the colonel asked Upton. "The Afghans have been stealing us blind for fifteen years. What will get them to change?"

"Well, where we start out from is important. The popular refrain that the Afghans are just a bunch of thieves will get nowhere. That's just Western bias," stated Upton.

This one's not afraid to speak her mind. Good, thought Trevanathan.

"Remember that this country has been war-ravaged and desperately poor for decades. Then our lot show up here with unlimited bags of money, require few controls on spending, and act shocked when theft happens. Fairly naïve on our part. Like setting a feast before a starving man and complaining when he eats too much and slips some apples in his pockets," she continued.

"Got it," said Trevanathan, "but recognizing that history may be valid, it has now spun way out of control. This is not a few random bad actors and isolated instances. The stealing is institutionalized at every level in the everyday operations of GIRoA. The prosecutors, cops, and judges are all on the take and there's no place to create a toehold to even start changing a culture where you're viewed as a fool if you're not lining your pockets. If we can't reverse this trend, *fast,* and those allies pull out, the entire mission will collapse, and we'll have a bunch of mullahs running this place again."

"Well, that's not completely true, colonel," countered Upton.

"Which part?"

"The toehold. There's a counter-narcotics justice center that has done some legitimate work in busting drug traffickers with ties inside the government. It's advised by some of our UK police advisors."

"I haven't heard of it," said Trevanathan.

"It used to be funded by our Embassy too, sir, until they started pulling back on their efforts to improve matters," said Brandt.

"Who runs it? How does it work?" Trevanathan asked, leaning forward in his chair.

"It's a separate organization with its own Tashkil[42]—police, prosecutors, and judges," said Upton.

"Operates relatively autonomously outside the Attorney General's direct control," added Brandt. "It was designed to go after the big fish who were moving heroin out of the south to Europe and elsewhere. They had some good results initially, but then they got flooded by low-level cases and became bogged down. Too many cases, not enough resources. When the U.S. Embassy pulled their money and trainers, the whole thing became log-jammed. It still exists but is suffocating under a crippling caseload and not enough resources."

"That sounds kinda' like what we need, isn't it?" said Trevanathan, getting energized, as his wheels started to turn. "The Attorney General's office is too big and too corrupt to fix, especially within six months, right? They'd just string us along. We can't recreate an entire justice system for the entire government —again not enough time. But what if we shrink the justice system into a bite-sized morsel that focuses only on high-level corruption? Make it small enough that we can keep an eye on it. Not let it get flooded with small cases. Target only big fish with big dollar cases and the highest-level defendants—generals and ministers, for example. Create the modern equivalent of putting prominent heads on stakes at the city gates to deter misconduct."

"Do you think your embassy would get on board?" asked Upton.

---

[42] Tashkil – Dari phrase for an organizational chart of personnel and equipment. The phrase was adopted and widely used by NATO personnel working in Afghanistan on manning and logistics issues.

"No idea at this point," replied Trevanathan. "We might not want them, considering how they bailed on the narcotics center. We can't get three months into this and have them pull the financial rug out. There won't be time for do-overs. What about yours?"

"I can certainly take the pulse of some people I know. The other embassies–the international community–would need to present a united front on any corruption reform project. The Afghans are masters of playing us off against one another, so that no reforms take root. They are very effective at playing the colonialist card…"

"…while they steal our colonial money?" finished Brandt.

"I did not say that, Charles," laughed Upton.

"What about your ambassador? Where is he on counter-corruption?" asked Trevanathan.

"I think he wants to make a difference. Doesn't seem like the type who's just watching the sand go through the hourglass for his time here. I sense he's ambitious, but cautious as well. If he's presented with a good idea he may well get on board, but it would have to be solid."

"You know, not to overdo it with the analogies, but this idea reminds me a bit of that play in American football we call a 'Hail Mary.' It's a desperate long pass with a low likelihood of success, where everything must go right. Most often it ends in defeat, but when it works, it's glorious. Seems like our situation," said Trevanathan.

"Never understood the game," smiled Upton. "But I do get the reference. Penalty shots in our football are similar."

"Likewise, never understood a couple dozen guys running in circles for an hour and a half and then deciding a game by one guy making a kick," teased Trevanathan.

"What haven't we covered?" asked Major Brandt, bringing the conversation back to the nuts and bolts.

"A hundred things, I'm sure," replied Trevanathan. "But if we forgot something, we'll make it up on the fly. We're caught in a bad situation. Ideally, we'd take months to study this and come up with a detailed plan thinking through all the angles. But we don't have that time. So, the best we can do is grab an idea that almost worked—the narcotics center—and try to fix what made it broken when we apply it to corruption. *Ready, fire, aim.* We'll do the work and give the Afghans all the credit. That's key. We need to lure them into taking ownership as soon as possible."

"Interesting, but isn't that merely theater? If we're doing the actual work?" asked Upton.

"It would be if we ran it permanently. This has to proceed in stages because of the time constraints. I'm looking at this like triage for wounded. This country needs immediate life-saving intervention. The first step is stabilizing the patient and keeping him alive. If the international money leaves, the Afghan army collapses, and the patient dies. So, we can't get too religious about the nationality of the field surgeon that stabilizes the patient. That's us for the next six months."

"But, if we can keep the patient alive, then we'll move onto a second stage, which is getting the Afghans to take ownership of the corruption prosecutions and understand that the path to more money in the long run is not stealing it, but by maintaining credibility with the donors."

"Aren't you concerned this might fail? It seems we're moving awfully fast. What if the Afghans don't get on board?"

Trevanathan shook his head. "I'm absolutely concerned, but not that we'll fail—we're already at failure. The problem is everyone keeps spinning this failure as a success, because they don't want to link their name to a corpse. We haven't moved the needle much in fifteen years in terms of stabilizing the country: people are still dying, the treasury is being drained by its officials, and those who have been paying the bills are about to turn off the cash spigot and leave. Failure is already here."

"Hmm, we do see things similarly. I'm sure you know this, Colonel, but of every country on the planet, only Somalia and North Korea are currently ranked as more corrupt. This won't be easy."

"Our competition for last place is a failed state and another one run by a deranged hobbit? How can we do worse?" interjected Brandt.

"In that view we have nowhere to go, but up," observed Upton, trying to smother a laugh. "Much to think about."

Upton, changing the subject, asked, "Colonel, out of curiosity, is your family Cornish by any chance?" asked.

"Yes, they are," Trevanathan replied, surprised that his family roots had been recognized. "Came over after the war."

"I thought so, by your name. Lovely country. I've camped up and down the coast there. St. Ives, Port Isaac. Gorgeous."

"It is when it's not raining," the colonel agreed.

"Quite right. I did catch a miserable cold hitchhiking in a rainstorm."

Trevanathan was impressed. Upton was obviously confident and personable. She had taken the initiative in this conversation, had charmed him by their mutual connection, and had a steely look behind vivid blue eyes.

"Well, I am certainly glad I stopped by," Upton added. "I was coming back from the gym when I ran into the major and he mentioned your assignment. So, I will make some inquiries as to interest levels in this concept within my channels, and then we should meet again, I think, to flesh out where the weaknesses with the counter-narcotics center could be corrected in this new context."

"We need to move fast," reminded Trevanathan.

"Brilliant," replied Upton.

"Major," she said, standing and extending her hand to Brandt.

Somehow Trevanathan sensed he had been set up, that the idea he thought he had just developed was pre-scripted by his two visitors. Yet it was all good, and he accepted being outmaneuvered with humor. *We have a plan.* He felt himself exhaling for the first time since meeting with General Crist.

"Jodie," Brandt replied with a nod and a smile, confirming Trevanathan's suspicions that the two of them had steered the outcome of this meeting.

"Is there anyone in this town you don't know?" Trevanathan asked.

"Only those not worth knowing, sir," Brandt replied with a grin.

Chapter 12

Afghan Ministry of Defense Headquarters, Kabul, December 2015

Major General Sadat's office was located on the fourth floor of the Ministry of Defense (MOD) Headquarters. As the chief military lawyer for the Afghan National Army, he possessed broad powers. He was both the chief prosecutor and in charge of the military judges. He had significant influence over defense counsel assignments for any soldiers facing courts-martial. In short, he controlled all aspects of the Afghan military justice system and had the power to tilt the scale in whatever direction he, or the Minister of Defense, wanted. Due to this great power, he was the first Afghan official with whom Trevanathan wanted to discuss the concept of a corruption justice center—to test if there would be resistance.

Trevanathan worked his way through the labyrinth of the MOD headquarters, surrounded by his security detail. Being constantly shielded by bodyguards was something new, and he was still adjusting. Whenever he went off Camp Resolute Support, in whichever direction he walked, Trevanathan was led by two infantrymen and trailed by two more, assigned from the command's VIP security detail. Although only a colonel, the fact that he was serving in a brigadier general's position on the organizational chart necessitated an extra layer of protection. His role at the hub of counter-corruption activity for NATO also put him at greater risk from those skimming Western aid to the tune of billions per year.

Today, he was also accompanied by Major Brandt, who was what was called an "Afghan hand," an officer with specialized training, who spent a substantial amount of his career rotating in and out of assignments focused on stabilizing the Afghan government. Trevanathan was quickly finding Brandt to be an encyclopedia of knowledge on the way things really were in Afghanistan—not the sanitized way they were packaged in headquarters' briefs.

The group passed an internal Afghan security checkpoint dividing the newer and older portions of the MOD headquarters. The new half was comprised of wide hallways with fresh paint and a large marble-floored foyer paid for by the Americans. The older half reminded Trevanathan of a shabby, former-Soviet headquarters he had been stationed at in Hungary after the Iron Curtain fell, full of cheap wood paneling, peeling paint, and the smell of mildew. One's office location within the building sent a clear message as to their importance to the Minister of Defense. If an officer was relegated to the older section, the message conveyed was, "try harder."

A bored Afghan soldier sat next to a metal detector arch between the two halves of the building. "That thing hasn't worked in over three years," Brandt commented as they passed through. "We paid for it on my second tour. It broke within a year and there was no maintenance plan. So, now it's modern art—and that same private's been sitting there watching it not work for three years."

The detail turned and climbed a narrow stairwell at the back of the building, stepping on broken, yellow and black linoleum tiles illuminated by cracked and dirty windows. "No shiny elevators back here," Brandt muttered. An Afghan general with a long, ragged beard, descended the stairwell, glaring at the Americans as they passed. Trevanathan attempted a smile but received only a glare of pure hatred.

"What's that guy's issue?" Trevanathan asked Brandt in a low voice.

"He's Muj," Brandt replied.

"Moozh?"

"Mujaheddin. Hard core fundamentalist. The guys who kicked the Russians out of here. Hates Westerners. After the Soviets left, MOD gave a bunch of them general officer rank to get them down from the hills and buy them off to support the new government."

"What's his job?"

"Wearing a uniform. Modeling shitty beards. Glaring at people. Fucker probably can't even read—other than the Qu'ran. But it keeps the Chief Executive, Abdullah, happy and stops the other Muj from cozying up to the Taliban."

Trevanathan knew Brandt was referring to Chief Executive Abdullah Abdullah, a power broker and Mujaheddin himself, who had become Chief Executive when the vote had narrowly split in the last election between Abdullah and President Ashraf Ghani amidst mutual allegations of fraud. Faced with the prospect of a second civil war erupting over the results, the United States had stepped in and massaged a power sharing arrangement, using its huge financial contribution as leverage. Ghani received the top job as President and Abdullah became Chief Executive, a made-up position, with guarantees of a free hand in his areas of interest.

"There's always another level below the surface from what you can see here, isn't there?" observed the colonel.

"Sometimes two or three, sir. Most loyalty here is based on blood and tribal loyalty, or who has paid you off. There's no commitment to institutional political parties—all loyalty is personal. Few local players think about what's in the best interest of the country, because *country* isn't a priority at all."

"This is it, sir," Staff Sergeant Ford announced from the top of the stairs, his head swiveling back and forth as he checked the hallway.

"Great," Trevanathan puffed, stepping up to join him in the dimly lit hallway. Wood paneling covered the lower third of the hallway, with greenish masonry walls above. Half of the fluorescent lights in the passage were out or blinking their death knell. "Let me catch my breath a second before we go in," the colonel wheezed, hating to admit the elevation was getting to him, after walking up four flights wearing eighty pounds of body armor and equipment. The incisions from his recent surgery were talking to him, as well: they weren't happy.

"You get used to it fast, sir. Takes a couple weeks," encouraged Ford. "Even though we're in a valley, we're still six thousand feet above sea level. And it doesn't help that the locals are burning crap to stay warm."

"Yeah, I smoke a carton of Camels every week just to improve the air going into my lungs," joked Corporal Hawthorne, the round-faced, second-ranking NCO on the security detail.

Taking advantage of the pause, Ford reminded the colonel what would happen next. "Sir, that green door three doors down to the left, leads into the general's outer office. We'll enter there. Hawthorne and I will go first. The other two members of my team," he nodded to two specialists who were the rear guard keeping an eye on the stairwell, "will remain in this hallway unless you direct otherwise."

"I'll defer to you and Sergeant Ford on that. You know the turf."

"That's how I'd do it, sir," replied Ford. "Two years ago, one of your predecessors used to take his security team right into the meetings with the Afghan generals and they took it as an insult—like we didn't trust them."

The colonel smiled. "Do we?"

"Fuck no, sir," interjected Brandt. "We just can't look so obvious about it. There was one knucklehead in another section who used to have his team 'clear' an Afghan general's office for threats before he'd even go in. He literally sent a squad into the general's office with their rifles raised to clear out any threats. Imagine how much cooperation he got there."

"Hmph," replied Trevanathan, beginning to catch his breath.

"So, there's smart ways to be ready and dumb ways," added Brandt. "The smart way is you're never anywhere off base without being armed. The boys will be outside the door here and can take care of business for any external threat. But things can happen really fast. I wouldn't trust that Muj we saw on the stairway with the spare change in my pocket, let alone with my life. The local Afghan security will sometimes try to bullshit you that you can't take a sidearm into this or that meeting because Assistant Minister so-and-so is extra important. What I do if I'm going into any meeting with an Afghan VIP is take my pistol and stick it in the small of my back, like this." Brandt lifted the long tail of his blouse and slid his 9mm pistol between his T-shirt and the band of his trousers. "Tighten the belt and it acts like a makeshift holster. Drop the blouse back down and you walk in looking unarmed and all kumbaya. They never frisk us because they're scared of us."

"How real is the threat?"

Ford and Hawthorne gave each other a knowing look that Trevanathan caught. "Sergeant Ford, don't sugarcoat it," said the colonel. "I need to know the ground truth."

Ford grimaced. "It's very real, sir. We don't even worry about the Taliban much here in Kabul. They throw a rocket in once in a while and blow up a bunch of civilians with a car bomb every few weeks, but they don't fuck with us directly too often. They've learned that the payback is too painful. The main threat to you is the police and soldiers who pretend they're on our side but have become radicalized. They're bad news because they're right around us, with loaded rifles, and we can't mind read."

"Got it," replied Trevanathan.

Ford continued. "Do we expect any trouble from General Sadat, today? No. He's a known quantity. But he has outer office people that change over time that we don't always know. And if his tea boy's family has been kidnapped by the bad guys and their lives can be ransomed by him killing an American officer, you need to be ready to rock and roll."

"Greaat," Trevanathan replied, removing his pistol from his shoulder holster and securing it in the small of his back under his shirt, as Brandt had demonstrated. "Homicidal tea boys. What else?"

"Drink two cups of tea," suggested Brandt. "The shit is half sugar. Not bad really. But as long as you keep drinking it, they'll keep refilling your glass and you'll get a sugar buzz. When you don't want more put the flat of your hand over the cup. But you gotta' drink at least two cups to not insult. Don't expect a lot out of this first meeting beyond some pleasantries and some tea."

"Right. It was that way in Iraq."

"OK, we better go. We're five minutes late, which is good enough to show you're important enough to be late, but not so late as to insult the general." Brandt turned toward the door, then paused to let Ford and his assistant squad leader, Corporal Hawthorne, take the lead.

General Sadat's outer office was the size of a medium-size walk-in closet. Behind a cheap metal desk was an Afghan sergeant who jumped to his feet upon the entry of the Americans. Hawthorne moved to the left of the door and greeted him. Ford entered right on his heels and moved directly to the guard with the AK-47 across his lap, lounging in a cheap plastic lawn chair. "Salaam Alaikum," greeted Ford, touching his heart chest with his right hand in the traditional Afghan greeting and extending his hand to the armed guard in a traditional Western handshake.

Smart, thought Trevanathan, looking into the small room over Brandt's shoulder. *The handshake required the guard to take his hand off the weapon.* Brandt stood in the doorway, as there was no more room for him to enter.

To the immediate left was another door. It opened outward, bumping into Hawthorne. A smiling face popped out from behind, surveying the group. "Major Brandt! You're back," he declared.

"I came back to see you, Major Wasim," Brandt replied to the young Afghan officer, smiling back.

"We're good, sir," Ford said over his shoulder, continuing to politely engage the guard with the AK-47.

"Pardon me, sir," said Hawthorne, slipping past Brandt back into the hallway so that the colonel could enter. He put his mouth to the colonel's ear before stepping aside. "Ford will keep the guard busy, sir. Go right into the general's office. Don't pause outside."

Trevanathan marveled that the bodies stumbling past each other in the tiny space was a well-choreographed security operation shielding him from harm. "Roger," he replied, slipping through the inner door into the luxurious office of Major General Sadat.

The contrast between the shabby outer trappings and the general's inner office was marked. Inside, two massive red velvet couches created an "L" shaped arrangement across from two large, matching chairs. Between them, a low, gilded coffee table between the furniture was set with gold-trimmed glassware. French paintings in gold frames hung on the walls. The general was seated at the far end of the office, behind an impressive cherry wood desk. He rose deliberately to his feet, conveying he was in no hurry, and walked across the room, a tight smile on his lips that did not reach his eyes. He was in his early fifties, with a well-groomed salt-and-pepper beard. Piercing blue eyes beneath mostly white brows searched Trevanathan's face.

Major Wasim offered introductions. "My honored colonel, I am privileged to meet you, and to introduce the Legal Advisor for Military Affairs to the Minister of Defense, Major General Massad Sadat."

"General Sadat, it is my great honor to meet you. General Maywood has told me of your productive friendship, and it is my hope that we will be able to continue that friendship for the benefit of both our great nations." *These introductions make me want to hurl,* thought the colonel.

"It is my honor as well," the general responded in a resonant baritone voice. "I have no doubt this will be the start of a long and successful relationship." *Will this one be as useless as the others?* the general pondered. He extended an open palm to the couch along the wall for the colonel to sit, while he took the chair opposite.

The colonel and Brandt removed their sweat-stained flak jackets and sat them next to the opulent furnishings. As Trevanathan sat with his back to the wall, Brandt took a seat on the couch to his left. General Sadat sat across from them, while Major Wasim remained standing at the general's right elbow.

An old man who had stood so still against the far wall as to be unnoticed previously now went into action, serving tea to the general and the colonel, along with one cookie apiece on an accompanying saucer. He then served Major Brandt.

Hmm, Wasim, gets neither a chair, nor tea. Interesting power dynamic, observed Trevanathan.

Sadat said nothing, so Trevanathan opened, relying on his cultural experience from Iraq. "I hope that your family is well?"

"They are, thank you. And yours?"

"Very well, thank you. I understand you have a son who is serving?" Brandt had briefed Trevanathan before the meeting, explaining that Sadat's son was a military attorney under his father's authority, stationed in Herat.

A slight gleam grew in Sadat's eye. *The American is prepared.* "He is, thank you. And your sons?"

It was Trevanathan's turn to be impressed. It was either a lucky guess by Sadat, or he, too, had done his homework before the meeting.

"They are both well, thank you."

"Praise Allah," Sadat commented.

An awkward silence descended over the meeting. Not familiar with the Afghan major in the meeting, Trevanathan steered the conversation his direction. "Major Brandt, how do you know the major?"

"My apologies, sir. This is Major Wasim. He was the military prosecutor in Helmand in 2012 when I was doing a human rights investigation down there. Some of the Brits were a bit overzealous in their counter-terrorism ops and I was tapped as a joint investigating officer. The major was helpful in ensuring local cooperation and access to witnesses."

"Major, it is my pleasure to meet you."

"And you as well, sir," replied Wasim, touching his heart.

Major General Sadat, apparently annoyed by attention being focused on his underling, resumed the initiative. "My colonel, while it is a great pleasure to meet you, and I have no doubt you will do a superior job, is the assignment of your position to a *colonel* a signal by your command that legal matters have become a lesser priority? All of your predecessors were general officers, were they not?"

Trevanathan expected the question, knowing how status conscious Afghans could be. "Not at all, sir. The fact that they chose me is a sign that they consider this to be their most important mission. I am a judge in the United States. Not a military judge, but a civilian judge. Elected by the people. I also serve in our reserve military forces. The Pentagon specifically activated me away from my court to do this most important work, rather than assigning a lesser qualified general officer with more rank, but less skill." *Let him chew on that.*

This time the smile did reach Sadat's eyes. *This one knows word play. He could be an Afghan.* "Well, that is fortunate news. May I ask what your hopes are for the next year?"

Though Trevanathan had no official blessing for his plan yet, he needed to feel out any potential local roadblocks before presenting his ideas to General Crist. It wouldn't be helpful to brief an idea to Crist that was dead on arrival due to some objection the Afghans harbored. "Sir, I am new here and have much to learn. I have learned in the past to not arrive with preconceived ideas, but to be patient and listen to those with experience."

"That is very wise," said Sadat, surprised that this new American was not immediately trying to tell him how to run things in his own country.

"Our two countries have many shared challenges. The one of great concern to my superior, General Crist, is ensuring ongoing financial support for your government."

Sadat nodded, without commenting.

"General Crist is concerned that the misappropriation of aid by some officials is threatening continued support from our NATO allies. He has asked me to find solutions to this problem, in order to ensure ongoing financial support. You know your government much better than I do, so I was hoping to get your input." *Let's see if he is susceptible to flattery*, Trevanathan thought.

"That is of course, important work. Have I not said the same thing myself, major?" Sadat nodded toward Wasim.

"You were talking about that very thing this morning, sir."

"We have increased the number of corruption prosecutions this year 34 percent over last year," said Sadat. "The pilfering of supplies from our front-line troops has been drastically curtailed in seven provinces."

"If the judges would stop muddling about, the success rate would be even higher," suggested Wasim.

"Very true," reinforced Sadat. "Sometimes our judges are more interested in position and comfort than results," he said, pausing to let his servant refill his tea.

Trevanathan glanced at Brandt out of the corner of his eye, but the Marine was stone faced, revealing nothing.

"How would you propose to proceed, my colonel?" inquired Sadat, his voice exuding a new warmth.

"I am not certain yet, sir, but in America when there are special challenging issues, we have at times created specialty courts where the judge focuses upon only one type of issue. We have drug courts to deal with those who are addicted. Bankruptcy courts for financial failures. Rather than leaving something as important as public corruption to the general court system, I was wondering if a special corruption court focused solely on that issue might work here in Afghanistan?"

"I can see now why they chose you for this important mission, colonel. You are a strategic thinker. You do not accept the status quo."

"Well sir, the status quo has taken us to a place where the U.S. Congress and many NATO donor nations are starting to rethink their long-term financial commitments. I am new, but I can see that if things do not change it is possible that the European countries may lose interest in funding a mission where their investment simply disappears. That will not benefit Afghanistan or America."

"I need to see details of what you propose, of course. In our system one officer cannot make decisions alone. But I see great wisdom in what you propose. Is it possible to get a written plan that lays this out? Whenever you are ready, of course," added Sadat, reasonably.

"It will be my pleasure, sir."

"Well, then, that is much to think about for one day. If I may excuse myself, I have a meeting with the General Staff to attend." Sadat stood, signaling that the meeting was over.

Trevanathan stood and extended his hand, receiving a warm, two-handed handshake from the general. "I look forward to our next conversation, Colonel. I'm sure there will be many."

"My privilege, sir."

An Absence of Faith

Colonel Trevanathan exited the MOD headquarters through the cavernous ceremonial hall at the building's front. As per tradition, he paused before the large display in the lobby containing the Afghan flag and saluted the colors. The colonel and Major Brandt walked quickly to the front steps, a series of impressive marble slabs leading down to the street. Two Afghan ceremonial guards, who remained at attention, were posted to either side of the massive wood doors from which they emerged. Sergeant Ford had used his radio to alert the waiting up-armored SUVs the colonel was coming, so they were standing at the curb, engines running. It was never a good idea to stand still too long in Kabul, especially on an Afghan base, so entries and exits by NATO personnel were done quickly.

In contrast to missions in the countryside, where tactical vehicles such as HMMWVs or MRAPS[43] were the standard means of transport, in Kabul the coalition forces relied upon up-armored civilian Suburbans. It was never clear if someone up the food chain thought that these civilian vehicles would blend in better in Kabul's dense traffic. If so, it was a foolish belief, as the great hulking Western vehicles, with their darkened windows, screamed "Western VIP inside" as they bullied their way through, around, and sometimes over the small third world sedans and donkey carts plying the capital's streets.

As he entered his vehicle, Trevanathan noted that a Specialist Mendez stood at the rear bumper of the third vehicle, his rifle unslung, casually watching their *allies* in their ceremonial guard posts for any suspicious movement. Ford's men did this type of mission several hundred times per year for generals and other VIPs. It was an art to not look aggressive, while at the same time being ready to instantly suppress any threats.

Fortunately, today was not a bad day. Trevanathan settled into his seat and smiled in relief. "Pretty good meeting," he said to Brandt, who was sitting to his left. "I was surprised at how much interest we heard from Sadat."

---

[43] MRAP - Mine Resistant Ambush Protected vehicles that improved survivability to its passengers when struck by an improvised explosive device, by virtue of a unique V shaped hull design that absorbed and deflected the blast.

"Yessir," replied Brandt, without expression.

"If he's on board, we'd be in a position to test the idea with the Interior Ministry, assuming General Crist buys off on it."

"Yessir," responded Brandt again, not making eye contact.

"I had heard Sadat was difficult to work with, but I didn't feel any of that today," continued the colonel.

"It's all good, sir," Brandt confirmed.

The conversation lulled, as Trevanathan turned to look out his window on the short drive back from the MOD compound through the Green Zone to Camp RS. A collection of beggars, children selling war souvenirs, and people with no apparent legitimate purpose drifted along the sidewalks. *For the Green Zone being a secure area, it's surprising how many people just hang around on this street,* thought Trevanathan.

The small convoy reentered the front gate of Camp Resolute Support, passing between the massive magnetic screening devices that looked for explosives. They entered the concrete cattle chutes for additional screening, where they underwent a second physical inspection beneath the hood, were searched underneath by wheeled mirrors, and surrounded by enthusiastic bomb sniffing dogs.

Once cleared, the security team drove Trevanathan and Brandt to the small walled compound that was home to the EF3 section. "Thanks, Sergeant Ford," the colonel joked, alighting from his seat. "I'll recommend you to all my friends."

"Sounds good, sir. You gentlemen have a good day."

Trevanathan turned to speak to Brandt, but the major had already entered the EF3 compound. *Something is wrong there,* he thought, regarding Brandt. *Not sure what, but I'm going to find out.*

Chapter 13

Camp Resolute Support, Kabul, December 2015

Major Brandt's office was next to the Colonel's. Trevanathan stuck his head in and announced, "Let's chat," before returning to his own.

"Have a seat," the colonel directed to Brandt, as the major entered. Trevanathan eased into his seat behind the cheap metal government desk. "OK, spill it," he directed to Brandt. "You haven't said more than two words since we left the meeting, so I know something is up."

"Roger that, sir," replied Brandt. "You got slow-rolled by one of the masters of the game."

"What does that mean?" the colonel asked, rubbing his eyes.

"Sir, you know this isn't my first deployment. I've been dealing with these GIRoA types since 2012. They never give you anything in your first meeting. Never."

"I thought Sadat just did."

"That's their superpower. Giving you nothing while leaving you with the feeling you got something. Sir, remember how I said in the first meeting all you do is drink tea? That's it. It's like two dogs sniffing each other. There may be a mind-meld later, but in meeting number one it's only a sniff contest. That thing where we get together and talk about a real problem and come up with an agreed-upon solution in a quick and efficient manner? That's an American idea, not Afghan. Hell, they're not even interested in that. They're interested in who you are, who your family is, and whether after about a half dozen more meetings they can maybe start to trust you a tiny bit."

"Hmm, so what did he mean when he seemed to agree that a special corruption court was a good idea."

"He agreed to slow-roll you, sir."

"You used that term again. I don't know what that means."

"Sir, this entire culture is based on courtesy, honor, and saving face. They may not accomplish a helluva' lot, but they'll be polite while doing it. When you first meet someone, you never ask for anything. You never agree to anything. You never put yourself or the other person in the position of having to say no. So, if any issue ever comes up that needs a decision—even if it is something they don't want to do—they say yes." Brandt paused. "Then they don't fucking do it."

"Why?"

"Because if they don't say no, they don't put you in a position of being embarrassed or dishonored. Courtesy is more important than results. Always. They don't make an enemy of you by refusing your request. So, the easiest thing in the world is to agree with everything that you say, even when they don't mean a word of it."

"So the entire meeting was a lie then?"

"That's looking at it through an American lens. Yeah, to us Sadat was lying to you through that entire meeting because he has zero intention of doing anything you brought up. But, from his perspective, he was being a gracious host, and making you feel valued and important by politely agreeing with everything you mentioned. He let you save face by not saying no—especially in front of your subordinate—me."

Trevanathan laughed in amazement.

"Remember that bit he said about getting a written summary?" Brandt asked.

"Yes?" the colonel replied cautiously.

"He doesn't want that summary. He'll never read it. It's just a tool in the slow-roll. He knows it will take a week or two for you to create the summary, and during that time he doesn't have to do anything."

"What's the point of giving me busy work?"

"Time is the point. After he gets it, he'll claim he needs to show it to three other Afghan generals and get their feedback. That will buy him a couple months pretending he is waiting to hear from them—when he never spoke to them in the first place. Then he'll come back to you with some fictional questions they raised and give you more homework answering things he doesn't even care about. Poof, a third of your deployment is gone and Sadat hasn't done a thing, except pretend to be interested and keep you busy."

"And that's why you didn't say anything on the drive back, because you were letting me save face in front of our security detail."

"Like I said, sir, I've been in the 'Stan a long time. Some of this crap rubs off."

"So, I guess I went in with my expectations set too high and was probably being the FNG[44] by asking him to do things when I should have just been sipping tea." The colonel paused. "But then...how does anything get done around here when the Afghans are always going to say yes...but then aren't going to do what they said yes *to*? Am I making sense?"

"You're a quick study, sir. That's been the challenge from day one. We're looking for input and commitment, and they're stroking our egos. They know each one of us has a shelf life of one year in our deployment. We come in here full of big ideas about how we're going to fix this place, forgetting it's not really our house to fix. The Afghans have watched this process fourteen times since 2001. So, they've learned they need to agree with everything we suggest to make sure the money still flows in, but then not actually do any of it. By the time Colonel or General FNG figures out that the big plans he has brought to Kabul aren't going anywhere, it's his turn to pack up, and his replacement, FNG number two walks off the plane ready to conquer the world.

"And the process starts all over again..." noted Trevanathan.

"You got it, sir."

"Well, that's pretty disheartening. How do they ever expect to make progress?"

---

[44] FNG – Military slang for Fucking New Guy, i.e., the new arrival in a combat zone who has no idea yet what is really going on.

"In the words of Ronald Reagan, sir, 'There you go again...' The progress you're talking about—a Western concept. You think of progress in terms of more efficient and honest courts, better schools, more reliable infrastructure. The progress these cats in GIRoA are thinking about is growing their personal bank accounts and keeping Uncle Sugar and his NATO allies paying for their $8 billion annual budget. Keeping that gravy train flowing for as long as possible is their idea of progress, so when this place goes tits up, they have a nice villa in France to run to. In fact, if things got too good around here, the biggest worry is we'd declare victory and start cutting off the money spigot."

"You make me want to curl into a fetal position," commented the colonel dryly. "I can't believe that they've been able to carry out such a charade for fifteen years without Congress or the Pentagon getting wise to it."

"Ah, sir, I'm not being judgmental in telling you this. It's the way it is. This country has had the crap kicked out of it for forty years. The Russians rolled in and destroyed the place. They pulled out and left a power vacuum that got filled by the Taliban and their terrorist friends. We got rid of them, and Karzai and the Afghan mob took over and started lining their pockets at the average Afghan's expense. When Karzai became too inconvenient, we found Ghani, whose people steal as much as Karzai's, but he's less of a headache because he doesn't bite the hand that feeds him. Against that background it's hard to blame them for trying to grab as much money as possible for their escape fund before the next disaster hits."

"But they have a chance...to make a difference...to not have to escape again...if they don't steal themselves into defeat," Trevanathan spoke haltingly, as if unsuccessfully trying to get inside the Afghan mindset Brandt was describing.

"That may be true, sir, but again, we have the benefit of a perspective from a country that hasn't been occupied and blown apart multiple times in less than a half century. At some point people don't care who is fucking them over—they just know they've been getting fucked over for forty years, so stashing away as much cash as possible is their best defense against being on the receiving end again. Unfortunately, that leads to the situation where they don't believe in their own future. A lot of those in charge, who could make a difference, aren't trying, because they're playing a waiting game."

"Waiting for what? It's not going to get better if they don't commit to building their future."

"Respectfully, sir, a Western lens again. Many GIRoA leaders have already decided this is the way things are and it's not going to get better so they're gonna' skim as much cream as they can before the Taliban, ISIS, or the next group of fanatics show up and toss them out. We, and our NATO allies, are the only ones who have sincerely bought into the story that we're gonna' make things better in this neighborhood. Whatever 'better' means. So, we're back to my original point—when we talk to them about a peaceful and stable future, they see Iran on one side, Pakistan on the other, and China nibbling on the north, and they keep shoving our aid dollars into their bug out bags."

Lieutenant Ripple stuck his head in the door at that moment. "Sorry to interrupt, sir. Wanted you to know that General Porcher cancelled his meeting with you *again*."

Brandt snorted. "What, did a new shipment of pork rinds hit the PX?"

"Thanks, LT, I'll call his chief of staff and see if I can get back on his calendar," replied Trevanathan, before returning to his conversation with Brandt.

"So, what about the Afghan people?" asked Trevanathan. "The ones I've met—our translators, the Afghan women who work on post—they seem to want something better—better schools, stronger justice system, better hospitals for their kids."

"That's true, sir. Like in most places there's a big difference between the people who live their day-to-day lives and the people in positions of power. But remember, also, that in Afghanistan you need to be careful when using the phrase, "the people," because that means different things in different places. There's Kabul, with its more educated population that has had fifteen years' ongoing contact with the West through NATO, the UN, and Western aid organizations. Then there's the rest of the country, which is poor, uneducated, and exists at an iron-age level, herding goats and raising opium. Those people mostly want to be left alone by whoever is in charge, because the only experience they have with the government is bad. Taliban, GIRoA, it doesn't matter—they always get screwed. Kinda' like saying someone who lives in Manhattan and someone in rural Mississippi share the same world views because they're both American."

"Hmmm. OK. I get that."

"We have all these NATO generals and embassy pukes sitting here in Kabul declaring what the 'Afghan people' want, but unless they've lived for a year out in some mud-walled village in the mountains, they are making decisions based on a fantasy they've created to validate their own views."

"So, you think GIRoA has a legitimacy problem, beyond the Taliban threat?"

"The people here don't see the government as a positive at all. If you have a government job, you like the government because they pay you; otherwise, forget it. That's why the Taliban shadow government has more cred with the population once you get outside Kabul city limits. Even people who don't buy into the whole Taliban fundamentalist philosophy prefer a Taliban judge to decide private disputes, because the decision can't be bought."

"Shadow government?"

"Taliban has its own governors for each province, their own judges, police, all the functions needed to run a government. It's a government waiting in the wings for the day they grab the reins again. But some of it is active now, like they run their own justice system behind the scenes based on Sharia law."

"You don't hear much about that in the States."

"You won't, because an operating parallel government doesn't sound like the imminent victory that's been promised by successive administrations. Let me give you another example of why the Afghans despise their government. No one likes taxes, but did you know you have to pay a bribe here to pay your taxes?"

"Bullshit. You're kidding."

"No joke. You don't get any government services without paying a bribe. Getting a driver's license, a business permit—it's all pay-to-play. That's not unusual in a lot of third-world countries. Here, the corruption is so bad that you have to pay a bribe at the tax office to get them to take your money. Otherwise, you're ignored, or your tax paperwork gets lost."

Trevanathan stared at Brandt, speechless.

"It's true, sir."

"Incredible. So, what can be done—there's SIGAR[45], right? They've been keeping an eye on the cashflow for years for Congress. Why don't they make a difference?"

The two officers paused while a helicopter on approach to the landing zone roared over their building drowning out their conversation.

"Several things," Brandt continued moments later. "First, 9/11. No one in DC wants to be the guy to admit that all those people died on September 11, but we can't do anything to make this place better than it was when those shitheads flew planes into the twin towers. Admitting there's limits to what we can accomplish is political suicide. So, we keep pumping in more blood and treasure. It's the 'Hope-as-a-course-of-action' school of military operations."

"Second?"

"We're as much to blame as the Afghans for letting ourselves be slow-rolled. Maybe more. I lay that blame squarely at the feet of careerists—both military and civilian. No one is willing to be the messenger that gets shot for bringing bad news. Let's go back to basics—we all come in here for one year, right?"

"Yep."

"Trying to effect generational change in one-year bites is like trying to turn an aircraft carrier by pissing on its side. Everyone wants to go home with a nice medal and improved chances for promotion, right? How many generals and colonels do you think

---

[45] SIGAR – Special Inspector General for Afghanistan Reconstruction. A Congressionally created office intended to oversee, investigate, and account for the spending of U.S. tax dollars in Afghanistan.

submit a performance evaluation form at the end of their tour that says, "I had a lot of bright ideas, but they weren't turned into meaningful action because I got slow-rolled by the Afghans?" None, right? So, for fifteen years there's been a flood of exaggerated reports and SITREPS[46] streaming back to Washington declaring an uninterrupted path of success and victory, so people can get promoted. When none of it is fucking true."

"Like my meeting this morning. I could write that up as a glowing success, but it was all theater."

"Roger, sir. That will make a great line item on an OER[47] at the end of your tour if you decide to perform the Kabul career shuffle like everyone else, but it'll still be a fairy tale. The other group of liars I can barely spend any oxygen discussing are at the end of the tunnel in the Embassy—they're not even informed enough to know what's really going on, so their bullshit is a little less sinister in my view, but nonetheless still a fairy tale."

"OK, any other reason, Major Sunshine?"

"Bureaucratic knife fight, sir. SIGAR and the Embassy are at war with each other. Each is trying to establish they are top dog. If SIGAR tells Congress that Ghani is running a kleptocracy, then that means we're throwing away taxpayer dollars being here, and that means the Embassy isn't doing its job. So, the Ambassador and his folks try to first undercut anyone they think is trying to undermine them. That includes SIGAR, who is one of the few honest brokers in town."

"We're not in that food fight at least."

"No, we have our own fight with them. The Ambo is paranoid that we're going to make him look like he's retired in place when we come up with new ideas—like the corruption justice center. If you start something like that, people start asking uncomfortable questions

---

[46] SITREP – Situation Report. Military term for a status report, often to a higher authority.

[47] OER – Officer Evaluation Report. An annual report card received by each officer from his superiors that impacts future promotions and assignments. In practice, most supervisors have their subordinates write their own OER and then just sign it, saving the boss work.

like, 'Why wasn't the Embassy doing this before?' 'Why didn't someone think of this ten years ago?' The Commander of Resolute Support is a U.S. four-star, but he is also the NATO commander, so he doesn't answer to the Ambassador. He answers to NATO in Brussels, and to the Pentagon. So, the Ambassador and COM smile at each other, while their staffs send reports back to DC blaming each other for the lack of progress. After fifteen years of it, everyone in DC is bored with the internecine warfare, so they let it go on like watching two monkeys fuck a football – a lot of noise and activity, but no real progress."

Trevanathan sighed. "Major, I appreciate what you are telling me in your own unique, profane way, even though it makes my head hurt. I'm surprised you haven't been promoted or taken out and shot with your unvarnished view of the world. But I have no interest in spending the next year contributing the next chapter to 'Grimm's Fairy Tales—Kabul Edition.' I'm too old to care about making people happy. So, do you have suggestions on how we might do something meaningful in the eleven months, two weeks and 3 days I have left, even with all the obstacles you've described?"

"Absolutely, sir," Brandt said with a lopsided grin. "We're gonna' have to not ask permission, start breaking shit, and piss people off."

Trevanathan laughed. "Now, *that* I understand. Let's do it."

Chapter 14

Camp Resolute Support, Kabul, January 2016

Ten days after their first meeting, Trevanathan found himself back in the same dining room chair across from Major General Crist's desk.

"So, what do you have, Bill?" the general asked, leaning forward. "I didn't get your PowerPoint."

"Sir, I know It's heresy to say so, but I think PowerPoint presentations have become a substitute for thinking in the Army." He could see a widening of the general's eyes that suggested he had perhaps made a serious mistake.

"Ohhkay…" the general said, slowly.

"Sir, when we're done, I'll send over a PowerPoint if you want so you can run it up the flagpole. But I'd rather talk you through my idea without being married to some slides. Remember you asked me to think outside the box? PowerPoint is literally a box that confines ideas. It's also a time suck. Staffs spend so much time on graphics…little tanks popping up on slides, formatting, getting the font and spacing perfect, and that type of BS, that they forget the purpose of the presentation. Then they spend hours creating forty slides so they can spend hours discussing which ten to present to the boss. You asked me to think outside the box, and you don't get 'outside the box' with PowerPoint. You get canned crap nicely formatted, and you get predictable."

"It can be useful, though…" began the general.

Trevanathan cut him off without realizing it. "Hugely useful when you're measuring how much fuel has been consumed or tracking personnel levels, sir. Numbers stuff. But innovation can't be reduced to a PowerPoint slide, and efforts to do so kills the innovation in the process. I think that's one reason why we're in this situation. The Army is in love with numbers—with its metrics—and there's some things that need to be *reasoned*, not counted. When an organization thinks everything can be solved by counting, you usually end up counting the wrong things. Creating the metric becomes the end in itself, not the means to an end. We're surrounded by smart guys here, and they've been cranking out PowerPoint slides for a decade-and-a-half about corruption. It hasn't made a bit of difference. We're in a worse position today than five or even ten years ago. So, point number one of my pitch to you is our methodology is flawed when we're dealing with something as amorphous as corruption, and we're not going to PowerPoint our way out of this."

"I'll have you burned at the stake later, heretic." Crist threw back his head again and let loose with one of his unrestrained laughs, enjoying his own joke. "OK, Bill, so what is your idea?"

"The center of gravity here is a lack of political legitimacy," Trevanathan said. "The corruption is a major feeder into that, but merely focusing on corruption in isolation, without recognizing its broader consequences, misses the mark. If we prosecuted corruption cases and did nothing more, it would not fix the political legitimacy problem. And lack of political legitimacy is what is causing GIRoA, and its army, to fail.

"The level of theft has become so extensive, so massive in scope, that the issue is not how many dollars have been taken, it's that there is an aura of *impunity* to theft. It's *normal* to steal in the government. To steal the country's money is not criminal or even shameful. It is expected, and you are a fool if you do not do so. So, we're dealing in part with culture change—changing a mindset or philosophy of governance, a thing not easily quantified. We can prosecute a few representative cases and put some heads on stakes, but if we don't change the underlying culture, we're bailing against the tide and will not influence the political legitimacy problem."

"Go on."

"The lack of legitimacy is so pervasive that it has corroded both domestic and international anchors for GIRoA. The Afghan people do not believe in their own government—they don't believe it's looking out for them or their family's best interest. They tolerate the government—at best—maybe because they have some personal patronage involved. But they have little interest in investing their

An Absence of Faith

lives or their children's lives in defending the future of GIRoA. The international problem was clearly stated by you at our last meeting. The donors are getting ready to cut and run, take their money and leave, because they see the place as irredeemable. September 11 was a long time ago, and it's not enough anymore to keep our allies on board by referencing that attack when they have current challenges of their own."

"I agree with all of that. Good insight. But where does that leave us?"

"Belief. Faith. Feelings and emotions that do not fit nicely on a PowerPoint slide and which are responsible for the rise or fall of the world's greatest empires. Gibbon—<u>Decline and Fall of the Roman Empire</u>—was right: internal strife brings the Empire down, at least in part, and not just a bunch of barbarians coming over the Alps." Trevanathan noted the general's eyes light up. *Ahh, the old man's reputation as a history buff is clearly accurate.*

"When you boil it down, we're talking about whether countries have the will to finance this war and whether Afghan families are willing to send their sons to catch a bullet to prop up this government. Those feelings are at a low ebb. If they disappear completely the Taliban will walk into Kabul without having to fire a shot. Saigon '75 all over again."

Crist looked at Trevanathan through narrowed eyes, his fingers steepled in front of his nose. *I know that look*, thought Trevanathan. *He has mixed feelings and is weighing options.*

At the risk of overstating his case, Trevanathan continued. "There's a speech I give in court to veterans, sir, when they are in front of my bench and I'm trying to get their attention to change their behavior—to stop their drinking or using drugs or to go to therapy, so I don't have to lock them up. It goes like this: 'The day you enlisted in the Army you signed a blank check to the President of the United States for the value of your life, allowing him to cash that in at a time and place of his choosing to defend the Constitution. You were willing to dedicate yourself to something bigger than yourself at that time. Now I need you to do that again, but for yourself.'"

Crist nodded. "Good speech."

"The point is every soldier makes that choice whether to sign that check or not, and in our country there's shared values that make that choice clear for many. The issue in Afghanistan is not a matter of justice or crime anymore. The corruption has become so widespread and destabilizing here that it is having a sustained negative impact on mission accomplishment, because these soldiers and their families don't believe in the government that dehumanizes them and steals their future. Your average Afghan soldier is going to do the bare minimum possible, and run at the first opportunity, not because he's a coward, but because he doesn't believe in what he is being asked to fight for."

"I agree with what you're saying, Bill. I think you've put your finger spot on the challenge. But we change that how? Especially with barely six months until the donors decide on their next five-year investment."

"I've learned, sir, that how you define a problem often drives actions forward for years thereafter—even if they don't make sense anymore. That's why I've spent so much of your time today defining the issue. Spitting out solutions is easy. Asking the right questions is hard. This operation has been defined as a war on terrorism, which is why we've spent a trillion dollars over here on bombs and trigger-pullers, while letting the governance piece be an afterthought.

"So to get to your point—what do we do? A three-pronged attack. First, we put heads on stakes, sir—figuratively speaking. We need to change the narrative to change the belief system—to grow a mustard seed of faith. As you pointed out, there's no time for committees and commissions and reports and studies. We need to get the Afghans to set up a specialty court, with jurisdiction to go after corrupt generals and high-level bureaucrats—only up to the Ministerial level—can't let Ghani feel threatened; to hold those publicly accountable who are stealing tens and hundreds of millions in NATO-donated money. We need to put them in prison, and we need to do it before July. A huge challenge, but possible."

"And then?"

"Second prong is a coordinated information campaign, directed at our international partners, to convince them that the approach here has fundamentally changed—that it is worth their money and continued political capital to continue to invest in Afghanistan's security.

"Third, and later—maybe a year from now— is an information campaign coordinated toward the Afghan people, so they see actual change—officials who had formerly been above the law, being held accountable. To give them something to believe in—that there can be justice if they invest their loyalty and their sons in the country. This third prong is really where this initiative will succeed or fail, because it is aimed at the lack of political legitimacy, which is the core problem for this country's future."

"What's your timeframe?"

"Sir, the first two prongs are like emergency treatment to a dying patient. Gotta' be done fast and gotta' be done now. Four or five months to get the court doors open and then start the second phase information ops with our allies. That third piece is going to take years. You don't change culture overnight. It will take a long-term commitment both by RS, the State Department if they decide to play in the game, and a good faith commitment on the part of key Ministries in GIRoA to make the third piece happen. If the Afghan officials merely create a façade of reform, but the thieving continues, what we do in prongs one and two won't matter in the long run. The Afghan people will smell that it is a sham, and Ghani's government will come down like a house of cards from its own thievery. Same is true if the next CSTC-A commander or COM makes this effort an afterthought. Not that we can control that, but I want to share the potential pitfalls up front. Success will depend on sustained effort over years."

"Where do you place this court? At the Attorney General's office?"

"It has to be a separate hybrid, sir, made up of cops, prosecutors and judges. A parallel justice center, with special jurisdiction over the biggest, headline-grabbing corruption cases. The current system, from the Attorney General's office through the existing courts to the cops, is too big and too corrupt to fix in six months, even if there was the will, which there isn't. If we don't want to be stonewalled by those entrenched in getting rich off the status quo, we need to build something new from the ground up."

"What do you need?"

"So, if this is going to work, we're going to need the COM to talk to President Ghani and get his blessing and political mojo to set up this new Anti-Corruption Justice Center. We can do the work—we have to launch this because the Afghans won't—but it needs to appear driven by Ghani to get the Afghan ministries on board. Otherwise, they'll just stonewall us. It will be separate physically from the preexisting institutions, using handpicked lawyers and judges, who are vetted beforehand, and kept honest by polygraph tests every six months. Six months is not enough time to reform a deeply-corrupt and entrenched existing system. It might be enough time to put together a new organization with new faces."

"I don't think we've ever done anything like this before," said the general, still thinking.

"Same conduct gets same results, sir. We'll tweak it as we go along and make mistakes and fix those. Some people will weasel in and try to be dirty—it would be naïve to presume otherwise—but we'll hold them accountable, too. My people will have to be on the ground with eyes on the cases coming through the system, so prosecutions don't disappear for a bribe like they do now. There's enough corruption operating without consequences right now that catching someone with their hand in the cookie jar will not be a problem, because no one expects any good faith enforcement. And the ripple effect when they get sent to jail will be massive, because it has never been done before. It will be in all the Afghan newspapers, TV, and radio, sending the message that things are starting to change."

"What else?"

"Well, there will be some logistics needs. We'll need to find a secure place to operate from, without all the usual movement restrictions that shut down missions every week. We can't keep things honest if we don't have access, so we can't be shut down every time a car bomb goes off in this town, which as you know, is pretty often. Right now, the Attorney General's office isn't even on the list of places I'm allowed to visit, because our security people haven't cleared it as being *safe* enough."

"I can fix that. You'll have VIP helicopter access, so ground transport won't be a showstopper. I'll get the RS Chief of Staff to bless it."

"Great, sir. I also need to be able to go see all of the EU[48] and GIRoA stakeholders and get their buy-in without having to wait ten days to set up a mission."

"Why would it take ten days?"

"Sir, this is way below your level, but if you're not a U.S. General, that's how long it takes to get the security and movement authorizations processed through the RS bureaucracy just to get off this post. It holds everything up."

"I had no idea."

"Yessir, that's why it's so easy for the Afghans to string us along. I can meet with one of them, but if there's a need for a follow-up, it may not occur until a month later, with all the bureaucratic hurdles and clearances needed to get off post. At the second meeting the Afghan official has to consult with Minister X, and at the third meeting they need to go consult with Minister Y. A couple meetings get rescheduled, and six months pass without anything happening. Our security bureaucracy is well intentioned, but it's strangling our ability to do anything in a one-year deployment."

"Got it. Well, you're a colonel by rank, but you'll have general officer access to helicopter transport, and priority movement approval after today. You might get bumped if the COM, or *me*, needs a helicopter, but otherwise you should get approval within twenty-four hours."

"Great, sir. That'll make a huge difference."

"What about the courts? They're independent, aren't they? Will they go along?"

"Not so independent, but apparently the Chief Justice is a political ally of the President and will do what Ghani says. It's not like the States."

"Well, sometimes corruption works to our advantage, I suppose," joked Crist. "And the police?"

---

[48] European Union

"I'm still working on that, but I have an idea of a possibility. Again, it has to be kept small to work. The bigger it is, the easier to corrupt."

"OK, do it."

"Sir?"

"I'm convinced. Considering our time-constraints and goals, this makes the most sense. It's audacious as hell, but as you said, there's no time to rewire the entire system."

"That's great, sir. I expected more push-back, sir, to be honest."

"There are a dozen ways this could fail, but you're the only person I know in Afghanistan who has run his own court system. Everyone claims to be in charge of fighting corruption over here—the Embassy, the Afghans, used to be the FBI, but none of them are currently doing anything now. On the command wire diagram for Resolute Support, the Italians are still in charge of rule of law issues. Hell, they aren't even in the country, anymore. They keep threatening to send a general out here to run things again and never do. Everyone is watching this train wreck in slow motion but doing nothing to prevent it. You make it happen, and I'll back you."

"Roger, sir."

"And get me some slides, because I need to convince the COM too, and your eloquent rant against PowerPoint won't sway a four-star who teethed on PowerPoint in his cradle."

"Understood, sir."

"What's your next step?"

"I need to start building consensus with the other international players—the embassies here whose diplomats will be in Warsaw. I need to get them on board to support and finance the new court. I also need to find someone in the diplomatic community with a pair of balls who's not afraid to stand up to our Embassy. My deputy tells me I can expect no help from the State Department."

Crist frowned. "Ahh, that reminds me, I need you to cover the weekly staff meeting at the Embassy for me on Wednesday. I'll be in Qatar. You fill in for me and float your idea. See how they react."

"Roger, sir. Do I need to do anything else there?"

"No, just listen for any major policy shifts. Otherwise, mention the concept of the corruption court as an idea we're considering and gauge their reaction. Remember, we're not asking for their approval. It'll be useful to see if they are going to actively oppose the idea, or just grumble. I think your deputy is right that they won't actively help, but we want to avoid any open inter-agency dispute that could cause problems back in Washington."

"Will do, sir. Do a recon, but don't get drawn into a firefight."

Crist smiled. "Exactly."

Chapter 15

Lashkar Gah, Helmand Province, December 2015

Command Sergeant Major Mahmood entered the 225th Corps headquarters wearing his familiar scowl, glaring down the hallway as if every step pained him. Daniyal watched his approach without concern. He had learned that the scowl was a tool the sergeant major used to keep people from pestering him with frivolous questions. When he was in a genuine bad mood the large blue vein on his temple stood out, and when he was truly angry, it pulsed with a life of its own. No vein today meant no problem.

"Daniyal!" The sergeant major barked angrily, approaching his desk. *Or have I miscalculated?* thought Daniyal. Several weeks had passed since his mission to deliver the medical supplies. They had not spoken of it since that night.

"You are out of uniform, Daniyal," growled the sergeant major. "If you are going to work for me you need to be properly attired at all times."

"My apologies, Sergeant Major," Daniyal apologized, snapping to attention. He was confused as to his mistake but knew that one does not argue with the sergeant major.

"Good, put these on immediately. We can't have privates cluttering up the headquarters." The sergeant major threw a pair of shoulder boards bearing the three stripes of an Afghan Army corporal onto Daniyal's desk.

"Really?" was all Daniyal could stutter. The fact that he might advance in the army, rather than being its perpetual whipping boy, had never occurred to him.

"Loyalty has its rewards." replied the sergeant major. "Now get back to work," he ordered, striding into his office and shutting the door.

It's always theater with that man, thought *Corporal* Daniyal. *Probably from his wrestling days.* "Mental intimidation was as important as physical strength in defeating an opponent," the sergeant major had stated more than once.

Footsteps at the far end of the hallway caused Daniyal to raise his eyes. It was Mr. Rajish, the corps accountant. While most positions in the corps headquarters were filled by military officers, a few requiring special skills were filled by civilians. Mr. Rajish was one of those. He reported to the corps commander, as well as to the Defense Ministry in Kabul, ensuring money and materiel resources were being properly used. A pale, nervous looking man with darting eyes, his job required a combination of business acumen and creative writing, in view of the constant thievery prevalent in the corps.

He seemed to shiver for a moment, then turned to the staff sergeant sitting outside the corps commander's office door to announce himself. Daniyal's phone rang, momentarily drawing his attention away. It was the mess sergeant, Staff Sergeant Dostan, wanting to know whether the dietary plan he had submitted the week before had yet been approved. Daniyal had seen it. It called for watering down the enlisted men's food even more.

"The sergeant major hasn't signed it yet, Sergeant Dostan. Would you like me to go ask him to hurry it for you?" Daniyal asked with a twisted sense of pleasure, knowing the fear this would strike into the fat mess sergeant.

"No... no! I wanted to be sure it had not been misrouted or was laying on someone's desk."

"Well, it is not on my desk, so that can only mean it is on the sergeant major's desk. I will be sure to pass along your concern regarding the delay."

"No...don't bother...please. Please don't. Sorry to bother you." Click.

Daniyal was quickly learning that daily life in a corps headquarters is not merely issuing orders, but a constant maneuver by people to gain proximity to power. His desk outside the sergeant major's office gave him an aura of power, certainly not equal to the sergeant major, but undeniably far above his rank. He found it interesting that sergeants who previously would not have tossed him a rope if he were drowning, now greeted him by name when he walked across the post, hoping that he might someday grant them important access.

A clatter at the far end of the hall refocused his attention. The tea boy was bringing his obligatory tray of tea and cookies to the meeting between the corps commander and Mr. Rajish. He was dressed in traditional silks with small bells that Daniyal knew signaled a special and dubious status, which he did not envy. The benefits of power were many in Afghanistan, and the tradition of the jingle boy to those in power was widely known and tolerated with a blind eye. The boy was invisible in the headquarters. No one spoke to him or of him. Yet he was always nearby to entertain the corps commander and his special guests.

At first, Daniyal thought the young boy had tripped with his tray, but as he looked more closely, he saw that the door to the general's office had been thrown open, knocking the boy to the ground. The accountant emerged, stumbling and holding his mouth, blood pouring between his fingers. The general pursued closely behind.

"You have ruined us, you fool!" Major General Rahman bellowed, raining blows down upon the slight man with a thick wooden rod. Mr. Rajish futilely tried to deflect the blows with a raised arm.

"I cannot explain away 150,000 liters of fuel..." the man blubbered, flecks of blood spraying every time he spoke. "Or two million kilos of firewood."

The general shoved Rajish to the ground and kicked him in the stomach. "You are a traitor!" he screamed. The jingle boy was curled into a ball, sobbing, as several of the wild blows directed at Rajish found the boy instead.

Horrified, Daniyal was in a panic. *What do I do? I can't stop a general.* The beating continued, as Rajish tried to crawl toward the stairs. Heavy blows fell on his head and shoulders. *I don't want to watch this,* Daniyal decided, looking for an exit. He froze momentarily, before taking his only escape, back into the sergeant major's office. He slipped quietly between its two great wooden doors.

The sergeant major looked up from his desk. "Corporal Daniyal, what can I do for you?"

"Sergeant Major," Daniyal panted, "the corps commander is beating Mr. Rajish in the hallway. *Stomping him*. I didn't know what to do."

"Ah yes, well, you did the right thing, which is nothing."

"But he is *killing* him."

"Perhaps, but he is not killing you, is he? You must learn, if you are to last here, that knowing when to do nothing is as important as knowing what to do. I did not become Command Sergeant Major by charging into the breach every time some officer lost his mind. That would be a full-time job."

"So we do nothing?" the young corporal asked plaintively.

"Sit," he directed to Daniyal, who complied.

"You are smart. I've watched you. You are not the average fool who only prays for the day he might go home to his worthless village of goats and babies crying in the dirt. You are always thinking. In your thinking, what have you learned about this corps?"

"It is a very proud unit, Sergeant Major" replied Daniyal, obligingly.

"Don't lie to me again, or I will take those stripes back," growled the sergeant major.

I will risk the truth. It is what he seems to need. Daniyal took a deep breath. "It is a collection of haves and have-nots, Sergeant Major. Those with the right connections or the right uses survive and prosper. Those who do not are disposable."

"True, but only partially on point. Are we a fighting force?"

"Of course, Sergeant Major."

"Do not be so quick with your answers. *Think*. What are we primarily?"

Daniyal was silent. He wasn't sure he knew the correct answer to the sergeant major's question.

"*Think*. We obtain money—capital—from our international donors. We convert that to certain uses, some military, some not, that are beneficial to those invested in the success of this corps: the commander, the Minister of Defense, the General Staff, me—even the President. We issue reports of our *progress* and then our international donors reinvest in us."

"That sounds like a…a business, Sergeant Major?"

"Very good. I knew you were not any fool. The Americans came here to fight a war. We are here to run a business," he declared proudly. "Mr. Rajish has let a displaced sense of professionalism interfere with the success of that business. He feels it is beneath him to move some matters from column A to column B that would make our business operations so much easier for everyone.

"The Americans have unfortunately renewed interest in how we are conducting our business. That interest comes and goes like the phases of the moon. Usually, they only care how many Taliban we tell them we've killed. But they have a new commander who wishes to placate their politicians and allies. This attention will only last until the next distraction comes along, perhaps from Iraq or Iran, but for now their attention is focused on how their money is being used, so we need to tread lightly. It will pass—it always does. But that fool Rajish is panicking and making a manageable situation worse."

"He mentioned fuel and firewood," Daniyal offered, still confused.

"It is best you do not know too much…not yet," added the sergeant major. "Let's say that what was a minor diversion of supplies to a senior officer's relatives became too…ambitious in scale. People became greedy to the point that losses could not be explained away merely as collateral damage from enemy activity…the usual practice. Now the Americans have asked questions of the Minister of Defense, who has asked questions of the General Staff, who have asked questions of Mr. Rajish. His initial response to the MOD Inspector General was that the supplies must have been stolen by someone outside the corps—a foolish response that will undoubtedly only raise further inquiry and investigation. So, he is receiving…how do the Americans call it?—an after-action review from the corps commander."

"What will happen?" Daniyal asked, not seeing how beating up an accountant could possibly help matters.

"What always happens when people get too greedy and upset the balance of things. There will be an investigation. Kabul will send down a team of investigators to show our NATO friends that the Minister and the President are taking their concerns seriously. I will, of course, be the local liaison to that investigation team to ensure they get full access to exactly what I want them to see. Many promises will be made. Heartfelt declarations will be issued. A lieutenant, or maybe a captain this time, will be found at fault and prosecuted. He will dutifully do a year in prison before quietly being released and reassigned, while his family is well cared for. Those here now from NATO will go home and matters will return to their natural state within six to nine months."

Daniyal sat silent, his head swirling with the realization that his corps was a criminal enterprise dressed up to look like a military organization. Only it was not a game of dress-up, he knew. People died every day. Azir had died. He had almost died. The men in the burn ward. The Taliban doctor's patients. All to keep the money flowing. He felt ill.

"Sergeant Major, thank you for explaining to me. May I return to my desk?" he asked quietly.

"It sounds like it has quieted down out there. Go. Remember, you have seen nothing and heard nothing. Those stripes are the start of good things for you."

"Yes, Sergeant Major." Daniyal turned to leave.

"Corporal, I neglected to mention, your mother is very proud of you."

"Sergeant Major?" Daniyal turned back, not certain he heard correctly.

"I sent Staff Sergeant Raghab to visit your family when he was in Kabul last week—to let them know of your promotion. They were very proud." The sergeant major's words were warm, but his eyes were flat and menacing. "Your little brother had been unwell, so Raghab took him some medicine to ease his pain. You should thank him the next time you see him."

They've found my family, Daniyal realized, feeling ill, *and he is letting me know they own me.* "Thank you, Sergeant Major, I will." Daniyal opened the door and peered down the hallway. No one was visible.

Daniyal walked to the central stairwell. A pair of bloody shoe prints led down the steps, suggesting that Mr. Rajish had perhaps survived his after-action review. Outside the commander's door a puddle of tea and blood was punctuated with broken teacups. A tooth lay where the stairs met the second-floor landing. Daniyal averted his eyes and swallowed hard. His head pounded. He looked down at his new rank insignia as a brand of complicity. *I need to get out, but there is no way.* The walls were closing in on him. Unable to rationalize the day's events further, Daniyal ran down the stairs, a voice echoing in his head, *"There is no escape."*

Chapter 16

U.S. Embassy, Kabul, December 2015

The U.S. Embassy compound was dominated by two six-story buildings in a city where few structures rose above three stories, earning the pair the nickname, "the goal posts." The unfortunate moniker derived from the fact that the construction had given the enemy a very distinctive target for its rockets, even when fired from many miles away. Embracing that reality, the Embassy gift shop sold stuffed-animal ducklings wearing little black T-shirts that read, "U.S. Embassy—Kabul, Duck and Cover."

One entered the Embassy grounds from Camp RS by passing through an internal military checkpoint, traversing an underground tunnel, and resurfacing on the well-manicured grounds of the Embassy compound. While Camp RS was a muddy-street collection of trailers, aging Afghan buildings, and CONEX shipping containers, the gleaming U.S. Embassy could have sat astride any European capital's boulevards. After several twists and turns through the Embassy grounds, passing the Embassy's liquor store and recreation center, Trevanathan and his aide, Lieutenant Ripple, found the main conference room on the sub-level of the main consular building.

As people filtered into the meeting room, Trevanathan took a seat behind the placard labelled "CSTC-A Commander," near the head of a long conference table. Lieutenant Ripple sat against the wall behind him, with the rest of the support staff. The first thing that struck Trevanathan was that there were several people present whose job title placards read as if they were operating in his counter-corruption world, yet he had never heard of them.

Halfway down the table on the opposite side, sat a young Asian woman, maybe in her late twenties, with the title, "Rule of Law" in front of her. *Hmmm, I thought that was my job*, Trevanathan pondered. To her right was a gray-haired man in a rumpled suit behind the "Justice" placard. To his right was a hatchet-faced man, staring at Trevanathan from behind a placard titled "INL."

Trevanathan thought that was something to do with narcotics, but he had not heard what their mission was in Afghanistan. *If there's all these people here working legal issues, why haven't I heard of any of them yet?*

His thoughts were interrupted as a middle-aged, balding man entered, prompting everyone to stand. The colonel followed suit. *Must be the Ambassador*, Trevanathan concluded. The man took the head chair before reaching across the corner of the table to extend his hand. "Good morning, Colonel, I'm Rick Willoughby, Deputy Chief of Mission. The Ambo is stuck on a call with the Secretary, so I'm pinch-hitting. I hear you're the new EF3 Director?"

"Yes, sir; nice to meet you."

"Well, welcome, welcome," the DCM gushed. "I hope you'll have an uneventful tour."

Uneventful tour? wondered Trevanathan. Then, what's the point?

"OK," Willoughby continued, turning his attention to the full group. "Let's call the meeting to order. We need to be efficient this morning. I've a call with the Minority Leader in 45 minutes. Let's run the usual list.

"Mil?"

An Air Force colonel, apparently the Embassy's military attaché, spoke up from the far end of the table. "Nothing significant to report, sir. There was some minor enemy activity near Lashkar Gah last week, but no Blue involvement. Training on the Tocano platform continues, and the Ministry of Defense has indicated that it will be increasing its requests for HMMWVs and ammunition in the next fiscal year."

"Well, I guess you can't fight a war without jeeps and bullets, right Colonel?" the DCM smiled knowingly at Trevanathan, as if they shared an important secret.

Trevanathan gave an awkward half-smile in reply. *Jeeps?*

"Log?" The DCM turned his attention back to the others at the table.

A dour man in his sixties to Trevanathan's right raised his head from the spreadsheets in front of him; he was apparently the

An Absence of Faith

Embassy logistician. "Two pallets of currency left HKIA[49] on Monday. Another is due out next week. The drawdown of nonessential personnel is continuing. Due to the staff reduction, we will be consolidating everyone out of the old apartments into the new building over the next six weeks to save on costs. That's all I have."

"What's the status on the courts?" the DCM asked. "I believe I asked you to check on that last week?"

What is a logistician doing with the courts? Trevanathan wondered, turning to hear the response.

The older man sighed, blowing out his cheeks slowly before responding. "The tennis court repairs were completed yesterday. The large crack on the surface of the one nearest the traffic circle is most likely caused by poor workmanship in laying the original foundation. We've filled it for now, but it is likely to recur at some point in the future."

"But it's playable now?" the DCM pressed, earnestly.

"Yes, sir."

Trevanathan noticed a slight reddening of the logistician's complexion as he finished.

"Good! Any questions?" the DCM asked the group.

The young woman behind the *Rule of Law* placard raised her hand. "ROL," called the DCM.

"Is there any way we can get the temperature in the pool raised, a bit? It's brutal if you try to swim early in the morning."

The logistician stared at the paper in front of him. "The short answer is 'no,'" he replied through gritted teeth. "The longer answer is no, too, unless the Ambassador wants to approve shipping over a new $10,000 heating unit on a military aircraft—which I doubt would be appreciated by Congress when we're evacuating nonessential personnel."

---

[49] HKIA – Hamid Karzai International Airport, the main civilian and military airport for Kabul.

The ROL representative shrunk back into her seat, as the DCM cut off the exchange. "OK, well thank you much. So, the takeaway is more tennis, less swimming. *C'est le guerre.* Let's move on."

"Justice?" he asked, turning to the man in the rumpled suit behind the "Department of Justice" placard.

"Nothing significant to report," the gray-haired man replied. "Pursuant to the Ambassador's direction, we've reduced my shop from three personnel to just me. And I leave next month."

"Hmm, and there's no replacement, correct?"

"Correct, sir. The Ambo ended our mission so there's no need for Justice to send more people."

What the hell is going on? Trevanathan wondered, with growing frustration.

"Back to you, Rule of Law," the DCM said.

The young Asian woman smiled. "Nothing significant to report, sir. We're still working on trying to get the Chief Justice to visit us, but he hasn't returned our calls yet."

"I met him last year at a soiree at the Presidential Palace," the DCM offered. "Very dignified gentleman. What's his name, again?"

The young woman blanched and shuffled through her notes. "I had it right here... I think it's Muhammad, something..."

"Halim," Trevanathan said, quietly.

"What was that, Colonel?" the DCM asked, catching the comment.

"The Chief Justice's name is Halim, sir."

"Muhammad Halim?" the DCM sought to clarify.

"Sayed Yousef Halim, sir."

"That's it," the DCM declared happily.

"Sir, I don't want to get into anyone else's lane here, but my people go to the Supreme Court about every two weeks for coordination. I'm going next Tuesday. I can ask the Chief Justice to call your Rule of Law office if that's helpful. Or if you want, your folks can ride along with us."

The room went silent, and the DCM looked intently at his pen as if he had never seen such a thing before.

"I'm sure our ROL staff would be most appreciative if you could ask Chief Justice Halim to call," he began, "but right now our force protection posture is that we are not allowed to leave the Embassy grounds because of the threat."

"Is there a new threat, sir?" Trevanathan asked out of genuine concern. "I didn't hear."

"Errr, it's more that the Ambassador has made the decision, in view of the fallout over Benghazi, that we need to raise our readiness profile here. No nonessential missions are approved at this time."

"I believe his excellency's words were, 'There won't be another Benghazi on my watch,'" volunteered the DOJ rep with a tight-lipped smile.

The situation was suddenly clear to a stunned Trevanathan: the Embassy in Kabul was evacuating personnel and reducing operations because bad guys had attacked the U.S. mission in Libya three years earlier and three thousand miles away.

"Ahh, OK, sir," replied the colonel, leaning back in his chair. Then, without intending to, he made an awkward situation worse. "Sir, even though the Supreme Court is just across the street from the Embassy, your personnel can't go there?" Trevanathan was surprised that his question came out sounding much more accusatory than he wanted, his words seemingly hanging in the air as everyone looked away.

"I, I'm afraid so," the DCM replied.

"We haven't had any meaningful contact with our counterparts in the Afghan justice system in several months," added the DOJ man in a bored voice. "We can't go there, and they're offended that we body search them when they come here. Probably why they're not returning our calls. Supreme Court Justices don't typically appreciate being manhandled."

"Well, that wouldn't apply to the Chief Justice, right?" asked Trevanathan.

"Yes, well, umm..." stammered the DCM. "Everyone—all locals that is—get searched. Ambassador's orders."

Trevanathan tried to keep his face impassive. Inside, he was exploding. *These shirts think they're going to build relationships when they're body searching the Chief Justice of the country in which they're stationed? Why don't we just spit in his face for crissakes?*

"OK, let's continue," said the DCM. "INL[50]?"

"Nothing significant to report."

The remainder of the staff provided their reports, the majority of which were the standard "nothing significant to report." Trevanathan did learn that there was to be a disco night, complete with a DJ, in the Embassy ballroom a week from Wednesday, with prizes for best individual and group costumes. Everyone also had a nice time at the holiday party, with the DCM playing Santa Claus.

This is nuts, Trevanathan thought to himself. *Everyone's focus is either on getting out the door, or how to do as little as possible. "The threat" freezing them in place is the same damn war we've been fighting for fifteen years.* His thoughts were interrupted when the DCM turned toward him. "Just a few minutes left. CSTC-A? Do you have anything for the group?"

"Umm, yes, sir. This would require more explanation than we have time for here today, but the main point is we're going to reengage with the Afghans prior to the Warsaw donor conference, on reducing systemic corruption."

"Good luck," sneered the man behind the *INL* placard loud enough to be heard.

Trevanathan ignored him. "RS believes there's a causal connection between unrestricted corruption and the lack of success in the war effort. One is undercutting the other. Therefore, as a

---

[50] INL – Bureau of International Narcotics and Law Enforcement. A sub-agency of the U.S. State Department, whose declared mission includes combatting corruption by helping governments and civil society entities build transparent and accountable public institutions—a cornerstone of strong, stable, and fair societies.

matter of military necessity, we need to reduce corruption to increase Afghan army battlefield effectiveness. To do that we're going to set up a special corruption tribunal with the Afghans."

The INL representative lost his sneer and leaned forward, his face darkening. Trevanathan could swear that the ROL's mouth was sagging open, and that the DOJ representative had the hint of a smile on the corner of his lips.

"You *do* realize that the State Department is lead agency for Rule of Law reform in theater, *Colonel*?" the INL representative challenged him.

"That's great to hear. I look forward to hearing your plans," Trevanathan replied, not taking the bait. "However, NATO is lead on winning the war, so we're going to do whatever is needed to *win…the…war*." He dragged out the final three words as if speaking to a dimwitted person who might not understand the concept.

The INL representative's eyes bulged.

Before matters could escalate further, the DCM interjected, "Well, that all sounds intriguing. We should set up a study group to explore this further. Hiram, can you put that together?"

"Actually, no, sir. I'm leaving, remember?" said the DOJ man in the rumpled suit.

"Ahh, yes, well, umm, OK. Right." The DCM looked at the Rule of Law representative, but then looked away. "Yes, well, as you heard, I have my call, so the meeting is adjourned for today. Keep up the good work everyone. Colonel, thank you for coming." The DCM gathered a small handful of folders and quickly exited.

Trevanathan turned to find his aide at his shoulder, as the table emptied. "Making new friends again, sir?" Lieutenant Ripple smiled, as the INL representative stormed from the room, with the Rule of Law representative trailing in his wake. The Justice Department representative remained in his seat, chuckling and shaking his head.

Chapter 17

United Nations High Commission Compound, Kabul, January 2016

The UN High Commission's compound sat at the end of a long, shaded driveway within the Green Zone, one of the few that still had mature trees not sacrificed for firewood. The main road to the compound was bordered by the ubiquitous T-walls that sculpted the Green Zone into a rat's maze of narrow, twenty feet high concrete channels, interspersed with occasional Ministry of Interior checkpoints, whose guards were characterized more by apathy than by security.

The importance of the United Nations' mission had grown at first, when the focus of Western efforts was freeing Afghan society from the poverty and cultural taint of the Taliban. But it then ebbed over the years, as the West's focus shifted to its military campaigns. NATO, not the UN, was running the show in the country now. Yet, the UN Mission, UNAMA[51], still provided an important forum where nongovernmental agencies and non-NATO countries could have their voices heard to coordinate economic and social policy with other entities. The ongoing efforts to promote women's rights, to enhance health and education for all Afghans, and to promote democracy within Afghan institutions were all UN-led or partnered initiatives.

The UN's access and influence made it an important potential partner for the corruption court concept. If the Afghan government did not sense there was unanimity among its international financial supporters for the court, it would have little incentive to support the effort. Seeking that unity was why the colonel was attending today's law and justice committee meeting at the UN compound, where he expected many legal representatives from the various Western embassies that populated the Green Zone to appear.

---

[51] United Nations Assistance Mission in Afghanistan

After clearing the UN security checkpoint, Trevanathan's three-vehicle convoy drove into the lush compound. In contrast to the barren walls and dirty streets outside, a palatial two-story mansion sat in the shade of ancient trees. The team found a secluded place to park to the right of the house, against the exterior wall, where their oversized vehicles would not block later arrivals.

As Trevanathan exited his vehicle, he heard a voice booming voice from the front porch. "Charles Brandt! You've come home!" The source was a large man, wearing a Panama hat, a cape loosely thrown about his shoulders, and waving a polished walking stick in his right hand. Major Brandt, who had dismounted on the vehicle's opposite side, waved, and then turned back to Trevanathan. "That is our UN host, Michael Broadbent, Esquire," he said, with a smile.

"British?" Trevanathan asked.

"No. American eccentric," Brandt replied, still smiling.

The large man approached quickly with the flair of a drama critic entering Sardi's after a Broadway opening. "Charles, you are back!" he declared, belaboring the obvious. "Now we can generate some real excitement." He buried the major in a hug, his salt and pepper beard scratching the younger officer's cheek.

"Mike, this is Colonel Trevanathan, the new EF3 Director," Brandt sputtered, freeing himself from the ursine grasp of his host.

"My colonel," Broadbent, smiled broadly with arms thrown wide, placing fear into Trevanathan that he was also about to be mauled. But their host instead lowered his cane and head in a mock bow. "Welcome to Kabul, the city where dreams go to die."

Trevanathan grinned and extended his hand. "My pleasure; hopefully we can change that."

"Ah, an idealist—a man after my own heart. We'll get along *famously*."

Trevanathan shed his helmet and flak jacket, while Brandt and Broadbent caught up on old times. The colonel placed his equipment in the back seat of the armored suburban, much to the consternation of Sergeant Ford. "Can't build trust while all turtled up, Sergeant Ford," Trevanathan said in a low voice. Ford gave his best "*I don't like it, but I'm not saying anything*" look back at the colonel. To assuage the sergeant's concern, Trevanathan did a subtle pat of the waistline of his outer blouse, showing the NCO that he had slipped his pistol beneath the longer outer garment, into his pants' waistband. Ford inclined his head subtly in agreement. Within the walls of this compound the other diplomats and bureaucrats were, of course, not a security concern, but there were always local national employees who did maintenance and custodian services. Their loyalties could never be presumed.

"This is Mike's second tour here," Brandt told Trevanathan. "He did work at the MEC[52] when Karzai was in power."

"Yes, I knew the Godfather before he was the Godfather," Broadbent beamed. "In the early days, when we were trying to move the government forward, rather than bailing against the tide."

"What did you do before this tour?" Trevanathan asked.

"I was with the Southern Poverty Law Center for a number of years, slaying dragons. Preserving civilization against its darker impulses," he grinned. "Where else can an unrepentant child of the sixties still hope to make a difference?"

Trevanathan took an instant liking to his theatrical host.

"Who's showing up here today, Mike? Who are the players?" Brandt asked.

"The usual suspects," Broadbent declared, again throwing his arms wide, as if on a stage surrounded by an invisible cast. "The Brits are here looking to energize action on the corruption front before the donor conferences this summer. The Germans—they will sit and look dour, thinking deep Teutonic thoughts, but saying little. The Japanese are here—they will try to slow the process and commit to nothing, as usual, claiming they need direction from Tokyo—which will never come. The Italians have sent some junior staffer, a person with absolutely no authority. He's only here to make sure they don't get blamed for the lack of progress. The U.S. Embassy may or may not show up—depends on if they are having something good for lunch and if Captain Queeg has taken his meds today."

---

[52] The Independent Joint Anti-Corruption Monitoring and Evaluation Committee

"Captain Queeg?" Trevanathan asked.

"The Ambassador, sir," offered Brandt. "Nervous sort. Since the shitshow in Benghazi,[53] he made it clear he didn't want to be in an Arab country, so they sent him here. But he doesn't want to be here, either. He doesn't want anything to fuck up his chance to get posted to a nice quiet embassy in Europe for his last tour, so he's locking his people down."

"Yeah, I heard something like this at the staff meeting."

"Who else is coming, Mike?" asked Brandt.

"Those are the ones we know for sure. The rest are surprise guest stars. The European Union usually shows for the lunch. Norway? Danes?" Two vehicles came through the gate, interrupting the discussion. "Ahh, the frogs have arrived. They always show, to convince everyone they are still players. None of them are going to bring ideas, although having the EU behind any initiative is important for money reasons."

"So, what's the goal today, from your perspective?" asked Trevanathan.

"Inertia is our enemy, here. We talk corruption to death and admire the problem from a dozen different angles, but any action usually bogs down on core philosophical differences."

"Which are?"

"One group says Afghanistan is a sovereign nation and they must find their own answers. We can't do it for them. The argument runs that it is arrogant and colonialist for NATO to come here and try to impose change that the Afghans don't want. That, of course, ignores whose money is being stolen.

"The second group, often led by our military friends and the Brits, argue it is NATO money and troops that have been holding the country together for fifteen years, so they get input. Eight billion dollars per year worth of input. *It's our money, so it's our way*, runs the logic. Very arrogant, *very* American, and so other stakeholders

---

[53] The U.S. diplomatic compound in Benghazi, Libya was overrun in September 2012, resulting in the deaths of several U.S. personnel, including U.S. Ambassador Christopher Stevens.

instantly want to resist it, even if the best chance for GIRoA to survive is to not only lead the horse to water, but to smack it over the head with a two- by-four when it tries to steal the waterhole.

"Discussions on these two themes go round for hours. There are elements of truth in both views and so all of the stakeholders—those funding this adventure with cash and bodies—talk themselves to exhaustion until curfew or some contrived deadline by the attendees causes the group to disperse, and then we reconvene two months later and repeat the same Kabuki dance again."

"Mike," interjected the colonel, "if we wanted to actually do something—not just talk about it—to set examples that the same old way of doing business is no longer going to be tolerated, who would we need as allies? Who has the influence?"

Broadbent raised an eyebrow in thought. "You need the Brits. Where they go, others will follow, because the U.S. Embassy is a nonplayer. The UK ambassador *is* a player and is very interested in corruption issues. Their counter corruption rep is very highly regarded."

"I've met Jodie Upton. Very impressive. Well, let's go meet the rest," said Trevanathan, feeling this conversation might go on for some time if he didn't break it up.

"This way, *mon* colonel," invited Broadbent, gesturing toward the porch.

Like many of the embassies in the Green Zone, the UN High Commission headquarters exuded a faded opulence. Marble floors and staircases framed the foyer. A chandelier with half its crystals missing hung above a room of mismatched, scuffed tables and cabinets along the walls.

An oak door led into a conference room at the rear of the building, brightly lit by sunlight streaming through a wall of windows framing an elaborate garden. "Nice digs, Mike," commented Trevanathan to his host. A heavy wood conference table dominated the room, capable of seating two dozen people comfortably.

"We, too, serve, who sit and drink tea in squalid comfort," chuckled Broadbent.

Numerous faces scattered around the table turned toward the officers as they entered. Trevanathan, aware that their camouflage uniforms screamed a different message than the shirts and ties looking back, smiled and nodded toward the room. Only one face reciprocated: Jodie Upton smiled and waved in recognition. She quickly slipped past a man in a loud green jacket who had her trapped in a corner and hurried toward the new arrivals.

"Here is rock upon which to build your church, Colonel," beamed Broadbent, as Upton slipped past a cavalcade of high-backed chairs on the opposite side of the table.

"Thank God, you've come," she smiled. "Another moment in Antonio's grasp there and I would have needed to call in the SAS[54]."

"Ahh, but he is Italian. It is their way—to be romantic...and ineffectual," offered Broadbent, smiling.

"He can piss off and find his entertainment elsewhere, I say." The flush still on her cheeks, Upton turned to Trevanathan, "Colonel, good to see you again."

"Likewise," Trevanathan replied with a smile.

"Let's take our seats, shall we?" declared Broadbent, waving his arms toward the long table dominating the center of the room. Trevanathan and Brandt grabbed seats near Broadbent at the head of the table, looking out toward the gardens, and across from the Japanese and French representatives. Jodie Upton returned to her seat on the opposite side, next to her Italian counterpart, who was visibly pouting at having been rebuffed. Two latecomers slid in the door from the foyer, still clad in ill-fitting helmets and flak jackets.

"Who is that?" Trevanathan asked out the side of his mouth.

"Your friends from State," replied Brandt. "Guess you don't recognize them outside their starched shirts. She's Nancy-somebody, the Embassy Rule of Law advisor. New from the States. The sweaty guy is Nicholas Deepak, International Narcotics and Law Enforcement. He's a fucking snake. I dealt with him on my last tour. Hates the military. Actually, he hates everyone."

"So why is he here? I thought they weren't allowed off campus."

---

[54] SAS – Special Air Service. British Special Operations Forces.

"We are only a hundred meters from the Embassy back gate, so I suppose they got a Papal dispensation. He's the guy who is supposed to be working with the Afghans to fight corruption—funding courts, providing security, doing training. But he doesn't do Jack. His office is the one that stuck a fork in funding for the narcotics court."

"Because?"

"Well, the short answer is the Ambassador has told him not to engage, because they already believe the Taliban has won. But Deepak and the Ambo are of one mind. Their theory is that corruption is so pervasive in the country that if we do anything to fight against it, it'll destabilize the country politically, the government will fall, and the Embassy will get the blame."

"Huh," snorted Trevanathan. "So, it's like the patient has the clap so bad that if we treat it, we might cause them to die from what? Absence-of-clap-shock?"

"I didn't say it makes sense, sir. It's simply their excuse for not doing anything."

"So, again, why are they here then?"

"Probably spying on you, sir, since you let the cat out of the bag at that Embassy meeting about the corruption court. They don't want to get blindsided now that someone is doing their job for them."

"They're protecting their job of doing nothing?"

"Now you got it, sir. Welcome to Afghanistan." Brandt grinned.

"Welcome to our friends from the U.S. Embassy," smiled Broadbent from the head of the table. "It is nice to see you out."

Deepak merely nodded, his face still red from wrestling out of the unfamiliar flak jacket.

"The first item on the agenda is updates from the donor nations," stated Broadbent. He gestured to Deepak at the far end of the table, "Is there anything you'd like to brief the group on?"

"No new developments," announced Deepak in a clipped tone.

"Oh, I've an item," Nancy Something said, drawing an irritated side glance from Deepak. "We are planning to sponsor a regional rule of law conference in Qatar in 2021. It will bring together all of the regional players to support counter-corruption reform."

"What year was that again?" sneered the French representative, a dark-haired woman, with narrowed eyes.

"2021," repeated, Nancy Something. "We're hoping to invite regional Ministers of Justice and Attorneys General, so it's going to take a lot of coordination and planning. We want it to be a major success—so it can't be too rushed."

"Into the next decade. Brilliant. And what *regional players* are you intending to invite?" the Frenchwoman continued.

"All of them," Nancy Something continued. "Anyone with a stake in the stability of Afghanistan."

The French representative scoffed. "Pakistan has a stake. So, Pakistan. *Pakistan.* You're going to expect the Afghans to attend a conference with the Pakis about their internal justice operations. That will be a real diplomatic breakthrough when the Pakistanis are sheltering and funding the Taliban that are blowing up this country. *Mon Dieu.*"

"Well, we, we...," stuttered Something.

"Ah, and the Iranians," the Frenchwoman continued. "Yes, yes, they are stakeholders on the western border. I am sure they will love to come, as a regional stakeholder. I can't wait to see the U.S. Government inviting their dear Iranian friends to this *soiree.*" She spat the word, as only a disgusted French bureaucrat could.

Nancy Something looked bewildered, turning to whisper something to her embassy partner.

Unable to restrain himself, Trevanathan heard his voice inquiring, "2021? It's only 2016, right? You're assuming there's still going to be a country here five years from now if you wait that long to take corruption seriously?"

"Thought you were just going to listen today, sir," murmured Brandt.

"*Oui*, I agree with *mon* colonel," the French representative declared. "It sounds like a *bon* vacation to the Gulf for those stationed here in the distant future, but irrelevant to the serious problems today. France is not committing to fund five more years of its pockets being picked, without progress *now*."

"Well, it's going to take a lot of coordination and planning," repeated Nancy Something, her voice trailing off, suddenly no longer as chipper.

Deepak's eyes fixed on the new colonel, to whom he had taken an instant dislike during their previous encounter at the Embassy. "We do have to be *careful,"* he interjected slowly. "This government is at a critical juncture after the last election. The power sharing arrangement between Ghani and Abdullah is *delicate*. We cannot go charging in, as if this was some *military* adventure, and upset the *fragile* political balance that has been attained through extensive diplomatic negotiations."

"I agree," interrupted Trevanathan. *Nothing like agreeing with your opponent to throw them off balance.* "So, what's your plan to carefully deal with corruption amidst this delicate and fragile situation you describe?"

"The plan?" Deepak drawled, as if the word was distasteful.

"Yes, corruption reform is INL's job, as you've mentioned to me before, so you must have a plan. What's *your* plan to reduce corruption without overturning the *fragile situation*? I'm sure you've thought of one, because otherwise you're just marking time while the Afghans piss away our tax money and their future."

"Remember, no open warfare with the Embassy, sir," Brandt said under his breath.

"A colorful phrase," hissed Deepak, trying to buy himself time. He paused before continuing. "The plan is ongoing and extensive good faith negotiations, combined with constructive engagement amongst our international partners and GIRoA to reach a common understanding of our mutual needs." His heavy lids blinked once, satisfied he had deflected the matter.

"So that's another way of saying we're going to admire the problem until our replacements show up and we skip town. Ya' see Nick, the problem is that in July a bunch of people around this table are going to get orders from their governments to turn off the money. Without money the Afghan security forces collapse, and the

Afghan house of cards starts to *delicately* come down around our ears."

Deepak glared venomously at Trevanathan, unused to a *mere* Army colonel impeaching him so publicly. "You haven't..." he began.

Whatever accusation Deepak was about to cast toward Trevanathan was interrupted by the glass doors across from the colonel blowing open, as a shock wave hammered into the room. Amidst a whirl of flying papers and chairs being knocked askew, attendees dove beneath the massive wooden table. Trevanathan and Brandt looked at each other and remained in their seats: Camp RS was close to several major roads, and explosions were not unusual.

"Car bomb?" asked Brandt, looking out into the walled garden.

"Probably," replied Trevanathan. "Maybe three, four hundred meters away. Check on the men and have them report to Ops that we're OK. Try to get a SITREP on where it cooked off. Ask Ford for fighting positions if this is the start of something bigger."

"Aye, sir," replied Brandt, before double-timing out the door.

Trevanathan leaned over and extended a hand to assist Broadbent up. "I think it was out on the main road, Mike. But it's hard to tell the way noise bounces around these T-walls."

"Another day, another six hundred twenty-five dollars," joked Broadbent, regaining his feet and dusting off his knees. "It's become a Pavlovian reaction by now," he explained, slightly embarrassed to find himself on the ground.

"It's the smart thing to do," Trevanathan offered. "I could tell it wasn't too close when the glass didn't shatter." He gestured toward the wall of windows and doors framing the garden beyond.

The smell of dust and burning debris was now drifting in through the open doors. "Can you secure those doors and windows?" Trevanathan asked Upton, who was checking on the Italian representative on the floor next to her. "It'll keep some of the blast stink out."

"Yes, Colonel," she replied, moving to take care of business.

"Is everyone OK?" Trevanathan asked the disheveled room at large. Mosty attendees were still beneath the large table, out of sight.

He wanted to be sure no one had been struck by a piece of debris, knowing from personal experience the damage a small steel splinter can cause. Only a few murmurs responded.

"Mike, can you check on the far side of the table? I'll do this side."

Trevanathan quickly worked down his side of the large wooden table. People were mostly embarrassed and dealing in various ways with the adrenalin rush that typically accompanies a bomb blast. The Norwegian representative was staring at his shoe tips, as he rocked back and forth beneath the table. In contrast, the Japanese rep was talking quickly into her phone.

As he reached the table's far end, Trevanathan saw that Nicholas Deepak had managed to crawl into his flak jacket. Nancy Something was still curled into a fetal position under the table end, with her fingers locked behind her neck, and making small whimpers.

"I have to get back to the embassy. I have to get back to the embassy," Deepak repeated manically to himself as he crab-crawled over to his helmet. "They told me not to come," he continued his one-sided conversation, as he fumbled with his chin strap. "They said something like this might happen."

"It's OK, it's all over now," Trevanathan told Deepak, extending a hand to help the INL representative to his feet.

Deepak looked up at Trevanathan with unfocused eyes. "You don't know that. You *can't* say that," he accused. "I need to get back to the Embassy," he said, as he unsteadily regained his feet. "I need to go," he declared, before darting out the side door into the foyer.

Brandt returned a moment later. "We're not going anywhere for a while," he advised. "The men are OK, but I was right. VBIED[55] went off at Check Point Bravo near the German embassy. They were just inside the Green Zone. One of our convoys noticed the civilian sedan riding very low with a clean-shaven Haji in a white dishdasha driving–all the signs of a suicide bomber. He'd been let through the checkpoint, so it was definitely an inside job."

"How'd it blow?" Trevanathan asked.

---

[55] VBIED, mil. acronym – Vehicular Borne Improvised Explosive Device, i.e., car bomb.

"One of the security vehicles in the convoy swung around and tried to engage. The bomber tried to accelerate away, but crashed into the T-wall and the whole thing went sky high. We lost two guys in the security SUV and two more pretty badly busted up. The entire Green Zone is code black and locked down right now. Nothing's moving."

"Shit. Anyone we know?" asked the colonel.

"Don't know yet. They haven't released the names. The usual news blackout. Post internet will be down until tomorrow, so no one tips off the next of kin before official notice."

"Tough business," Trevanathan added flatly.

"Yes, sir."

"OK, I'll go fill in Mike and see if he wants to keep going with the meeting. See if you can unfuck what's-her-name here." The colonel gestured to Nancy Something. "Maybe get her a cup of tea? I don't think she's hurt, just shook up."

"Roger, sir."

Trevanathan walked to the front of the room, pausing to ask Upton, "Are you good?"

"Yes, Colonel, thank you. Rather jarring, wasn't it?"

"Rather," replied Trevanathan. "Can you do me a favor?"

"Certainly."

"That female staffer—I forget her name—from the U.S. Embassy. Looks like she is pretty shaken up—still laying at the end of the table." He gestured. "I think that INL puke ditched her. Can you chat her up to see if she needs anything?"

"Certainly, Colonel. She does seem rather young," Upton observed.

"I asked Major Brandt to talk to her, but now that I think of it, he'll probably say something helpful like, 'You're not fucking dead, so stop sniveling.' Marine, you know."

Upton snorted a laugh, immediately looking mortified, at the sound. "You Yanks do have a way with words."

Trevanathan turned his attention to Broadbent, who was finishing a call at the head of the table. He hung up, as the colonel reached his side.

"Letting our higher ups know we're in one piece," Broadbent explained. "Word is it was some sort of car bomb."

"Yeah, I just heard the same thing. The roads have gone Black, so we can't move. What do you plan to do, Mike? Any chance of continuing the meeting, or are we done?"

"I agree we don't want to lose the opportunity to discuss time-sensitive issues. I suggest we give everyone half an hour to recover, and then slowly start gathering in small groups to continue. As you said, no one can move on the roads back to their embassies, so we might as well grab the opportunity to proceed, after a break."

"Sounds good. I'm going to double-check on my guys, then I'll be right back."

Trevanathan stepped outside of the UN building, to the sounds of sirens warbling in the distance. A dissipating black cloud still hung in the air in the general direction of the German embassy to the Northwest. Staff Sergeant Ford saw the colonel walk onto the porch, and immediately moved in that direction, with Trevanathan's flak jacket and helmet in hand.

"You lookin' for these, sir?"

"Touché, Sergeant Ford. OK, from now on I take my gear into all buildings. No issues. Roads are Black, I hear?"

"Yessir. We're probably stuck here a couple hours at least, maybe more."

"Are our guys OK?"

"Yessir. Other than the big bang it all seems pretty quiet. If that changes, though, I'm coming in to get you. Small arms fire in the area—anything like that."

"You're the man." Trevanathan knew that while he held rank, when it came to matters of tactical security, Sergeant Ford was the voice to listen to. He had been doing this work a long time and knew when to get excited and when it was simply another lousy day in Kabul.

"You all have something to eat?" the colonel asked.

"Always travel with a pocket of jerky and power bars, sir. This ain't my first rodeo." Ford grinned.

"No doubt. OK, well, I'm going to be inside shmoozing and trying to cut some deals. As soon as the roads go Amber[56], come get me, and we'll go wheels up."

"Roger, sir."

"Oh, last thing—Did the embassy vehicles leave? They left someone behind."

"Yessir, some pasty guy came running out of the building yelling that he had to report to the Ambassador. They blew out the gate just as the roads were being shut down, so I have no idea if they made it back or not. It's not that far."

"OK, well, we may have to give a ride to this Embassy staffer inside. We can take her back to RS and she can walk back to the Embassy through the tunnel. Let Ops know she's with us, so she doesn't get reported as missing in action or some bullshit like that."

"Got it, sir. What's her name?"

Trevanathan paused, trying to recall. "Nancy...*Something!*" he declared triumphantly.

◊ ◊ ◊

Trevanathan never found whether the car bomb had been a Taliban, ISIS, or another group's operation. If he had, he might have sent them a thank you note. The consensus reached during the next several hours of informal discussions amongst the players trapped together at the UN compound surpassed his hopes for what might be accomplished at Kabul's normal, glacial pace.

With no other proposal on the table and the donors recognizing that time had run out on expecting the Afghans to initiate reforms on

---

[56] When roads were "Black" or "Code Black," there was no vehicular movement allowed at all in the Green Zone. This was often right after an attack or when intelligence knew an attack was imminent. "Code Amber" meant that it was a high-risk environment with a likelihood of danger, but movement by convoys was permissible with prior approval.

their own, the attendees embraced the idea of a new agency known as the Anti-Corruption Justice Center, or ACJC. Consultations would still be needed with their home ministries, as the Japanese delegate was quick to point out, but no one spoke against the idea.

Even the usual stumbling-block frequently raised by the EU representative, that any Afghan solution must originate with the Afghans themselves, was only half-heartedly mentioned. After fifteen years of Afghan inaction when it came to restraining themselves from pilfering from their own internationally-funded purse, that old chestnut had run its course. Ultimately, no one else had any other idea how to stop a country from stealing its own future, making the sole proposal on the table the most popular, by default.

In the days that followed, several critical components gelled. The British Embassy stepped up as the champion of the initiative, offering to use its broad base of police trainers and Foreign Ministry funding to provide the seed money for the Anti-Corruption Justice Center. The Germans agreed to support the Judiciary branch with new funding and training, including bringing German judges to Kabul to share their expertise in overseeing government embezzlement cases. Afghan prosecutors would receive additional financial and training support from the Italians, including substantial raises to try to reduce incentives for seeking bribes.

Trevanathan was not naïve. He knew that even with Western support, the key to success was Afghan political will to reform past, illicit practices. He knew this would not be a quick fix, as the ACJC was seeking a change of culture within a government that had embraced corruption as one of its founding principles. "They won't all buy in at first, but if we gradually change the culture through prosecutions so they no longer see theft as normal, we'll have come a long way," Trevanathan said in a subsequent meeting at the British Embassy with Jodie Upton.

"And if they don't come to believe in it?" Upton asked.

"You can't force belief on someone else," he answered. "You can only give them the opportunity. If they just play at this to keep us happy, like they have in the past, they'll have to live with the consequences when the roof caves in. We're giving them a chance for that not to happen."

"I think we have quite a good chance to succeed if we stay united," she said.

"I think we'll succeed at first, but then they'll piss it away if they see a way to make money off of it," said Brandt.

"We'll all find out together," said the colonel.

"I still have substantial work remaining to keep your Embassy from undermining the momentum we've built with their chronic gloom and doom predictions. What's your next priority?" asked Upton.

"I need to find some only marginally-corrupt cops," said Trevanathan.

Chapter 18

Major Crimes Task Force Compound, Kabul, January 2016

Brigadier General Yasif Baz was the newly-appointed commander of the Major Crimes Task Force (MCTF), a sub-unit of the Ministry of Interior, created and designed to function like the American FBI. The MCTF had a broad mission to investigate major felonies across the nation, including government corruption. For Baz, the appointment was a blessing and a curse. While he had been promoted from colonel to general with the appointment, his increase in power was only on paper. In reality, the MCTF had been relegated to a bureaucratic purgatory for several years, stripped of funding and responsibility by former President Hamid Karzai as punishment for too closely investigating the business dealings of the former President's allies.

General Baz was a rarity in the Afghan administration. He had been educated at UCLA when his father was a trade attaché to the U.S. in the late nineties and was familiar with American culture. Mere weeks earlier, he had been a peripheral player in charge of a border customs unit in remote Nuristan Province. But then his predecessor at the MCTF had been caught on film, meeting with several high-profile defendants at a well-known Kabul café immediately before their charges were summarily dropped. Such conduct was not unusual in Afghanistan but being foolish enough to do so while being filmed by an *Al Jazeera* news crew had forced the President to fire the former MCTF commander, creating a fortuitous opening for Baz.

It had taken two weeks for Trevanathan to meet Baz, due to the unusual circumstance that the Major Crimes Task Force was difficult to find. When it had been stripped of its funding, the Task Force had also been exiled to a pair of large underground bunkers in a remote neighborhood of Kabul, well away from other government agencies and buildings. It was also removed from the official government directories. It was as if the unit had been wiped from the face of the earth. Through the assistance of Upton and her connections in the President's office, Trevanathan had discovered the exiled MCTF's location and arranged a meeting.

Trevanathan's convoy approached the MCTF compound on the fringes of the city through an unmarked gravel driveway between concrete blast walls. It had taken some maneuvering on Trevanathan's part to get this mission to an unfamiliar neighborhood approved. Unlike other government compounds in Kabul, this one lacked any uniformed security, since no one cared what happened to the MCTF. Its anonymity was marred only by the middle-aged men in outdated, wide-lapel suits, who stood chain-smoking along the gravel entryway, assault rifles slung nonchalantly across their backs.

"This looks like a 70's detective show, sir," commented Sergeant Ford, from his customary front passenger seat.

"Definitely different," agreed the colonel. "Almost like prom pictures from my high school – lots of ill-fitting suits."

At the entrance to the concrete bunker, the MCTF's executive officer, a younger man with an unfortunate mustache, waited to escort Trevanathan's party.

"Nice Adolph-stache, sir. You'd look good with one of those," joked Ford, as their vehicle stopped.

"Behave," the colonel chuckled, as he waited for his detail to open the door. The young Afghan officer hurried over to meet him. "Good morning, colonel; the general is very anxious to meet you," he said, a broad smile dispelling his prior disturbing resemblance. "You are his first American visitor since he returned to Kabul."

"It's my honor. I've heard great things about the MCTF," offered Trevanathan.

"You are very kind. Let me show you to the office. We are located in these two main bunkers," the executive officer explained as they walked. "The investigators are in the right-hand bunker, which has three floors – two below ground– and the general and his staff are in the left."

"How many investigators do you have, currently?"

"We are authorized to have one hundred sixty. Currently, we have ninety-two. It is hard to keep people with our current…situation."

"I understand," said the colonel. Maybe we'll have a chance to work together and change that *situation*."

"It would be good to do meaningful work again," the executive officer said, his face flushing. "The general's office is this way," he gestured, pointing up a narrow staircase. Ford started to lead up the stairs, until the colonel laid a hand on his arm. "I'll be OK," the colonel said, giving Ford a knowing look that meant Ford was not coming. *I can't have the first impression Baz has of me being my security guys protecting me from him. Not if we're going to have trust,* thought Trevanathan.

"I'll be right here, sir," Ford replied unhappily, remaining at the base of the stairwell. He didn't like losing sight of his "packages" on unfamiliar turf.

The general's office was at the top of the stairs at the end of a short hallway. The executive officer led the way and knocked on the door, and then opened it for the colonel to enter, first. He then excused himself, leaving Trevanathan alone with the general. *This is different,* noted Trevanathan. *No tea boy, no assistant, no translator. Baz apparently likes to keep his meetings tight.*

Behind a wooden desk sat a round-faced man with brown, intelligent eyes. His short, dark hair was lightly flecked with gray, suggesting he was maybe in his mid-forties. He rose as Trevanathan entered, and the two men exchanged the usual greetings and best wishes for each other's families. Trevanathan knew that business was rarely discussed in initial meetings, but he was also running out of time. *No time to tip-toe around*, he thought, as he prepared to violate custom.

Trevanathan accepted the offer of a chair. Before he could begin, the executive officer again opened the door, admitting another detective, who brought in a plastic tray with two glasses of tea and the obligatory cellophane wrapped cookies. Trevanathan could not help but stare, as the man was wearing a powder blue leisure suit. "Tasakor,[57]" said Trevanathan, touching his chest with his right hand

---

[57] "Thank you" in Dari.

in a gesture of respect. The lounge singer smiled as both men withdrew.

Trevanathan obligingly sipped his tea then went to the point of his visit. "Sir, I come seeking your help. Have you heard of the Anti-Corruption Justice Center—the ACJC project?"

"I have," replied Baz, giving nothing more.

"Sir, I'm only a colonel, but the advantage of that rank is it puts me below the level of the politics that generals have to deal with. It gives me some ability to fly below the noise."

"I know what you mean, having only recently reached my current rank."

"The NATO donors' conference is coming up in July, and my chain of command is concerned that many of our allies may withdraw their funding. They're exhausted by the corruption, watching the money they give to the Afghan people go into private pockets. The U.S. will stick it out—for now. They have little choice because of the 9/11 attacks, but the Europeans are likely taking their money and going home—unless there's rapid improvement on countering corruption."

"And nothing moves quickly in Afghanistan, as I'm sure you've found," Baz commented.

"Yes. Things move slowly and Western money keeps pouring in. That has been the formula for fifteen years. I'm afraid your government's leaders believe that will always be the case, but it is about to end. In July, funding may dry up overnight for the Afghan military. In October, a second conference will address non-military aid, and we fear the same result."

"Why have I not heard of any such ultimatums?"

"Because there aren't going to be any ultimatums. We're past that. That's what makes the situation so dangerous. In the past, when the NATO countries were serious about a problem, they blustered and beat their chests and issued ultimatums. That let the Afghan government know they should pay attention amidst all the usual noise."

Baz smiled at the description, which he found apt.

Trevanathan continued. "I've learned that the one thing more dangerous than anger in relationships is apathy. This time there will not be ultimatums or last warnings. For years the U.S. and NATO countries have shaken their collective fingers at the need for corruption reform and watched the Attorney General's office and the courts respond with window dressing. A few low-level sacrificial lambs are prosecuted at best, with the expectation that will distract the Westerners."

"How long have you been in Afghanistan, colonel?"

"Just two months, sir."

"You have learned much in that time."

"I've had good teachers. Sir, my greatest strength and weakness is I tend to be direct. I hope you do not take that as discourtesy. I am simply trying to lay out the problem facing my country and yours, because time is running out."

"I was educated in America, colonel, so I am used to people being direct on matters of importance."

"Thank you for understanding. Here is my challenge. The U.S. Embassy is barely engaged. The fatigue of our European allies is more dangerous than their ultimatums. The only notice your government will get of their decision will be the sound of planes leaving for Europe carrying your former ally's soldiers and their money."

"Hmmm," Baz's eyes narrowed. "And why are you telling this to me?"

"Sir, I'm here because I need cops—police—for the ACJC. I can't rely on the usual MOI police; they are too infected with corruption. I need men who are willing to take risks and stand up to some powerful people who don't want change. Your men have done that before. Maybe some of them have had to take bribes to survive, especially after Karzai sidelined them. I don't care about that. I'm a realist. What I do care about is finding a partner who is willing to try a new path. To put saving the country above personal enrichment."

"And when charges are brought in your new court and the Attorney General still dismisses them?"

"I'm still working that piece, sir. We're going over the AG's head to the President. He has to commit that the ACJC will operate independently, without the Attorney General interfering in cases, or we're not going forward. If we don't go forward with the ACJC, he will lose billions in European aid money starting in July."

Baz looked thoughtful, and then laughed. "Ahh, so there *is* a threat involved."

"A consequence," Trevanathan smiled. "I think your President will agree to an independent court, whether or not he personally likes it, to protect his government's lifeline."

"Colonel, I have not been in this position for long. But, if one listens and watches, one can learn much in a short time. The morale of my men is low. They feel irrelevant. They have no pride. If they try to make an arrest—a real arrest—the perpetrator calls a friend in parliament or the Attorney General's office and the charges are dropped. My men have been humiliated—forced to apologize to criminals they arrested for stealing millions, *millions in your dollars,* from the Afghan people.

"The last commander of this unit would allow perpetrators to come directly to his office—*this office* in which you are sitting." Baz's voice raised with anger. "My detectives would see the suspect enter with a briefcase and leave without it. The charges would then immediately be dropped, with the commander claiming the Attorney General's office decided there was insufficient evidence. It only takes so many times of seeing that before my men think, 'Why bother? My work is making the commander rich and putting my family in danger.'"

General Baz paused before continuing, regaining his composure. "My men have become bad police and they know it," he said in a quiet voice. "They are not proud of it. They do not make enough to survive—to feed and house their families—so they take bribes. Traffic tickets, business license violations–all are made up to get money to survive. Those offenses are not even in our jurisdiction, but the people don't know, and a badge is a license to steal in Afghanistan.

"I see the shame in their eyes. I believe they can still be good officers. We do have several bad ones that need to be weeded out. I will take care of that soon. But the majority would take pride in a mission like you describe. *If* it is sustainable. How do you plan to police the police, though? The roots of corruption run deep."

"Polygraphs, sir," answered Trevanathan. "Anyone working on this project will have to agree to be polygraphed twice a year. If they fail, they're out. No excuses. Again, no one is going to ask them about past conduct—past *gratuities*. It will be from this time forward. A clean slate."

"The goals are noble. But my men have to survive, too, and our budget has been slashed. Noble intentions will not feed their children."

"There are a lot of moving pieces to this idea, sir. If you agree to come on board, the British Embassy is preparing to ask its government to fund greatly increased salaries for everyone working at the ACJC-police, prosecutors, and judges, due to the increased risks involved. I can't say what those salaries will be today because that's up to the UK government. I don't want to promise if I can't actually deliver. Once we get going and show some positive results, we may be able to get the FBI back to provide training and maybe equipment."

Baz raised his eyebrows. "That sounds expensive."

"It is much cheaper than the two to three billion dollars a year that is getting stolen right now, and a great deal cheaper than countering a fundamentalist Islamic government under the Taliban for the next fifty years, if Ghani's government collapses."

"You put matters in very clear terms, colonel."

"I know you went to UCLA, sir, so this phrase may mean something. This entire project is a 'Hail Mary'—like in American football. We are losing right now. There're two possible outcomes. We may accomplish something miraculous—a long shot that hasn't worked before. If it fails, the consequences to Afghanistan will be disastrous. Half-measures or modest success will be the same as failure. I believe if this doesn't succeed, Afghanistan's soldiers will lose their remaining hope, and that opens the door for the Taliban."

"You do not speak like a regular Army officer, colonel. I hope that isn't offensive."

Trevanathan laughed. "I've heard that before. I'm not a career officer, sir. Most of the time I am a judge in a civilian criminal court. My government sent me here because I've had some experience setting up court systems elsewhere."

"Such as?"

"I've done work in Iraq, Bosnia, and the Congo."

Baz nodded thoughtfully. "Those sound challenging. Were you successful?"

"Sometimes yes, sometimes no. It always depends on the willingness of the people to grab the lifesaving rope you're throwing to them. I'm not coming here with a magic solution. I'm coming with an opportunity. Success or failure will not come from my plan. It will come from people like you who decide they want to fight for something better for their families."

"Colonel, the idea is intriguing. It could work with the right support."

"Your example will be the most important matter in that regard."

"Go on."

"Sir, if your hands are clean, it will send a message to your men that there's a new way of doing business. If they sense that you are the same as others in authority, then we can expect little from them."

"You Americans are always to the point," Baz laughed. "Good thing that I lived in your country for so many years, or my honor might be offended."

"There is no slight intended, sir. We have an unhealthy culture here because America and her allies poured a flood of money into this country, without requiring accountability. *Too much money* is now destabilizing your country's very existence. That can only be remedied by men of vision changing how they conduct the people's business."

"You want me to be a revolutionary? That is not a healthy occupation in this part of the world."

"A reformer. A leader who places duty above personal interest." Trevanathan was beginning to take a liking to Baz. He did not try to bury the colonel with flowery language or double-speak. His candor was refreshing in a country where no one said what they were truly thinking.

"It still sounds like the recipe for an inspiring but short life. Colonel, may I ask how you reached your current rank?"

"Umm, like everyone else, sir. It's basically a competition based on one's career performance. You go to certain military schools, take the right jobs, and get good performance reviews. Then there's a certain amount of luck involved as to whether there's enough colonel positions open when you come up for promotion."

"Do you know how an Afghan general becomes a general?"

"No idea, sir."

Baz paused to sip his tea. "We buy it."

"I'm sorry?"

"Of course, you must be in good standing with the President and the Minister of Defense, but there is a fee schedule–known to all senior officers. A brigadier general pays one million U.S. dollars for the privilege of making a salary of roughly thirteen hundred U.S. dollars per year." Baz made a tight-lipped smile. "A two-star general must pay two million, and so on."

"Paid to who, sir?"

"The right people. They then see that the other right people agree to the promotion," Baz explained.

"That's remarkable. I didn't know." *Why is he telling me this*?

"I'm sure. It is something we do not talk about openly to our Western friends. But you and I need to be honest with each other from the start if there is to be trust. The money is considered an investment, as paying one million dollars opens a world where you can make many times that amount by virtue of one's position. I tell you this as a sign of good faith on my part. And so you understand what my price is for becoming this *reformer* of which you speak. You are asking me to dedicate my investment, for what? A sense of accomplishment? Patriotism?"

"Sir, I can't pay you anything near that."

"There are many types of payment. I did not get to my current position simply by paying money, although that is a requirement. The road to becoming a colonel in the MOI is treacherous. Your competition is always seeking to embarrass and derail you. So, I am very adept at assessing risk."

"I'm sure."

"So, if I choose to lead my men into investigating some of the most powerful men in this country, I will be placing my life in imminent danger. I recognize this, and it is of little consequence. But I will also be putting the lives of my family at risk, and that is of consequence."

"I understand that's a possibility, sir."

"That's a *certainty*, colonel," declared Baz, his eyes flashing. "My family must be given asylum out of the country. Before this unit was neutered, our investigations probed too closely to powerful supporters of the former President."

"I heard. It led to funding for MCTF being pulled."

"That is only part of it. The lead investigator's young son was kidnapped and tortured as a...disincentive to continue his activities. He had to listen to his child plead on the phone. But rather than give in to such coercion, he pursued all the honorable options—sought to have the NDS[58] and our special forces rescue the child. But his every action was telegraphed to the kidnappers—who had their own sources within those same agencies. The boy was recovered, dead, blinded, and mutilated from a sewage ditch on the outskirts of the city. That man was, as you would say, *a reformer—a patriot*. A most effective message, would you not agree?"

Trevanathan had no response.

"It wasn't always this way. When I was a boy, we were led by men of courage. Those who united us against the Soviet invaders. We didn't consume ourselves from within. Such violence cannot define us as a people or a nation unless we allow it. Unless we will be a nation of sheep," added Baz, his jaw working back and forth. "I do

---

[58]National Directorate of Security. In addition to gathering intelligence, the Afghan equivalent of the CIA also conducted anti-terrorism operations.

not intend to live as a sheep. For this reason, I will help you retore Afghanistan's honor, but I refuse to let my family be victim to my own *heroics* as payment. My price to support your court is for you to get my family out of Afghanistan."

"That may be a tall order, sir. The U.S. Embassy controls such things, and they aren't exactly supportive of this project or me."

"That is your issue, colonel. You know my requirements. Besides, I am not actually interested in going to the U.S. I have family in Britain and Germany and would prefer either of those locations. I find America a bit disorienting."

"But you will stay?"

"Yes, of course. I cannot leave without the President's blessing. If my family is safe, then I will be able to commit to your project and rally my men."

"What about their families?"

"They will need protection too."

"I don't think there's a chance of getting all of those families out, sir. It sets a precedent that's unsustainable. You have like a hundred or so detectives? If everyone who fights corruption gets their families evacuated, it undermines long term stability. It'll become a flood of people playing at fighting corruption just to get visas and that gets the whole idea shot down."

"Not everyone must leave. We can develop safety protocols in the country for my detectives. Security systems, bars on windows, cameras for their homes. Maybe relocation to secure neighborhoods. But my family must go. I insist."

"I understand."

"Thank you. The final matter is your own situation."

"Yes, sir?"

"You are challenging the power arrangements and income of very powerful people, both inside and outside the government. When they become unhappy, reformers become martyrs. Do not forget that."

"I'm getting that warning way too often, sir, but thank you. I'm doing my best."

Chapter 19

Lashkar Gah, Helmand Province, February 2016

Daniyal's life had changed over six months. He had entered the hospital a shattered man, physically and emotionally broken, without hope he would see his family again. He had been powerless in a world where the weak were consumed by those using the war as a springboard for personal gain.

The chance meeting with the sergeant major had improved his situation. Now, he was on the inside. Protected. *Valued*. Still controlled, he understood, but now he went to bed in his basement room in the headquarters with a full belly and did not fear the arbitrary violence of his barracks mates, nor death from his own artillery. So long as he was compliant, and closed his ears at appropriate times, he was secure.

Life was better in many other ways. He wore a clean uniform each day—a requirement for working in the headquarters. He now had three of them, of good quality, instead of just the one ragged-issue uniform he had worn everywhere. He ate fresh fruit and meat every day, delivered to his desk from the headquarters mess hall. Things had improved so much that he felt guilty when he saw groups of hollow-cheeked privates being harangued across the base by their sergeants. *That was me,* he shuddered. Those same sergeants would give him a nod of respect now, in recognition of his position, instead of focusing their abuse upon him. It made Daniyal feel relieved and ashamed.

Daniyal's relationship with the sergeant major was still precarious: Mahmood was not a trusting man. He had not reached his position by embracing the goodness of human nature. He regularly tested Daniyal's loyalty. Money left on a desk; an intentional mistake in counting cash to see if his new corporal would take advantage of the oversight to fill his own pockets. He left a gold ring on the window ledge in his office, where Daniyal would undoubtedly spot it. As Daniyal ignored each temptation, the sergeant major merely grunted or growled as usual, but assigned Daniyal duties of increasing sensitivity.

On the first Friday in February, the sergeant major called Daniyal to his office. While normally a day off, the sergeant major was not prone to recognize such trivialities when sensitive work was required. Often it was better to have fewer ears around. "Sit," he ordered.

Daniyal obeyed, sitting erect across from the sergeant major's desk. He never deluded himself that he was welcome to relax in the sergeant major's presence.

"General Rahman has lost faith in Mr. Rajish as manager of his special accounts. Do you know the accounts of which I speak?"

Was this a trap? To answer yes was to acknowledge that he knew their commander was keeping two sets of books for the corps funds. To deny that knowledge was to lie to the sergeant major, whose infallible ability to detect deception Daniyal witnessed daily.

"Yes, Sergeant Major," replied Daniyal, hopefully taking the safest path.

"He is aware that you have a background in accounting, and I have vouched for you as a possible replacement."

"I have not finished my degree..."

"Do I look like I care if you have a degree?" the sergeant major challenged, his brows knitting together over his impressive nose. "You can add, can't you?"

"Yes, Sergeant Major."

"Can you perhaps subtract as well?"

"Yes, Sergeant Major." Daniyal knew he was being baited but kept his usual expressionless face.

"Wonderful, then my confidence has not been misplaced. Pick that up," he ordered, pointing to a red leather notebook on the corner of his desk.

Daniyal did as he was told. The ledger, several hundred pages thick, was heavy. He waited.

An Absence of Faith

"Open it," said the sergeant major. "This is the record of special accounts by which both the commander and I track the...disposition of corps assets. Can you understand it?"

Daniyal sampled the pages quickly, knowing the sergeant major was not a patient man. "I believe so, Sergeant Major. There are certain short-hand notes and abbreviations used here, with which I am not familiar, but the methodology is a basic accounting approach with which I am familiar."

"Good, good," the sergeant major exclaimed, coming as near to smiling as Daniyal had ever seen. "The scope of our operations is necessarily very complex, and I, and the General, do not expect you to master everything immediately. But you are to spend the next several weeks learning this document."

"Yes, Sergeant Major."

"Mr. Rajish will continue to be the corps accountant during that time, but the day is rapidly approaching where his services will be no longer needed." A hardness came to the sergeant major's eyes as he spoke. "When he is...replaced, you need to be ready to step in. Do you understand, Sergeant?"

"I do, Sergeant Major." *Wait, wha...?*

"Good, now this is the last time I will warn you about being out of uniform. Get it fixed, immediately." The sergeant major lightly tossed a set of epaulets onto the desk before Daniyal: they were marked with the four stripes of a sergeant[59]. "We can't have a mere corporal working on such important duties," he clarified.

"Thank you, Sergeant Major," Daniyal mouthed, stunned at his new authority. It would normally take years to reach the rank of sergeant in the Afghan army.

"Hmph," grunted, the senior NCO. "These ledgers–they never leave my office or the General's office unless you are actively working on them. If you need more ledgers, there are more in the supply cabinet outside the General's door. In an operation this large they fill quickly. Nothing is to be copied, photographed, or put into a

---

[59] Afghan enlisted ranks insignia are illustrated in the Appendix.

computer. Keep just one ledger at a time. This avoids *complications.* Is that clear?"

"Yes, Sergeant Major."

"At night the ledger is to be locked in my safe," the sergeant major gestured at the floor safe in the corner behind his desk. "I will put it there myself. Only if I am away on a mission will you do so. Is this understood?"

"Yes, Sergeant Major." *I will be given access to his safe? Incredible.*

"You will eventually be trained on the computer system that is used to talk to the Americans about our supply situation. But not yet. That is for their world and is unimportant, except to account for the large combat losses in equipment we regularly suffer. The *special losses* then appear in the red ledger as capital inflows.

"Yes, Sergeant Major." Daniyal was amazed at the numbers he saw in the ledger. If these were correct, it was as if there was a corps within the corps. Dozens of trucks, HMMWVs, fuel and water tankers—even artillery pieces—were listed among the private assets of Major General Rahman. Hundreds of rifles, hundreds of thousands of rounds of ammunition; the list went on. The cash accounts were staggering. *Surely there must be a misplaced comma?* Hundreds of millions of Afghanis[60] came and went through phantom accounts and business fronts.

"General Rahman is not a patient man, but he does recognize loyalty. If you do a good job, both you and your family will be rewarded. Your brother and sisters will have the chance to attend the best schools in Kabul. If there are problems...he will feed your remains to the dogs behind the military police station."

"I understand, Sergeant Major. I will not disappoint." Their stealing is not my problem, thought Daniyal. My goal is to get out of here alive. If I have to move some numbers around on a page to get back to my family, it is a small price to pay.

---

[60] The unit of currency of the GIRoA was the "Afghan Afghani," with the international code, "AFN." Within the society, it was more common to use "Af" for singular, and "Afs" for multiples. One U.S. Dollar was worth roughly 65 Afghanis (Afs) during 2015–2016.

"Good. Now, your first duty as sergeant is to represent me at the shuttle to Kabul leaving this afternoon."

Daniyal remained silent, tilting his head in inquiry.

"The special shuttle that departs each week for Kabul?" repeated the sergeant major, raising an eyebrow.

Daniyal stared blank-faced.

"How did you ever survive before I rescued you, *sergeant?*" the sergeant major mocked. "Each Friday, a shuttle departs from the mosque gate at 1300 for those who have gathered sufficient resources to fund their *leave*, back to visit family."

"I am sorry, Sergeant Major, this is the first time I have heard of this program. I was told there wasn't leave for the enlisted because they will not come back."

"It is not for everyone," the sergeant major continued patiently. "They have to be able to prove their ability to fund their trip home and back again. They do this by providing an envelope of their funds to me or my representative—you, today—for accounting purposes. It is received, *accounted for,* and then they are permitted to depart."

"And what funds do they show, Sergeant Major?"

"350,000 Afghanis for the enlisted men. More for higher ranks, but today it is all enlisted. They will be escorted by one of their sergeants, who will receive 50,000 Afs each prior to departure. You will collect 300,000 Afs per man from their sergeant—not one Af less. That returns here, goes into the safe, and is recorded in the ledger."

A deserter's shuttle. Operated by the same corps leadership they are deserting from, realized Daniyal. *There is no limit to the rot.*

"I understand, Sergeant Major. It is all clear. Thank you for your patience." Daniyal could feel his ear tips burning and hoped that his internal disgust did not reach his face. Even amidst the widespread embezzlement and sale of materiel to the enemy the idea that the corps commander profited by helping his own soldiers desert was shocking. *If Azir had had enough money, he could be home with his family now,* Daniyal realized. *But because he was just another poor fool, he is rotting in the cemetery at the end of the runway.* He did not know if it was rage or despair that was sending spasms through his guts.

"Good," replied the sergeant major. "Now get out."

Daniyal stood and turned to depart.

"Sergeant," snapped the sergeant major, "Do you not want your promotion?"

Daniyal turned back. A sneer creased the sergeant major's face, as he gestured at the limp rank epaulets on his desk. A fantasy flitted through Daniyal's mind of lunging across the desk to slap that sneer away, but his survival instincts overcame the unwise urge. "Of course, Sergeant Major," he replied, forcing enthusiasm into his voice. "Thank you again." He picked up his new badges of authority with a feeling of disgust. *I am a prince in hell.*

◊ ◊ ◊

It was called "the mosque gate" because the rusty metal barrier sat next to an old administrative building that had been used as a mosque by other soldiers, years earlier. Now, the building was empty. Nothing of its bland exterior suggested anything of a traditional mosque—no onion domes or minarets. Today, it was just another, unremarkable, two-story building with cracked, dirty windows and crooked blinds.

Daniyal wasn't aware that this part of the camp's external wall was even manned by a regular guard force, and perhaps that was the point. The mosque gate wasn't a regular exit from the camp, usually being chained and bolted shut. Normal base traffic entered and exited through the main gate, two kilometers away. That meant fewer eyes and questions about the day's *leave shuttle.*

When he arrived at the gate a half hour early, Daniyal was surprised to see there was already a battered bus idling next to the old building. Shipping containers that normally sat in front of the gate had been hauled aside. In the meager shade of the gate, a pair of disinterested guards were vainly trying to shield themselves from the intense afternoon sun. Next to the bus, five soldiers stood in a circle, examining their feet and trying to crawl inside their own shirt collars. Their noncommissioned officers (NCOs) stood nearby, loudly joking, a sign of their own nervousness.

Daniyal felt conspicuous in his new sergeant's epaulets. A *fraud*, he thought. But in his short time in the headquarters, he had learned an important lesson about the Afghan army: it ran on fear. Those who exhibited fear were prey; those who inflicted terror were left alone. So, despite his doubt, he pushed confidence into his stride and crossed the road toward the waiting men.

A staff sergeant from the corps artillery turned and eyed Daniyal narrowly. "Where is the Sergeant Major?" he snapped. Rather than answer the question, Daniyal shot back, "Who are you?" Being the sergeant major's orderly had taught him that he who asks the questions is in charge, and he who answers them is subordinate. He gestured with the folder given to him by the sergeant major containing today's roster.

"I am Staff Sergeant Kaaliya," the man declared imperiously. He was a heavy man with a badly pocked complexion.

"Kaaliya… I don't remember you on the list," declared Daniyal. "Who is your soldier?"

"Ali, Private," Kaaliya replied, suddenly slightly less sure of himself.

Daniyal casually opened the folder he had been given and spent two seconds looking at it. "No record of it," he announced firmly, slapping the cover shut, though he knew both names were prominently displayed on the list given him by the sergeant major. "You wait until the end, and I will see what can be done for you."

Sergeant Kaaliya momentarily met Daniyal's stare, and then dropped his eyes. "Thank you, Sergeant," he replied, now understanding that his share of the day's take depended upon the good nature of this young sergeant. His pocket stood to receive more than two months' pay in bribe money, and Kaaliya knew how things worked.

The other sergeants greeted Daniyal with the warmth of a long-lost brother. Two, attached to subordinate headquarters units, knew him as a corporal and congratulated him on his *long-overdue* promotion. This made Daniyal smile inwardly, as he had reached this rank in record time. Nods of mock appreciation and sincerity greeted his every pronouncement now that it was clear who was in charge. He led the NCOs into the vacant building to conduct business out of the sun—and out of sight—beginning by telling them to produce their thick envelopes and count their contents, *twice*. "A wise precaution," they complimented him on his thoroughness.

Following the sergeant major's instructions, Daniyal ordered, "I will have you bring your men in, one by one. They may be going *on leave*, but that does not mean they take any corps property with them. No weapons, no contraband. They will enter, be searched, and wait to get on the bus. Any problems, and they will be returned to their units. Clear?"

"Yes, Sergeant!" the NCOs responded in unison, anxious to get the job done and secure their *bonuses*.

A sergeant named Barukh was first on the list. Barukh had a heavy Mongol appearance, as did many in the country that had been conquered by Ghengis Khan and his horde in the 1200s. He entered the room with his man, who looked like a beaten dog even by Afghan army standards. The private stared at the floor, shifting his weight uneasily back and forth, with occasional nervous side glances. His uniform was rent in multiple places, barely preserving his modesty. He flinched when Daniyal raised the folder to check his name. "Abdu Khwarei, Private?" inquired Daniyal.

The man nodded vigorously, not raising his eyes, wringing his hat tightly between two balled fists.

Slap! Sergeant Barukh smashed his beefy hand across the back of the private's skull, driving the man to his knees. "You will answer the sergeant when your name is called, donkey!"

"Abdu," the man wailed. Tears ran down his face in a stream of despair. "I am A-Abdu," he continued, his voice rising. The sergeant's foot lashed out, catching the soldier in the ribs, pitching him sideways onto the dirty concrete floor. "Silence, you idiot! Quit babbling."

Abdu curled into a fetal position, whimpering to himself. "Abdu...."

"That's fine, sergeant," Daniyal, said, trying to keep his voice from shaking. "I have what I need." The sergeant nodded to Daniyal, as if the two of them understood that the private had been properly disciplined.

Daniyal knew that he should not involve himself, but he stepped past the still babbling private to speak to Barukh in a low voice. "What is wrong with him?"

"He is *mayub*[61]...broken brain. His brother enlisted him to get rid of him, and he ended up here. He is a constant problem for me–can't follow the simplest directions. It would be quicker to let him wander into a minefield, but apparently his father is a prominent physician in Kabul and wants him back."

"So that is where the money for his *leave* came from?"

"I do not ask such questions. The captain was summoned to the headquarters and then told me what I told you. Here we are. I am not even sure he will make it to Kabul. It is a two-day trip and the others on the bus may take care of what the minefield hasn't. It's happened before."

Daniyal nodded and stepped back past the now still form of Private Abdu. He leaned over, "Private, go sit in the corner," he directed. Abdu looked up with vacant eyes, his face a smear of tears, dirt, and snot. "Abdu, go sit in the corner," Daniyal repeated. This time, Daniyal pointed to the far-left corner of the room behind him.

The private croaked out something unintelligible and staggered to his feet. He looked quickly over his shoulder for more blows but seeing none coming stumbled to the corner and sat down, burying his head in his crossed arms.

Daniyal looked at his papers, appearing to be searching for information, but in fact buying time to compose himself. *The only person without a hateful soul on this base is that private. I have sold myself for a safe place to hide,* Daniyal realized. *The cruelty, the greed...the longer I stay...someday soon I will be one of them and won't even realize it.* Daniyal looked at the clipboard and folder in his hands–the sergeant epaulets on his shoulder. An icy fist grabbed his heart. *Soon? It has already happened.*

---

[61] Urdu for faulty or unsound.

"Do you want the next man, sergeant?" asked the next NCO in line, the motor pool sergeant, who had taught him to drive the cargo truck.

Daniyal was too heartsick to lash the man for trying to hurry him. "Yes, send him in."

The next three deserters were brought in one at a time, checked against the list, searched, and then told to stand near Abdu. When the first NCO offered to search the *mayub* private, Daniyal declined, indicating he would do it before the young man boarded the bus. *He's been beaten enough.*

As the fourth man took his place along the wall, Staff Sergeant Kaaliya stood nervously in the doorway, hoping to not be forgotten. He feared irritating the powerful young sergeant, now recognized to be Sergeant Major Mahmood's right-hand man.

"*You*, I will see your man now," Daniyal ordered, pointing to the staff sergeant as if he was addressing a recruit.

"Thank you, Sergeant, I will get him," Sergeant Kaaliya smiled and practically bowed back out the door. *I need a shower when I am done with this filth*, Daniyal told himself.

Kaaliya quickly returned. "Here he is, Sergeant. Thank you for your consideration," he groveled. He jerked the man behind him violently by the arm. There was something familiar about the man, Daniyal thought, but his face was averted.

"Ali bin Ali, Private?" asked Daniyal, looking up from his folder.

"Yes, Sergeant," the man mumbled, staring intently at a crack in the floor.

"Let me see your face."

"Let the sergeant see your face, dog," repeated Kaaliya, seizing the man's head and twisting it toward Daniyal.

Ali.

His Ali. The man who had left him for dead.

"You…you aren't in the artillery," Daniyal stammered, his brain trying to process what he was seeing.

Ali did not speak. He kept his eyes downward. The staff sergeant, unsure of what was happening, tried to be helpful. "Sergeant, this man was sent to my unit on rehabilitative assignment five months ago. Too much fighting, even drinking. We thought he had potential, but he has been a continuous disappointment."

"I know this man," said Daniyal coldly.

"Then I'm sure you will agree that letting him go on leave will be of no detriment to the corps."

"As I said, his name is not on the list." Daniyal looked at Ali, feeling hatred. *There's no way I'm letting this animal escape while I stay. While Azir remains here forever. How did Ali obtain 350,000 Afs? Stealing and beating it out of the weaker members of his unit, no doubt.*

"I had an understanding with the sergeant major…" pleaded the staff sergeant.

"I *am* the Sergeant Major. Do you not understand that yet?" Daniyal raised his voice. "Shall I return to the headquarters and inform him that you were a disruption today?"

"No…no, of course not. I meant no disrespect."

A choking sound interrupted their exchange. Daniyal glanced back, irritated by the interruption. Large, muddy tears were streaming down Ali's face. His chest heaved, as he tried to stifle his sobs. *What is this? This was not the Ali I knew.* Ali's efforts to control his emotions failed, a dam giving way to irresistible pressure. He dropped to his knees, wracking with sobs. "I need…I h-h-have to…go…," he begged between convulsions. "Allah, please."

Daniyal watched in horror. *I hated Ali, but at least I knew who he was. Who is this creature?*

Kaaliya pulled his arm back to strike Ali's head. "No, wait," Daniyal ordered, holding up his hand. As if in a game, Kaaliya froze in place, his arm cocked to deliver the blow.

"Everyone out. Except Private Ali. I will interview him alone," Daniyal directed.

"As you wish, Sergeant," nodded Kaaliya, certain that Ali was about to receive his comeuppance in a particularly brutal way, where no witnesses were desired.

"Give me your envelope, Sergeant Kaaliya," Daniyal ordered. "Private Abdu can stay as well."

"Of course. Of course," the excited staff sergeant, although confused, saw that there was still a chance he might profit from the day's strange events.

Everyone exited the room, leaving Daniyal and Ali alone with Abdu, who was oblivious in the far corner.

Daniyal had no fear of Ali. All the power had shifted in their relationship.

"What is wrong with you, Ali?"

Ali shook his head, kneeling over tear splatters in the dust.

"I am not going to ask you again, Private. Get on your feet and answer my question," Daniyal commanded, seeking to reach the soldier inside Ali.

Ali looked up, confused. "Daniyal?" he mouthed, as if recognition had just come to him.

"Sergeant," Daniyal replied firmly.

Ali reached up and grabbed Daniyal's sleeve, as he struggled to his feet. "Daniyal, I need to go home. I need to leave this place."

Daniyal momentarily ignored the use of his first name. "We all need to leave this place, Ali."

"No…no. They have done terrible things to me. I was sent away from our unit for fighting."

"Yes, I'm familiar with that, if you recall."

"I was afraid, Daniyal. I was afraid that if I didn't show I was the toughest man in the unit, everyone would see how scared I was."

"So, you put me in the hospital, where I almost died?"

"I was a fool. Forgive me. Forgive me, please."

"Now that you want to desert, you want forgiveness?" Daniyal spat the accusation.

"No, no, I *need* your forgiveness, because I know now what it feels like to be used."

Daniyal shook Ali's hands loose from his uniform. "How is that possible? You are the greatest bully on this camp."

Ali gulped for air. "When I went to the corps artillery unit, I was the new man. They had all been together. I was only one man. I tried to assert myself, and they humiliated me. They trapped me in my bunk. They used me, Daniyal. They made me a woman, do you understand?"

Daniyal pulled back, his eyes wide in revulsion. Ali was the most feared person he knew, after the sergeant major. He personified that strength ruled the weak. Now he was a broken, pitiful victim. If he could be destroyed, what hope was there for Daniyal, hiding behind his stripes?

"Ali..." was all he could utter.

"My family sent the money. I am the unit's joke. Their toy. I will not be that staff sergeant's whore every time he gets drunk. Please...please, help me..." Tears were again freely running down Ali's face.

Every fiber of Daniyal's being called for retribution. This was the retribution that Allah, or the universe, had brought down upon Ali's inhumanity. It was fitting that he, Daniyal, was now the judge of this evil. He hated Ali for his brutality, for his weakness, and for trying to play upon their former affiliation.

"Do not ever call me Daniyal again, Private," the new sergeant directed in a clipped tone. "Daniyal died to you back in that barracks room."

Ali shuddered as he lowered his chin to his chest, defeated.

Daniyal regarded the remnants of the man before him in disgust. He shook his head and took a deep breath before speaking. "You have earned no compassion. You have only been a misery," declared Daniyal. "I remember where you live in Kabul. You will escort Private Abdu there and keep him safe until his family comes to pick him up. You will send me proof that this has been accomplished. If you fail to accomplish any of that, I will have you arrested for desertion and returned to your unit for more *discipline*. Do you understand?"

Ali raised uncertain eyes to look at the sergeant.

"Private Abdu cannot take care of himself. He's *diwana*[62]. Brain damaged. But it is important to me he gets home. You said you understand now what it is like to be powerless. Prove it. Get him home.

"Ye-yes, Sergeant," replied Ali, bewildered as to the connection between this hard-faced young sergeant and the slobbering mess sitting in the corner.

Daniyal reached into his pants and pulled out three one-thousand Afghani notes. He reached up and shoved them into Ali's shirt pocket. "Make sure that both of you eat and drink something on the trip. It is long and hot."

Ali could not believe what was happening. The man he had beaten and abused was saving his life and giving him money to ease his travels. *Either he or I am crazy.* "How can I thank you, Da...Sergeant?" Ali choked out in a thick voice.

"Live. And make sure he lives. Nothing else matters."

Ali looked into Daniyal's eyes and realized he was before a different man. There was no fear in this man's eyes. There was steel. They were the eyes of a man who has made a decision. Ali nodded, and then looked away, unable to hold the look of such a man.

Daniyal turned and walked over to Abdu. He feigned searching him but slipped another one thousand Af note into his pocket, in case Ali reverted to his old ways. "Private Ali will be your friend on the trip, Abdu. There he is. Do you understand?"

"Ali. My friend," the man on the floor repeated.

I hope he is, prayed Daniyal.

---

[62] Urdu for crazy. The Afghan vocabulary is not replete with polite names for people suffering from intellectual deficiencies.

Sergeant Daniyal walked across the room and threw open the door to the mosque, announcing, "Everything is in order. Five men ready to go *on leave*. Let's move them out."

"Get moving. Move it you donkeys…" barked the collected sergeants in their usual abusive manner, as the soon-to-be-former-soldiers scrambled aboard their life raft. The two guards forced the rusty metal gate open, its hinges squealing in protest. The bus belched a cloud of black exhaust as the driver shifted into gear and the weekly desertion shuttle lurched out the gate. Daniyal's last view of the bus, as it turned along the road parallel to the wall, was Private Abdu framed in the back window, happily waving.

Chapter 20

Camp Resolute Support, Kabul, February 2016

The pieces were slowly coming together for the Anti-Corruption Justice Center. After some arm twisting by Jodie Upton, the Brits had agreed to bankroll the first two years of operations and to increase the salaries of the Afghan police, prosecutors, and judges who would work there, to remove poverty as an excuse for graft. Despite the fact that the U.S. Embassy itself had no plan to deter the widespread theft of aid funds, its functionaries nevertheless worked behind the scenes to undermine the ACJC project: they were politely ignored by the other embassies as the Ambassador had idled himself into irrelevance.

Trevanathan now had his cops and had just finished a successful meeting with Chief Justice Halim, who was supportive to providing judges to the new court after the colonel promised to get new blast barriers installed around the Supreme Court's own buildings. "Of course, your idea is very ingenious," admired Halim. "I have thought of such an approach myself, several times, and would be able to support it if I were not daily distracted by our vulnerability to attack here," he said, as he gestured toward the busy boulevard that passed close to the Supreme Court offices in which they were sitting. *Everything has a price tag in Kabul,* Trevanathan was beginning to understand. *A drowning man here would demand a bribe before grabbing his own life preserver.*

A meeting with the newly installed Attorney General had yielded less enthusiasm. The prior Attorney General had been removed by President Ghani just weeks before, amidst an internal disagreement. This was no great loss in the colonel's book, as the prior Attorney General had presided over years of inaction on corruption reform. The new AG was being cautious on any new initiatives until he got his feet under him. "I will have to study this proposal in some detail," he offered noncommittally. Reading between the lines, Trevanathan felt that the new AG, Hamidi, would support the project if Ghani supported it, and oppose it if Ghani opposed it. Getting Ghani on board was a job above his pay grade, so Trevanathan was not letting the Attorney General's current ambivalence dissuade him.

For all that, Trevanathan knew one major piece was missing. *Where?* Where could he put a hybrid court so it would be independent and physically safe from attack by the Taliban, ISIS, organized crime, and those in GIRoA who want the embezzlement free-for-all to continue? He had inspected several possible locations in existing facilities but knew that any Afghan government ministry providing space would gain *de facto* veto power on investigations into their own corruption. Prior reform initiatives in Kabul had been suffocated over the past two decades when a minister cut power and water to a reform organization under his roof when its activities began sniffing too close to home. *It's hard to accomplish much when the computers won't turn on and toilets won't flush. This project can't be beholden to the very people it is meant to keep honest*, the colonel knew.

After an unproductive week visiting squalid buildings owned by the Ministries of Interior and Defense, a possible solution appeared in the unlikely form of a U.S. Army Special Forces sergeant who appeared in Trevanathan's doorway unannounced. Typical of his branch's operators in-country, he wore his hair below his ears, a full beard and mustache, and sported a raggedy baseball cap. Rank insignia on his collar and a collapsible-stock automatic rifle across his back were all that revealed his military affiliation.

"Hey, sir, I'm Sergeant First Class Frame. Word on the street is you're looking for a home for your court project. I think I may have a place."

"Sergeant Frame, if you have real estate, I'm all ears," replied the colonel, leaning back in his chair and gesturing Frame to the rusty metal chair across from his desk. Frame exuded a calm, surfer-dude vibe that Trevanathan had learned was typical of Special Forces personnel: low key, affable, and deadly. SF operators were trained to integrate into local areas and operate independently. They could play diplomat or strike enemy targets deep within their own territory.

"Would you like some coffee?" Trevanathan offered. "One of my guys got a care package with some Starbucks in it yesterday."

"Damn sir, you know how to sweet talk a girl. Thanks a lot."

"LT, coffee for the sergeant, please," Trevanathan bellowed out his door. Ripple appeared in moments with a steaming cup. Frame thanked him, then pulled a well-worn map from his blouse pocket and spread it on the colonel's desk.

"There's an empty compound not far from the Counter-Narcotics Center, here," he pointed to a spot on the western fringes of Kabul, where the city tucked up against some large hills. He shifted his finger slightly south. "My ODA[63] is in this next compound. Half of it, anyway. My commander is up north trying to teach the ANA not to run away as soon as a round snaps over their heads." He shrugged and continued. "The empty compound is called 'Camp Heath,' and has been empty since last year. It's big and high-walled, with three major gates. Four guard towers on the corners have nice fields of fire. There's the potential to drop another LZ[64] to the west, but currently there's already an underused LZ about 500 meters to the north." He pointed to a small brown square.

"What's in there?" Trevanathan asked, putting a finger on the green square of Camp Heath.

"Buncha' medium-sized, one-story office-type buildings. There's one two-story building that looks like a cheap hotel back home: lots of external doors that open into one-room hooches. One larger central building that maybe could be your courthouse, but I don't know much about that sort of thing. That's your area, sir," he grinned.

"Sounds promising. Who owns it, Afghan-wise, I mean?"

"It was a training base for the customs police. They signed it over to the Afghan colonel I work with now, who is doing counter-narcotics work."

---

[63] ODA – Operational Detachment Alpha. A twelve-man Special Forces team that is the operational core of the Green Berets structure. Comprised of a commanding officer, a deputy commander, and ten sergeants of varying combat skills and specialties.

[64] Landing Zone – A place for helicopters to land, take on or let off passengers, or take off. Some may include support elements such as fuel, munitions, maintenance, and communications.

"And who does he answer to?" Trevanathan wanted to know who might be turning off his water and lights if the corruption court investigated the wrong—*or the right*—suspect.

"He works for the counter-narcotics center."

"Really? So, your guy answers ultimately to the Chief Justice then?"

"I think that's how it works, sir. I mean they've got some weird-ass chains of command 'round here, but I know he's not under the usual MOD or MOI chains of command. We're left pretty much alone."

"That could have possibilities. I can't have someone who's going to cut the lights as soon as we investigate his cousin."

"Understood, sir. We've had no issues like that on the narco end of things. If you occupy that turf, I see it as a win-win. Sometimes we have trouble getting in logistical support—meds, mail, chew, important stuff like that, so having a big next-door neighbor could help us piggy-back supply drops. And we could be your cavalry if shit goes south, and some bad guys show up. A QRF[65] of sorts."

"Not that that ever happens," said Trevanathan dryly.

"Roger, sir, every day's a love-fest in the Stan."

"How about roads in and out?"

"Not bad by Kabul standards. It's roughly forty minutes from here, depending on traffic, so that's why commuting by rotary wing might be preferable to driving every day. Plus, if you get predictable on your ground routes, you'll get hit, eventually. This entire quadrant is controlled by guard points here and here," Frame pointed on the map. "But those aren't foolproof since they're manned by MOI personnel. Somebody pays enough, they'll get through. But your compound has huge-ass metal gates on the front, so you have another layer of defense where you can set your own access controls."

"Hmmm..." Trevanathan stared at the map, as if doing so would bring the center to life. It's good that it's away from Camp RS and the

---

[65] QRF – Quick Reaction Force.

Afghan Ministries. We don't need a bunch of generals sucking up our time being tourists and getting their photos taken. Trevanathan knew from multiple prior deployments that anytime a general descended on your operation for a "fact finding tour" it consumed two days to prepare for the visit, a day to cater to the general's security and personal needs during the tour, and then another day to send the general a follow-on memo with the show-and-tell slides reminding him what he had just seen with his own eyes. Also don't want to make it too easy for perps or their cronies in Parliament to gain access to spread cash around. But it's close enough that international donors can visit and see its more than window dressing. We could probably get it added to the air taxi routes. UH-60 Blackhawk helicopters were ubiquitous and the main means of movement beyond the Green Zone, where travel by vehicle was vulnerable to ISIS and Taliban car bombs.

"What do you think, sir?" prompted Sergeant Frame.

"I think I need to take a road trip."

◊ ◊ ◊

Six days after his conversation with Sergeant First Class Frame, Colonel Trevanathan dropped a flak jacket over his head, tightening the Velcro side straps for a snug fit. Weeks earlier, the forty pounds of armor had felt like he was carrying a sack of cement up a hill. Now it was a light second shirt. His stitches had healed, and he had dropped eight pounds of weight from around his middle, fat that had accumulated while sitting on a bench in court eight hours a day. "A novel middle-age weight loss program," he joked to Brandt: "Get your ass shipped to a war zone."

For the day's mission he had drawn an urban-friendly M4 rifle from the Camp RS armorer. The M4 was a compact version of the older M16 semi-automatic rifle, useful for tight spaces and city corners. He had two different assessments of Camp Heath: Frame said it was a quiet but remote area on the fringes of Kabul; Trevanathan's security detail described it as "an unsecure neighborhood where NATO had 'no eyes on,'" aside from Frame's team. For his own reconnaissance, Trevanathan resolved to err on the side of caution, carrying the M4 in addition to his usual 9mm pistol. With these weapons, the additional ammunition, first aid kit, water, helmet and flak jacket, and miscellaneous personal items stuffed into his pockets, he had increased his load to half his body weight.

"Ready to go, sir," announced Staff Sergeant Ford, standing in his doorway. Major Brandt stood silently behind him, wearing khaki-colored Marine field gear.

"One more thing," replied Trevanathan, hooking a six-inch Marine Ka-Bar knife onto his pistol belt. Ford's eyes widened. "If you need that, sir, we're in a world of hurt."

"My good luck charm, Sergeant Ford," replied the colonel. "Been carrying it for fourteen years, and I've only been blown up once."

"Helluva' good luck charm, sir," laughed Ford.

"Good to go," declared the colonel, grabbing his helmet. Today, they were departing from the small Camp RS helicopter field, just one hundred meters from the EF3 office. Dozens of helicopter flights arrived and departed daily, rotating troops in and out, while also ferrying various NATO general officers to meetings at Bagram, Hamid Karzai Airport, or other NATO compounds.

As the three of them approached the former soccer field, Trevanathan saw dozens of troops from the 101st Airborne Division lying about the pavement. A SAW[66] machine gun, heavy with a hundred-round ammo drum, lay across the stomach of one snoozing troop. A sergeant was reattaching a grenade launcher beneath the barrel of his rifle. Several other soldiers engaged in the never-ending pre-mission routine of checking and rechecking the lubrication on their rifles. A staff sergeant was doing knife tricks to the amazement of a couple wide-eyed privates. A dog handler walked his Belgian Malinois back and forth between piles of equipment, letting the dog sniff about as practice—*Bomb detection*, recognized Trevanathan.

"Where are these guys headed?" joked Trevanathan to Ford. "Normandy?"

"These are yours, sir," replied Ford. "Today is a BFD."

---

[66] SAW – U.S. M249 Squad Automatic Weapon, a light machine gun firing 5.56 mm NATO ammunition.

An Absence of Faith

Trevanathan stopped. "What?" He paused, taking in the entire scene again. "Umm, isn't this overkill?" *This was definitely overkill. I'm trying to keep a low profile on this effort.* "Why wasn't I briefed about this? This has to be most of the trigger pullers on the camp."

"Not my call, sir," replied Ford. "Late last night the mission brief went up to my battalion commander. He heard it was a movement into an uncleared area with a VIP, and he ordered the company commander to upgrade the mission profile to reduce the risk…to you. We've got two full platoons. They were going to send the update to you early this AM over SIPR.[67]"

"Never saw it. Chuck, you?"

"Negative, sir."

Ford interrupted, "Here comes Captain Darr. He's the OIC[68] today."

A broad-shouldered officer, who looked like he had spent a fair part of his life rappelling out of helicopters, approached at a quick stride. "Good morning, sir. Sir," he repeated, nodding to Brandt.

"Good morning, Captain Darr. Quite a show here today. Makes me feel loved," quipped Trevanathan.

"Roger, sir. Our intel guys dug around a bit yesterday and no one could confirm that anyone, including ANA or MOI, had occupied this compound in the past five years. It's been sitting there empty, but no one knows what's inside. Could be mined and booby trapped all to hell, just waiting for someone to wander in. So, we're treating this as a movement into a likely hostile environment."

"The A Team up there seemed to think it was used by a customs unit for training until last year," said Trevanathan.

"We heard the same thing, sir, but no one in the Ministry would confirm that for us. We're not betting *your* life on some oral legend," said Darr.

---

[67] SIPR – Secure Internet Protocol Router. Secure internet employed by the military to convey sensitive or classified information.
[68] OIC – Officer in Charge.

Trevanathan sighed. He knew that conflicting intel was the norm in a combat zone and the captain was right to be cautious. "OK, it's your show. Where do you need me?"

"We have two Chinooks[69] inbound. You will be in the second platform, with the major."

"You can get Chinooks into this little airfield?"

"Roger, sir. Leastways, the *pilots* can." He grinned for the first time.

"OK..." replied Trevanathan, feeling a bit overwhelmed that his brief real estate inspection had ballooned into a major military operation.

"Two MH-60s will provide overwatch in case we run into any trouble on the ground. Between my boys, the 240s[70] on the Chinooks, and rocket pods on the Blackhawks, there's nothing in this AO[71] we can't handle. MEDEVAC is on standby at HKIA four minutes away."

I need to act like this is all normal to me, thought Trevanathan. "Got it. What else?" he said, imitating the confident tone he had heard General Crist use.

"When you reach the LZ, let the platoon dismount and secure the area before you exit, sir. Sergeant Ford is going to get the high sign from First Sergeant Alvarez that the area is secure, and then he will bring you out."

"OK, and if it's not secure?"

"If we run into unfriendlies, the primary job of Sergeant Ford and the pilot is to get you the fuck out of there. We stay and kill the bad guys. You are exfiltrated."

---

[69] CH-47 heavy cargo helicopters. Dual rotor utility helicopters used for movement of heavy cargo and large numbers of personnel.

[70] Chinooks have M240 machine guns mounted on each side, and sometimes on the ramp, to provide defensive fire capability.

[71] AO – military acronym for area of operations

An Absence of Faith

"No way, Captain. I'm not flitting off to safety, leaving your guys to fight it out after I drag them into some shitshow. It's my mission; I'm not running if things get warm."

"I know it may feel that way, sir. But *you* are the mission to us. *Our* mission is to keep you alive. If you hang around, it's going to get more of my people killed trying to protect you. If you're safe, it frees my men up to do what they do best."

As if to confirm that statement, First Sergeant Alvarez, a tall, dark-haired, ruddy-skinned NCO approached the group. "Is this the package, sir?" he asked Darr, while saluting the colonel.

"Yes, First Sergeant," replied Darr. "This is Colonel Trevanathan and Major Brandt."

"Gentlemen," nodded Alvarez, sizing up his charges, his eyes pausing momentarily on the rifle carried by the colonel, not the usual weapon for a senior officer.

I'm now "The package?" Wonderful, thought Trevanathan.

Brandt tugged at the colonel's sleeve. "Captain's right, sir. Success for the bad guys is knocking off a colonel. And then what happens to the court project?"

"Sir," added Captain Darr, "I checked your shit out. Valor citation, Purple Heart. You've nothing to prove. But I don't need you in the middle of a firefight distracting my folks just by being there."

"OK, I get it. I hate it, but I get it. What else?" The deep and unmistakable *BUP, BUP, BUP* of the approaching helicopters signaled that the show was about to start.

"That's it, sir. Stay with Sergeant Ford and enjoy the ride."

The colonel gave a quick thumbs up, as the roar of the approaching aircraft made further conversation impossible. He fumbled to get his foam ear plugs into place as the first of the two large helicopters broke over the trees a hundred meters above them. The right-side gunner was leaning out his window, looking directly down at Trevanathan as he passed over.

Several hundred feet above the Chinooks, two Blackhawk helicopters circled above the camp. Trevanathan noticed that while he had been engaged with Captain Darr, the disorganized piles of humanity, weapons, and equipment had formed into four straight lines, or *sticks*, immediately outside the narrow, gated entrance into the soccer field. Dust was still swirling around as the first stick on the right double-timed through the gate, followed closely by the second.

Ford yelled something unintelligible in Trevanathan's ear and then guided him to the rear of the fourth stick, on the left side of the grouping. They had barely joined before the soldiers ahead of them lurched forward, following the third stick into the small stadium, down a short set of stairs and out onto the grass. Both Chinooks had landed, their rear ramps lowered, their rotors still spinning. The lead aircraft was in the forward right corner of the soccer field, with the second at eight o'clock, behind, in the opposite corner. The first stick climbed into the first aircraft as its crew chief signaled the second to wait.

Even while idling, the wash of the four rotors in the small area was impressive, driving dirt into everyone's faces. Combat goggles protected their eyes. Sticks Three and Four jogged to the open ramp of their machine. Brandt, Ford, and the colonel followed, and Trevanathan could feel his heart thumping under his flak jacket. This was a full-on sensory experience: as the blades spun overhead, the engine roar drowned out all other noise, and the ground seemed to shake beneath their feet. To Trevanathan, it felt like the swirling air was more difficult to breathe. After just a moment's pause, the second aircraft's crew chief pointed at Stick Three and waved them forward while Stick Four and the VIP party waited. Trevanathan glanced at the lead Chinook on the far side of the field and was surprised to see that Stick Two was already aboard and the ramp was rising. Seconds later, the troops ahead of him surged forward, and he followed them up into the long, dim interior.

Sergeant Ford led Trevanathan and Brandt to the front of the aircraft. As they passed between the two rows of soldiers lining the bulkheads, Trevanathan felt their eyes on him, each perhaps wondering who "the package" was, and why this mission was important. They'd been briefed on their piece of today's mission, but the details of the corruption court project as a priority within the scope of the broader war effort—not so much.

Trevanathan dropped into the furthest forward troop seat on the right front side of the aircraft, opposite Brandt, and buckled in. Ford slid into the seat on the colonel's left and did the same. Trevanathan pointed his rifle barrel toward the floor. An accidental discharge was always bad, but an accidental discharge upward could kill everyone aboard if the round hit the complex rotor assembly.

A familiar feeling came over the colonel—one first experienced in Iraq: he was numb. Not a *tingling sensation* kind of numb, but rather the absence of emotion. In his civilian life, people would occasionally ask him how he had been able to function in combat in Iraq, inevitably qualifying the question by claiming that they could never do such things. For Trevanathan, there were really two answers. The first was usually easy for people to understand, that training simply kicks in—you don't stop to consider "is this a good idea or not?" You just do what you're trained to do.

But the second answer that he usually didn't bother to explain was that *stuff* happens very quickly in war. Once things start to move, individuals get swept along like leaves in a storm. Half an hour earlier, he had been finishing coffee in his office; ten minutes ago, he was chatting with Sergeant Ford and watching knife tricks on the roadway; and now he had just run up the ramp into a flying war machine, without a second thought, on his way to an unsecure LZ, in a country where life was cheap. All of those moments did not move at the same speed. The closer he came to the helicopter, the more time accelerated, and he was swept forward into events over which independent thought and action was nonexistent. He simply acted. And now, he was sitting with a rifle between his knees waiting for who knows what on the other end of this flight.

The noise in the Chinook grew louder, if that was even possible, as the pilot throttled up. Trevanathan clumsily adjusted his ear plugs, a simple task complicated by wearing leather combat gloves, and trying to do it one-handed, without letting go of his rifle. Momentarily, the engine noise snuck past his hearing protection. *It's like having your head underneath a massive lawn mower. Hearing protection or not, these Chinook crews must be deaf by the time they're sixty,* he thought.

With surprising agility, the giant machine lifted into the air. Cocooned inside, Trevanathan's only view outside were slivers of the sky he could see past the left side door gunner. It would be a short trip. What would have been a forty- or fifty-minute drive would today be an eight-minute flight.

Trevanathan looked back toward the ramp. *Amazing, half these guys are already asleep,* he noted, seeing slack jaws and lolling heads scattered along both rows of seats. Across the aisle, Brandt sat back with eyes closed and chin tilted toward the roof of the helicopter.

Trevanathan tried to avoid thinking of the multiple bad things that could possibly happen in the next ten minutes. His tour in Iraq had ended abruptly on a mission much more routine than this one. He knew that things could change from routine to chaos in a heartbeat. The roar of the helicopter, the smells of sweat, canvas, and gun metal. He felt himself on the verge of flashing back to that day outside Al Hillah when half his intestines had been ripped out by an exploding roadside shell. *Today is NOT that day,* he reassured himself. *Keep your eyes open. Deep breaths. Mind in the present.* Iraq faded as Trevanathan focused on his breathing and the mission ahead.

The Chinooks were heavily armed, with a 40 mm grenade launcher in a chin turret, in addition to the side machine guns. But they were also vulnerable as they landed—like large ungainly birds. *In that last hundred meters before landing, a blind man could hit one of these things with an RPG,* the colonel mulled. But then he chided himself. *Knock it off. Focus on what you can control. Don't generate fake stress. Deep breaths.* He checked his M4 for the tenth time since leaving the office minutes ago. *Safety on, magazine seated, round chambered.* Anywhere else, the flight crew would have made everyone clear their weapons before boarding, but this was Afghanistan. Nobody wanted to exit an aircraft into enemy fire with a weapon that wasn't ready to shoot back. Hence, the nervous habit of soldiers going over their equipment again and again, repeated endlessly ever since there have been soldiers.

Next to Brandt was a broad-shouldered specialist carrying the SAW with the large ammunition drum slung underneath. *The ammunition alone must weigh twenty pounds,* thought the colonel.

First Sergeant Alvaraz walked down the aisle toward the cockpit, shaking soldiers awake by their vests or smacking them on their helmet if they failed to respond immediately. "Two minutes," he yelled, audible even over the massive rotors. He leaned in toward Trevanathan. "Two minutes, sir," he repeated, as if the colonel needed his own special notification. Trevanathan replied with a thumbs up.

The specialist sitting next to Brandt stirred. Ford waved his right hand to catch the young soldier's attention. As the first sergeant turned and retreated to his seat next to the ramp, Ford extended his green covered combat glove into a middle digit salute. The specialist broke into a huge grin, returning the gesture. The specialist nudged the corporal next to him and then passed on the gesture to him. This triggered a wave of laughter and competing middle-digit exchanges that rippled down the length of the aircraft. As they banked into their LZ the atmosphere within the aircraft was bizarrely festive. *These guys are crazy*, thought Trevanathan.

Yet, in the ten seconds before touchdown, the atmosphere among the combat troops inside the Chinook shifted, and everyone was back to business. Faces were tight; hands rapidly rechecked weapons, and then settled on seatbelt releases to ensure a quick exit at touchdown. Trevanathan felt the nose of the aircraft pitch up as the ramp descended. The aircraft was sufficiently loud that any incoming fire would be drowned out, but any sudden holes in the bulkheads would be hard to miss. *No incoming, no incoming*, the colonel willed, as no holes appeared.

The rear wheels touched, and the nose came down. Thick brown dust swirled around the rear opening as two ribbons of warriors streamed out in one smooth motion. Trevanathan could see the shadows of two soldiers who had gone prone at the base of the ramp to cover their exit. Ford laid a cautioning hand on the colonel's chest to make sure his officer did not sweep out the door in an initial adrenalin rush. Trevanathan looked at the two side gunners on the crew, and saw they were vigilant, but not firing. *Hating this*, he thought, feeling helpless, as adrenalin flooded his system, calling for him to do *anything* but just *sit* there.

"Wait," barked Ford in his ear, and then he too was gone, out the rear of the aircraft. Trevanathan noted jealously that Brandt had gone out with the first wave, apparently unconstrained by the safety bumpers placed on the colonel. Trevanathan could feel his battle blood getting up. "I'm not sitting here fucking forever," he said out loud to no one, his voice washed away by the rotors. He undid his seat belt and stood, checking his rifle again, and then Ford was back. *Had it been seconds? Minutes?* Time was meaningless.

"Let's go, sir!" he barked, gesturing for the colonel to follow.

Trevanathan exited through the dust into the bright morning air of a shallow dirt bowl at the base of large, rocky hills. Instinctively, he crouched, an old habit for a tall guy around whirling helicopter blades, as he got his bearings. The platoon from the first helicopter occupied an arc along the northern edge top of the of the bowl surrounding the LZ. Sergeants ran back and forth, communicating with hand signals as they adjusted their assigned sectors of fire. Closer, the second platoon was moving into position along the southern side, closing the perimeter. On the ground behind both helicopters, machine gun teams waited to reinforce as needed. The two Blackhawks zoomed low overhead, less than one hundred meters above, adding to the deafening noise of the idling Chinooks. White smoke spread from cannisters thrown to obscure the fledgling invasion.

"This way, sir," directed Ford, jogging ahead of the colonel toward the slightly higher ground at the bowl's edge. Though the Chinook rotors were many feet above his head, Trevanathan stooped as he followed, determined to keep his head attached to his shoulders.

Huddled against a small bank of dirt and gravel at the LZ's western edge, they found Captain Darr and First Sergeant Alvarez, huddled over a map. Nearby, a soldier spoke into a radio, relaying reports back to their headquarters adjoining Camp RS. "Sierra 3, this is Whiskey 6. We are Sierra India.[72] No red contact, over."

Darr smiled at the colonel. "Everything is good so far, sir: just a walk in the sunshine."

---

[72] A unit may use the NATO alphabet with a prearranged code to communicate a successful landing to their higher headquarters. In this instance, "Sierra India" meant a successful insertion of troops.

An Absence of Faith

"I appreciate that. Thanks," replied Trevanathan, taking a knee next to the captain and trying to look inconspicuous to any snipers who might not share Darr's optimism.

To their south, two dune buggy-type vehicles were moving in their direction along a gravel road, at a remarkably high rate of speed.

Trevanathan noticed that Brandt had reappeared at his side. "How is *your* war going?" the colonel asked, slightly irritated that his deputy had left him.

"No Navy Cross today, sir," Brandt replied, grinning.

From their vantage point, Trevanathan saw that two 101st troopers stopped the dune buggies about fifty meters short of the perimeter. One of the two vehicles was driven by Sergeant First Class Frame. "That's the SF NCOIC[73]," Trevanathan advised Captain Darr. "Sergeant First Class Frame—our welcoming party."

"Nice toys. McElligot, tell Second Platoon to let them through," Darr told his radioman.

A minute later, they were joined by Frame and another member of his team, who skidded their vehicles to a stop. Trevanathan climbed up to the road to greet him.

"Hey, sir, good to see you," welcomed Frame. "You know how to make an entrance," he laughed, extending his arms out toward the heavily armed LZ. As he spoke, the Chinooks made ready to depart, raising their ramps and throttling up their rotors. The small command group turned away, covering their eyes as soil and stones pelted them.

As both aircraft cleared the LZ and banked toward the nearby HKIA airfield, Frame spat out a mouthful of dirt and exclaimed, "Those fuckers love doing that," gesturing at the departing aircraft. "What's the drill now?" Trevanathan asked.

Darr answered first. "We'll send two squads to recon the compound. It's about 400 meters straight down the road the Sergeant came up. They'll make sure it's clear and then take initial positions around the wall. If it's not clear, then they'll deal with it.

---

[73] Special Forces Noncommissioned Officer in Charge

Once we get word it's clear, Sergeant Frame can bring you and the Major up there to do your assessment."

"Always last to the dance," Trevanathan joked, looking at Brandt.

"It was clear last night," added Frame. "We didn't have the gear for a full EOD[74] sweep, but two of my boys went up there and poked around. No one gave them trouble."

"Good. Let's hope it stays that way," said Alvarez.

"Although you do have a welcoming committee of sorts, sir," chuckled Frame.

Trevanathan lifted an eyebrow. "What do you mean?"

"I don't want to spoil the surprise, sir. It's pretty funny. You'll see." Frame smiled.

Trevanathan noted that a platoon of the 101st troopers were already moving down the road in a loose tactical formation, spaced well apart. Ford excused himself to go with them, sensing that the greater threat to the colonel likely lay down the unknown road than in this LZ where he was surrounded by heavy firepower. Trevanathan probably had twenty minutes or more to kill, so he took a moment to assess the terrain around him. The small LZ on which they stood was tucked on the east side of a gravel road that ran parallel to the large hills marking the western boundary of Kabul. *Anyone up on those hills would have a field day shooting down into this area*, Trevanathan thought. *But they'd have a helluva' time getting away, afterwards.* He remembered the map Frame had shown him, and the flat, open terrain that surrounded the hills above him.

To the east, the land fell away, covered by endless walled compounds dropping gradually toward central Kabul. The city itself was obscured by the gray cloud of pollution that perpetually hung over the valley this time of year. To the north, further up the road a half-kilometer or so, was the Counter-Narcotics Justice Center compound, where major drug producers and dealers were supposed to be detained and tried.

---

[74] EOD – Explosives Ordnance Disposal. The army branch responsible for bomb and explosives disarming and disposal.

There was almost no vehicular traffic in the area. This neighborhood looks a lot more isolated and easier to secure than putting the court in the middle of downtown Kabul, where it's a weekly parade of car bombs and suicide vest bombers, Trevanathan thought.

A gunshot report snapped from the far side of the perimeter, echoing off the hillside above them. Trevanathan was instantly on the ground. The infantrymen surrounding him seemed to shift as a single organism, tensing in anticipation of a massive response. The colonel crawled to the edge of the bowl and slid back down for better cover. "Accidental discharge. Stand down," came a voice from the opposite side.

"Who?" barked Alvarez. "Goddamn it, w*ho*?" The first sergeant was marching across the LZ like Godzilla through downtown Tokyo, all pretense of tactical concealment cast aside. Darr looked embarrassed. "Sorry, sir. No matter how much training, there's always one fuck-up in the group."

"*Jordan*, you sorry sack-of-shit. I wouldn't trust your worthless ass with a pea-shooter. Give me that goddamn rifle." First Sergeant Alvarez' wrath could be heard loud and clear from the far side of the bowl, in full glory.

"PFC Jordan, I would have bet on it," muttered Captain Darr.

Trevanathan wasn't interested in the unit's internal issues, but knew this *Jordan* was about to lose a stripe, or more, depending on his prior record. "Main thing is no one is hurt," he replied, trying to sound magnanimous. He knew the battalion or brigade commander would not share his charitable disposition later.

"Let's try not to shoot each other," roared Alvarez, stomping back across the landing zone. Jordan's rifle was now in the custody of his squad leader. "Let's resist the overwhelming goddamn temptation to blow each other's brains out, shall we, ladies?" he declared in mock disgust. No one smiled, knowing the first sergeant's bad mood would now shadow the rest of this mission.

Darr's radioman spoke up. "Sir, Sergeant Ford says it's clear for the colonel to come up. The exterior is clean. They're still checking inside some buildings, but he can start outside." Sergeant Frame looked at Trevanathan and gestured for him to climb aboard. The colonel nodded and scrambled up the gravel slope to board the metal-framed buggy. "Got an air bag on this thing?" he asked, as Frame jumped behind the wheel.

Frame had the same expression as a kid who has been given his first dirt bike. Showing off, he hit the gas and fishtailed one hundred eighty degrees, accelerating rapidly toward Camp Heath. "*Local Judge Dies in Afghan Dune Buggy Accident*," Trevanathan imagined on his hometown newspaper headline, as he tried to appear unconcerned. In a few moments, they crested a slight rise to see the beige-walled compound. Trevanathan could see the promised guard towers on the corners facing them, which were already occupied by the American troops. *These guys move fast.* A large, brown, metal door, wide enough to admit a deuce-and-a-half[75] awaited them, outside of which Ford and two more 101st troopers waited. A pedestrian door built into the larger door was already open.

Frame skidded to a gravel-scattering halt, laughing like a teenage boy at the high-speed ride he had given the colonel.

"Thanks, I think," offered the colonel, climbing over the side onto slightly wobbly legs.

"They're still clearing the buildings, sir, so I wouldn't open any doors or windows inside until the EOD guys give the green light," advised Ford, stepping up to advise on the situation inside the compound. "Looks clean, but that's when they bite you on the ass."

"Yep, been there," echoed the colonel.

"Let's check it out," Trevanathan nodded to Brandt, who was climbing out of the second dune buggy.

Stepping through the pedestrian door, the colonel saw a large, well-maintained compound, something rare in the filth and poverty of Kabul. Several buildings immediately in front of him had intact windows, and the area was remarkably free of trash. *Doesn't look like it's been empty too long*, thought Trevanathan, who knew most real estate in Kabul was either occupied or used as a dumping ground. To his right, the dog handler was moving toward a small one-story building in his search for boobytraps.

---

[75] Two-and-one-half-ton truck.

What Trevanathan did not expect were the children, a group of which had set up a makeshift market on several colorful blankets inside the gate. "My friends! My friends!" greeted a young boy, wearing a red fez with a black tassel. His arms were thrown wide, and a bright white smile stretched from ear to ear. "My name is Jesus. Welcome to my kingdom!"

"Not again," groaned Trevanathan to himself.

"General, my General, come. Come see my fine wares. Buy something for your beautiful wife. Your lovely daughters. I have lapis jewelry, fine art, rugs. Best prices in Kabul!" The boy latched onto Trevanathan's sleeve before anyone could interfere and dragged him toward his small emporium.

"Get something nice there for the missus, sir" joked Frame, over the colonel's shoulder. "Just keep a hand on your wallet."

"Fine art, from a rich home in Kabul," the boy schmoozed, holding up a ceramic plaque of a woman drinking from a teacup.

"Jesus...is that your real name, kid?" Trevanathan asked.

The boy giggled, grabbing his stomach with both hands. "Hakeem, I am Hakeem, General. 'Jesus' is my business name." He giggled again. "I get better deals with the soldiers when I say I am Jesus." Two young girls behind Hakeem laughed, hiding their faces in their hands. They were maybe eight or nine years old. "Hsshh," Hakeem ordered over his shoulder, annoyed. "I am doing business."

"Who are they?"

"My sisters. They follow me everywhere." Hakeem rolled his eyes in a manner that transcended all cultures.

Trevanathan looked around the compound where the 101st troops were still clearing buildings and setting up security. He turned back to the boy, who was perhaps his best potential source of intel.

"So, Hakeem, what are you doing here? There's no market here, nobody to sell to."

"You're here, General!" the little man declared happily. "I have beautiful pictures, look," he insisted, opening a large notebook that contained beautiful, embossed pictures of a tiger hunt, with Arabic script in gold leaf on the pages.

"Yes, but how did you know we were coming today?" the colonel asked.

"Everyone knows, General. The men who work in the dining hall on your base heard it this morning from the soldiers at breakfast. They talked about it to the people who clean the toilets. They talked to the merchants who run the small bazaar inside your base, and that is where I heard. My cousin works in the shop that sells chess sets. I caught a ride up here in a truck that was taking away the trash from your base and made first claim to this spot. It is now Camp Hakeem and the Jesus market! Welcome to my business!" he grinned proudly.

"Do you know if anyone else has been here…recently? Taliban?"

Hakeem said something in Dari that Trevanathan did not understand and spat. "No Taliban or Daisch here, General. Bad for business. There are too many soldiers nearby. This was a soldier school, but they gave it up to move closer to the border. The building there in the middle," he gestured to the large central building that had its own surrounding wall, "is sometimes used as a mosque by the soldiers down the road."

"It's in pretty good condition," the colonel, said out loud, while really speaking to himself.

"They would not put a mosque in a dirty place, General."

"I suppose you're right…Jesus." The colonel smiled. "How much for that picture, of the guy hunting the tigers?"

"Ooh, that is extremely rare, General. You have an eye for quality. It is very old too. I could not part with it for less than fifty dollars."

"I'll give you five."

"Oh, you are taking advantage of a poor orphan child, General. For shame." The boy clutched his chest and closed his eyes in pain. "How will I feed my sisters? Twenty-five."

"Do you have access to a phone?"

Hakeem wrinkled his brow. "Yes, my General," he replied, cautiously.

"You don't have to tell me your number. I'm going to give you mine. I have an Afghan civilian phone. I will give you ten dollars for the picture. And I will give you twenty dollars every month, if you let me know if you hear that anyone is planning to cause any problems for this compound. Understand?"

"What if I don't hear anything, General? What if there is no news?"

"That's fine, you still get twenty dollars. I don't want you making things up to get paid. If there's nothing to report, you still get paid."

"So, you will pay me if I do nothing?" the boy looked skeptical.

"No, you will always keep your eyes and ears open. That is what I'm paying you for. If there are no problems or dangers that you hear about, you still get paid. If you do hear something that could create problems for me or my men, then you let me know right away."

"Ah, so I am like 007—secret agent man," smiled the boy.

"Exactly," replied Trevanathan. "Except you don't try to stop anything yourself or do anything risky to get yourself hurt. You just make a call and say…you say, 'This is Jesus, and we have an issue.'"

"A tissue?"

"An issue—it is a fancy word for a problem, a *danger*. How about just say, 'There is a problem.'"

"That is all, and I get twenty dollars? Every month?" the boy asked, wrinkling his nose.

"That's it."

"I will do it, General." The boy extended his hand to seal the deal. As they shook, he declared, "But I want twelve dollars for the picture."

Trevanathan laughed as he turned over the money.

Having completed his negotiations, and being thirty-two dollars lighter, Trevanathan turned back to the business of evaluating the compound as a potential court site. To his surprise, the buildings throughout the compound were furnished. That was unusual in a country where anything not nailed down usually disappeared in minutes. To the right of the gate, Trevanathan inspected a one-story building that might serve as the prosecutor's office. It had a large common area where the staff could share space, and a separate section with individual offices for supervisors. There were also two large steel cages in the rear that would be equally suitable as an arms locker or as a temporary holding cell for a defendant in custody. *Well, that'll be for the Afghans to decide,* the colonel thought. *Don't get bogged down in details.*

The wall around the large building that had been used as a mosque shielded all but its roof from direct sight within the compound. This barrier afforded additional cover from small arms or rocket fire. *Could be a good emergency shelter*, thought the colonel. Inside, a spacious foyer opened onto hallways left and right, leading to large, conference-style rooms at either end of the building. *Here are my court rooms. We'll only need one to start, but if this project picks up steam, we can refurbish the other and have two trials going on at the same time.*

There were several other smaller buildings in the compound that offered additional space for the project. One building, the size of a small ranch house in the States, could be for judges' chambers. *There're several individual offices in the front and a bed and bathroom in the back. Couldn't have asked for anything better. Judges can stay here overnight during sensitive trials and not get whacked by the bad guys during their commute,* Trevanathan assessed. There was a similar building next door, without the bedrooms, that could house offices for the defense attorneys.

A large, metal-roofed building on the far end of the camp looked as if it had been a gym—at least it smelled like an old gym, Trevanathan thought—and could probably be repurposed into a training center for the police and prosecutors.

Trevanathan worked his way to the far wall of the camp and climbed to the guard tower that was occupied by a young sergeant from the 101st. Ford remained at the base of the stairs. "Sir," was the short greeting he received, as the NCO was keeping close watch over an extensive junkyard that began fifty meters away from that corner. Rusting cars, trucks, and buses were piled as far as the eye could see on uneven terrain to the south. *May need to push some of this back*, the colonel thought. *Creates a blind spot.* Trevanathan turned and surveyed the compound's interior from his elevated position.

The last building on the camp, and the largest by square footage, looked almost like a two-story, drive-up motel. Noting there were at least thirty-two individual room units on the front and back, Trevanathan realized this could be workspace for the many coalition personnel who might play a role in keeping the justice center honest—FBI trainers, German judges, and advisors from Trevanathan's own EF3 shop. The colonel knew it would take several years of oversight and encouragement before the Afghans would choose to follow the rule of law, instead of embracing get-rich-quick as a governing philosophy. The steady presence of his office and other Western advisors was essential to that change of mindset. Trevanathan tried to keep himself from getting too excited as he imagined the possibilities, but Camp Heath looked like a gift in a country where nothing was ever easy. *This is the place,* the colonel decided.

The metal staircase groaned, as another person climbed to join them. "What do you think, sir?" asked Brandt, interrupting his thoughts.

"I think it's perfect. There's no need for new construction, just some tweaking. We could have this thing up and running in sixty to ninety days, even at an Afghan pace."

"I agree. Sixty to ninety to get the water and lights on. Fix up some rudimentary courtrooms. Identify the startup personnel and bring the first charges. Super-fast but do-able. Get it going and then fine-tune it. Build the plane at thirty thousand feet," said Brandt.

"So, what are we forgetting?"

"Well, none of it's gonna' happen with the Afghans 'less the COM convinces Ghani that it's a priority."

"Think so?" Trevanathan asked, already knowing the answer.

"Yessir, this is the land where good intentions go to die, right? Need Presidential mojo on this, or the Attorney General, the courts, and every crooked bastard in between will find a way to slow-roll and tear away at this idea until you and I are both gone."

"OK, I'll work that."

"Captain Darr also wants to know if you want him to clear those kids out by the gate."

"No, we're designating them special liaisons." Trevanathan laughed when Brandt raised his eyebrows. "Our mission here today, that we thought was such a secret, was known to every Hajji on and off Camp RS before we went wheels up this morning. We need eyes and ears outside the wall letting us know what's coming at us before it happens."

"Agreed, but they could be working both sides, sir. I've seen it happen."

"I know, but we gotta' start somewhere. Right now, we're running blind, and the locals aren't. The kids might give us shaky intel, but right now we get zero intel."

"OK, sir."

"And if you can't trust Jesus, who can you trust?" asked Trevanathan.

Brandt groaned, shaking his head as he turned and descended the rusty metal stairs to the ground. "Wheels up in 20 mikes, sir," he called over his shoulder.

Chapter 21

Camp Resolute Support, Kabul, February 2016

Every soldier uses some form of mental gymnastics to get through the monotony of a deployment. Some become gym rats, pumping their frustration out on iron. Younger troops in garrison environments often lose themselves in video gaming and social media when off duty. Some troops keep up with college courses through long distance learning systems.

Trevanathan's pressure relief valve amid sixteen-hour duty days was The Blue Café. The Blue, as it was called, was a coffee bar built above the small Camp RS post exchange and laundry drop-off. It was run by twin Afghan brothers. They created espresso and lattes that provided enough jolt to get an aging colonel through another day. On sunny days, when he was able to grab a rickety table on the small rooftop deck outside their shop, and if the smell of burning sewage was blowing away from camp, Trevanathan could close his eyes and for a few moments be in Rome or along the Seine. If it wasn't too late in the day, scoring a chocolate croissant was even a possibility. A small sliver of joy in a land of chronic misery.

When his schedule allowed, the colonel would pop his head into Lieutenant Ripple's cubby outside his office at 1430 hours and say, "I need to see a man about a horse." That was notice that the colonel was off the clock for the next half hour to recharge at The Blue.

Although it was February, it was unseasonably warm in Kabul. Snow was visible on the mountains, but there was none in Kabul. Temperatures were pushing up into the low fifties during the day. At his usual time, Trevanathan made his way across the camp and climbed the metal stairwell to the Blue, relieved to see that there were only two civilians inside. *Not going to have to talk shop with someone,* Trevanathan gratefully realized. The other four tables inside were empty, while out front on the small rooftop deck, a lone woman in civilian clothes sat at a picnic table engrossed in her book.

"Good afternoon, sir," greeted the proprietor with a broad smile, as the colonel entered. "Your usual?" Afghan Brother Number One (or was it Two?) was dressed in new blue jeans and a black polo shirt. His black mustache, well-trimmed beard, and coal-dark eyes always left Trevanathan with a "Wolfman Jack" impression of the barista. *I'm coming here way too frickin' much if I've got a "usual"*, the colonel warned himself.

"Yes, please," Trevanathan replied.

The owner quickly busied himself with the art of the medium latte, which seemed to involve a large production of knobs, spouts, and much hissing.

"Good afternoon, Colonel," greeted one of the two men to his right, in a German accent. "Can I persuade you to join us?" The balding man with pale blue eyes, perhaps in his mid-forties, stood stiffly and gestured to a chair across from himself. He wore a nicely tailored suit of green tweed. His partner, a red complexioned man of similar age forced an awkward smile that revealed it was not an expression he often made. *Flat snake eyes,* thought the colonel.

"I don't believe I've had the pleasure," replied Trevanathan, extending his hand, while inwardly lamenting, *there goes my coffee break...*

"I am Hans Juergen, from the Deutsch...that is, German Embassy. This is my associate, Dieter Klimpt." Klimpt stared, unblinking, and Trevanathan would not have been surprised to see a thin, forked tongue flick between the man's lips.

"A pleasure," replied Trevanathan. "Bill Trevanathan, Rule of Law Advisor."

"Ahh, we know. Everyone knows," schmoozed Herr Jurgen. "You are the man who is going to stop corruption in Afghanistan, *nicht wahr*?[76]" He smiled warmly, while his words gently mocked. "Please join us."

Trevanathan's latte and croissant arrived on the counter at that moment, giving him several seconds to think while he paid and collected his order. *They know who I am. They know what I'm*

---

[76] Nicht Wahr. German Tr. – "Isn't that true?"

doing. They were waiting for me, and Dieter boy there would cut my throat without flinching. Intel. Maybe German, maybe just playing as Germans. Let's find out.

Trevanathan returned to the table and took the offered chair. "Herr Klimpt, *was machen Sie in der Botschaft*?[77]" inquired the colonel, inquiring as to Dieter Klimpt's role at the embassy.

Klimpt's eyes twitched slightly, caught off guard that the American spoke German. "*Alles*," he snickered. "Everything. I am what you call in your baseball a utility player. Economics, political analysis, security matters." He had recovered, and the eyes were dead again.

Herr Juergen intervened to regain control of the conversation. "If I may ask, how do you think progress is going with the corruption court?"

OK, so they need to answer someone up their food chain about the ACJC and need a primary source to quote, Trevanathan calculated. Nothing to hide here, so I'll give it to him straight.

"It depends on how one defines progress, doesn't it? If one is naive enough to think any new project will change the government here overnight, then progress is slow." Herr Juergen nodded slightly in acknowledgment. "But if we define progress as starting change from a culture of complete impunity for theft to one where stealing the national budget is not acceptable, then we are off to a solid start."

"Is a start enough, I wonder? After so much time has passed," replied Juergen, leaving the question hanging.

The roles were suddenly clear to Trevanathan. Juergen was probably some type of political analyst who needed to send an assessment back to his Ministry in Berlin about the viability of the ACJC. Klimpt was probably a field officer—an interrogator, most likely—someone professionally skilled at detecting deception.

Trevanathan leaned forward, pointing steepled fingers at Juergen. "You tell me. This is about will. Do the Afghans have the will to change? Do the Americans have the will to stay the course until they do? Do our NATO allies—Germany, for example—have the

---

[77] German Tr. - Mr. Klimpt, what do you do at the embassy?

will to give this time to work before domestic issues force you to cut and run?" Trevanathan noticed both men stiffen at his expression. "Everyone has a different level of will in this game. Everyone, including the U.S., is mentally, morally, and physically exhausted by this war. Some, I'm sure, are hoping this project will fail, so they will have an excuse to leave. They are scared it will succeed because it will mean a longer commitment here. Change is slow; quitting is quick." Having made his point, Trevanathan leaned back. "So, is a start enough for Germany? Do *you* have the will?" The colonel took a sip of his drink while he let them ponder the gauntlet he had thrown down.

Herr Juergen gave a tight-lipped smile. "That is a question that those above me will have to answer," he replied. "If they do have such will, as you put it, what would you need? From us?"

Trevanathan considered a moment before responding in his usual unvarnished manner. "One of the repeated failures in this mission is that the United States acts as if its allies are bit players whose sole function is to support its political goals, whatever they may be." A look of surprise came to Herr Jurgen's eyes, and even the corner of Klimpt's lip twitched. "That leads to acquiescence, not success. What this effort needs is your expertise—as true full partners. I'm told by my British counterpart that you have great expertise with judge training programs. If Germany were to volunteer such training support—not wait for the U.S. Embassy to ask, because that is never going to happen—then others may also feel welcome to volunteer support."

"I've noticed a sense of fatalism ever since I arrived in country—from our Embassy, from the Afghans, even from some allies. It's as if everyone is resigned to getting hit by the truck coming down the road, instead of taking action to avoid the collission. If each embassy sits on its hands, waiting to see what everyone else does, or waits to see if the project fails, it will fail—from lack of movement. We need allies who are fed up with the past misconduct but won't use their frustration as an excuse to run."

"You are direct, Colonel," commented Jurgen.

"Very direct," murmured Klimpt.

"The curse of being an American, I'm afraid," laughed Trevanathan. "But we have lost too many lives and spent too much money here to do a subtle pantomime about intentions and needs. That type of gamesmanship has led to the current stagnation, with the Afghans looking at NATO as a rich and dimwitted uncle."

A snort escaped Klimpt, who instantly flushed even redder than normal from embarrassment. "Entschuldigung,[78]" he apologized.

"This has been a most productive conversation, Colonel," said Herr Juergen, standing and extending his hand. "Is it possible for us to speak again in the future, as the project matures?"

"It will be my pleasure. But next time, here is my number, so you do not have to stake out the coffee shop waiting for my arrival." Trevanathan smiled and passed Herr Juergen a business card.

"Colonel," stated Klimpt, standing and nodding curtly, before walking out the door.

"I bet he's a hoot at Embassy parties," Trevanathan cracked, as Herr Jurgen put on his coat.

"He is a true believer, as we say in the trade," observed. "Auf Wiedersehen, Herr Oberst."

"Auf Wiedersehen, Herr Juergen."

Trevanathan settled back into his chair, as the Germans left. *Well, now maybe I can have my lukewarm latte and croissant in peace,* resolved the colonel, checking his watch to ensure he made it back to the office in time for the 1600 staff meeting.

He heard the door open behind him. "Sir, could I have a minute of your time? Outside, if possible?"

Trevanathan looked up to see the willowy young woman who had been reading on the deck. "I'm not getting a warm croissant today, am I?" Trevanathan said aloud to himself.

The woman smiled and extended her hand. "Jennifer Reed, Embassy," she said, as if there was only one. "OGA," she whispered, leaning in, so that the proprietor clattering his cups nearby would not hear.

---

[78] Tr. from German – "Pardon."

Other Government Agency, recognized Trevanathan. CIA. Nope, no croissant today.

"Why don't we step outside and catch up?" offered Trevanathan. He had no doubt that the barista, as well as every other local national hire that kept the post running was regularly debriefed by the Afghan intelligence service. Some were probably shaken down by the Taliban for information, as well.

After moving to a table outside, Trevanathan raised his eyebrows in inquiry. Reed was obviously a junior officer, maybe on her first or second assignment with the Agency. He thought she couldn't be older than her mid-twenties.

"Thank you for taking time to talk to me," she said, in a Midwestern twang. Her U.S. Embassy access badge completed her bona fides, for the moment.

"Sorry you had to take a number to see me. The Reich beat you to the punch," Trevanathan explained.

"Those two...?"

"I thought you guys were all in the same club? Yeah, they said they were German embassy staffers, but at least one was clearly a spook. The guy with the reddish face—Dieter Klimpt, he said. Carried himself like an operator. Hans Juergen, was the other—not so sure about him. He smelled of paper clips."

Reed smiled, as she jotted names in a small notebook.

"So what flavor are you?" Trevanathan asked.

"Pardon?"

"Operations or intel?[79]"

Reed smiled again. "Intel, of course. If I was ops, I'd say intel anyway, you know."

---

[79] The CIA has field officers (sometimes called spies by foreign nations) that fall under the Deputy Director for Operations (DDO) and Intelligence Analysts under the Deputy Director for Intelligence (DDI), who examine facts collected from various sources and write foreign policy assessments for consumption by U.S. policy makers.

"Fair enough. So, what can I help you with? I really need to find a new hangout if every agent in Kabul knows when and where to find me."

"It's more a matter of what can we do to help each other. You are making some people uncomfortable with your new court project."

"You mean people other than the State Department?" Trevanathan rejoined.

"Unfortunately, yes. We have picked up on some traffic from the Afghan National Security Directorate.[80] It looks like the former regime is taking a jaundiced view of your efforts and wants it to stop."

Trevanathan was confused. "The former regime? Taliban?" he asked, uncertainly.

"Karzai's[81] people. They became extremely wealthy when he was in office. They have become even more so since he left power. Drugs, black market transactions with neighboring countries, rare earth minerals. They control large segments of the trade and are concerned about anything—or *anyone*—that might upset the profitable status quo."

"And why are you telling me this?"

"The intercept we obtained mentioned that the Americans need another strong reminder to not interfere in Afghan justice matters."

"Hmmm, well people talk all sorts of crap. How reliable is this information?"

"Considering the source, we view it as highly reliable."

Trevanathan did not bother to ask the source, as the Agency wouldn't compromise its sources and methods. "Great, well other than telling me that there's danger in a war zone, why are we having this discussion?"

---

[80] The NDS is the parallel intelligence organization to the CIA within GIRoA.

[81] Hamid Karzai was the U.S.-backed president of Afghanistan from 2004 to 2014. His relationship with the U.S. soured over time and he became an outspoken critic of U.S. policy and operations in Afghanistan. He was succeeded by the last President of Afghanistan, Ashraf Ghani.

Ms. Reed leaned across the table. "This was not a generalized threat, Colonel. You were mentioned by name. There is a fifty-thousand-dollar bounty on your head as of yesterday. You might want to consider cutting back on coffee brewed by local nationals."

Trevanathan sat silently, pursing his lips. *OK, she has my attention.*

"Later today or tomorrow morning, you'll get a visit from someone at DIA.[82] It's their ball to provide intelligence involving force protection issues, such as this."

"Why are you here then?"

"Because their role is keeping you alive. I want your information and access."

"Access?"

"Sir, with POTUS[83] and Congress nervous as cats about taking any U.S. casualties in theater, there's few people moving about Kabul, except generals, and they won't talk to us...or when they do, they won't share anything of worth, because they don't want to be quoted. Those VIP travel orders you have in your pocket make you the most interesting guy at the dance. You can come and go at will—to see the Attorney General, the Chief Justice, and basically anyone up to the President. You're working with the Afghan cops and all the other embassies and learning a lot of dirt, I expect. That's access."

"And you're looking for...?"

"A reality check. Few share intel in this town. State won't share with us, not that they have anything worthwhile to share. The military is afraid to talk to us because they always need permission from someone in the Pentagon, and by the time they get it, if they get it, the information is old. The Ambassador has gutted the FBI presence here, so our contacts there are dead. We have our own local sources, of course, in other arenas, but you're running in a crowd where our game is weak."

---

[82] DIA is the Defense Intelligence Agency, which engages in counter-intelligence activities to protect U.S. forces.

[83] POTUS – President of the United States

"OK, I appreciate the info to watch my back, but my mission here is not to be a source for the Agency. I work for DOD."

"That's not what we're asking."

"What *are* you asking then?"

"If we have discrete areas where we might have overlapping interests, whether you might be open to having a discussion once in a while to compare notes..."

"Give me an example," Trevanathan interrupted.

"Tomorrow morning you're going to go meet with General Crist."

"I am?"

"Yes. Because he has been asked by the COM to investigate allegations of growing 225th Corps corruption. They operate in Helmand and that's home to the opium trade that funds terrorism all over the world. We have interest in that area. It might be mutually beneficial to compare notes as your investigation goes forward."

"My investigation?"

"You'll be going to Lashkar Gah in Helmand with a team to look into allegations that the Taliban are being supplied from 225th Corps."

Trevanathan sat silently. He was stunned that this, whatever she was, knew his orders before he did.

"We can't get in there—inside the corps itself—but you will be an invited guest. We need to know the scope of this problem. Is it an Afghan colonel making a few thousand dollars on the side, or something more significant? And how, if at all, is it tied to transnational terror group funding? The Haqqani Network,[84] for example."

"So they're going to send the guy with the fifty-K price tag to Lashkar Gah to investigate corruption that might be tied to funding

---

[84] The Haqqani Network is a militant Sunni faction with reputed ties to Pakistani Intelligence. While part of the Taliban, it operated semi-autonomously, frequently targeting embassies and civilians with indiscriminate bombings that caused mass casualties during the Afghanistan War.

terrorism? And I'll be surrounded by what? Twenty thousand trigger-happy Afghan soldiers? Nice."

"Weighing the competing options, I believe the conclusion is that you'll be safer out of town for a few days. No one knows you're going."

"Except you...and whoever gets leaks out of the Embassy," Trevanathan replied, irritated. *If this is as secret as our mission to Heath, I'm a dead man,* he realized. *I'm starting to feel like a pawn in other people's games.* The colonel looked at a large cockroach that had climbed up between a gap in the deck's floor and was crawling toward the coffee shop. Before he could comment further, a large black bird swooped in and snatched the insect in its beak in one smooth motion before flying off. *Yeah, like that*, he mused.

"OK, I'm not making any promises, because I don't know how tight this noose is you're asking me to put my neck into. But I'll think about it," replied Trevanathan. "Does General Crist know about our meeting today?"

"He will. Thank you, Colonel. I'll be in touch when you get back." Reed rose and walked to the top of the metal staircase back to street level. "Have a safe trip," she called over her shoulder.

"I will. Could you send up the North Koreans next?" Trevanathan replied, regarding his lukewarm latte with disappointment.

Chapter 22

Lashkar Gah, Helmand Province, March 2016

Five days after the desertion shuttle left his camp, Daniyal received a call from Ali. "I have done what you asked, Sergeant. Everything is fine on this end."

"How do I know that?"

"He can tell you himself." Ali spoke to someone on his end of the line in a muffled voice, "Say hello to your old friend."

"Abdu," slurred a voice on the line. "Ali take me home. Good friend."

"Hello, Abdu, it is good to hear your voice," replied Daniyal, smiling slightly. "Be well. Let me speak to Ali again, please."

Ali came back on the line. "Yes?"

"Why is he still with you?"

"Why do you care?"

"Because you're supposed to take him to his family. Why is he still with you?"

The line was silent for a moment. "He *is* with his family. I took him there as soon as we arrived in Kabul."

"So why is he with you now?"

"Just leave it alone."

"No. I don't trust you. If you are up to your usual…"

"He needs someone to look out for him. His brother tried to get him killed, remember?"

"Yes, I know," Daniyal replied. "That doesn't explain why he is with you. You don't care about anyone."

"Because of you. Damn you. You shamed me. I nearly killed you, and you took pity on me. Who does that?"

Abdu's voice echoed softly in the background.

"So, I thought I might try…my life…it's been a mess. I thought I needed to always fight, but that brought me more pain. You were never a great soldier, but you helped others. When Hassan was sick, you shared your rations with him, when they were not enough for one man. I thought you were a fool then. But now I think your way might be better. I don't know how to do that, so I'm starting with this…Abdu."

"My way is that I want to live and get back to my family," Daniyal said, lowering his voice. "Nothing else matters."

"You say that. But you worry what happens to others. Azir, Abdu, even me for some reason."

"I care about surviving," said Daniyal, feeling irritated that Ali felt free to lecture him.

"We all do, Sergeant. But only surviving nearly broke me. I don't know where my life leads from here, but I'm going to start with this one thing. I take Abdu out every other day because he likes to see birds. I don't know why. The stupid things just make a racket and shit on everything, but he is happiest when we go to Ka Faroshi market and see the parrots."

"Magpies," echoed a happy voice behind Ali.

"What did he say?" asked Daniyal, a chill running through him.

"I don't know. Something about magpies. He likes birds that can talk."

"I don't know what to say," murmured Daniyal.

"You gave him a thousand Afs. The fool gave it to me as soon as the bus left. Can I use it to buy him a fucking parrot?"

Daniyal laughed, his eyes welling up, despite his best efforts. He shielded his eyes behind fingers so no one in the headquarters would notice. "Yes…yes, buy him a fucking parrot…or a magpie."

"Okay, I need to get him home. Try not to get killed."

"You as well." The line clicked dead. Daniyal was dazed. Ali is an evil bastard. Now he's befriending a mental case that the world wanted dead. It makes no sense. Good and evil are upside down.

The door to the sergeant major's office opened. "Sergeant Daniyal, come in," the sergeant major ordered. "Leave the pad."

Daniyal entered, and the sergeant major closed the door behind him. "I understand you had some difficulty with the bus roster the other day?" the sergeant major inquired.

"No, Sergeant Major," Daniyal replied. Before he could elaborate, a massive fist pounded into Daniyal's abdomen, knocking the wind out of him and dropping him to his knees.

"It seems you've forgotten the basic rules of our relationship," Mahmood explained through gritted teeth. "Let's review."

Daniyal was on his knees, his forehead on the cool tile, as he gagged for air that would not come.

"One, you belong to me. Two, don't lie to me. Three, this is a business, and your total compliance ensures our profitability. Does that sound right?" he growled.

Daniyal could feel the sergeant major bending over him. Daniyal could still not find air to speak, but he nodded quickly, in the hope of avoiding another punch.

"Yesterday, while I am trying to enjoy my midday meal, I am approached by Staff Sergeant Kaaliya, from corps artillery," continued the sergeant major. "He tells me that you tried to shake him down for more money by pretending that his man was not on the roster. Is that true?"

Air had slowly begun to creep back into Daniyal's lungs. "N-no...didn't shake him down."

"He is lying then?" Daniyal could feel the sergeant major hovering above him and braced for the next blow.

"I told him...I told him his man was not on the roster. B-but not to shake him down." The words were coming now, and Daniyal lifted his head a few inches off the floor, while still kneeling. The room was spinning.

"Why would you do such a stupid thing, then?" the sergeant major probed.

"Because he was an asshole."

The sergeant major scoffed. "You did it because he hurt your feelings?"

"N-no, Sergeant Major. I was there as your representative. You had just given me these stripes, from your own hand. I knew what an honor that was. It felt like he was disrespecting this office by his conduct. So, I tried to teach him a lesson by showing him he was not in charge. I was wrong." Daniyal looked directly into the sergeant major's eyes as he spoke this, knowing that the big man would find this credible. He left out the part about Ali.

"You never asked him for extra money?"

"Never, Sergeant Major. I would not do something so stupid."

Sergeant Major Mahmood stared at him intently.

"If you ask him how much I demanded he will lie, and you will certainly be able to tell," Daniyal offered.

"I did," replied the sergeant major. "He didn't answer, so that part of his story was weak." To Daniyal's relief the sergeant major walked behind his desk and sat, perhaps signaling that the beating was over.

"I have no issue with you ensuring proper respect for this headquarters and for me," the sergeant major continued. "But next time there is a problem, you let me know before I hear of such a thing from someone else. I do not appreciate surprises. Understand?"

"Yes, Sergeant Major. It was my mistake."

"Don't ever let me get blindsided. There can never be any side deals. You understand that, too?"

"You have made that clear, Sergeant Major."

"Alright, get on your feet. Sit there. We have business to discuss."

Daniyal rose on knees of jelly. He was sure that the sergeant major had pulled his punch. If he hadn't, he would have ruptured internal organs. The man's fists were the size of melons. Daniyal eased into one of the two upholstered chairs.

"We have another special mission."

Daniyal looked blankly. They were all special missions in the headquarters.

"A truck. To the same place. This time it is a German truck. Off the official books, as usual, and operates manually–the same way as the Romanian one from before. Still, I want you to get familiar with it. There can be no problems."

"Yes, Sergeant Major. How soon?"

'I will let you know the day, but you should have ten days at least to prepare."

"The same procedure?"

"Mostly. This time you will get a full cargo list in advance so you can account for the supplies in the ledger, as well. That will save me work. Some of it will be…fragile. So, make sure you are comfortable with the truck and how it is packed. We can't have this mission go up in a puff of smoke."

"Fragile, Sergeant Major? Those are very rough roads."

"Not like glass, fool. Older munitions. Mortar rounds from Soviet times. We have old star flares that we know have been unreliable for years. They might not appreciate being banged about too much. They are of little use to us, so we're going to…redistribute them."

Daniyal remembered Azir writhing on the ground. *So, that wasn't an accident.*

"Yes, Sergeant Major. I will be prepared."

"Good. Now, one more matter. There will be an investigation team coming within the next week or two. An investigator from Kabul, and maybe an American to give it an air of seriousness. The MOD Inspector General has tipped us off. We're trying to delay it, but we don't know if that is possible because of pressures from the Palace. I need you to get us prepared for when they come."

"What can I do?"

Craig Trebilcock

"It requires your accounting skills. Let me explain…"

Chapter 23

Lashkar Gah, Helmand Province, March 2016

Trevanathan was impressed that events played out as Jennifer Reed had predicted. He was indeed summoned to General Crist's office the next morning, to be briefed on suspicions that supplies were being redirected from the 225th Corps. The idea of Afghan corps commanders skimming resources for personal enrichment was hardly a new idea, but the scope of this suspected conduct was audacious. A confidential informant had come forward, claiming evidence existed showing over two-and-a-half million cubic feet of firewood had been stolen, and that the family members of senior officers were routinely siphoning off petrol from military shipments to run private gas stations in and around Kabul. Those same family members were allowed unlimited access to free gas, while selling the balance to the public. Munitions were being requisitioned at a rate that did not match the operational pace of the corps—a lethargic pace that could be verified by American drones, not the ANA's claimed level of offensive activity that would have won the war several times over by now, if true.

More seriously, the source claimed that food was being rerouted to the enemy in both Helmand and Kandahar Provinces on such a scale that the corps was becoming the *de facto* supply depot for the Taliban, while Afghan soldiers lived lives of hunger and sickness. Recent encounters between NATO and Taliban forces in the south suggested the insurgents were gaining increased access to Western weapons and ammunition. Taliban bodies were found with Western military rifles, whose serial numbers had been filed off to avoid tracking. Sensitive items, such as U.S. night vision goggles, had also been increasingly found in Taliban hands in Helmand. All these items were available from only one common source: 225th Corps.

Yet it was not only the scope of the thievery that raised the issue to the level of the COM, General Peterson. It was the timing. If these allegations were to surface in advance of the NATO donor conference, without someone being held accountable, it would be the last straw. Weak-kneed allies, such as Japan, would seize upon this news as their palatable excuse to leave the morass of Afghanistan, without worrying about long-term political cost or embarrassment. No one could blame them for choosing to not fund Afghan units that pursued illicit profit from the enemy, instead of battlefield success.

Yet, there were still political sensitivities that had to be observed in investigating these allegations. Afghanistan was a sovereign country. U.S. forces could not simply launch their own investigation inside an Afghan army unit. So, the COM had conferred with President Ghani, who had agreed to have his own investigators take the lead in the inquiry, with the Resolute Support counter corruption representative, Colonel Trevanathan, acting in an advisory role. Behind these niceties, the reality was that the COM had told Ghani that unless the source of the materiel drain was located, and someone held accountable, Western military aid would certainly end in July.

President Ghani was not happy with the timing of this development, but he also saw it as an opportunity. He selected the newly appointed commander of the Major Crimes Task Force to be his lead investigator. If Brigadier General Baz were to confirm a significant case of corruption, it might provide Ghani with an enforcement triumph to trumpet at the Warsaw conference, assuming he could do something about it.

Another member of the fact-finding team was Major Wasim, Major Brandt's old friend from General Sadat's office, representing the ANA's interests. The Afghan army connection he provided would hopefully minimize attempts at stonewalling by 225th Corps leadership. Efforts to coordinate the visit had been delayed a week already by the claimed illness of the corps commander, and a report from the corps intelligence section that the Taliban were planning an imminent attack on the base. But after a week had passed with no attack, the sense that this was the old Afghan slow-roll trick, rather than reality, led the Minister of Defense to announce that the investigation team was going whether the 225th Corps leadership cooperated or not.

Accordingly, as the ramp of the U.S. Air Force C-130 cargo plane lowered onto Lashkar Gah's Airfield, Colonel Trevanathan was accompanied by Major Brandt, Major Wasim, and Brigadier General Baz. The difference in the weather from Kabul was obvious as soon as the team stepped off the aircraft. It was only March, and the heat smacked them in the face. *This is like Iraq*, Trevanathan recalled, already feeling his uniform sticking to him, as dirt devils swirled across the tarmac.

As the investigation team walked toward the terminal, two HMMWVs entered the airfield through a gate next to the control tower. The vehicles turned toward the investigation party, then stopped twenty meters in front of them. A seeming giant dismounted from the lead vehicle and marched up to them.

"Command Sergeant Major Mahmood, 225th Corps," the man declared, stomping his boot heels together and saluting.

As the senior officer, General Baz took the lead, returning the salute. "Good morning, Command Sergeant Major." He then introduced the members of his team.

"Major General Rahman regrets not being able to greet you personally," declared the sergeant major. "He was delayed by a call from the Minister. He is awaiting you at the headquarters."

Trevanathan could not put his finger on it, but each time the sergeant major spoke, he felt like he was being told to drop and perform pushups. *Not his words, but his delivery.*

"Let us go. The general and the colonel will ride with me," the sergeant major said. He was halfway to his vehicle before anyone moved, leaving them to scramble to keep up.

Trevanathan climbed into the rear passenger-side seat behind the sergeant major, while General Baz sat behind the driver, a young, thin sergeant who stared straight ahead.

They rode in silence at first. Trevanathan sensed that an opportunity to gather information was being lost, so he broke the silence. "Command Sergeant Major, your English is perfect, where did you go to school?"

"Paris. My father was a diplomat, so I had access to the best schools." His tone was matter-of-fact.

"He must be proud of you, being the Corps Sergeant Major."

"He is dead."

Ouch, stepped on that one, Trevanathan thought.

"How long have you been here?" Trevanathan asked.

"Why do you ask? Is this part of your investigation?" The sergeant major turned in his seat and fixed Trevanathan with an unfriendly stare.

Undeterred, Trevanathan replied. "Yes. The longer you've been here the more *valuable* you may be as a witness." *Don't dance with me, buddy,* Trevanathan thought.

The sergeant major nodded, turning back toward the front. "I have been in Lashkar Gah for eight years. I have been the Corps Command Sergeant Major for three. But I'm afraid that you may have traveled a long distance for nothing. The case is already solved."

Trevanathan turned and raised an eyebrow at General Baz, who took up the conversation.

"Why do you say it is solved, Sergeant Major? How do you even know what we are investigating?"

"Sir," the sergeant major said, although it sounded like he was spitting the word. "There are no secrets in the army. You are here because traitors have dishonored this corps by stealing its equipment and selling it for their personal profit. Petroleum, yes? Firewood, yes? Medical supplies, yes?"

Trevanathan noted that the young sergeant who was driving was shifting uncomfortably in his seat. His fingers grabbed the wheel with white knuckles.

"Go on," Baz encouraged.

"Sir, you will find Major General Rahman to be a thorough officer. We have been tracking these irregularities ourselves for some time. He will be able to explain more, but we know who the culprits are, and are ready, with your assistance, to arrest them. They have betrayed their comrades and need to be put down like dogs."

"Watch out!" Trevanathan blurted. The young sergeant had driven through a stop sign into the path of a cargo truck. The truck swerved to the right, missing the rear of their vehicle by inches, as its horn blared. A burst of profanity exploded from the sergeant major's lips, as he cuffed the sergeant on the side of his head. "Pay attention," he repeated in English for the benefit of his passengers.

"My apologies, gentleman," the young sergeant mumbled in thickly accented English. His comment drew another censure from the sergeant major.

That's interesting, thought Trevanathan. Not many enlisted speak English over here.

Trevanathan knew only a handful of phrases in Dari, which included, "Halt or I'll shoot," "thank you," and "shut up." The sergeant major had distinctly said, "Shut up," as he glared at the young NCO.

After their near-death experience, the chance for further conversation faded. They arrived at the main entrance of the corps headquarters in silence, where an overweight, balding man wearing the rank of Afghan major general was waiting.

Major General Rahman greeted Trevanathan and Brigadier General Baz like brothers he had not seen for years. His embrace revealed surprising strength in Rahman's short arms. "General, Colonel, thank you for coming so far out of concern for my corps," he said in English. "It does my heart good to know that our efforts here at the front do not go unnoticed in the capital."

That's weird, thought Trevanathan. Never been hugged during an introduction before.

Rahman escorted the team up to his second-floor office where a nervous private waited to serve tea. The general's office was the usual senior officer's layout—a work area in one part of a massive suite, partnered with a U-shaped collection of velvet couches on which he received visitors.

In the middle of the U was a large glass table on which stood an ornate tea set and a tall pile of green leather ledgers. "Please sit," General Rahman gestured. "We have tea and ledgers for refreshment today." He chuckled deeply at his own joke.

"I do not know if the sergeant major had the opportunity to explain to you yet, but we have uncovered an extensive network of theft within the corps, which we have brought to a stop. Here is the evidence," he gestured at the ledgers.

"This is impressive," said General Baz, as he sat. "The ledgers I mean, not the tea." He laughed at his joke, which Major General Rahman joined. The sergeant major remained standing near the door, stone-faced.

"It appears that our financial manager, Mr. Rajish, was engaging in duplicity," continued Rahman. "I had long suspected him. His mother is Pakistani after all. But everything seemed to always add up. That is, until we discovered that one of our battalion commanders was working in league with him to divert supplies to private buyers. I'm afraid that several hundred thousand dollars were stolen before we detected it. These records were found in the battalion commander's office shortly after he was killed."

"Killed?" asked Trevanathan.

"Yes, my dear Colonel. Unfortunately, this is an unhealthy environment for those who do not fully think through what they are doing." The corps commander paused, while maintaining eye contact with Trevanathan, then continued. "Lieutenant Colonel Naveed's vehicle hit a land mine in Sangin while returning from a meeting. Everyone in his vehicle died. When his personal effects were being assembled, these records were found. One set shows what should be in the battalion's inventory and the second set shows what was improperly diverted with assistance from Mr. Rajish. A second set of records mirroring these was found in a search of Mr. Rajish's quarters. The connection is irrefutable."

The link between the two sets of records was indeed irrefutable. It had to be after the sergeant major ordered Daniyal to spend the late hours of the past two weeks creating the fictitious paper trail incriminating Rajish and the battalion commander. Lieutenant Colonel Naveed had indeed been killed by a mine, but that was merely a happy accident that was not involved with the corps' embezzlement scheme. His death provided a convenient fall guy, one who could no longer defend himself. The corps commander had planned to pin the blame on another brigade commander to whom he had taken a dislike, but this was much better. A dead culprit was much preferable to a live one, General Rahman realized, when informed of Naveed's accident.

The work of transcribing the complex financial records was sufficiently voluminous that Daniyal was left in the office alone until the early hours each morning copying helpful sections of the red corps ledgers into the fake green ones, before returning both sets to the sergeant major's safe. Not everything was copied—just enough to provide a taste of truth to the alibi.

"And where is Mr. Rajish now, sir?" asked Major Wasim.

General Rahman looked irritated for a moment at being questioned by a mere major but quickly recovered his jovial veneer. "He has fled, I am afraid. Missing. He is apparently aware of my displeasure in his actions tarnishing the reputation of this corps. And that is where you gentlemen can help me. If we can locate him and give him the opportunity to admit his wrongdoing, the honor of this corps can be restored." General Rahman looked about the room with great affection, as if a group of old friends had agreed upon the most reasonable idea in the world.

General Baz spoke up. "Sir, you have my personal guarantee that we will locate this villain Rajish and ensure that justice is done. May we take these records with us back to Kabul?"

"Certainly, certainly," General Rahman replied. "That is why I brought them here. I want to assist in any way I can. Now I apologize, I have been a bad host and let business precede tea. "Private," he snapped. "Pour."

Only half the tea made it into the narrow cups due to the private's shaking hands. He had been brought in from the mess hall at the last moment to perform these unfamiliar duties after the sergeant major had reminded General Rahman that using his usual tea boy, dressed in a girl's silks, might lead to awkward questions from their American guest. After the table was sufficiently doused with tea, Sergeant Daniyal was summoned to complete the service, with the private dismissed under the sergeant major's menacing glare.

Daniyal had endured so much in the past year that pouring tea for a group of senior officers was nothing to him. *I've been kidnapped, beaten, shelled, and forced to conspire with the enemy. What is pouring tea?* In such meetings the person who serves tea is usually invisible amid the business. Yet something about this young sergeant struck Trevanathan as different. His knowledge of English. His reaction in the vehicle when the sergeant major had spoken about catching the real perpetrators. That was an overly convenient story that had yet to convince the colonel. *There's intelligence there,* Trevanathan thought. *I wonder if it hides a story worth knowing?*

Due to the layout of the room, the young sergeant had to step in front of Trevanathan to hand him his tea and obligatory stale cookie. "Tasakor,[85] Sergeant Daniel" Trevanathan said in a low voice. The young NCO met his gaze. Daniyal wanted to tell him, *"This is all a lie. Don't believe it. They killed my friend Azir."* But he could only stare silently into the colonel's eyes, his hand on one side of the saucer, the colonel's hand on the other. Trevanathan could sense a message in the eyes but didn't know what it meant.

"Sergeant! You can return to your duties," commanded the sergeant major. Startled, Daniyal released the saucer and stepped back. Before he turned away, he saw the colonel's camouflage backpack next to the couch. He looked from the backpack to the colonel's face and back again. "You are welcome, my Colonel," he stated in English, before exiting the room.

The meeting lasted perhaps another hour, as Major General Rahman detailed how the ledgers explained each step of the conspiracy by Rajish and the dead battalion commander. Trevanathan felt increasing irritation as General Baz nodded and smiled with each explanation, rather than asking any probing questions. He was doubly irritated when Baz declared that their trip would now be cut short, since all the answers lay before them.

On the flight back to Kabul, Trevanathan chose a moment when Major Wasim had gone to the latrine to question General Baz. "You seemed persuaded by the story we heard in the corps commander's office," Trevanathan opened.

"Did I?" laughed Baz. "Or maybe I didn't want to hit a land mine like that battalion commander, eh?"

"So, you don't believe them?"

---

[85] Tasakor – Dari for "Thank you."

"Do you, Colonel?" Baz narrowed his eyes.

"No. It's all too tidy. 'The bad guy is dead. Nothing to see here.'"

Baz steepled his fingers and spoke to the air above his seat. "This is the way the game is played. They are obviously lying. They know that I know they are lying. But they also expect me to take their silly ledgers and wave them around Kabul as irrefutable proof that they are innocent. If you look closely at the ledgers, one can see they are recreations." General Baz pulled a green ledger from his bag and opened it for the colonel. "See, there are ink smudges in the same place on the edge of many pages where the writer had ink on the side of his hand. Yet those separate entries were supposedly made on many different days? Did the ink stay wet on the writer's hand across multiple days? No. These pages were all created at the same time. For us."

"Very good," commented Trevanathan, leafing through one of the green ledgers and noting what Baz described.

"If I do as they expect, I will see a large anonymous gift in my accounts that will put me well on the way to buying my next promotion," said Baz. "It will appear without explanation and there will be no doubt as to its source."

"And if you don't?"

"Perhaps they will kill me, or more likely someone close to me, as a sanction for breaking the unwritten code. Which is why you need to get me those visas, my friend. The axe cannot drop on Rahman until my family is safe."

"I spoke to my contact at the British Embassy. She is working it. I have found her to be very persuasive, and if you are OK with me explaining this new development, I am sure it can be expedited."

"Certainly."

"She said that she needs the full legal names and birthdates of your wife and children exactly as they appear on their Afghan passports. Can you get that to me?"

"Of course, I can give that to you now."

"Great. Let me get my notebook." Trevanathan pulled his backpack from beneath his seat and unzipped it. He had to double-check that he had grabbed the right bag, as there was a red leather ledger inside.

Chapter 24

Lashkar Gah, Helmand Province, April 2016

Daniyal prepared for the next special mission as before. He became familiar with the German cargo truck, which differed only superficially from the prior Romanian one. As the possible day of the mission neared, his anxiety increased. He expected to be summoned to the sergeant major's office at any moment for an interrogation about a red ledger missing from the supply cabinet. He knew he would not be able to withstand the sergeant major's probing glare. Yet, nothing happened. Now, twelve days after being informed of the new mission, he was driving the German truck toward the camp's rear gate, with the sergeant major leading in his HMMWV. The sun was still above the horizon, but the sky was taking on a pinkish hue as evening approached.

As they exited the base, Daniyal noticed a weathered magpie, sitting on the rusty perimeter fence, cocking its black head to look at him. "Go away, bad omen," Daniyal declared out his open window. "You have brought me enough bad luck."

The black and white bird chortled a response in its throaty, mocking voice. To Daniyal's discomfort, the magpie took to the air and flew beside the truck for a few seconds, continuing its raucous song, before peeling away. He shuddered. *All superstitions*, he tried to convince himself.

Following the sergeant major's vehicle, Daniyal found himself wondering why he had risked his life giving the ledger to that American. *I don't know why I did it. No, that is a lie. I know exactly why. Azir. Azir died because of the greed that defines the corps. We did our duty. We had manned our post. We had tried to summon help. But we were betrayed. When we fired the flare signaling enemy on the perimeter, the headquarters had not sent help. Had the corps commander been pleasuring himself with the tea boy, or just planning his next act of treason when the barrage was ordered? The salvo obliterated the entire area, making it clear that both the enemy and the corps' soldiers were equally expendable.*

What Daniyal didn't know was why he had trusted the American colonel, a man he had never met before. If the colonel had pulled the ledger out of his pack at any point before departing and asked, "What's this?" *I would now be dead. Something in his manner...? Maybe I'm a fool. Maybe I have a death wish?*

As the kilometers drifted by, Daniyal felt the weight of the anxiety of the past several days. It had taken him eleven nights to copy the records from Mr. Rajish's red ledger into the replacement volume that now sat in the sergeant major's safe. His work had been slowed by the need to also create the fake green ledgers the corps commander had given to the investigators. Frequently, he had despaired that he would not finish either task in time. Sheer determination, and fear of discovery, helped him finish the job the day before the investigation team arrived. He had to send Mr. Rajish's original red ledger with the American colonel, knowing a copy in other handwriting might be discredited as a fake.

Swapping the two red volumes had been easy enough, as he had late-night access to the sergeant major's safe. Getting one into the American's bag had been no challenge either, as one of his *prestigious* jobs was loading the bags of VIPs for transport to the flight line. But once the switch had been made, he knew that if the corps commander or the sergeant major made a thorough inspection of the ledgers, his copy might not survive their scrutiny, despite his best efforts to mimic Rajish's handwriting. Each day since the switch he had felt like a man awaiting the gallows. Would his duplicity be discovered before he could get away?

Despite the fading light, Daniyal thought that they were driving the same route as his prior "special mission," although he could not be sure. There were so many turns. He suffered a brief moment of terror when the thought crossed his mind that the sergeant major might be taking him into the wilds to kill him. *Maybe my switch has been discovered*, he thought. He breathed easier when he recognized the walled compound, and the sergeant major pulled aside after giving him the same instructions as before. "Take the right-hand turn down the narrow road. Speak to no one." The bicycle was again there. As he turned onto the narrower road, Daniyal wondered, *I should be nervous, so why do I feel such relief? I am driving a truck filled with unstable munitions on a bumpy road to meet the enemy. Yet I feel free.*

Daniyal slowed as he neared the end of the road, where he had met Doctor Baseer. He was looking forward to possibly seeing him again. *So strange that a man who is my enemy seemed to be so compassionate.* In the dim light of his truck's running lamps, he appeared to be alone, however. No one was on the rocky ledge.

Daniyal felt concern building. *This is not what...*

"Get out of the truck!" a harsh voice ordered from the darkness. Daniyal turned off the key and slowly dismounted, bringing his backpack with him. *This is not the doctor.*

"On your knees," the voice ordered.

"I was told to deliver the truck and walk away," Daniyal spoke to the darkness.

A sharp blow to the side of his head dropped him to the ground. "Tie his hands," he heard the same voice ordering, as his head spun. Two men threw him on his belly and tightly bound his hands behind him.

"Kill him. He's a sergeant," a deeper voice on his right offered. A foot plowed into his abdomen from the left side–*Yes, definitely two*, confirmed Daniyal.

Daniyal tried to remind them who he worked for. "My commander will..."

"'Your commander likes little boys,' is that what you want to say?" laughed the man on his right before smacking Daniyal hard on the back of his head, driving his face into the dirt.

"Don't damage him too much," ordered the sharp voice.

"Only a little," laughed the man on the right, to whom Daniyal was taking a growing dislike.

"What's in the bag, sergeant?" asked the sharp voice. "A weapon?"

Daniyal spat, his lips and teeth packed with dirt. "No, just clothes."

"Check it," the sharp voice ordered.

There was a pause and the sound of rustling. Daniyal could not see and dared not raise his head in fear of giving the man on his right an excuse for further entertainment.

The voice behind Daniyal reported, "Yes, clothes, and money...a lot of money. Child of a dog!" The man swore. "Everything is covered in dried blood."

There was silence for a moment. Daniyal could then see the tips of sandals before his eyes. "Sit up," ordered the sharp voice. Daniyal struggled to comply but failed. Two hands grabbed him and roughly pulled him to a sitting position.

"Tell me a story," the man with the sharp voice ordered. "And don't lie. It makes me unhappy."

Daniyal hesitated. "I'm dead either way. So, you can fuck each other," he replied calmly.

"Wrong answer."

An iron grip seized Daniyal's left hand, seconds before a searing pain shot up his arm. A scream burst from his lips, as his hand throbbed and cramped into a claw.

"That is one finger. You have nine remaining. You don't want to make me ask the same question nine more times. Why is the clothing and money bloody?"

"This is taking too long," growled the man from his right. "Someone may have heard his scream. We need to go. Kill him."

A blanket was thrown over Daniyal's head. Beneath it a second face appeared, holding a dim flashlight. Daniyal knew the blanket was being used to shelter the white light. The man's breath was foul. His face was heavily scarred beneath a black beard. A patch covered one eye.

The remaining eye was piercing, even more so than the sergeant major's glare. "I need to know what is happening here. I need to know if my men are in danger. You are going to tell me. If you hesitate, I will cut off each of your fingers and then your balls. You will tell me. It is simply a matter of how many body parts you will lose before you become wise." It was the sharp-voiced man, Daniyal recognized.

It was almost enough to get his foul breath out of his face to motivate Daniyal to break his silence. "I'm deserting," he blurted. "After I walk back up that road, I am leaving the shirt in the road to make it look like I was killed by you, or bandits. It doesn't matter."

"I don't believe you."

"I can't help that. Check the shirt. It has bullet holes in the front and back. I pulled it out of the hospital waste bin and sewed my name on it."

The man disappeared, then returned.

"Why such a charade? Why not just disappear, like everyone else? Buy a seat on the famous coward's bus?"

"I know too much," said Daniyal, instantly knowing the words were a mistake. "I work for the sergeant major…"

"I know who you work for. Do you not think we have people within your camp? We also know this truck is full of worthless munitions."

"Then you know what I do. If I desert, they will hurt my family. They will hurt my mother, brother, sisters. To make me come back…or to punish me if I don't. If I am believed dead, then maybe they will be left alone. I can maybe go home someday."

"You ask a lot in Afghanistan," the one-eyed man replied. He held Daniyal's gaze, as if assessing a horse at the market. Then the light went out and the man was gone.

Daniyal heard intense whispered voices, before the conversation ended with a declaratory, "Enough!" from the sharp-voiced man.

The blanket was whisked from his head, and he could feel the iron grip on his hand again. "Nooo," moaned Daniyal, anticipating the coming pain.

"Silence, donkey," whispered the deep-voiced man. "I am binding your wound. Tomorrow, the Hajji will probably kill you, but tonight I bind your wound." He snickered at his own joke.

"Bring him. Leave a bloody 500 Af note on the ground with the shirt," the sharp-voiced man ordered. "Then bring down the pack animals. We will take what is useful and leave the rest."

Chapter 25

Unknown Location, Afghanistan-Pakistan Border, April 2016

Daniyal awoke. His face was pressed into the dirt with a stone wall inches from his nose. Only his right eye seemed to be working, as the other was caked shut with dirt. He was desperately thirsty, and his tongue felt too big for his mouth. His hand, still tied behind his back, throbbed in waves of pain radiating up his arm. He tried to shift his position, which sent pain shooting through ribs that had endured being tied across the back of a donkey for several days.

"Salaam Alaikum,[86] my friend," greeted a familiar voice behind him. "I see your career as a truck driver has come to an end."

"Doctor Baseer?" Daniyal croaked through parched lips.

Two strong hands grabbed him beneath his arms and helped him to a sitting position. "Indeed. Now, have a drink," the doctor offered. Daniyal opened his mouth and drank greedily from a stream of water from a goat skin.

"That's enough for the moment," Baseer cautioned, stopping the flow before Daniyal was ready. "Your body needs to adjust."

Remembering his manners, and with his voice returning, Daniyal replied, "Alaikum Salaam. It appears so. But it is good to see you again, Doctor."

"Is it? I would have thought talking with the *enemy* would not be your wish." Baseer smiled, remembering their first conversation.

"Well, my friends don't cut my fingers off," Daniyal countered.

"Really? They did not tell me. Let me see." The doctor was suddenly all business. He cut the ties behind Daniyal's back and laid the bandaged hand on a plastic tray across his lap. "Don't try to flee," he warned. "There are guards outside who would happily kill an ANA

---

[86] Tr. - Peace be unto you.

sergeant." Daniyal saw that they were in a small cave, perhaps four meters across, that connected to a larger cavern through a narrow gap in the stone wall.

Baseer unwrapped Daniyal's hand and bent down to sniff it. He wrinkled his nose and sniffed a second time. "No gangrene, but an ugly wound. You should have kept it clean. The danger of infection is still high."

"My nurse was the same man who cut off the finger to get me to talk, so my hygiene hasn't been a high priority," replied Daniyal. It had taken four nights to reach this location, wherever it was. Daniyal only knew they were moving east by the position of the rising sun each day. His hosts would not travel openly during daylight hours and knew places to hide that were big enough for them and the animals carrying their recently-acquired supplies. There had been an ongoing debate during those days between the sharp-voiced man and the one who enjoyed kicking him, over whether to speed their journey by killing him.

The doctor opened a small canvas bag sitting on the ground near the gap in the wall. He pressed a large, oblong pill into Daniyal's good hand. "Take this, and don't tell anyone I gave it to you—it will prevent infection. Our drugs are not plentiful and giving them to an enemy soldier would be frowned upon."

"Even though my army provides them?"

"Even though," Baseer replied.

"Where are we? Is this still Afghanistan or are we across the border?" asked Daniyal.

"It is best for someone in your situation to not ask too many questions."

Daniyal nodded, understanding.

"I can't figure out why you are still alive," the doctor said. "The man who led that mission has no love for your army. I have seen him do much worse than take a finger from a captive."

"Muhammad? That's what the others called him."

"Yes. Your army killed his brother the night before his wedding. That's where he lost his eye too, I hear," said the doctor. "Let me see how much you can move your hand," Baseer directed.

Daniyal complied, slowly stretching his palm flat, despite the pain from the missing index finger. "They kill everyone's family. So do those." Daniyal waved at the back of a sentry now visible in the larger cavern room. "No one is innocent."

"So, you never killed anyone?"

"I'm an accountant. Or would have been, had I been allowed to graduate." I'm not sharing too much, even with this doctor, Daniyal decided. He is very good at putting people at ease.

"Accountants can kill, too," Baseer observed, as he began to clean the wound.

Daniyal hissed through his teeth as the disinfectant did its work.

"Maybe," he replied, his eyes watering from the pain. "But I am done with this war. Who has the power? Who wants it next? Who wins or loses? It's all the same. For me and my family it is only a choice of who will hold the whip. I want a life, a family. For them to be safe and not killed by the government—or *these*." He gestured toward the guard again.

"You ask for much…" the doctor replied.

"…in Afghanistan," Daniyal finished his sentence. "Yes, you're not the first person to tell me that."

"Maybe someday when the foreign troops leave, you can have those things. Until then…"

Daniyal snorted. "Let me ask you this, Doctor, who do we hold responsible for the Afghanistan we live in now? Do we always get to blame the foreigners? The Russians, Americans, British? Or the Pakis? Because I don't see any foreigners here right now. I'm a prisoner in a hole with nine fingers from an Afghan knife, running from an Afghan commander who is stealing money from the Afghan people. You're pulling Afghan bullets out of Afghan bodies. Isn't it *convenient* we have so many foreigners to blame for our troubles.…" Daniyal's voice trailed off.

"You know much for a young man," a gravelly voice interrupted. Daniyal looked up to see an older man with a prominent gray and white beard standing in the space between the two caves. He wore an off-green waistcoat and turban with white trousers and a matching shirt that fell to his knees. He leaned on a worn wooden cane. "I am Hajji Khan. You are the soldier, yes?"

"Yes," replied Daniyal in a low voice. The Hajji was an impressive-looking man. Some of his eyebrows were as long as some men's hair and turned up at the corners to give the elder a distinct owl-like appearance.

"I wanted to confirm that, as you sound more like a philosopher than a soldier."

Daniyal said nothing.

"Salaam Alaikum, Hajji Khan," greeted the doctor. "This is the soldier I spoke to you about from my last mission. He has an unhealthy habit of telling the truth."

"Hmm, that is very unhealthy in a nation at war. So, what am I supposed to do with this truth teller?" asked the Hajji, observing Daniyal closely. "I cannot let him go. He has seen too much. I do not want the ANA to know we took him, as they may feel that breaches our agreement– even though their truckload of worthless shells is also a breach. And I have no need for philosophers. Muhammad says he may have valuable information. Is that true?"

"I am not a fighter, Hajji," replied Daniyal, unsure whether to affect a tone of respect or defiance to this man. "I worked for the corps sergeant major. What I know is the money business of the corps, not their combat operations."

"Hah! Well, that is of little use to me. I am their best customer, so I know their business well. I suppose I will simply have to kill you," he stated calmly.

Daniyal was so numb to being threatened with his life, that he reacted to the words as if someone had asked him to pass the yogurt at breakfast.

"I could use him, Hajji," the doctor offered.

"As what? Does he have medical training?"

"Only that given to every soldier," replied Baseer. "But he can read. He was a student at Kabul University. I can teach him, and when we have many casualties, having another set of hands will free me to focus on the serious cases. He is intelligent. I can teach him the basics—how to administer medicine and treat minor injuries."

"So, he can be a...medic?" the Hajji asked, skeptically.

"Yes, yes, he can learn," answered the doctor.

The Hajji looked at Daniyal doubtfully. "He doesn't look very strong. If I grant this, you will be responsible for him. If he tries to escape or communicate with the outside world, he will be killed. No second chances."

"Do you understand?" the doctor asked Daniyal.

Daniyal had followed the exchange closely, recognizing that his life was being negotiated before his eyes. "I will not fight, but I can help your sick," said Daniyal. "I am tired of death."

"Hmph. There is plenty of death ahead for all of us," observed the Hajji. "Grow a beard. You look like a boy," he directed, before shuffling out of the cave.

There was a moment of silence as they listened to the Hajji hobble away. "Thank you, Doctor," said Daniyal.

"There are no politics in this medical area, do you understand? And no path back. If you try to go back to your old life, or to reach your family, they will kill you. And they will hold me responsible for speaking on your behalf," emphasized Baseer.

"I will not betray your trust, doctor."

"I hope not. Now let me finish cleaning your hand, before gangrene sets in and I have to cut more away."

Chapter 26

Camp Resolute Support, Kabul, April 2016

Colonel Trevanathan worked for General Peterson, the COM, but so did eighty-five hundred other troops in the country. Trevanathan had spoken to him only once since arriving five months earlier, but that was not unusual. The COM was spread thin, leading a fifteen-year-old war of several dozen squabbling allies, while trying to motivate the Afghan military into doing, well, *anything more* than sitting in their camps.

As the senior U.S. military authority in Afghanistan, Peterson's days were filled trying to satisfy the insatiable appetite for metrics, projections, and analysis from Central Command[87], the Pentagon, and The White House. But he was also bombarded with demands for information from 532 members of Congress, and the media. It did not help that he was also battling Ambassador McKinley's efforts to undermine his policies back in Washington, where a wary Congress was increasingly skeptical that the aging mission was worth the expense and political headaches.

In addition to the military and political demands of his position, Peterson was also the Resolute Support *fireman*. Every time Afghan forces were caught committing human rights abuses, or U.S. forces suffered casualties, his planned schedule for the day went out the window as he switched to media and political damage-control mode.

In comparison to everything else competing for the COM's attention, Trevanathan's mission had largely been a sideshow. *Until now*. The discovery of the red ledger, and the potentially explosive consequences for the upcoming NATO conference, placed Trevanathan at the top of the COM's calendar. Trevanathan had briefed Major General Crist as soon as a cursory translation of the

---

[87] CENTCOM is a U.S. Combatant Command with responsibility over the Afghanistan area of operations. Its headquarters is in Tampa, Florida, with a forward in-theater headquarters in Qatar.

document revealed a roadmap of how NATO money and equipment coming into 225th Corps was stolen. The records traced Western aid being diverted into intermediate holding accounts and locations owned by the corps commander before being liquidated and distributed as cash to General Rahman, Command Sergeant Major Mahmood, select members of the ANA General Staff, and various Afghan inspectors general whose job was to ensure such corruption was either prevented, or at least punished.

The trail of corruption did not end there, however. The red ledger tracked regular and sizeable payoffs to other logisticians, military investigators, military prosecutors, military judges, and virtually anyone who might play a disruptive role in enforcing accountability. There was a complex, interdependent web of co-conspirators who cooperated and grew wealthy from the war and by keeping their Western allies chasing their tails in search of individual culprits, when the entire Afghan military was built upon a foundation of fraud.

Hundreds of millions of Afs, totaling millions of American dollars in food, petroleum, medical supplies, ammunition, and other logistics, had been directed into accounts belonging personally to Major General Rahman and his family businesses—gas stations, foodstuffs, hardware, and heavy equipment. Other than maintaining double books, the general seemed unconcerned that the money trail was so obvious, a sign of his confidence that he would not be investigated by a government where everyone fed together from the same trough.

A list of corps supply vehicles was annotated, which although not stolen outright, were apparently allocated solely to support Rahman's businesses. Petroleum tankers that were supposed to support ANA vehicles in operations against the Taliban were frequently noted as redlined for repairs, when in fact they were daily hauling tens of thousands of gallons of NATO-financed petrol to Kabul to be sold at commercial gas stations owned and operated by Rahman's family. HMMWVs that had been listed as *destroyed* on official corps records were a primary tool to deliver smaller shipments of goods to civilian buyers.

Among the more disturbing revelations was that a significant quantity of medical supplies, food, and ammunition had been diverted to a recipient identified only as "H." It was not clear who "H" was, but he or they appeared frequently in the ledger, and often paid for their supplies by the kilogram. Payments made by "H" were often flown out of Lashkar Gah—flight numbers and destinations were included—to several military air bases jointly operated by the U.S. and regional governments across the Persian Gulf. The scope of the deception and profit was more complex than anyone might have imagined.

General Crist summarized Trevanathan's evidence to the COM. The colonel's phone had rung minutes later, with the COM's aide politely asking if he had time to see General Peterson the next morning at 0730? Trevanathan smiled. *Like I would say, "I'm too busy?"*

The COM's office occupied a suite of rooms on the first floor of a two-story, masonry and marble building in the heart of Camp Resolute Support, across from the camp's small park from the EF3 offices. Rose and yellow marble walls with dark wood stairways gave the interior an air of opulence, even though cheap military furniture and whatever tables and chairs could be bought off the Afghan economy filled its rooms.

Trevanathan entered the COM's suite, after having his ID badge inspected by a large military policeman at the entrance. General Crist was already in the snug waiting room, where the receptionist's desk was yet unoccupied at this early hour. "Morning, Bill," he greeted.

"Morning, sir," Trevanathan responded.

"Can I give you a piece of advice?" Crist asked, quietly.

"Yessir," the colonel responded, leaning in for advice.

"Don't screw this up," Crist replied, a mischievous grin on his face.

Before the colonel could collect himself, the interior door to the COM's office swung open and General Peterson charged out with the energy of a retriever let off his leash. "Skip, Bill, thanks for coming by. Come on in."

"Sir..." was all Trevanathan stammered, before his boss practically pushed him into the COM's office, pointing to a large, low chair across from the four-star's desk.

"Sorry to keep you waiting," the General apologized. "A certain senator back in D.C. likes to call me every week and tell me how to win the war. Since he was a Navy pilot thirty years ago, I need to listen with rapt attention.

"OK," the COM continued; "Tell me what we have." His eyes, suddenly all business, bore into Trevanathan.

"Sir, I was sent to Lashkar Gah to look into irregularities in 225th Corps."

"Theft, right? Don't sugarcoat it."

"Roger, sir. It's no big news that the ANA has a serious corruption problem, and a big share of what we give them gets siphoned off."

"Yep," confirmed the COM.

"What makes recent events different is that we've come across evidence that the scope of the corruption reaches to the corps commander level, as well as into the MOD four-star ranks in a systemic manner. Almost engrained into their daily operations—not *ad hoc*."

"Hmm, mm," followed the COM.

"The other thing that makes this significant is timing. The Warsaw conference is three months away. By then our allies are going to decide whether to sign up for five more years of support for this operation...or not."

"Great timing, huh?" commented Crist, shifting in his chair. Teeing up the issue for his boss, he continued, "So, what do we do? If we go public, we risk our NATO allies packing up and going home. It would be hard to blame them. Yet if we don't hold GIRoA accountable, we'll watch the mission bleed to death from self-inflicted wounds."

The COM turned and stared out the window at the park across the street, his mental wheels spinning for a moment before turning back to Trevanathan.

"Bill, how do we know this is true?" the COM asked. "Like no-shit true, not just probably true? Isn't it a bit convenient that the evidence to hang this corps commander walks itself into your backpack? All these guys have enemies. Political, tribal, and otherwise. How do we know we aren't being used once again to settle an old score by some malcontent, or the next guy in line who wants Rahman's job?"

"Sir, we didn't take this ledger at face value. It led us to other evidence–like the corps accountant. I'm working with the Major Crimes Task Force—Brigadier General Baz. We tapped his phone, the accountant that is."

"You tapped an Afghan national's phone?" The COM's eyebrows went up.

"Negative, sir. I just advise the MCTF. They tapped his phone, under Afghan law. From that tap we found out the accountant has an axe to grind against Major General Rahman. Apparently, Rahman kicked out a couple of his teeth over a disagreement about a prior investigation. MCTF brought the accountant in for questioning and the accountant flipped and validated the ledger we have as authentic. He said that medical supplies, weapons, and food are all being sold to the Taliban out of the corps. We have it on tape."

"OK, but doesn't the accountant have some bias? Hardly a neutral witness against someone who knocked out his teeth."

"Roger that, sir. That was just the start, but there's more. The ledger shows the transfer of fuel from the corps to private gas stations owned by Rahman and his family here in Kabul. NATO—*We*—give them the gas. Rahman diverts it and sells it for personal profit through the family stores. I...rather, *General Baz* sent his detectives to several of those gas stations under the ruse of getting a kickback for safety violations. Businesses are used to such shakedowns. While one of the detectives was distracting the manager, the other went through their shipping records. Those records corroborate the ledger. From them we have the date and the number of liters of fuel that corps oil tankers brought from Lashkar Gah to these gas stations. They are so confident of not being investigated they didn't even cover up the identity of the delivery trucks."

"Damn," the COM whispered. "They can get that info without a search warrant?"

"We had one, sir. Sometimes these tribal ties can be used to our advantage. I don't want to go into too much detail, but let's say that General Baz basically has an inexhaustible supply of search warrants in his top drawer from his cousin being a judge."

The COM laughed ruefully. "I guess we're finally learning to think like Afghans."

"We've a couple other sting operations underway with MCTF, sir, especially on the drug front. Looks like someone may be using some of our aircraft out of Helmand to smuggle opium for the corps commander."

"Who's supplying the opium?" Peterson asked, already knowing the answer.

"I don't have the evidence on that yet, sir, but there's only one group in charge of the opium trade in the south."

"So, you're saying this record shows we're providing ammunition and medical supplies that go to the Taliban, and then they pay for it with opium that's smuggled out on our planes?" Peterson turned and looked at Crist with raised eyebrows. "It's no wonder they never run out of supplies. We're their Goddamn ammo dump! It never made sense that they could bring enough across the mountains from Pakistan to supply an entire war. This makes more sense...unfortunately."

Trevanathan continued. "One last thing, which I know you are familiar with—ghost soldiers. Rahman's official manning reports, the ones that he sends to us for payroll purposes, claim he is at eighty-nine percent manning levels. It will take more investigation, but the ledger I received suggests that the corps is operating at forty-five percent manning levels. Rahman and his accomplices are pocketing forty-four percent of the salary money we provide because those soldiers don't exist. It's not just theft—they're operating at levels that are combat ineffective and getting rich off the deficiency."

The COM looked pained. "OK, what about the timing? Can we keep a lid on this until after the donor conference? As bad as it is, we can't afford for everyone to stampede for the exits. POTUS isn't going to authorize more troops—he's made that clear—and if our NATO friends pull out, I won't have enough warm bodies to hold this place together."

Trevanathan said nothing. He looked at Crist.

"Don't look at me, Bill. Tell the boss what you told me yesterday."

"Now is not the time to be shy, Colonel." The COM leaned forward on his elbows, appearing to increase his size. "I need your best counsel. The future of this operation might depend on it."

Trevanathan took a deep breath. "Sir, the old maxim is that out of chaos comes opportunity."

"'In the midst of chaos, there is also opportunity.' Sun Tzu," clarified the COM, with a smile.

"Roger, sir. My best advice is that we don't ignore this or delay it; we seize it as an opportunity."

"Explain."

"Sir, every country supporting this mission knows the Afghans have been stealing us blind for fifteen years. You aren't going to lose any allies by telling them a truth they know already. But imagine if we do something different this time. We not only hold the thieves accountable; we push *the Afghans* to hold them accountable. On the global stage. Instead of some lieutenant colonel or mid-level bureaucrat taking the fall, which is the usual theater, this time it is a two-star corps commander convicted in an *Afghan court* by *Afghan judges*. That change in the system will become the focus of our allies' attention—not the theft itself. And it's much more powerful than us just revealing the crime."

"That hasn't happened in fifteen years," said the COM.

"There's gotta' be a first time, sir, and I'm not saying that to be a Pollyanna. The conditions are right. We have this corruption court project underway, already. There is real-world pressure on Ghani to get his people in line or the NATO cash goes away. We have my people embedded into the police, prosecutors, and court staff as advisors, so cases and evidence don't disappear like in the past. That has never existed before."

"Corruption runs deep here," the COM said, almost to himself.

"This country is going to take a generation or longer to change the way it does business," Trevanathan continued, "but we have a tight window here over the next few months to bring a perp into the light who is undermining the war while betraying his own soldiers—committing *treason* against the sons of the Afghan people. If we can convict him before Warsaw, even our allies who are looking for an excuse to hit the exits may reconsider. Who wants to be the quitter when positive change is finally occurring?"

"There's a lot of 'ifs' built into that plan, Colonel. They could equally say, 'this validates my instinct to get out of this cesspool,'" the COM observed.

"Absolutely, sir. But what operational plan doesn't have risk? I can't guarantee success. I can guarantee that if we try to keep a lid on this current corruption and the word gets out—which it always does in Kabul—the fallout will be worse. We *will* lose our allies and someday soon we'll be sitting across from a Congressional panel back in D.C., answering questions under oath as to why we covered it up."

"Bill..." cautioned Crist.

"No, Skip. I asked the colonel for his unvarnished advice and he's giving me both barrels of it." The COM's face creased in thought for a minute, then relaxed. "We're going your way, Bill. It's the smart way and the right way. Those two things don't always align, but it's nice when they do. What do you need from me?"

"Something big, sir. The President—Ghani—needs to be on board 110 percent. There can't be any of the usual back-alley deals on this one. No agreeing to it verbally but then resisting it behind the scenes, like they usually do. No payoffs, no favors, no old political debts being satisfied to make cases go away. This corps commander needs a fair trial, but if he is convicted, we need his head, as a deterrent to all the other corrupt generals and ministers. That's how we keep *our* allies."

"He's a pretty big fish to make your test case," observed the COM. "Going to be a lot of political fallout."

"That's why it's worth it, sir," emphasized Trevanathan. "It's time to be audacious. General Rahman is getting rich off the suffering of his men. That's a measure of how far things have fallen. If this is only a show trial with no real-world consequences, we may as well not do it. If we only go after low-level offenders, we may as well not do it. Because it won't change the culture of impunity and it won't get our allies to stay. They've seen all those reindeer games before. This is a high-risk, high-reward endeavor–there's no middle ground."

"Ghani needs to hear these things from someone he respects in an unambiguous message," Trevanathan continued. "I don't have the juice to deliver that. To him a colonel is someone not smart enough to have stolen the money to become a general yet."

The COM tilted his head and looked at Crist.

"I told you he wouldn't sugar coat it, sir," said Crist.

The COM nodded. "I'll make it clear to him this is a fork in the road. I believe it is. One path gives this country a future. The other is helicopters from the roof of the embassy."

"Great, sir," replied Trevanathan.

"What I need from you, Colonel, is to brief our senior staff. I can tell them the broad strokes, but you'll be able to answer their detailed questions. A lot of the senior leadership knows you're doing some sort of court project, but they don't understand how it fits into the strategic picture of stabilizing GIRoA. I need you to fill that hole and educate them how this is integral to our strategic plan."

"Will do, sir."

"Just leave the bit out about Congressional hearings."

Chapter 27

Presidential Palace, Kabul, April 2016

The COM's weekly meeting with the President of Afghanistan took place at the Palace in the west end of the Green Zone. It was a mere five-minute drive from Camp RS, but the two areas could have been in different worlds. The Palace grounds were lush and dominated by a nineteenth century stone palace. Crumbling ruins on the grounds suggested a continuous presence on this location even more ancient. Peacocks strutted the grounds, while the Presidential Guard, grim-faced in their distinctive tiger stripe uniforms, sent a message of strength. It took longer to walk across the massive compound to the President's office than it did to drive there from Camp RS.

The relationship between the two men was complex. General Peterson was a large, fit man, consistent with his career as an airborne infantryman. He had multiple combat tours in Afghanistan under his belt, including as a brigade commander in Helmand Province. He knew the Afghan people and respected their culture, while recognizing many flaws in their government. He respected Ghani's many political challenges, but also knew he could trust the President only so long as the U.S. presence benefitted Ghani politically. Former President Karzai had turned on his U.S. sponsors late in his presidency when it was politically convenient, and Peterson did not expect any better from Ghani.

Ashraf Ghani was a former World Bank bureaucrat who returned to his country after the Taliban were expelled in 2002. After serving in various roles under former President Karzai's regime, he became President in 2014, narrowly defeating his opponent. He stood barely five feet tall, although he would argue the point, being widely known for his mood swings and temper. He had been educated in Lebanon and at Columbia University, before teaching at Johns Hopkins University. Unlike the COM, who regularly delegated critical decisions to his subordinates, Ghani was notorious for trying to restrict virtually all decision-making authority to himself. Western critics accused him of being a micro-manager, while locals knowingly recognized that he who controls decision-making also controls the flow of wealth.

Ghani understood Americans and the tremendous military power the U.S. could wield on his behalf. He also knew that the United States cared little about Afghanistan, itself. They cared about retribution for September 11, 2001, and very much about not looking weak. Al Qaeda had made them look weak, and the last fifteen years of war had been payback for that embarrassment. He respected Peterson's competence, but also thought him too idealistic when dealing with Afghan political realities.

These dynamics were at play as the COM strode into the President's working office, past the sentry outside. "Good evening, Mr. President," announced General Peterson, saluting as was his custom, a show of respect. Ghani was standing next to his chair, behind an ornate desk.

"Ah good evening, good evening, my General, it is a pleasure to see you. I trust your family is well?"

"They are, sir. And yours?"

"They are well. Thanks be to Allah."

President Ghani's policy advisor, Thomas Breed, an Australian national and one of Ghani's longtime friends, sat on a red velvet couch to the COM's left. He nodded at the general, with whom he was well acquainted. Breed was always present in the President's meetings, sometimes participating, and sometimes the silent second set of eyes and ears, gathering his impressions for later discussion.

"I believe you wanted to speak to me privately before our meeting with the full staff?" inquired Ghani.

"Yes sir, I appreciate your consideration."

"Always, General, always. How may I be of service?"

"Sir, I know you are aware of this Anti-Corruption Justice Center project that is starting soon?"

"Yes, yes, a noble idea. Modeled on my Counter Narcotics Court, is it not? I was discussing it with the Chief Justice earlier this week.

We both believe it is a forward-thinking idea. I think that there are some issues with the banking system that deserve its attention immediately."

"I agree. However, there are some recent developments that are…sensitive in nature that may well affect the priority of cases."

Ghani inclined his head without saying anything, waiting for more information.

"I believe we are at an inflection point—in terms of political will—for certain of our NATO allies to continue supporting security efforts here."

"There are always those who follow and those who lead, which is why we are so grateful for your presence," said Ghani, taking his seat behind the desk.

"As you know, the Warsaw conference will determine which countries will continue to provide funding and logistical support for the war. The weeks between now and then are important to send a message that your government is fighting corruption. Specifically, that the pace and intensity of such efforts has increased from the past."

"Are you suggesting to the President that his efforts have been inadequate?" interjected Breed.

Not one to be intimidated, Peterson replied, "I'm not suggesting. I'm speaking plainly that come July you are going to lose billions in aid because the donors have already decided there has been only strong words and weak action. These nations have their own domestic problems, and those of Afghanistan are becoming secondary in their political calculus."

"Are they not paying attention to the prosecution of corrupt officials that have happened over the past two years?" Breed offered.

"You're wanting to have a debate with someone not in the room," Peterson countered. "I'm not here to argue. I'm here to deliver the message that your money is leaving. The Europeans are unimpressed when prosecutions are reserved for those stealing thousands of dollars, while billions are embezzled at high levels."

Ghani steepled his fingertips in front of his face, saying nothing.

Peterson turned to the President, adding, "Sir, I am not telling you anything that your own sources have not told you already, I'm sure."

"Perhaps not as impolitely," Breed added.

Peterson had had enough of the sniping from the cheap seats. "I'll be sure to be polite when you're being evacuated by my men, Tom. If those NATO troops leave, my President is not going to backfill them with American ones. Your army can barely hold its ground now. There's a strong possibility of a negative chain reaction that ends this government."

"General," interjected the President in a soft voice. "What is the path to a more positive outcome that you envision? I'm sure you have a plan."

"I do. There are only a handful of people right now who are aware that there is hard evidence that Major General Rahman of the 225th Corps has been stealing petroleum, food, and medical supplies from his corps to sell to private buyers. Those private buyers are believed to include the Taliban. He has also been embezzling soldier pay for ghost soldiers, an issue I have discussed with you previously in more general terms. I propose that you have him arrested and placed on trial at the ACJC as its first case."

"Rahman is a national hero," observed the President, his eyes widening slightly.

"Sir, Rahman has created a mythology that he is a hero and is trading on that. We believe he is a traitor undercutting the security and stability of your government. If you prosecute him and lock him up, there will be no one among the NATO donors who will want to back out in Warsaw once the message is sent that serious change has finally come."

"And if he is not convicted?" asked Breed. "No Afghan general or minister has ever been convicted of corruption before. You will have created a martyr and undermined the President's relationship with his military."

"No one has ever been convicted because no one has tried to enforce the law. Under your logic, no one ever will. Tell me how I make that into an argument to get the Europeans to stay."

Breed was silent.

"What is this hard evidence you have, General?" interrupted the president.

"I do not have all of the details, Mr. President," General Peterson dodged, "but my legal personnel have reviewed it and tell me it is very strong under your law. It is financial records and testimony from insider whistleblowers."

"This sounds extremely risky," Breed commented. "With no assurance of success."

"Only corrupt justice systems can guarantee outcomes in advance," replied the COM. "You need to let the system work, not preordain the outcome. The one thing that is a certainty is that if this action is not taken, come July, I will be standing here with a list of NATO countries who have announced they are withdrawing their troops and ending their financial support to your government."

"And America?" Ghani asked.

"I can't speak for the President or Congress on future political matters. Obviously, our country has a long history here. This is the longest armed conflict in American history. But, if the cracks begin developing with others changing course, I can't promise where things will be in two or three years, or under the next U.S. President. Neither of the top presidential candidates in our country have taken a strong stand on this mission. My suggested course of action is to stop cracks from forming in the first place, rather than trying to fix them when it's too late."

Ghani did not speak for a moment. He stared ahead. This was usually the time when he would turn to Breed and ask him for his views, if for no other reason than to buy time. Breed was expecting it and formulating his usual response about not rushing into a hasty decision. "My General, you will have my full support in this matter," declared Ghani, to Breed's surprise.

"General Baz is the commander of the Major Crimes Task Force, is he not?" Ghani continued. "I will meet with him and the Attorney General this week to inform them Rahman will be the test case for the ACJC. Neither guilt nor innocence will be prejudged. We will, as you put it, *let the system work*. This is, of course, for the greater future success of Afghanistan, and although difficult, it is right and just, despite the political allies General Rahman has in parliament."

"You have made a courageous decision, sir. I will let my men know of your support. If you have any questions, please contact me. Otherwise, I will prepare for the staff meeting now."

"Thank you, General," Ghani nodded, as Peterson departed.

Ghani continued to stare over his fingertips, as silence filled the room.

"That was...unexpected," said Breed, after several moments.

"Did I disappoint you?" the President mocked.

"No, but isn't Rahman your cousin?"

"The Americans can be naive, but that doesn't mean that they are always wrong. General Peterson is correct about wavering resolve among our funders. Our intelligence has been reporting that to me for a year, and it is this corruption issue that always leads the list of reasons. It is not the lack of battlefield success that is the potential wedge, it is the diversion of money and equipment," explained Ghani.

Breed had spent many years with Ghani. Enough to know that he never acted without a reason that benefited Ghani. The President could have easily deflected Peterson's request about the charges to "discuss it with my advisors," but he had immediately agreed with the COM. Breed's curiosity was piqued.

"Do you really think NATO will pull out, unless you charge Rahman?"

"Not the major players. Germany, Britain. They are not here for our sake. They are here because they need the Americans to stand with them against the Russians. That hasn't changed. Some of the minor countries might shrink. But they are unimportant."

"Still, their political support is valuable, isn't it, to defeating the Taliban?"

A sneer crossed Ghani's face. "You are naive in the extreme, if you believe that is what is occurring here." "It would be a disaster for Afghanistan if we were to defeat the Taliban. Over eighty percent of our budget comes from the Western nations. Do you think that money will remain if there is no enemy here to fight?"

Breed inclined his head, indicating he understood Ghani's point.

"If we were to achieve victory, it would be catastrophic," continued the President. "The Americans and their allies would congratulate us, have a parade, and immediately go home *with their money*. Our nation—this government—*my government*—would collapse within a year. There would be no services, no salaries, no economy. We would not be able to feed our army or police. Being surrounded by unhappy men with guns is not a healthy platform from which to govern."

Ghani paused to consider the future. "No. Our success depends on military victory being the ever-elusive carrot dangling just in front of the donkey's nose. Always promised—within view—but never delivered. An equilibrium of war is required for Afghanistan, where there is neither defeat, nor victory, but where the money consistently flows."

"They—the West—they'll tire of it eventually," countered Breed.

"They already have, but they are addicted. The addict does not continue to use the drug because he wants to, but because he doesn't know how to stop. He lacks the will to quit."

Breed always enjoyed it when someone else was being marginalized, but this conversation was making him uncomfortable. "What are they addicted to? The war?"

"No, they are addicted to their own myths. They have convinced themselves that victory is merely another campaign season away; that to stop the madness would dishonor those who died in 2001; that Americans always win." Ghani laughed lightly. "Watch their American movies and you quickly learn what buttons to push. There must be a hero, a helpless maiden, and a villain. We are the maidens. Not the preferred role, but I embrace whatever combination of their fantasies keeps the money coming."

Breed was having trouble following the analogy of Afghanistan as a helpless maiden but could tell Ghani was unusually philosophical tonight. "So, if that's true—that there needs to be an equilibrium in the war—when will the country have peace?"

Ghani looked at his friend, as a teacher regards a likeable, yet slightly dim pupil. After all these years in Asia, he was surprised that Breed was still so linear in his thinking. "When has this nation ever known peace? Our tribes have been in a state of perpetual conflict for hundreds of years. Before the Taliban it was the Russians, and before them the British. When there is not an external threat, we fight each other. If we attain your "peace" and the Americans leave, we will be gnawed upon like a bone between the Pakis to the East and the Persians to the West. The only thing that keeps us free from those future wars is the current war. That is an Afghan peace."

Breed hesitated. "I see what you are saying," he said, trying to be deferential to the President, who was increasingly irascible, the longer he was in office. *I think you underestimate the staying power of the Americans though,* he voiced only to himself.

Ghani continued. "Today, the Americans pay our bills, provide air cover when things go badly, and deliver our food and equipment. They fund our social programs, and there is still enough fat left over for *intangibles* if the current equilibrium is ever thrown out of balance. We have the full backing of the world's largest economy—*that* is stability. That stability goes away if we achieve *victory* over the Taliban. Ghani shuddered. "No, no, Allah forbid, I would not wish the peace you propose upon my worst enemy. We would lose everything."

Chapter 28

Camp Resolute Support, Kabul, April 2016

Trevanathan spent the next two days preparing and editing his briefing for the senior staff generals who ran the NATO mission behind the scenes. While he still had little use for the time suck of PowerPoint, he was going to be briefing a room of two- and three-star generals who consumed briefing slides like oxygen. To such an audience, the best idea presented on bad slides would be dead on arrival. So, he needed to condense the complexities of fifteen years' worth of Afghan corruption and the planned prosecution of General Rahman into a dozen unambiguous slides.

At a certain point, the editing and reordering of the slides became a blur, so he was almost relieved when Major Brandt appeared in his doorway. Almost.

"What's new, Chuck?" the colonel greeted, relaxing back in his wobbly chair.

The look in Brandt's red-rimmed eyes told him it was one of *those* visits.

"Who?" the colonel asked, bracing himself.

"Ford," was all the major could choke out. His eyes were welling.

"How?"

"One of those guards on the front steps of the MOD got him while trying to whack Porcher. Ford shielded Porcher and took the rounds. His vest stopped some, but..." Brandt shook his head, as a deep groan rose from his throat and paused additional details. "Fuck!" he bellowed, slamming his palm against the door jamb.

Trevanathan was gutted. He put his face in his hands for a moment. He breathed deeply. Neither officer spoke.

Major General Porcher had been called to meet with the Minister of Defense, because there was trouble once more in Kunduz in the north. Porcher was the senior U.S. military officer advising the Ministry of Defense on the best use of resources provided by NATO. An artillery officer by branch, he was the product of a West Point engineering education and a believer that if the Afghans were given enough ammunition, artillery pieces, and HMMWVs, victory was inevitable. He viewed matters such as courts, a legitimate economy, and civilians supporting their government as distractions to be worked out by people wearing ties after the war was won.

Neither Trevanathan nor Brandt could look at each other, as they struggled to adjust to the news. Brandt spoke first, recovering his usual no-nonsense demeanor after just a breath or two. "Corporal Hawthorne greased the bastard who got Ford. The Afghans then tried to lock them down in the MOD compound, but Hawthorne put his M4 in the face of the gate guard, and he let them out so they could get Porcher back to camp."

"Where's Ford now?"

"I don't know. Here somewhere. Probably the clinic. They threw his body in the back of the trail vehicle. He was KIA[88] at the scene. That candy-ass Porcher was screaming they needed to leave before they recovered Ford, but Hawthorne said he wasn't going anywhere without him. The team loaded him while all the MOD guards were still running in circles."

"Good for them."

"Agreed, but Hawthorne's probably going to get busted for disobeying Porcher."

Trevanathan shook his head. "Unbelievable. Let me know if you hear of that getting any traction."

Brandt said nothing.

Trevanathan breathed deeply, slowly regaining his composure. He slid his hands underneath the desk when he noticed them shaking. "OK, Ford's unit is going to be pretty stressed out today, so let's not add to it," said the colonel. "In a couple days I'd like to see Hawthorne and express my regrets—let him know how much I appreciate what he and Ford have done for me. I'd also like to get

---

[88] Killed in Action

Ford's family's address, if possible. Not going to write them now, but maybe in a month or so when they've had time to absorb this."

"Roger, sir."

"Dammit," said Trevanathan.

"Dammit," confirmed Brandt.

Chapter 29

Camp Resolute Support, Kabul, April 2016

In Afghanistan, one week often seemed to slide into the next, without much change. In other weeks, the world turned upside down in a few hours. So it was in mid-April, 2016. Trevanathan met with the COM on Monday. The COM spoke with Ghani Tuesday night. The news about Ford crashed the colonel's world on Wednesday afternoon, and the senior staff meeting was scheduled for Thursday at 1300 hours[89].

An additional complication to the week was that the enemy did not cooperate with NATO's neatly-planned schedule. Mild winter conditions that year allowed the Taliban to launch their spring offensive early in the far north. On that same Wednesday, the Taliban were celebrating victory in the streets of the provincial capital of Kunduz before the Afghan army even understood they were being attacked. GIRoA plans to defend the city, a perennial Taliban objective, were irrelevant when the enemy simply walked into the city in small groups, past inattentive Ministry of Interior guards, carrying their weapons beneath bulky winter clothing.

Later inquiry revealed that bribes at key checkpoints ensured that no one was too vigilant in screening the infiltrators. When the shooting began, the enemy was not in front of the Afghan army, but behind them, inside the city, intermingled with the civilian population. This triggered the usual reaction among the low-morale Afghan soldiers: they dropped their weapons, hid their uniforms, and found safe places in which to ride out the chaos. A few of the more elite units unsuccessfully tried to maintain the semblance of a defense until the Americans once again came to the rescue, but even those forces melted away by the second afternoon of the attack. Once more, what had been described since 2014 in Washington as an

---

[89] 1:00 PM local time. Afghanistan is one of the few countries that sets its time ½ hour off from the rest of the world. So, when it is noon in the Eastern United States, it is 8:30 PM in Kabul.

"Afghan war fought by Afghan soldiers," came down to U.S. military intervention to prop up the teetering Afghan government.

These operational developments meant that the COM would not be present for Trevanathan's briefing. Nor would Major General Crist, as both were scrambling to move supplies and reinforcements north. The Resolute Support Chief of Staff, Lieutenant General Kraft of the Bundeswehr[90] would lead the meeting, with Trevanathan representing the interests of CSTC-A. The British Deputy Commander of Resolute Support, Lieutenant General Smith, was also present, as were the senior advisor to the Afghan MOI, Major General Crantock of the Royal Marines, and the senior advisor to Afghan MOD, Major General Porcher.

Trevanathan knew all of these men and had a good relationship with each of them—except Porcher. Trevanathan's efforts to get on Porcher's schedule to explain why reducing corruption within the Afghan Ministry of Defense was important had been repeatedly rebuffed. Porcher's chief of staff had eventually made it clear to Trevanathan that his efforts to meet with the MOD Advisor would not be successful, and Trevanathan had stopped banging his head against the wall. But he kept notes of his attempts in case General Crist ever asked him about not keeping Porcher in the loop.

General Kraft opened the meeting, and after the usual staff reports on weather and supply levels, he turned to the intel section. "Intel, I understand there have been further developments in Kunduz?"

A bespectacled, balding lieutenant colonel in Air Force blue spoke from the far side of the semi-circular table that centered the room before a large drop-down screen. "Sir, all this information is preliminary, and none of it can leave this room, not even to your staffs with clearance. The COM wanted this briefed today to the senior staff because there's the possibility a real CNN moment is about to occur."

No one spoke, but the body language changed in the room, with each senior officer leaning forward. With that intro, everyone knew that whatever came next would not be good. A map of the Kunduz

---

[90] German Army. The Germans maintained a significant troop presence in Afghanistan as part of their NATO treaty commitment.

An Absence of Faith

area appeared on the screen. "At 0100 hours today an AC-130U aircraft out of Bagram engaged what it believed was a large concentration of Taliban fighters in Kunduz. Using its airborne weapons systems it destroyed *this* facility." A red circle appeared around a nondescript cluster of buildings.

The colonel paused and cleared his throat. "Rather...rather, than a concentration of Taliban fighters, preliminary indications are that the facility was a *Doctors Without Borders* trauma field hospital."

Someone in the back of the room uttered a low groan into the silence.

The briefer continued. "Remember there is an investigation underway and none of this is confirmed, but Doctors Without Borders has already gone public that dozens of its medical personnel and patients were killed in a barrage that lasted well over 45 minutes. They claim that they contacted our ground forces to identify themselves as a hospital, but that the barrage continued for another thirty minutes afterwards."

Another map, a larger blow-up of the hospital compound, appeared on the screen, with a central building circled in red. "The gunship crew estimates they serviced this target with 100 high-explosive rounds, mostly a mix of 105 mm and 40 mm projectiles. There are no known survivors there."

The room was quiet as the Air Force officer stopped speaking. For several moments, the only sound in the room was a quietly-squeaking ceiling fan at the back of the room.

"Jesus Christ!" thundered General Porcher, jolting everyone out of their silence.

Brigadier General Milligan, the command's public affairs chief, spoke in a firm voice. "The COM wanted you gentlemen briefed so that you did not get blindsided. While he does not want you to share any of the information with your staffs, as this is still under investigation, and as misinformation will grow and become distorted with the telling, he does want you to speak with your staffs *generally* about the importance of not communicating with family or friends back home when there are operational developments—good or bad—over here. This will certainly hit the American press within the next day and the email will start flowing in, asking questions. Anything one of your people puts in an email that ends up in the New York Times is going to cause a bad day around here."

Trevanathan considered the irony of a bad day being a quote in the Times, compared to a hospital obliterated by friendly fire.

"*Danke*...thank you for your reports, gentlemen. I am sure we will all be most mindful of information discipline on this matter," reminded the chief of staff.

"Colonel Trevanathan, I believe you have a report?"

Trevanathan was still trying to digest what he had just heard. From long experience he knew that incidents such as this could derail civilian and congressional support for an entire war. *I'm not sure my report is even important anymore*, he pondered. *We may all be out of here in three months if Congress uses this as an excuse to end this campaign. Destroying a hospital is a war crime—not sure "oops" is going to cover it.*

"Colonel, your report, please?" General Kraft repeated, pleasantly.

Trevanathan brought himself back into the room. He could see General Porcher had already gathered his papers and was moving toward the door. The MOD Advisor's continued lack of interest in the corruption undermining the war effort pushed a button with Trevanathan. Perhaps it was today's news or learning of Ford's death, but today he was not sugar-coating his message—especially knowing that the Afghan army was Porcher's specific area of responsibility.

"Yes, sir," Trevanathan replied. "We have evidence the 225th Corps Commander is stealing NATO aid and supplies to aid the enemy."

Porcher pivoted back and dropped heavily into his chair, fixing Trevanathan with a hateful glare.

That got his attention. Trevanathan continued. "The evidence shows that 225th Corps leadership has been systemically embezzling funds. Major General Rahman, the corps commander, has also redirected materiel to civilian businesses he owns for personal profit, while denying his soldiers the food, medicine, and military supplies they need to prosecute the war."

"Now, wait a Goddamn minute!" thundered Porcher. "You have no right to come in here and slander the reputation of one of the finest field commanders in the Afghan army. That man fights. He has killed more Taliban than any other corps commander currently in the field."

A calm descended over Trevanathan. He had never intentionally mixed it up with a general officer before: that was usually a very bad, career-ending idea. But something about Porcher, and what he represented—linear, unimaginative thinking that had drawn this war out over fifteen years—struck a nerve. Trevanathan had also been in Kabul long enough now to recognize that Porcher had been infected by the "My Favorite Afghan" disease.[91] He was deaf to any criticism of his Afghan counterparts.

"Slander isn't the correct term when it's true, *sir*. This isn't an opinion—we have the hard evidence. The fact that he kills some Taliban doesn't keep him from also being a thief...*sir*." The last word was gratuitous, but Trevanathan had learned if he hung "sir" on the end of a sentence and didn't call a general an asshole to his face, he could be fairly direct within the Resolute Support hierarchy. *What are they going to do, send me home?*

Porcher's face was purple. A blue vein bulged on the left side of his neck, and his eyes watered.

"It is shameful that you come in here, *Colonel*," he spat the last word, "and malign a man that I would trust with my life."

---

[91] The 'My Favorite Afghan' theory is a concept whose importance should not be underestimated in relating the failure of the U.S. mission in Afghanistan. The Resolute Support Headquarters was divided into different areas of responsibility – one staff section was responsible for coordinating logistics with Afghan counterparts, another for police liaison, yet another for financial affairs and economic development with the Ministry of Finance. The longer an American advisor stayed in Kabul, the more likely they identified with and came under the sway of their Afghan counterpart. This occurred to the point where the petty grudges and agendas that existed between bureaucrats within the Afghan government often became mirrored within the staff sections of the NATO headquarters. It was remarkable to observe the extent to which American advisors forgot what team they were working for, as they became flacks for their Afghan counterpart's agenda.

"It's important to know you have such a close relationship, sir, because he will need character witnesses." *OK, that was really unnecessary. I better tamp it down a bit,* Trevanathan thought to himself. "On the legal side of this, we are following a trail of facts and evidence, not weighing who we like or don't. The evidence shows that General Rahman is the central hub of a complex conspiracy that reaches across southern Afghanistan and up into the highest levels of the Defense Ministry. His activities may extend across this entire theater, but that has yet to be determined. What *is* clear is that he is bleeding away the fighting effectiveness of the Afghan military by diverting its money and supplies for self-enrichment."

"What does a lawyer know about fighting effectiveness?" shot back Porcher, venomously.

"I am not combat arms, sir. I do know that we all just heard a briefing where a group of Taliban walked through MOI and ANA lines and took a provincial capital with barely a fight. That does not sound like fighting effectiveness to anyone, can we agree?" Trevanathan's courtroom skills had awoken. The general either had to agree or look stupid denying the obvious proposition. Trevanathan glanced at General Kraft to see if he was going to break up this exchange. The German officer appeared intensely occupied with staring at his hands.

Porcher's jaw hung open, quivering.

Damn, is this guy going to stroke out? wondered Trevanathan.

Porcher did not get two stars by letting a colonel embarrass him publicly, however, so he shifted position and reattacked. "Colonel, you know MOD is my area of responsibility. Why have you not briefed me on these so-called claims? That's a failing on your part."

"Negative, sir, you've refused to meet me on the multiple occasions when I've asked to see you."

"That's not true," countered the general.

"My calendar is in front of me, sir. I contacted your office on December 6th, 12th, 18th, 27th, January 3rd, and January 10th for an appointment. On January 10th, your chief of staff finally said, "The general is too busy to meet with you for the foreseeable future.""

Colonel Bridle, Porcher's chief of staff, shifted uneasily in his chair behind his boss, recognizing the truth of Trevanathan's claim.

"I'm not here at your beck and call, Colonel," Porcher continued, trying to again shift tactics. "I want to see this evidence you have. Today. In my office. I'm not trusting *your* assessment."

"Sir, respectfully," everyone in the room knew that anything following that intro was going to be anything *but* respectful, "I'm not here to convince you of anything. As you've already acknowledged, you have a close and trusting relationship with this man. I believe you'd trust him with your life, you said. It's clear you've already made up your mind." *The old tools of cross-examination—use the witness' own words to box him in.*

"You will show me the evidence, Colonel, and you'll cease disparaging this patriot right now. That's an order!" Porcher crumpled a piece of paper in his fist, his voice shaking with rage.

The others in the room had slowly inched several inches back from the table, trying not to be caught in the exchange between the two officers.

Trevanathan replied, "Sir, with great respect, I do not work for you, and you are not part of this investigation, so I will *not* be going over this highly sensitive evidence with you, which has already been presented to the COM, who is in fact convinced. You have no legitimate role to review the evidence, and, if you were to see the evidence and the investigation was later compromised, *obviously unintentionally*, it could be unfortunate."

Trevanathan noted with interest that Porcher's face that had been a deep purple seconds before, had now drained of all color.

Tired of the exchange and Porcher's attempt to prove who had the bigger pair, Trevanathan turned his attention to others about the table. "Gentlemen, I'm here to brief you on this information at the direction of the COM. He has reviewed this evidence, and he believes that there is a bona fide basis to take this matter further. He asked me to brief the senior staff, so that you would not be surprised when this evolves into more formal proceedings. President Ghani is also in the loop and supports this course of action. The stakes are certainly high within the 225th Corps and the ANA, but they are higher for the legitimacy of the Afghan government going into the Warsaw conference later this year. The bad news of this general's misconduct actually presents a historic opportunity for the Afghan legal system to establish itself as legitimate."

Each of the senior officers was nodding in Trevanathan's direction, recognizing that this was a pivotal moment. Except Porcher, of course, who sat and stared blankly ahead, his face expressionless, realizing he had been outmaneuvered. While he thought he had been berating a colonel, he had been publicly impeaching the conclusions of the COM and President Ghani, and now looked a fool.

"The COM recognizes that the fighting will of the Afghan soldier depends on his faith in his leaders. Corruption destroys the work each one of you does daily to sustain the Afghan military. As with the briefing on Kunduz, this overview must be kept compartmentalized in order that the investigation may continue unimpeded. It cannot leave this room." Trevanathan dared to look at Porcher as he said these words, but the general was oblivious.

"The COM believes that you, his senior advisors, needed to know, as you are the ones most likely to be approached by Afghan officials seeking details on the investigation when the news breaks. We can't give them any inside information. The goal is to break through the culture within GIRoA that the powerful can do whatever they want without consequences. Their being left uncertain and uncomfortable is part of that reform process. They need to experience pain to break from a habit of viewing the national treasury as their personal account. We are using both human and signals intelligence to corroborate the significant body of evidence we already possess, and it is likely more arrests will occur." Trevanathan threw that last morsel out, as he did not know how far Porcher would take his misplaced loyalty to Rahman, and wanted the man to understand he might be recorded.

Lieutenant General Smith had remained silent during the jousting between Trevanathan and Porcher. When he cleared his throat, all heads turned toward him. "The COM briefly explained this situation to me before he was sidetracked by the Kunduz debacle. Although he could not be here, he wanted me to emphasize that this matter is of the utmost importance in his mind and deserves our attention *and support*. An army that does not trust its leaders is doomed to fail, as we all know." The Deputy concluded with a twinkle in his eye, "I want to thank our Cornish ambassador, Colonel Trevanathan, for bringing this matter to our attention."

"Thank you, sir," replied Trevanathan, resolving to escape through the door as soon as General Kraft adjourned the meeting. *Never presented a damn slide,* he reflected, realizing two days' slogging through PowerPoint had once again been a waste of time.

Chapter 30

Lashkar Gah, Helmand Province, April 2016

Major General Rahman was finishing his morning meeting with Sergeant Major Mahmood, when his office door swung open.

"I said not to interrup..." he snarled, without looking up.

Brigadier General Baz entered the room, accompanied by Major General Sadat and four Afghan military policemen.

"General Rahman, by order of the Minister of Defense, you are relieved of command," announced General Sadat.

The color drained from Rahman's face. He tried to stand but could not.

Mahmood did stand, his face flushing with anger. He opened his mouth, but no words came. Two of the military policemen carried assault rifles, which were now pointing in his direction. A third approached the sergeant major with handcuffs, while the fourth went to help General Rahman find his legs.

Brigadier General Baz spoke next. "Sergeant Major Mahmood, you are under arrest by the Major Crimes Task Force pursuant to order of the Attorney General and the Minister of Defense. You are charged with treason, embezzlement, and conspiracy to theft of government property. You are hereby remanded to the jurisdiction and custody of the Anti-Corruption Justice Center."

The sergeant major eyed his options, but decided active resistance was not realistic. He knew the system and that he could press the right buttons to be released before the sun went down. *Then there will be payback*, he thought.

Baz continued. "Major General Rahman. You are under arrest by the Major Crimes Task Force pursuant to order of the President and the Attorney General. You are charged with treason, embezzlement, dereliction of duty, and conspiracy to theft of government property.

You will be flown to Kabul and are under house arrest, effective immediately."

The President? Had Rahman heard correctly? *That's not possible.*

"This is...," was all he managed to squeak out before he and Mahmood were escorted out of his office. A young two-star Afghan army officer was waiting in the hallway, tapping his foot impatiently for his new office to be vacated.

◇ ◇ ◇

Sergeant Major Mahmood found he had been overconfident in his anticipation of imminent release. After the short flight to Kabul, he was not taken to the Attorney General's office, where he had many friends and business associates, but to an unfamiliar compound on the outskirts of the city. Before the afternoon call for prayer, he was brought before a panel of three judges, two men and one woman, who bound his case over for trial and denied him bail on national security grounds.

Mahmood seethed at the humiliation. *Handcuffs, ankle chains...do they not know who I am?* A military attorney was appointed to represent him at the hearing. That captain informed the sergeant major that his was a test case for the new anti-corruption court. That didn't sound promising to Mahmood, who was used to matters working according to *his* rules.

His anticipation of preferential treatment at the detention facility was also frustrated. The corruption center had its own detention facility, forestalling the frequent practice in Afghan jails of well-connected prisoners exiting through the back door in return for a gratuity. As he was led from the courtroom following the formal reading of charges, another sight surprised the sergeant major: that American colonel who had come to Lashkar Gah with General Baz was seated in the back of the courtroom, next to a blonde woman. *He's looking at me like I am a bug*, the sergeant major fumed, glaring at the officer as he departed, his ankle shackles clattering on the hallway linoleum. *This is all being orchestrated by the Americans*, he realized.

Mahmood had been driven to the courthouse from the airport with a hood over his head, but he was now being walked outside to a waiting van, with his head uncovered. Looking about, he saw that the guard towers seemed to be manned by Ministry of Interior personnel, but the compound also buzzed with American and British personnel, some military, and some civilians. *What is this place?* he wondered, as worry began crawling up his spine. *Where are the people who normally handle these things?*

His escort pushed him into a seat in the back of the van but could barely close the doors because of his size. Just before they managed to latch them shut, Mahmood saw Major General Rahman being escorted into the courthouse by two military policemen. He noted that while he, the *corps sergeant major*, was now wearing a filthy prison jumpsuit, the general was allowed to appear in uniform. *That little swine is no doubt living in his grand home, that my efforts paid for.*

Inside the courtroom, Trevanathan turned to Jodie Upton. "One down, three to go," he jested.

"Three? I thought only Rahman was still scheduled for today."

"He is. But yesterday the MCTF busted an Inspector General in the Interior Ministry. I didn't have a chance to tell you. We have him on a buttonhole camera promising to make an embezzlement case go away in return for a briefcase filled with nine hundred thousand Afs sitting on his lap. When they cuffed him, he dimed-out his deputy to try to make a deal, so we picked him up, too."

"Brilliant! How long do you think it will take before these *master criminals* start being more careful in how they conduct business?"

"I don't know, but now we have two generals, a corps sergeant major, and an MOI colonel on the chopping block. I expect that will send some shockwaves."

"Speaking of MCTF, I confirmed appointments for General Baz's family on the twenty-seventh at our consulate," said Jodie. "They are to keep it quiet, of course. We can't have a stampede to the exits."

"Excellent. I know you had to call in some favors to fast track this, so I appreciate it. The project would be dead on arrival if the head cop's family were abducted or killed."

"I'm happy for Baz. However..."

"Yes?"

"I've been asking myself can we call it success if we have to hide the family of the police, or the judge, or the prosecutor every time they simply do their job?"

Trevanathan looked down at his hands, a frown on his face. "You're right. We shouldn't get too intoxicated with the progress we've made. It's still a corrupt system from top to bottom, and they've years of work ahead of them. But it's a start, right?"

"Yes Colonel, it is definitely a start," Upton beamed, as the next case was called.

Major General Rahman did not intend to remain as stoic as his sergeant major. As soon as the case was announced, he jumped to his feet and demanded that the charges be dismissed. He slapped away his military lawyer's attempts to pull him back into his seat.

"This is an outrage!" Rahman continued in Dari. What he was saying was unintelligible to Trevanathan and Upton, but they could see the judges looking with impatience at the officer, who was waving his arms and raising his voice.

"Not a wise start," Trevanathan commented. "Rule number one: don't piss off the judge."

Rahman's blustering and table-pounding continued uninterrupted for five minutes, before his lawyer was successful in pulling him back into his seat.

The chief judge, named Massad, was a somber man in his mid-fifties, with a great wave of black hair. He spoke from a script to both lawyers. When Rahman attempted to interrupt, a chop of the judge's hand and a short admonition sent Rahman contritely back into his seat. When the judge finished speaking, all three judges closed their binders and departed the courtroom. Rahman hung his head.

The lead ACJC prosecutor was a young man named Abdul Malik, with whom Trevanathan was acquainted from screening staff for the ACJC. Malik had been a prosecutor in Herat in western Afghanistan for several years and had not been in Kabul long enough to be contaminated by the revolving door practices at the Attorney General's office—or so the colonel hoped. Trevanathan walked up to the prosecution table to get his feedback on the session.

"The judge has set trial for June 5th for both the sergeant major and the general," informed the prosecutor. "They will be tried together since there is a conspiracy charged."

"That's quick for such serious charges," said Trevanathan.

"The defense raised that argument as well. The judges were not sympathetic."

"What was all the drama about?" Trevanathan asked.

The prosecutor snorted. "The general did not appreciate that this was simply a preliminary charging and bail hearing. He tried to argue his case on its merits. He is used to being in charge, no?"

"What did he say?"

"Rahman said he was a victim. That the sergeant major and an accountant named Rajish were stealing from the corps to enrich themselves and set him up. He argued they altered records. He recited his record of victories over the Taliban and how he has protected the people, including this court, from the enemy's lash."

"The judges didn't look too impressed."

"They're judges. It is hard to know what they are thinking. But Judge Massad admonished him he would not tolerate future outbursts. He reminded the general he is on house arrest at the discretion of the court, and if he can't obey basic courtroom rules, they would revoke his status and jail him."

"So, now that things are finally moving, are you concerned about prosecuting someone as powerful as Rahman?"

"Of course, I'm concerned. I'd be a fool not to be," Malik rejoined. "It was much easier when all I had to do was show up and take a bribe." He half-smiled at the joke. "Now, I am positioned between the President, who I understand wants to make an example of Rahman, and Rahman, who has many dangerous allies. Thank you for creating this wonderful career opportunity for me, Colonel."

Trevanathan admired the black humor of the prosecutor. *If he can still joke about it, maybe we have a chance.*

"You can take great pride in what you're doing. It gives your country a future," the colonel offered.

"That's very inspiring," Malik replied, putting the last of his papers into a large folder. "Maybe they can carve that on my tombstone."

Chapter 31

Camp Resolute Support, Kabul, May 2016

Despite a carefully planned timeline to open the ACJC, the arrests of Major General Rahman and Command Sergeant Major Mahmood pushed the court into operation before its intended grand opening. In a country where the smallest details of governance were debated nonstop, often smothering any efforts at reform or efficiency, the opening of the Anti-Corruption Justice Center within just six months was indeed a geopolitical *Hail Mary*. The support of General Baz at MCTF, the unexpected, good condition of the Camp Heath compound, the influence of the COM and the President, and the leadership of Jodie Upton at the U.K. Embassy in mobilizing financial and political support with the other embassies, had brought the project to life mere weeks before the Warsaw NATO conference, which would decide the fate of Ghani's government. Had any of the key pieces not fallen into place, the game would be over.

The expected opposition from the U.S. Embassy to the court had failed to mature. Inasmuch as the Embassy hated the military stepping into what they perceived as its area of responsibility–legal reform–the Embassy's perpetual disengagement had sacrificed the normal influence a U.S. ambassador would wield. While the Ambassador's toady, Nicholas Deepak, did his best to convince the other Western embassies in Kabul that the sky would fall if the ACJC became a reality, NATO allies were tired of seeing their aid being embezzled. A State Department approach that was little more than running in circles crying "the sky is falling," was weak sauce to those tired of the war and watching their aid being diverted to enrich Afghan politicians. As the French Ambassador said to the INL representative, "Your best guidance is to give my wallet to the thief, so that the other thieves are not upset? *C'est merde*."

Jodie Upton organized the grand opening VIP event at Camp Heath for May 9, 2016. President Ghani and the Chief Justice of Afghanistan would cut the ribbon. The Attorney General would give inspiring words about a new day for justice. The COM would speak on behalf of Resolute Support. The British Ambassador would have his moment in the sun, as the leader of the international donor community supporting the project. Most importantly, representatives from every NATO donor nation, the European Union, and the United Nations High Commission would be treated to a VIP tour of the prosecutor's offices and judge chambers, with the principles underlying the corruption court being carefully explained by Afghan prosecutors, using a script of talking points written by Trevanathan's EF3 section.

Yet, despite all the work done on the project by the British and Resolute Support, Trevanathan and Upton reminded themselves repeatedly during their meetings that the long-term success of the court would be measured not by their work, but by the Afghans themselves—deciding that prosecuting corruption was in their own best interest. More than once, Trevanathan had used the training wheels analogy. "Anyone can ride a bike with training wheels. We need them to keep moving forward when they no longer have us as their training wheels."

Trevanathan was almost letting himself grow optimistic, a dangerous thing in Afghanistan. Having decided it was unlikely he would be poisoned by his barista—that would likely hurt business—he was walking over to the Blue Cafe on the first Saturday in May when his cell phone buzzed.

"Colonel Trevanathan" he answered.

A voice with a local accent said, "This is Jesus."

Trevanathan paused. *Is this a joke?*

"They are digging."

"Who is digging?" the colonel asked carefully.

"I do not know. But I hear them...at night. They started beyond the junkyard, and now they are almost to the wall."

The ACJC compound! The kid—Jesus. It all came together through the recent swirl of activity. "Jesus—*Hakeem*, right? Where are you now?"

"I am at my shop, outside the gate. They will not let me inside any more since the prisoners arrived."

"Can you be there tomorrow?"

"I am always here, General. I have a family to support."

"If I show up there tomorrow, can you show me where the digging sounds are coming from?"

"Most assuredly, General. Although I will lose a lot of profit if I have to leave my shop…"

Smart kid. Always has an angle. "I'll cover your lost profit, OK? But be sure about where you think the sounds are coming from."

"No problem, General. I know exactly. I listened for two nights before I called to be sure."

"Did you tell any of the guards at the compound? Any of the Interior Ministry police?"

"No, General."

"Why not?"

"Because they would not give me money." The boy giggled into the receiver.

"OK, Diamond Jim, I will see you tomorrow, probably in the afternoon."

"I am Jesus, not Diamond Jim," the voice sounded offended.

"My apologies, Jesus, I will see you there. Don't tell the guards and don't go near the digging tonight, OK?" Trevanathan didn't want the kid to get overly ambitious in his attempt to earn a few dollars and walk into something nasty, nor did he want the guards to tip anyone off.

Tomorrow would be an interesting day.

Chapter 32

Eastern Kandahar Province, May 2016

The twelve men moved in a loose line along the ridge, eyes looking all directions for anything out of place. They were behind schedule and dawn was approaching. Their nerves were taut.

"We cannot be caught in the open during daytime," Farzaad whispered to Muhammad. The bow-legged second-in-command was increasingly agitated, as he watched the sky lighten to the east.

"Do you think I don't know this?" hissed Muhammad.

"How is it possible that the police found our cave?" Farzaad fretted.

"Does it matter?" Muhammad replied. "They did, so we need to find new cover."

"I think it was the soldier," Farzaad accused. He turned to look at Daniyal, climbing up the path behind them. "He gave our location away."

"How?"

"I don't know."

"Then stop speaking foolishness. Did he not help set your shoulder last month?"

"Yes, but..."

"And he helped the doctor pull shrapnel out of your brother after he was stupid enough to trigger that mine?"

Farzaad did not answer this time.

"Don't let fear cloud your brain."

"He will not carry a weapon," Farzaad accused.

"Could he fix your shoulder with a weapon?"

"That is not the point. If he will not kill, how do we know his loyalty?"

"He has killed. That is why he no longer carries a weapon. Baseer told me. Each man must find his place in this war. He has found his. Let it be."

"I still do not trust him."

"Until the next time you separate your shoulder," Muhammad mocked, turning his attention back to the trail.

Muhammad knew that Farzaad was right about one thing. They needed cover. They were on a mission to establish a new forward headquarters in eastern Kandahar province. His men had been moving in the darkness to a cave they had used for earlier missions—one well hidden among these hills. But, on approach, they found it occupied by government paramilitary forces, who were not nearly as careful about making noise as the Taliban had learned to be. Perhaps it was a coincidence. Perhaps it was not. Either way, their mission was not to fight today, it was to find a new headquarters for Hajji Khan, so they kept moving.

Now, they were in danger of being caught out in the open. With few trails to choose from, they would soon be visible to anyone looking up from the valley. It was every insurgent's nightmare—open terrain during daylight. The next safe hole was twelve kilometers away. It would be mid-day before they would reach it, leaving them vulnerable that entire time. Muhammad looked nervously at the orange horizon. Aircraft would be up soon. Drones were always about. *Should we just shelter in the open? Movement always draws eyes. Or risk making it to the safe hole?*

A scream and the sound of tumbling rocks made Muhammad wheel about. One of the men had fallen, sliding down a steep incline toward a drop-off into the valley. The man let out a second, panicked shriek as he grabbed futilely for a handhold. There was none amongst the rubble, which slid with the man toward the edge. Muhammad held his breath as he expected the man to disappear over the lip, but at the cliff's edge he stopped suddenly, his leg catching under the ledge of a large, flat rock.

Muhammad leapt back down the path. It was that boy, Zaram. Farzaad's brother. *Always trouble.* He now hung partially suspended over the cliff, his torso in the air and his leg twisted at an ugly angle beneath the rock. And he was screaming again. *Damn him. He's giving away our position.*

"Help me, Allah!" Zaram shrieked, before his voice lowered into guttural, animal-like sounds.

That noise is carrying to every corner of the valley below, Muhammad knew. He started to unsling his rifle. One clean shot was preferable to a continuing chorus that would surely draw that police unit to them.

Before he could take aim, another man was sliding down the steep slope, a rope about his waist: Daniyal.

Muhammad cursed and shouldered his weapon, before descending the path. "What happened?" Muhammad demanded, as he reached the spot where his men had unwisely bunched together.

"I don't know. He must have tripped," blurted Farzaad.

"Not paying attention, again," Muhammad accused. "He is your responsibility. Now the world knows where we are."

Farzaad did not answer.

"Spread out, you fools," Muhammad ordered his men. "The enemy could be on us any minute."

"A rope," Daniyal called. "I need another rope." Baseer was holding the end of the rope tied around Daniyal's waist. Muhammad pulled another length from his pack.

Daniyal reached the boy. "Zaram. Zaram!" he shouted to get the panicked boy's attention. "I am here. You are safe now. I am not going to let you fall. Do you trust me?"

The boy, of perhaps twelve summers, nodded his head desperately, tears streaming down his face.

"I am going to tie a rope around your middle and through your legs and then your brother will pull you up. You and he will have lamb for dinner tonight. Won't that be good?"

Again, the boy nodded, his shoulders and head dangling over the edge.

"But I need you to stop screaming. You are going to bring the police to us, do you understand?"

The boy looked confused.

"The police we passed last night. They will hear your screams and come kill us. You must stop screaming."

Zaram nodded, but looked down into the valley, terrified, anticipating his fall.

"Don't look down. Look up the slope to your brother. He is waiting for you there. Your leg is hurt. When they pull you up it is going to hurt more, but you will live. I need you to swallow your pain. No screams. Understand?"

The boy nodded. Daniyal's reassuring words calmed him slightly, despite his fear.

Muhammad gently tossed his rope to Daniyal, making sure it landed above him. Daniyal was perhaps only ten meters below, but the slope was steep and unforgiving. Daniyal carefully wrapped it around the boy's waist and then through his legs, tying it off tightly so that the thin boy would not slip out of the makeshift harness. He had seen such a harness used before, but this was his first attempt at tying one. "Pull, but slowly," Daniyal called to Muhammad and Farzaad, waiting on the path. "I think his leg may be broken." To Zaram he instructed, "Grab the rope with both hands and don't let go."

It worked. First the boy's mid-section, then his shoulders were reclaimed from the precipice. As the men dragged Zaram slowly back onto the slope, Daniyal freed his foot from beneath the boulder. It was not easy, as it was already the size of a large gourd. Something was clearly broken.

The pain of his injury being dragged across rocky terrain was excruciating, but the boy obeyed Daniyal and did not scream. The color drained from his face, and he thankfully fainted after only a few feet.

Daniyal climbed back up to the path, aided by Baseer, and shaking from the adrenaline pumping through his system. He had not thought of the danger when he went down the slope, but now calculated a dozen ways he might have died, had the boy panicked or the crumbling cliff edge had given way. He put his head between his knees, while Baseer busied himself setting Zaram's broken ankle. As the events replayed in his mind, Daniyal turned and vomited…onto Muhammad's feet.

"You are a fool. Why do I keep you alive?" Muhammad said flatly, looking at his soiled sandals.

"S-So…sorry, Muhammad."

"You should have slit his throat instead of saving him," Muhammad criticized. "He has given our position away to everyone within a day's march."

Daniyal did not respond.

"Doctor," Muhammad addressed to Baseer, who kneeled a few feet away, tending the boy. "We must move. Now. What is his condition?"

"His ankle. It is a serious break, but not life threatening. With treatment he could be fine."

"I have no hospital with me," said Muhammad. "And I cannot leave the child to tell the militia where we have gone."

"He cannot walk. We could build a field litter, but it will be slow going," said the doctor.

"With us exposed in the daylight, carrying wounded, and the police following?" Muhammad frowned.

Baseer nodded.

"I will stay behind with him," interjected Farzaad. "I can find a safe place for him."

"You will not," denied Muhammad. "You know too much to fall into their hands."

"But I can…" began Farzaad.

"No," Muhammad cut him off. "You are thinking like a brother, not a soldier. I need you to take the men and go. We cannot stay here or remain in the open. Head for the next safe hole. Keep your eyes on the sky. That is where death will come from."

"And Zaram?"

"I will take care of it."

Tears welled up in Farzaad's eyes. He knew what had to be done. He knelt by his unconscious brother, taking his hand. "Goodbye, my brother. I will see you in paradise." Tears fell onto the unconscious boy's dirty face. Everyone looked away as Farzaad bent and kissed his brother.

Farzaad stood and snarled at the others. "Stop wasting time. We need to move. NOW."

The men lifted their packs and moved up the path, no one making eye contact. Several glanced back nervously toward Zaram until they disappeared around a bend. Baseer and Daniyal were the last with the boy, together with Muhammad.

Daniyal grabbed Baseer by the arm. "What do you have to cause sleep?"

"I have drugs that will put a man out for a half day."

"Give them to me. Please."

Baseer dug into his kit and produced two large, white pills.

"Thank you. Do you also have those canvas straps for carrying the wounded?"

"Yes, but Muhammad said we cannot take him."

"I know. Can I have them?"

Baseer produced the heavy straps, which allowed one man to carry another a short distance, on his back.

"Thank you, my friend. Be safe," said Daniyal.

Baseer headed up the path, as Daniyal returned to Muhammad's side.

"Go," Muhammad snarled. "I have a job to do. Alone."

"So do I," replied Daniyal. "I will carry him."

Muhammad regarded Daniyal with his one piercing eye. "No. We cannot be delayed by one man."

"I know. I will do it alone."

Muhammad snorted. "The boy weighs nearly as much as you do. Go with Baseer. I have no time for this. That militia could come up this path any minute."

"I can do this."

"When this child screamed, he gave the enemy a map to find us. When they find you, you will be shot for desertion, after they torture you. You have told Baseer of your sergeant major. Do you want to see him again?"

"He is a boy. He hasn't lived yet. My fear doesn't justify ending his life."

"I will do what is best for my men," replied Muhammad, kneeling over the boy, and drawing his knife.

"Would you say that if it was your brother?" Daniyal challenged.

"Do not speak of my brother," Muhammad warned.

"I speak only out of respect. He was taken by senseless violence. What would he say, if he were here?"

Muhammad did not move. Daniyal could see the muscles in his jaw clench and blood flush the skin on his neck. His knuckles gripping the knife were white. *Perhaps he will finally kill me*, he realized, thinking he had gone too far.

Slowly, Muhammad stood. He stepped toward Daniyal, knife in hand.

"How would you manage it?" Muhammad asked.

"I will strap him to my back," Daniyal replied.

"You won't make it a kilometer."

"I will."

"How will you find us?"

"Give me directions. I have learned much living in these mountains."

Muhammad knew the wisest choice was just to run his blade across the boy's throat. Why was he listening to this mad idea? *Damn him for mentioning Tamir.* Muhammad stared down into the valley. A large vulture soared on the updrafts, looking for its next meal. "Are you trying to escape?" Muhammad asked quietly.

"Escape to what?" Daniyal scoffed. "To my family, where word of my return will reach my old unit within days? There are informers everywhere. Back to the army, where I will be shot? When have I not done what I said I would? I will bring him."

Muhammad shook his head. "You will be dead by noon."

"If it is Allah's will."

"Pah," Muhammad declared. "We will wait at the next safe hole until the moon rises. Then we must move. This trail leads down to a bridge, which will likely be guarded. If the militia do not capture you, the bridge garrison will. Beyond the bridge—a kilometer to the east at most—is a curve in the road that conceals the beginning of another trail. The safe hole is up that trail—two kilometers maybe. Try not to die painfully." With those encouraging words Muhammad turned away up the trail.

◊ ◊ ◊

"I told you he would not come," said Farzaad, watching the moon starting to rise.

"He will come," said Muhammad. The ten remaining men of Muhammad's team had made it to the safe hole by early afternoon, still alive to their great surprise. A police checkpoint at a bridge in the valley had delayed them, but a few moments of concentrated gunfire had motivated its small garrison to run away. *The Americans must have their eyes focused elsewhere,* reasoned Muhammad. *There is no other explanation why we are still alive.*

"He is in the valley right now, giving our position to the militia." Farzaad's eyes flicked nervously to the left and right.

"You say this after he saved your brother from the blade? Was that you on the end of the rope by Zaram's side this morning? Do not let fear replace your brains."

"He should have been here by now," suggested Baseer, concerned.

"He is carrying much. He will come," repeated Muhammad, as if the saying would make it true.

"We need to move," said Farzaad. "We cannot assume he will find us. When dawn comes, the aircraft will come. We ran that garrison off the bridge, so they know we are in the area. If we reach the river before light, there are many places to hide. If we stay here, the American drones will surely find us."

Farzaad's constant worrying is wearing, but he is not wrong, realized Muhammad. *He is nervous because he has seen much.* "As soon as the moon is fully above the horizon we will go," ordered Muhammad. "I will not move in the blackness. We can afford no more broken ankles."

Another half hour passed and there was no more time if they were to make the river before daylight. The moon had risen enough to guide them. They would follow the trail along the crest for another five kilometers, before the path descended into the valley and led them through rolling hills to the river. The wind cut through Muhammad's clothes as they began to climb higher.

At the crest he looked back down the trail. His men were strung out over a hundred meters, the last man barely visible, except as a shifting shadow moving against the rocks. Further below in the valley, the bridge they had crossed earlier was visible in the moonlight. It cut the stream, which shone like a silver thread, and on the bridge...*Movement? No. Yes? Barely discernable.* But for the nearly full moon it would be invisible. *A man? If so, moving slowly. Achingly so.*

"Farzaad, keep the men moving," Muhammad ordered, as his second-in-command moved up beside him.

"Yes, Muhammad. Where are you going?"

"To save a fool," he replied. "Keep moving to the river. Do not wait for me."

◊ ◊ ◊

It was a blessing that Daniyal could no longer feel his shoulders or his bleeding feet. The weight of the boy strapped to him like a backpack was taking its toll. He no longer walked, as much as he lurched from leg to leg. He had almost lost hope that he was still on the right path when he came to the bridge. It was blocked at the far end by a small hut and a boom barrier, just as Muhammad had said.

He could not go around with his load, and he knew that the guards would likely just execute him if he was captured. His clothing, and moving at night, would instantly see him labeled as *Taliban*. These rural militias were known for their swift and brutal justice. He stared at the outpost, a hundred meters before him. Daniyal was out of ideas. *So, is this where I finally die?* Daniyal saw no movement. No noise. *Maybe they are all asleep?* he hoped, remembering his days as a bored airfield guard. The boy, Zaram, had been unconscious for hours, aided by exhaustion, injury, and the drugs from Baseer. *I will stay to the far side of the road and simply walk across*, he concluded. *If I don't go, the boy dies. If I do go and am caught, the boy dies. The only chance is to go and not be seen. Allah will decide.* Bolstered by his logic, Daniyal started up the road to cross the bridge.

An owl broke the silence, its cry bringing him to a halt. *Is that a good omen or bad?* he wondered. *Just no more magpies*, he prayed. Daniyal moved forward once more. He was on the bridge over a rushing mountain stream that gurgled noisily from the spring thaw. Fifty meters to the guard shack. *Nothing.* Twenty meters. *Noth...wait, someone is there.* A man stumbled out the side door of the shack into the middle of the road. He turned to face Daniyal. Daniyal froze.

An earth-shaking burp tore through the air, followed a moment later by the sound of the guard emptying his bladder onto the road. Daniyal did not breathe. *Was this a man or a horse?* Daniyal wondered, as the pissing continued for well over a minute. The crescendo of the performance was a massive fart and a satisfied groan. *Allah, protect this boy*, Daniyal prayed. The man again appeared to look directly at Daniyal before staggering back into the shack.

Daniyal could not move for a minute. His legs were shaking. *How am I not dead? He must have seen me.* Daniyal willed his legs to move again. He took one tentative step forward, then another. His knees were not working—he was stumping forward on two unbending wooden beams. Daniyal was now even with the sandbags and the boom barrier. *Now they will come.*

But no voice challenged him. No blow fell. The sound of snoring echoed from the small shed. He moved forward, slowly shuffling toward safety.

Have I ever known a moment without this weight? He couldn't recall it. *Forward.* The shack was now slightly behind him. *Will a voice cry out "Halt!" from behind?* Daniyal staggered forward. No voice sounded the alarm. He knew the road would eventually come to a curve in another kilometer and Muhammad said that was where the path to the next trail was hidden. How he would find it in the dark, he did not know. *It doesn't matter. Just keep moving.*

Daniyal fantasized about sitting down for maybe just two minutes, to remove the weight tearing at his shoulders, but knew he would not get up again if he did so. *Maybe I am hallucinating*, he considered. *Maybe I am still on the road before the shack. The man will walk out and stare at me soon.* Time had no meaning, distance had no meaning, pain had no meaning. He could not feel his legs moving, but something propelled him forward. He thought there was a slight curve in the road ahead but could see no path. *Have I gone a kilometer? Is this the curve? Did Muhammad mean a sharper curve?* He stepped off the road and began to push the bushes aside with his hands. Sharp thorns discouraged further attempts. He could feel warm blood running down his hands. *What do I do? If I wait for more light, the others will be gone.*

An iron hand clamped over his mouth.

"If I was the enemy, you would be dead right now," a fierce voice breathed in his ear, before releasing him.

"If you were the enemy, they would make you brush your teeth," he replied to Muhammad, trying not to reveal his terror. "What *have* you been eating?"

"How is the boy?" asked Muhammad.

"Alive. He is strong and his ankle is well set. If we can get him to a place of safety, he should recover."

"Ah, 'place of safety.' Do you forget what country you are in?"

"Where are the others?"

"Gone ahead."

"What now?"

"We build a litter. There are some small trees across the road we can cut into poles without much noise. Then we must make time. It will be light in a few hours. We need to get over this mountain and to the river before they start hunting us again."

"There are police in a guard shack back there." Daniyal gestured the way he had come.

"We scared them off earlier so we could cross the bridge," Muhammad confirmed. "They must have returned. How did you get across?"

"They were asleep."

"Good, I will go cut their throats while you build the litter."

"Don't. I won't have their blood on my hands."

"You are more trouble than you are worth, have I told you that?" Muhammad asked.

"Daily."

"Remember it. Now hurry. We can still get there by dawn."

Chapter 33

Anti-Corruption Justice Center, Kabul, May 2016

A flurry of activity followed Trevanathan's phone call with Jesus. His first stop was to brief Major General Crist on the news. They agreed that, if true, there was no reason anyone would be digging toward the ACJC compound with anything other than bad intentions. They also agreed that the kid could be making the entire thing up to score a few bucks. But with the stakes so high, they needed to assume it was true until proven otherwise. The grand opening was days away, with attendees including President Ghani, the COM, and a host of Western ambassadors. There was no room—or time—for mistakes.

The next afternoon, Trevanathan's UH-60 Blackhawk touched down at the small landing zone near the ACJC. Accompanying him was his security detachment, now led by Corporal Hawthorne, but also a captain and a sergeant from the explosive ordnance disposal detachment, with their Belgian Malinois, named Smoke. With a potential threat to the Afghan President, the COM had also ordered a ground-penetrating radar team from Parwan prison at Bagram to meet them. That team was normally kept busy looking for people tunneling out. Today they would be looking for people tunneling *in*. Their NCOIC joked that it was a nice change of pace.

Trevanathan was impressed with how many moving pieces were dedicated to the corruption center project. After nearly thirty years of Army bureaucracy demonstrating the many ways the Army could find to say *no* to ideas, he was impressed at what the Army could pull together when it said *yes*.

Hakeem, or *Jesus*, as he preferred, was waiting outside the main gate to Camp Heath, as promised. Trevanathan saw that the boy's market had grown since his last visit. The presence of Interior Ministry security guards, along with prosecutors, judges, MCTF investigators, and their corresponding coalition advisors, brought the number of daily personnel at the ACJC to nearly two hundred.

All of them got thirsty, hungry, and wanted breaks, so Jesus was now proprietor of *The Justice Fresh Market*, with cases of water, boxes of fruit, and even a tea kettle simmering over an open flame, all ready for business.

"General, my General," declared Jesus, opening his arms wide and flashing his best salesman's smile, as the colonel approached. "Welcome back."

"Looks like you're doing alright for yourself, kid." Trevanathan noted the boy was wearing a shiny gold vest and a finely-woven, red Uzbek hat, replacing his tattered fez. "You look like a successful businessman."

"*Insh'allah*. The court has been a great blessing to me and my family, although the local commander takes his share." The boy frowned.

"What? The MOI commander here? Captain Shafiq?"

"Yes, he said my stand was a security risk to the court and had to move...until I agreed to give him ten percent of the profits. Then suddenly I wasn't a security risk anymore."

"Is that a problem for you?"

"No, he is too stupid to know how much I really make here. I keep a record of sales that are just for him, what do you call it—a fairy tale—and he accepts it. He is no businessman."

"You learn young, don't you?"

"You can tell how honest a man is in Afghanistan by how poor he is," shrugged the boy, with the cynicism of an older man. But he suddenly brightened. "Coke? Ice cold! Stolen from one of your trucks just this morning!" He giggled infectiously.

"Sure, kid, sounds great."

Jesus went behind a counter built from old boards and empty petrol barrels to fish a can of Coca Cola out of a chest. Trevanathan could hear it was stocked with ice. *How does he get ice up here?* Trevanathan wondered, marveling at the ingenuity of the Afghan people, who had so little.

Jesus handed the colonel a Coke and Trevanathan handed him sixty dollars, holding onto his hand for a second as he spoke. "I told you I'd take care of you, right? I appreciate you calling. This is very important."

"You treated me with respect, my General. It is my pleasure to help you. The money is welcome too, though." The boy wrinkled his nose and giggled again.

"So, here's the drill, Jesus. You see those two guys over there by the gate with the dog?"

"Yes, General."

"They are experts in finding bombs. So is the dog."

"The dog has special powers?"

"Yes, even more so than the two men. He can tell when there's a bomb anywhere nearby. We think maybe someone wants to put a bomb under this camp. What I want you to do for them is to point to where you heard the digging noises."

"Of course, General."

"There are some other men still coming up from the landing pad that have some equipment that can see through the ground."

"Like a medical machine," Jesus replied.

"Exactly. They are going to look around the area that you point out with their machine and see if they can see any tunnels."

"General, may I ask you something I wonder about?"

"Sure, kid."

"How is it that with magic dogs and machines that can see through rock you have not yet beaten the Taliban? They have no such miracles."

Trevanathan laughed. "Jesus, that is an outstanding question. I don't have an answer, other than sometimes the biggest guy in the fight doesn't win. You should be a lawyer, though, with good questions like that."

"No General, I want to be a rich merchant and live in a big house."

"Fair enough. Now, the sergeant with the magic dog is the only one going out to the junk yard. He said that if someone is trying to dig a tunnel, they may have trip wires or mines set out to protect the tunnel from being discovered. He knows what to look for and you don't, so he wants you to go up on the wall with his captain and point out where he should look. Can you do that?"

"Of course. Am I allowed to go into the compound?"

"Absolutely. You are my honored guest."

Jesus smiled and his shoulders went back at hearing himself called an honored *anything*.

As soon as the dog and its handler were in position, the EOD captain went into the tower with Jesus and Trevanathan. The captain marked the locations Jesus pointed to on his tablet for further investigation. Armed with this information, the professionals went to work. The radar team laid out a search grid to help them determine if the earth beneath had been disturbed. The sergeant and Smoke carefully scouted the area inside and around the piles of junked cars and trucks, suspecting that a tunnel, if it existed, would likely originate beneath a junked vehicle or a large piece of debris.

Trevanathan watched the two teams from the relative security of the southwest guard tower, which he shared with Corporal Hawthorne. Jesus returned to selling drinks and fake war souvenirs.

After an hour without significant discoveries, Trevanathan grew bored and left the tower to wander the compound. He rarely had time that was not scheduled, so he took advantage of the quiet to make an informal inspection of the ACJC. *Is there anything I'm forgetting? The courthouse is ready to go, needing only additional chairs in the public gallery. The prosecutor's office and evidence room are ready. The judge's chambers are almost ready, waiting for delivery of their computers.*

The buildings in the earliest stages of refurbishment were those to be occupied by the Coalition advisors. Right now, those were largely empty, except for a dozen rooms occupied by Trevanathan's people and some British police advisors. They needed to not only watch that cases didn't disappear, but also that the court did not become a political weapon with which Ghani could derail his political critics.

Either approach would cause the ACJC to fail and could eventually bring the government down under the weight of its own malfeasance.

As Trevanathan pondered which future would likely occur, Captain Shafiq, the MOI garrison commander who was shaking down Jesus, passed by and rendered an unenthusiastic salute. *Hopefully, that was not an answer to my question,* Trevanathan thought.

The day dragged on, with Trevanathan increasingly convinced that Jesus had been at best mistaken, or at worst, had played him for a few dollars. *Well, if they find nothing, that's good news. It won't screw up the grand opening.* Trevanathan secluded himself away in the coalition advisors' building and took the luxury of some down time to write to his parents, who did not do the email thing.

Six hours into the monotony, Hawthorne stuck his head in the door and announced, "Here's Captain Carlson, sir." Trevanathan looked up to see the EOD officer entering.

"Nothing, huh?" Trevanathan asked.

"Negative sir. The kid was spot on. We have two parallel tunnels running from the southwest to the northeast, originating in the junk yard. We found the entrance to one tunnel under the hood of a rusted out Russian truck. It had been marked with a wire so that the diggers would know if anyone uncovered it, but we were looking for that sort of thing. We left everything as we found it. But that also made us back away from finding the other entrance, because we didn't want our efforts to be discovered—if they haven't been watching us already—which is always a possibility."

"Holy shit," uttered Trevanathan.

"Smoke alerted on Tunnel One—the one with the entrance we found. So, there's something either down there or been near there that's got Smoke excited."

"So, by 'excited,' you mean he's detected some type of explosive?"

"Roger that, sir. We don't know how much. Could be they have the tunnel boobytrapped with some sort of antipersonnel device while they're away, or the entire tunnel could be packed to the rafters. Neither we nor the ground-penetrating radar boys can tell without going down there, and we aren't prepared to do that. Not today, anyway."

"Holy shit," repeated Trevanathan. "I'd convinced myself this was a wild goose chase."

"Sometimes they are, sir. Not today." Carlson was matter-of-fact.

"So, now what?"

"Well, subject to your approval, sir, and I have to run this up the chain to the G3[92], I'd like to bait the trap."

"I like that," muttered Hawthorne.

"How so?" replied Trevanathan.

"The radar guys say that Tunnel One is still about twenty meters short of the wall. That makes me think they haven't packed it with explosives yet. I mean why bother? Tunnel Two, we don't know the entrance location, but it is not far from that of Tunnel One. Tunnel Two has reached the wall but is not yet inside the perimeter."

"OK, let me ask some maybe dumb questions. Why do they have two tunnels? Seem like it'd increase the chances of being detected."

"Sir, I'm an EOD guy, not a tunnel expert, but I know enough to be dangerous. Tunnels are notoriously risky. They collapse. They run into shit that turns them into dead ends. If you have two, you have double the chance of being successful. Look at the fact that one of the tunnels is twenty meters ahead of the other. Shows that one of them is maybe having more problems than the other."

"OK, second question. Any way to know what their intent is? Is their plan to blow up the wall…and then do a ground assault, or are they planning to tunnel into the compound and place charges inside, to like blow up the courthouse—maybe when it's full of VIPs?"

"No way to know at this point, sir. Could be either or both since they have two routes. Only way to know for sure is to let them keep at it, which I don't recommend."

"So, what do you suggest?"

---

[92] G3 – The staff officer and section responsible for carrying out military planning, operations, and training under orders from the commander.

"We put a few of those Special Forces bubbas up on that north hillside with NVGs[93] and sniper rifles. Then wait. Let them come back and resume digging. When they're down in the hole we take out the guys on top. When those down below come up from digging, we pop them too. If intel wants any of them alive, that could be arranged, but with explosives involved it's better to just cap 'em."

"And what about the tunnels?"

"We can collapse them. We can send a robotic camera down to make sure they aren't already set to blow first. When their entire mining team ends up dead, they probably won't try it again any time soon."

"How soon can this be put together?"

"It's late afternoon now. I'd say we get the guys with the NVGs up on the hill tonight to make sure the bad guys don't pack the tunnel full of explosives before tomorrow. If they keep digging, let them go at it, and then tomorrow night, it's lights out for our friends."

"OK. Corporal Hawthorne, I can sense you bursting at the seams. What's your input?"

"Sir, I think it makes all sorts of sense. I also think you'll want some type of air piece in case one of the snipers misses. You're not going to want to chase bad guys through a junkyard at night and we don't want anyone getting away. They might have their route in and out wired and only they would know the safe lanes in and out. Being able to hit them from above would be a good backup option. We always have helos in the area, so their presence shouldn't tip anyone off."

"OK, that's all out of my lane, but it makes sense. I'm sure your commanders and the G3 will work out the tactical details. I'll brief General Crist, so he can think deep thoughts about who else needs to be read in…or not."

"My two cents is 'the fewer the better,' sir," said Captain Carlson. "I don't totally understand what you guys are doing up here, except you're going after corrupt Afghan politicians…which is really every Afghan politician, right? The bad guys digging this hole aren't

---

[93] NVGs: Night Vision Goggles, a/k/a NODs – Night Optical Devices.

necessarily Taliban, right? They could be ISIS, or friends of these corrupt politicians…could be Karzai's people…now that we're making a list, basically anyone who wants Afghanistan to stay weak and corrupt. The Pakis, Iranians, Russians, or even the Afghan Government itself, right?"

"They are talented at saying one thing and then doing the exact opposite," confirmed Trevanathan.

"My point is that by sharing info in the name of being a good ally, we may be talking to the very guys who are digging that hole out yonder. It's sure interesting the guards here haven't reported any digging noise, but a kid did, know what I mean?"

"Got it," said Trevanathan. "I'll be sure to remind Crist of that. Now let's get packing before our friends show up for the night shift."

◇ ◇ ◇

The *night shift* did indeed report as expected. Seven men in dark clothing passed like wraiths through the junkyard just after midnight. But for the night vision scopes of the Special Forces team on the hillside, their movements would have been invisible. *These guys are pros*, noted Sergeant Frame, peering through his scope. Patience was rewarded when Frame watched some of the men move toward an abandoned bus 150 meters from the wall. *Smart*, granted Frame, as he saw them enter the bus. *The tunnel opening must be beneath a false floor, inside.*

During planning sessions the next day, the bus became a complication to the original plan of picking off the diggers as they emerged from the tunnels. Because the large vehicle would provide too much concealment, and maybe some cover, to the diggers, trying to take them out one-by-one might just result in a protracted gun fight, with the advantage going to those hiding in the junkyard. Major General "Pop" Anderson, the G3 for Resolute Support, was not interested in such a lopsided battlefield, especially with a high risk that some of the diggers would escape.

Because he had walked the ground where the fight would happen, Corporal Hawthorne was included in the planning session, something unusual for someone so junior. He earned a modicum of respect from the room full of experienced officers when he suggested, "Sir, how's about we freeze 'em in place with small arms fire and then put a couple antipersonnel missiles right in the middle of their party? Avoids any messy firefights and will take care of anyone above or below ground."

Anderson liked the idea. And so, for the next twenty-four hours, the ACJC became the primary focus of operations, with Hawthorne's suggestion at the hub of the plan. "It's kinda' nuts," noted Trevanathan to Major Brandt. "This project didn't exist six months ago, and now has the full attention of the COM and the G3, with priority for resources."

"Sir, I used to think I had seen it all, and then I came to Afghanistan," said Brandt. "I've dropped the expression, 'It can't happen,' and replaced it with, 'When does the next shitshow begin?'"

Trevanathan choked on his coffee.

"So, do you get to watch it go down?" asked Brandt.

"The COM said he wanted me in the Operations Center to provide local knowledge, if needed. Crist vetoed me being anywhere near the compound. Said it's too hard to replace stubborn judges. But he agreed I should be available *in case*... Whatever that means."

"I don't suppose you can sneak a Marine in there?"

"Not my party, bub, or I'd give you a front row seat. These things used to be run by the Special Operations Commander in theater, but since the downsizing in 2014, the G3 is running the show tonight. He's having Frame's A team take the tactical lead since they know the ground."

"Well, shoot me a message afterwards, because I won't be sleeping anyway—if you don't mind."

"You got it."

◊ ◊ ◊

Inasmuch as there was a G3 Plans section at Camp Resolute Support, that element's location was more for the convenience of the COM, General Peterson. Because a significant portion of the COM's duties fell into the *political* sphere, it was necessary that he and his immediate staff be located at Camp Resolute Support, near the center of Kabul and—not coincidentally—the GIRoA leadership, not the least of whom was President Ghani. But conduct of RS *combat operations* was another animal, requiring communications capabilities, personnel, and defensible facilities that Camp RS could not provide. Unlike past wars, technology permitted geographic separation of the commander—Peterson—from the people who directed and monitored combat operations within the theater: the RS G3 Operations cell. As Trevanathan learned shortly after his arrival, this meant that the people who were responsible for "making things happen and shaking the rocks" were 64 kilometers north, at Bagram Air Base.

Major General Anderson would be overseeing the ACJC threat intercept operation from Bagram. That the COM might be present was understood, but execution of the mission would be Anderson's responsibility. Unless everything went sideways, of course, in which case the COM would take the blame. But in the modern Army there was almost always another layer of bureaucracy to keep in the loop, and for the Resolute Support effort, this was U.S. Central Command, located over 1,100 kilometers from Kabul, in Qatar. In theory, CENTCOM would be monitoring the feeds from overhead drones but leaving operational details—and control—to Anderson.

Shortly after dusk, Trevanathan flew from Camp RS to Bagram, by Blackhawk. Hours earlier, before dawn, the Special Forces A team had moved its two best shooters, which included Sergeant Frame, and their spotters into position above the ACJC, where they had remained immobile to avoid detection. At HKIA, just four minutes away, two MEDEVAC Blackhawks were on standby, just in case.

To maintain operational security, also known as "OPSEC," the Afghan security commander for Camp Heath, Captain Shafiq, had not been read into the plan. The Americans did not know that the Afghan contingent could not be trusted, but they also did not know that they *could*. Based on experience, it was smarter to remove the possibility that Interior Ministry forces would sell operational information rather than trust that they wouldn't. Shafiq's questions about the bomb dog and the radar team had been deflected as a routine precaution ending in a "dead end." His people would be contacted just before the drone released its payload, so the Afghan security detachment would know why there was a robust explosion just outside their perimeter. Blast analysis calculations had determined that no one in the guard towers would be at significant risk from the air-to-ground missile being used, though the Americans smiled that their Afghan allies might need to change their shorts afterwards.

The COM had briefed President Ghani on the situation earlier in the day, since the threat assessment concluded he was likely the intended target of the tunneling operation. Analysts believed it likely that a complex attack was being planned, timed to occur during the Grand Opening ceremonies over which Ghani would be presiding. The most damaging scenario would be an explosion that brought down the exterior wall of Heath, another that maximized casualties by exploding underneath the compound, and a follow-on ground assault–likely by suicide vest-wearing martyrs who could use the decrepit bus as a place to conceal themselves beforehand. Although there was no guarantee the Palace would not be the source of a leak, the need to ensure the President's ongoing support for the court project tilted in favor of not letting him be blindsided by an undisclosed operation in his capital.

The miners had arrived at midnight the previous evening. It could not be assumed that they would follow the same schedule the following night, as the enemy's varying of routine was to be expected. Tonight, the sky was clear, at least as clear as the polluted skies above Kabul ever were. Trevanathan slipped into an observer's chair at the rear of the Operations Center's "war room" at 2130 hours. Three large screens dominated the room, with many smaller ones tracking operations elsewhere in the country. The COM and General Anderson were standing at the rear of the room, deep in discussion. The COM had nodded when Trevanathan entered, but the colonel knew he was only there to observe and answer any questions. His primary job at the moment was staying out of the way.

The room was laid out like a large college auditorium with multiple tiers of workstations leading down in descending tiers to a front wall on which the screens and several digital clocks tracking time around the world were mounted. It was an impressive space. Each workstation was equipped with a computer and several phones. *Local, unsecure, and secure lines,* guessed Trevanathan. Each station was labeled with its assigned function, conveniently identifying the players in the intricate choreography of combat missions: Air (Air Force assets in all their many flavors), Aviation (primarily Army rotary wing elements), Fires (artillery), LOG (logistics), MEDEVAC, and many others. Trevanathan noticed a young Army officer sitting at the JAG station, there to give legal advice pertaining to any sticky targeting issues under the rules of warfare. Even the Chaplain had an assigned position, an important role in a country where a misstep over religion could inflame the region against the NATO presence.

The center screen was already displaying an aerial view of the area surrounding the ACJC compound. An Air Force captain at the Air desk spoke into a microphone to the entire room. "Shadow 6 is five-by-five, on target, and providing continuous feed. Predator 1 is ready to launch, on order." While not completely familiar with Air Force jargon, Trevanathan understood that there was already one drone providing camera coverage of the ACJC area. A second drone, armed with high explosive missiles, was sitting on the tarmac several hundred yards from where he sat, ready to launch toward the ACJC compound.

General Anderson interrupted his conversation with the COM, ordering "Launch Predator 1."

"Launching Predator 1," confirmed the captain.

This is getting very real, thought Trevanathan, irritated at himself that his palms were moist.

Moments later, the same Air Force officer announced, "Predator 1 is airborne and inbound."

"SOF.[94] SITREP?" queried Anderson to a Special Operations major sitting at a workstation near the front of the room.

"Team One is green." He paused to listen to a receiver at his station. "Team Two is green."

---

[94] SOF – Special Operations Forces. All forces assigned under U.S. Special Operations Command, which includes U.S. Army Special Forces, a/k/a Green Berets, Rangers (Army), SEALS (Navy), Special Tactics Squadron (U.S.A.F.), and Marine Raiders, among others.

The snipers are in position and ready, thought Trevanathan.

Anderson nodded and returned to his conversation with the COM.

Ten minutes passed. "Predator 1 is on location and standing by," announced the Air Force captain.

Another thirty uneventful minutes passed. Waiting for a jury verdict has nothing on this level of tension, thought Trevanathan. No idle chatter in the room, either.

Another five passed. "Movement," declared the SOF officer, sending a jolt through the room. "Team Two detects movement at the south end of the junkyard."

"They're early tonight. Remind the teams the order to fire belongs with me, SOF," Anderson ordered.

"They know, sir. These guys are pros."

"Do it," repeated the General.

"Roger, sir."

The SOF officer muttered into his microphone, somewhat irritated the general was micro-managing the men on the ground.

"Multiple movements," the SOF officer declared. "Four, five, six pax."[95]

"I want a visual," said Anderson.

"Roger, sir," replied the Air Force captain. The large screen in the center switched to night vision mode, with its greenish hue, but the level of clarity was still astounding. There was little doubt they would be able to find their targets tonight.

Thirty seconds passed, while the drone's camera scanned the area, without result.

"Where's my picture?" the G3 demanded.

The Air Force captain was rattled. "Yes sir—err, no sir. We have the correct picture on screen. We're just not seeing the reported movement."

---

[95] Pax – Mil. Shorthand reference for "Personnel."

"SOF?"

"No movement sir, they've gone to ground."

Anderson folded his arms across his chest and shrugged, while whispering something to the COM, who kept a poker face.

Several minutes passed. An Army lieutenant, manning the medical console, drummed his fingers nervously until a dirty look from the Special Forces major caused him to press his hands between his knees. The room was quiet.

Nothing.

Nothing.

"Movement," declared the SOF major, relaying the transmissions from his sniper teams.

"I've got movement," declared the drone officer simultaneously, as his cameras showed a blurry shape cutting through the wreckage.

A collective exhale across the room could be felt.

"Zoom in," ordered Anderson. All eyes focused on the large center screen where the drone feed from Shadow 6 appeared. "Sniper teams stand by."

Trevanathan could see a smudge of movement, as the camera refocused. It looked like several streams of green light running across the screen.

"Dogs. It's fucking dogs," declared the SOF officer.

"Keep it professional, SOF," snapped Anderson.

But the SOF major had accurately captured everyone's reaction as the drone camera refocused on a pack of wild dogs cavorting through the junkyard, jumping on vehicles, chasing each other, and searching for food. There were seven or eight of them, a mixture of breeds likely abandoned at some point during the war, now gone feral, and hunting as a pack.

All eyes in the Ops Center followed the antics of the dogs, as they weaved amidst the debris. Several had gathered near the entrance to Tunnel One and were digging at the edges of the rusting hood that covered the hole.

"Well, this is unexpected," murmured the COM to Anderson, who merely shook his head in reply.

"Maybe they left some food down there. I dunno'," the G3 commented, as the ferocity of the digging increased.

"Shots fired," announced the SOF officer.

"I need more than that, SOF," replied the G3.

"Team One reports shots are fired. Shooter unidentified. Target unidentified. Team Two confirms," the SOF major responded.

"What the hell…?" Anderson said to no one, but turned to the COM.

"Sir, it looks like one of the dogs is hit," announced the Air Force captain. Anderson swiveled back to the screen where a large dog, a German Shepherd mix, was dragging its hind quarters across the ground, pulled by its front paws. It started and stopped, then lunged forward again, before rolling onto its side.

"Team Two sees gunfire coming from the wall of the ACJC compound," announced the SOF major.

"Another dog is down," announced the Air Force captain, as another stray pitched forward and was still, dirt kicking up around its body.

"Team One confirms. They can see three guards—two with AKs and one officer with a handgun in the southwest tower, using the dogs for target practice. They're laughing," he added unnecessarily.

"Goddamn it," Anderson swore, just loud enough for Trevanathan to hear. "Should we have read them in?" he asked the COM, second-guessing their approach to operational secrecy.

"No, Pop," replied the COM firmly. "Might as well put up a billboard announcing the operation, as let the Interior Ministry in on it. The intel would have been sold in hours, making our people targets."

"The rest of the dogs are taking off, sir," announced the Air Force captain, the cameras turning to record their departure.

"Any sign of enemy activity?" asked Anderson.

"Negative, sir," replied the Air Force officer.

"SOF?"

"Negative sir. Just those heroes up on the wall."

The G3 hesitated, thinking over his options.

"The teams are requesting orders, sir."

"Remain in place. This Op is not over," replied Anderson. "It's been a goat screw so far, but maybe we'll get lucky, and the diggers will come once everything calms down." The G3 did not believe a word he was saying.

"Team Two says that first dog isn't dead, sir. It's howling," reported the SOF major.

"We aren't the SPCA, SOF. Tell them to stay in place, and to *not*, I repeat *not*, put that animal out of its misery. They shoot that dog and we'll end up in a firefight with the MOI. They don't know we're out there, remember?"

"Roger, sir. It's just with that dog howling, it's less likely the targets will come in," the SOF officer replied.

"I know, SOF. Believe me, I know. These are the cards we've been dealt."

The COM clapped General Anderson on the shoulder, gave him a knowing look, and walked out of the room. It was over.

Chapter 34

Anti-Corruption Justice Center, Kabul, May 2016

Though delayed by almost two weeks, the ACJC opened without further incident, thanks to Jesus. Sergeant Frame's sniper teams remained in place for another seven hours after the dog shooting, with no additional contact, before they pulled out. The wounded dog's cries became weaker and then went silent after an hour. There was no sign of the miners the following night or on any night thereafter. Whether they had been tipped off, or the shooting had spooked them into believing their plan discovered, the tunnels were abandoned. After three days of uneventful surveillance, the demolition team returned, feigned discovering the tunnels for the first time, and destroyed them.

The Major Crimes Task Force was assigned to investigate the likely perpetrators behind the tunneling effort but came up empty. There were too many potential suspects in a land where everyone profited from instability. There was a growing ISIS presence in the country. The Haqqani network—an independent and particularly brutal offshoot of the Taliban—was also a likely suspect, although the necessary patience shown in a tunneling effort over a period of weeks was not their trademark. The President's political opponents, the prior President's allies, and numerous groups within the government vested in a successful kleptocracy all had equal interest in seeing the ACJC fail. To close the matter and satisfy all appetites, the matter was blamed on the Taliban, without any real evidence to support the conclusion.

With heightened vigilance and increased security, the grand opening ceremony was a success. A *Who's Who* of Kabul attended. President Ghani made a stirring speech in which he announced *he* had initiated the ACJC project and had "given it my personal attention since day one," which earned Trevanathan a knowing side-eye from Jodie Upton.

In their turns, the Chief Justice and the Attorney General both made remarks condemning corruption by *other* branches of the government, being careful not to admit any wrongdoing in their own, rampantly corrupt, organizations. They were also quite adept at not upstaging the President, who was known to have a thin skin about such things. To everyone's surprise, the Chief Executive, Abdullah Abdullah, attended. This was unusual, since he and Ghani were bitter political rivals who rarely appeared together by choice. It was a positive sign for the ACJC's future that both rivals supported the project—at least coming out of the gate.

The most important attendees from Trevanathan's perspective, however, were the diplomats from the donor nations, whose countries could choose to bow out of the war at the Warsaw conference. The British Ambassador, who had championed financial and political support for the ACJC with the other embassies, was widely commended for his insight and resolve. Trevanathan knew that the name of that insight and resolve was "Jodie Upton," but experienced staffers were used to their bosses grabbing the limelight. U.S. Ambassador MacMillan had begged off the event, noting an important conflict, but sent Nancy Something to represent the United States.

The donor nation ambassadors received a VIP tour of the prosecutors' office, judges' chambers, and investigators' offices, the latter where Brigadier General Baz had ensconced a team of his Major Crimes Task Force investigators to show off the hidden cameras, listening devices, and other electronic gadgetry they now routinely used to pursue corrupt officials. During the tour, emphasis was placed on the number of accountability measures created to ensure that cases could no longer be dismissed through contributing to the Attorney General's retirement fund. The joint tracking of cases, the presence of NATO advisors at each stage of the case from charging until sentencing, and the use of semi-annual polygraphs to ensure bad actors were weeded out, were all reinforced during the tour so that those details enhancing the rule of law would be reported back to decision-makers in Europe.

Upton had been the eyes and ears into what the donor nations truly thought throughout the development of the ACJC initiative, as she lived in their world. Whenever one of the allied embassies began to get cold feet about supporting the initiative, which occurred with some frequency, Upton was the one- person emergency response team that encouraged, badgered, and arm-twisted that embassy to bolster their resolve. Diplomats have an inherent suspicion of those in uniform, and when doubts crept in, it took a civilian advocate, like Upton, who spoke their language, to settle them down.

After the ceremony, Upton confided to Trevanathan that there was now mild optimism even among the skeptics. "Except your lot, of course," she indicated, referring to the U.S. Embassy officials, who had continued to pester the British ambassador that the ACJC initiative was reckless. "There's legitimate concern among several embassies Ghani might miscalculate and turn this into a political weapon," she explained, "but they also recognize the alternative is 'do nothing and watch our NATO allies take to the lifeboats.' That would not only be disastrous for this mission, but for future defense cooperation in Europe."

"Mild optimism is a big improvement from where we were in November, when they saw GIRoA as a total cluster," Trevanathan observed.

"Cluster?" asked Upton, always fascinated by American military slang.

"Umm, let's leave it at a 'bad situation,'" laughed Trevanathan.

"Well, there's still time to fumble the ball before Warsaw, as you Yanks like to say."

"Rahman's trial," Trevanathan agreed, confirming her thoughts.

"Yes, Colonel. With the mountain of documentary evidence obtained, if he is acquitted, this entire effort may be viewed as just another round of window dressing."

"I agree. But there's no choice but to let the Afghans present the evidence and live with the outcome," replied Trevanathan.

"Agreed. Yet it makes me nervous that all our work comes down to one case."

"Me too. Who would have thought Afghanistan's future might be decided in a courtroom instead of the battlefield?"

Chapter 35

Anti-Corruption Justice Center, Kabul, June, 2016

The trial of Major General Rahman and Command Sergeant Major Mahmood began on a Sunday—a workday in a Muslim country. For fifteen years, persons in position of power had operated without consequences while stealing the wealth of the Afghan people. Suddenly, this ACJC *thing* was challenging that system, and the political elite in Kabul were nervous.

Many Afghan politicians were in denial. This was not how things were done, after all. Surely, the charges will be dismissed. Apologies will be offered. In the meantime, rumors abounded that the 225th Corps had been destroyed in battle, so its commander was being court-martialed for incompetence. *That* fiction was more palatable. The idea that he was being charged for corruption was unthinkable. *This new court is chaos*, representatives in Parliament whispered to each other. *Why is Ghani allowing it?*

The gallery of the ACJC courtroom was full, with an audience mostly comprised of representatives of Western governments, although several nonprofits and Afghan news organizations were present. Tolo News[96] was allowed to film the interior of the courtroom before the proceeding began. Common Afghan citizens were absent, having learned long ago to stay distant from government proceedings.

Trevanathan took a seat in the third row, sandwiched beside Jodie Upton and Major Brandt. The defendants were seated at two separate tables, with their counsel, on the left side of the courtroom. The two prosecutors sat at a table on the right. *Everyone looks nervous*, Trevanathan thought, being used to his Pennsylvania courtroom where the lawyers tended to be fairly confident–or were at least good at faking it. Three judges entered through a side door

---

[96] The national broadcast news network in Afghanistan.

behind the defendants. For this first, high-profile proceeding, simultaneous translation into English had been arranged, with testimony and the judge's rulings appearing on a screen on the right wall of the courtroom. There was no jury in the Afghan system: the judges would act in a hybrid role of judge and interrogator before reaching their verdict by majority vote.

Trevanathan was worried. He was concerned the defense would present some last-minute argument, supported by a behind-the-scenes deal, killing the entire effort at the starting line. Trevanathan knew these judges only by a generally positive reputation, but they had been selected by the Chief Justice of the Supreme Court, and not with any input from Trevanathan or other Western stakeholders. Unlike with the police or prosecutors, EF3 had kept its distance when it came to judge selection. To do otherwise would lead to accusations of *undue influence*, which would open the court and its supporters to criticism that this was all just a NATO sham, rather than something representing the Afghan people. Accordingly, the colonel had no idea how they would handle the case. If they dismissed it, there was nothing he could do, and months of work would evaporate in an instant, as the diplomats in the courtroom would scurry back to their embassies to report that nothing had changed.

As Trevanathan expected, motions to dismiss were immediately made by both defendants, based on the grounds of illegal seizure of evidence—the red ledger—which was the key to the entire case. To Trevanathan's relief, these objections were peremptorily dismissed. "It is not a violation of Defendants' rights that they carelessly stored their illegal records," Chief Judge Massad ruled. *"Illegal records," I like that*, thought Trevanathan. *The Chief Judge doesn't sound very sympathetic.*

Given permission to proceed, the lead Prosecutor methodically presented the documentary evidence to the court, responding to the judges' questions. This was new to Trevanathan. It was almost as if the judges were questioning the Prosecutor as a witness.

Mr. Rajish, the former 225th Corps accountant, was called as a witness. He identified the infamous red binder, maintained by himself as a business record of the general's criminal empire under Rahman's direction.

An Absence of Faith

Defense attempts at cross examination went badly, as Rahman had apparently failed to disclose his assault on Rajish to his own lawyer. When Rajish was asked why he had flipped from supporting General Rahman to testifying against him, Rajish pulled a plate containing two false teeth from his mouth and described in detail how Rahman had kicked them out during a fit of rage. The impact of that testimony was apparent when Judge Salari, the other male judge on the panel, asked the defense attorney if he had finished trying to convict his client.

The prosecution had its own moment of drama, when they asked Mr. Rajish if the red ledger was an accurate record of transactions. He replied "yes," but then equivocated on two points. He reminded the prosecutor that the entries had been made by him only up until the time that General Rahman had kicked out his teeth. He could not testify to the accuracy of entries after that, which had been made in someone else's hand. Over a new defense objection to exclude the ledger, he confirmed that the later entries were of the same type as those he had personally entered, and consistent with the general's business practices, so the court allowed the full ledger into evidence. "Dodged a bullet there," Trevanathan whispered to Upton. "That could have gone either way."

Mr. Rajish then added a gratuitous detail that neither lawyer had noted previously. On the final page of the ledger, in handwriting Rajish did not recognize, someone had written in Dari, "For Azir." Sergeant Major Mahmood's head snapped up at that, his face darkening. He made his lawyer show him the exhibit. He bit his lip until blood was nearly drawn. "If he is not dead already, I will kill him," he muttered to himself, suddenly understanding how he had come to this end. He did not realize, however, that his words had been picked up by the microphone and translated onto the wall screen for all to see. His lawyer intensely whispered into his ear for Mahmood to shut up, but the damage was done.

Trevanathan was surprised when General Rahman testified. As often happens when indignant defendants take the witness stand, Rahman's testimony did nothing but squash any doubt of his guilt. Rahman tried to claim that he had been set up by Rajish and Mahmood, when they had taken advantage of his generosity and trusting nature to steal corps property and create a false paper trial leading back to himself. At his seat, Mahmood looked like he was going to snap the defense table in half, while Rahman wove his fantasy.

Rahman had not adequately anticipated cross-examination, however, where he was asked to reconcile his claim that the deliveries of corps petroleum to his gas stations were fabricated, with the delivery records originating from *his* gas stations that were obtained by the MCTF. His response that "they were thorough in setting me up," drew smirks from all three judges. Similarly, his inability to explain millions of dollars transferred into overseas accounts bearing his name did not help his cause, not when his official salary was 2,500 U.S. dollars per year. This latter evidence had become available through a new partnership between the MCTF and the FBI, coordinated by a U.S. Department of Justice attorney sent home from the Embassy in January, and to whom Trevanathan had reached out for help.

By the time the case focused upon Sergeant Major Mahmood's role in the alleged conspiracy, there was little maneuvering room left for his lawyer. Mahmood was a highly intelligent and brutal man. Although the right to remain silent did not exist in Afghanistan, he refused to answer questions raised by the judges. He recognized his predicament. If he attempted to shift blame to Rahman, as had been done to him, the general's powerful allies would ensure he never left prison alive. Or, if he did survive prison, he would not last an afternoon on the streets once released. *I will not grovel before these dogs,* he resolved. He knew his foot was in the snare, and he would bear the humiliation.

The sergeant major knew now that he had no one to blame but himself. He had made a mistake in bringing that private into his trust and now must pay the price for his hubris. *I was right that he felt he had nothing to lose. I miscalculated what that meant.* Mahmood was already crafting his plans as he sat at the defense table. *I will start over—first in prison. Build a new organization. Then, I will get revenge when I am released.* He had learned much while running the general's interests. He had also heard that if one paid a sufficient sum after being convicted, prison gates could still magically open after a prisoner had served a year or two. *I am likely facing four or five years. Patience. I will have my day.*

◇ ◇ ◇

After a four-day trial, the judges retired to deliberate. With the number and complexity of charges, Trevanathan did not expect a verdict until the following day, at the earliest. *If they come back too soon, it is probably a bad sign—an acquittal,* he reasoned, based on his experience. *It doesn't take much work to say, "Not guilty." You don't even need to support your reasoning. Just say that the prosecutor didn't bring enough evidence. But analyzing each charge against the facts and deciding that the prosecution has met its burden of proof requires deliberation, reasoning, and time. Further, here we have three judges, not one, so there's the possibility of disagreement and debate on a number of points.*

Trevanathan was sitting in the ACJC advisor's building talking to Upton about next steps to secure long-term funding for the court when Major Brandt popped his head in the door. "They're back," he announced. "They have a verdict."

"Shit," Trevanathan declared, glancing at his watch. It had only been 90 minutes.

"That's not good?" asked Upton.

"Too soon. They would have barely had time to make their tea and start reviewing the facts. This is a complex case with hundreds of transactions. I have a bad feeling it's a clean sweep against us."

"Well, let's go see. We've done what we can. It's up to them. Always has been, in the end," she commented stoically.

Trevanathan, Brandt, and Upton glumly resumed their seats in the courtroom. The judges were not yet present, but no one was talking. *Sixty people sitting in silence is a lot louder than it seems*, thought Trevanathan. General Rahman was staring at his hands. Sergeant Major Mahmood was glaring at everyone he felt responsible for his situation. "It's nice you've made new friends over here, sir," murmured Brandt, noticing the sergeant major's focus on his boss.

"Not now..." whispered the colonel.

The side door to the courtroom flung open and the judges entered as the court was called to order.

Chief Judge Massad spoke for the court, "The Defendants will rise," he ordered. Trevanathan tried to read his expression, but it was inscrutable. The other two judges were busying themselves with paperwork.

"In the name of Allah, the Just and Merciful, this court has done its duty under the laws of the Government of the Islamic Republic of Afghanistan and reached a unanimous verdict," Massad announced. This was the moment that Trevanathan and his team had worked for over the past year. He watched the Chief Judge's words appear on the wall, as if this historic moment was being narrated in real time. The moment where Afghanistan would choose a new path, or double-down on its corrosive culture of graft. The verdict as it came, was a shock to Trevanathan, which he had to have Brandt repeat afterwards.

Chief Judge Massad announced: "Major General Rahman, in Anti-Corruption Justice Center Case 00001, you are Guilty of Count One, *Treason*; Guilty of Count Two, *Fraud in the performance of government duties*; Guilty of Count Three, *Theft of government property in excess of six million, five hundred thousand Afs*; Guilty of Count Four, *Conspiracy to theft of government property in excess of six million, five hundred thousand Afs*; and Guilty of Count Five, *Bribery*."

Rahman's legs gave out before the verdict was finished being read, and he sank heavily into his chair.

"Although you have been afforded military counsel due to your position, this is a civilian court, not a military court. The Afghan National Army, through the Minister of Defense, is reserving the right to court-martial you, as well, for Dereliction of Duty and other military charges, in a future proceeding."

Sergeant Major Mahmood's verdict was then announced. He was found guilty in case Number 00002 of the identical crimes, with the addition of a sanction for contemptuous behavior in refusing to answer the court's questions. Neither man was acquitted of any charges.

The General's defense attorney rose to request a delay before sentencing to develop additional evidence regarding the general's outstanding military character. Judge Massad denied the request, adding, "General Rahman is not accused of being a bad military tactician. He is convicted of betraying his nation's trust. How many enemies he claims to have killed or how well he reads a map will have no bearing on this court's disposition."

The hearing then proceeded immediately to the sentencing phase, where both the defense and prosecution were permitted to present evidence and argument to sway the court as to an appropriate sentence. During the sentencing phase, General Rahman gave a meandering and self-aggrandizing speech to the court where he once again blamed everyone around him for his predicament. He discussed his many medals and made it sound as if his personal bravery was the sole reason that Afghanistan had not yet fallen to the Taliban. "I have made mistakes," he declared, "but they were not intentional. I was let down by others." By the time he finished, the judges were staring at the ceiling, bored.

The General's lawyer argued for a fine, and a term of one year of house arrest. Abdul Malik, the lead Prosecutor, pointed out in disgust that under that argument General Rahman would be paying the fine from stolen money, while living in a luxurious home bought with that same stolen money. He then nervously asked the court for a period of confinement for only five years, seeming to remember mid-argument his personal vulnerability in a country where the powerful are not criticized without consequences.

"Five years for treason? Is he shitting me?" Major Brandt stewed.

"Yeah, that's pretty weak," whispered Trevanathan. "I sense he's worried about payback. We'll have to work on that going forward. It's not going to impress the donors if you can steal millions, sell out to the enemy, and only get five years."

Sergeant Major Mahmood spoke briefly on his own behalf during sentencing. "I am a man. I will take my punishment like a man. I will not whimper like a woman." This bit of bravado, apparently directed at his co-conspirator, did nothing to help him with the third judge on the panel—Judge Amari—a woman.

Again, the judges recessed to consider their sentence, which apparently was a formality, as they returned minutes later, with their judgement. Judge Massad again spoke on behalf of the court.

"Major General Rahman, you have disgraced yourself and betrayed the people of Afghanistan. This court was founded to renew the rule of law in our troubled land, where the powerful have become used to no consequences for their excesses. Those days are over. For your criminal acts against the Islamic Republic of Afghanistan, you are sentenced to twelve years in prison and fined seventy-five million Afghanis. A written opinion will follow. This court recommends to the Minister of Defense that you be stripped of all rank and military entitlements and discharged from further service."

"Someone was paying attention," whispered Brandt whispered to Trevanathan.

Rahman's eyes were unfocused, and his chin trembled. He gripped his lawyer's arm tightly, and asked, "What does that mean?" The lawyer merely shook his head.

Massad continued. "Sergeant Major Mahmood, you have disgraced yourself, and betrayed your nation." Mahmood sneered as if bored with being lectured. "I knew your father. A great man. You have tarnished his family's name." The sneer disappeared. "This court sentences you to 22 years in prison and a fine of 50 million Afs. A written opinion will follow. This court recommends the Minister of Defense strip you of all rank and military entitlements and that you be discharged from further service."

Upton leaned toward Trevanathan. "Colonel, why did they sentence the sergeant to so much more time?"

"He forgot lesson number one: Don't piss off the judge. Look at her."

Upton looked up at the bench. The two male judges were gathering their papers and preparing to leave. Judge Amari was sitting with her glasses on the tip of her nose and her fingers steepled before her lips, staring a hole through the sergeant major. "That bit of grandstanding cost him ten years," observed the colonel.

After the court recessed and the defendants were removed, Trevanathan congratulated prosecutor Abdul Malik. "Has to feel good to get that first one under your belt," the colonel offered.

"Under my belt?"

"American slang, sorry. Means to get a tough job finished."

"Perhaps," the prosecutor said without emotion.

"This is going to send a strong message that there's a new way of doing business, and you were part of it," Trevanathan enthused. "This could be a historic moment."

"Putting generals in jail *is* new, Colonel," Malik observed. "There is no doubt. But…don't let that blind you that the way cases are going to be decided will change very soon."

Trevanathan was confused at Malik's dour mood. "Meaning?"

"Chief Judge Massad had dinner at the Palace last night. I don't think my challenge today was as great as perhaps you believe."

Trevanathan was stunned. "The President told him how to decide the case?"

"I did not say that, Colonel. I am a low-level prosecutor and would not be so bold as to put words in the President's mouth. I merely said that the judge had dinner at the Palace. You are a man of the world. You decide the rest."

All the sense of accomplishment drained out of Trevanathan. He paused before speaking, struggling to find words. "You…you realize that if this court…if it isn't allowed to function like a real court—one where the outcome isn't predetermined by pressure…or bribes—this government doesn't stand a chance, right? The people have had it with corruption. Your allies have had it. It doesn't matter whether the corruption is to let the bad guys go or to convict them—it all kills people's belief."

"Colonel, I have great respect for you. Your opinions are noble, but perhaps they do not fit Afghanistan. Like a nice suit bought in the wrong size. We have a different way here. The expectations are…different."

"Doesn't everyone want fairness?" Trevanathan asked.

Malik replied, "There is a story one of my professors used to tell that went like this: 'Once a man was chosen as the town judge. He took his place prior to the start of an important trial and spoke to the opposing lawyers. 'I have been given a bribe from each of you,' he declared sharply. Both lawyers looked ashamed and could not meet the judge's gaze. 'You, Ahmed, gave me 1,000 silver pieces. And you,

Abdul, gave me 500.' The judge reached into his drawer and pulled out a heavy bag, handing it to Ahmed. 'I'm returning 500 silver pieces to you, Ahmed, so we're going to decide this case fairly.'"

Malik paused. "*That*, my Colonel, is impartial justice in Afghanistan. Someone is always getting rich off the result. It is simply a matter of who and how much."

Trevanathan closed his eyes, biting back comments he knew would not be helpful. "You're right," he spoke slowly. "I shouldn't pretend to know everything the Afghan people want or expect. But I do know soldiers. I've worked with them all over the world. Yours have lost the will to fight. We see it every day from our drones and intelligence reports. The Afghan fighter is known throughout history as a fierce warrior. They defeated the British Empire, the Soviet Army, and have a proud history back to Alexander the Great. Today they drop their rifles and flee at the first sign of danger. What explains that other than a lack of belief in what they are fighting for?"

"You may be right, Colonel. But in Afghanistan, we put our faith in Allah, not in men. Trying to change bad behavior is an admirable goal, but one where you may be casting your seeds among the rocks. Now, if you will excuse me, I need to hurry home and hope my wife and children are still alive when I get there." Malik exited the courtroom, leaving Trevanathan to ponder if the past seven months had been a waste of time.

Chapter 36

Camp Resolute Support, Kabul, October 2016

Representatives at the Warsaw conference still had deep skepticism over the will of Afghans to fight corruption, but the conviction of General Rahman could not be overlooked. It had taken fifteen years, but a senior Afghan official had finally been held accountable for his misdeeds. It was a start. The donors agreed that perhaps Afghanistan was not as irredeemable as they had feared, and the ACJC's success suggested continued progress could occur. No donor country backed off from its security commitments to the U.S.-led mission, and each NATO partner signed on for another five years' funding.

Trevanathan shared the conversation with General Crist about President Ghani dining with Chief Judge Massad before General Rahman's trial. Crist decided that the allegation should stay between the two of them. "We don't know the truth, only the accusation, and we can't undermine the mission based on suppositions," Crist reasoned. "Besides, Bill, it would be naïve to think the Afghans would have a 'Come to Jesus' moment all at once on corruption reform just because they tried their first case." The multiple permutations of that statement in a Muslim country where Jesus sold stolen Cokes back to those he stole them from caused Trevanathan to laugh for the first time since his talk with Abdul Malik.

That there might still be hope for reform, despite the stink of political interference with Rahman's conviction, seemed warranted when the convictions of Major General Rahman and Command Sergeant Major Mahmood were soon followed by additional high-level convictions. The inspector general from the Ministry of Interior, who was filmed with a lapful of cash, was convicted and sentenced to eight years in prison. A high-level official within the Attorney General's office was indicted for fixing other cases. Those who had routinely embezzled international aid began to do a risk analysis. *Millions are nice, but what value is it if I'm sharing a cell with Rahman?* It was the deterrence effect that Trevanathan had hoped for when he first talked about putting heads on stakes when the ACJC was only an idea.

Ghani and his GIRoA Ministers now had the tools to maintain legitimacy in the eyes of their citizens, and more importantly, their soldiers. Those who undercut the welfare of the soldiers *were* being punished. Rations improved under the new 225th Corps Commander, and the desertion shuttle disappeared. But as he neared the end of his one-year deployment, Trevanathan had mixed feelings. *This only works long-term if the Afghans care enough to make it work,* he knew, but they had a chance. His redeployment clock and ability to influence matters was running out. In three weeks, Trevanathan would be out-processing back to the reserves and civilian life at Fort Bliss, Texas. He would be home with his family in Pennsylvania before Christmas. *It's someone else's turn to run the circus.*

Escaping his office for an hour, Trevanathan retrieved his clothing bag from the surly counter man at the laundry drop off window, perused the mini-PX to see it was still selling the same twelve giant jugs of protein powder that had been there since last November, and then climbed the adjoining creaky, metal staircase to his favorite haunt.

"Hello, Colonel, nice to see you again."

"Ms. Reed...."

"Jennifer."

"Jennifer, how are you? I assume this is no coincidence?" Trevanathan inquired of the CIA officer.

"Who is to say what is or isn't a coincidence, sir?" she teased.

"Well, today I'm getting my coffee first, as I've found our conversations leave me without my afternoon boost."

"What a coincidence, sir. I happen to have an extra latte and a chocolate croissant right here at my table."

"Like the serpent in paradise," Trevanathan joked. "But thanks. Now how can I be of assistance to those who shall not be named."

"I'm hoping we can be of assistance to each other."

"Sounds ominous. What do you have?"

"I have to be quick, because in 28 minutes, some new *friends* from Swedish intel are coming up those stairs looking for you. They're delayed at the security gate right now with a false dog alert."

"OK..."

"They will be proposing to you that the ACJC not pursue a case against a man who works for the National Security Directorate— Khalid Naguib. They're going to ask that his case be dismissed for reasons of national security, as Naguib is a key operative in infiltrating an ISIS cell that has taken root near Jalalabad. They think that two of their Swedish nationals—aid workers, they claim, but who knows— are being held by that cell somewhere near the Paki border, and that Naguib is key to ultimately obtaining their release."

"I recognize that name. He was selling military electronics that were being turned into remote timers on rockets fired into the city. MCTF found his house full of restricted tech. Pretty tight case. But I only helped get the ACJC set up: I don't control what cases are brought or not brought against anyone."

"I think you're understating your influence, Colonel."

"Seriously, I don't have a role in that," Trevanathan insisted. "MCTF investigates the cases. The ACJC prosecutor decides whether to charge, and the judges decide if there's enough evidence. I set them up to be able to do that—hopefully without being bribed or threatened to dispose of cases improperly—which sounds a lot like what we're discussing doing right now, as a matter of fact."

"Someone once said that 'you can calculate the worth of a man by the number of his enemies.' Well sir, under that assessment you're about the most valuable man in Kabul these days. You and I both know there's billions being misdirected within GIRoA and the only person those people fear is you and your court. No one else is holding them accountable."

"Let's assume that's true for sake of this discussion. You're making my point. The second I start using my position, such as it is, influencing a case, even to help get some hostages released, I've corrupted the system too. I just spent a year setting up a system to avoid that."

"And what if it's your country that is making the ask?"

"What do you mean?"

"The Swedes are coming here to make the ask. But we don't want Naguib touched either."

"Why?"

"I can't say."

"If you can't say, then I don't care. Let's not be cute."

Reed sat quietly, fingering her coffee cup, her wheels turning.

"I'm sure you've done your homework," Trevanathan interrupted. "What do I do in the civilian world?"

"You're a judge, of course. Pennsylvania."

"Exactly. Judges don't put their finger on the scale and fix outcomes because somebody needs a favor, or it might help the war effort. The fact I'm wearing this pickle suit doesn't change that."

"This isn't exactly the same situation as Pennsylvania."

"And it never will be, so long as Ghani, every GIRoA politician getting rich here, and you intel guys justify cutting corners to meet your needs. If we want the long-term benefits—stability, the rule of law—we gotta' let the Afghans experiment with an honest court system. You can't be honest on Monday but call a time-out on Tuesday to fix a case so you can accomplish some unrelated political or military goal. If Ghani wants to pardon someone after the fact, that's his call, and he has to justify that to the Afghan people. But you can't break the system before it has a chance to work, or the whole thing just falls apart."

Reed said nothing.

"You know that even though most people in this country don't like the Taliban medieval justice crap, they take their disputes to Taliban judges anyway, because they know they'll get an honest verdict. Think about that—they trust the terrorist system of justice more than their own government because it isn't fixed. That's a bigger problem for us in the big picture of winning this war than whether Naguib ends up charged or not. The bad guys are preferred by the population because their laws don't shift depending on who is on trial. We're losing that war of trust."

An explosion reverberated from the direction of the Presidential Palace. Small arms fire could be heard stuttering shortly thereafter. Trevanathan and Reed continued their conversation, as a plume of black smoke rose in the distance.

"I admire your principles, Colonel. I really do. But the court you're trying to protect may not be as insulated as you think. Ghani is going to fire your General Baz, because he's doing his job a little too well. Did you know that?"

"Really? How did you know?"

"That's a question you can't ask someone in my line of work, sir."

"OK, how about, what does replacing Baz accomplish for him?"

"Five of the six high-profile perps that have been convicted in your court…"

"…not my court."

"As you wish. Those five have all been either relatives or political allies of Ghani. Rahman was his cousin; did you know that?"

Trevanathan shook his head.

"Another—one of those MOI generals—was the brother-in-law of a senior player in Parliament important to Ghani. Both those cases have brought Ghani considerable political heartburn from his supporters who wonder why he is not targeting the corruption surrounding Abdullah Abdullah. So, they are pressing for a new head cop who is more *user friendly* to their side. Baz is the sacrificial lamb."

"Unbelievable," said Trevanathan, shaking his head. "The games never end."

"I'm just saying, sir, you've given them their best chance, and they have to make it work or not. But there's two Swedish aid workers who aren't going home if Naguib ends up in the dock, and we have our own *insider* interests with him as well. Think about it."

"Think about whether I want to join Ghani in stacking the deck? Whether to piss away what we worked to build the foundations of this year? No thanks. I'm not deaf to the stakes, but the long-term damage to this country's future is too great. Now, I'm out of here before I have to give the same civics lesson to our Swedish friends. Good luck to you." The colonel walked away, knowing that this was the last time he would patronize The Blue. *The price of coffee has become too high.*

◊ ◊ ◊

Trevanathan knew before he left the country that he had to confirm whether the information about General Baz being relieved was true or not. He invited the general to lunch at the pizza parlor on Camp RS, which he knew Baz liked. Baz arrived promptly at noon, a punctuality rare among Afghan officials. The two men greeted each other warmly, recognizing the difference each had made. Baz had helped give the ACJC life and Trevanathan had given Baz's men their pride and purpose back. They sat down at a table at the back of the restaurant.

"Is your family well?" Trevanathan asked.

"Yes, thank you. They have settled near Stuttgart. It appears I may be joining them soon after all." General Baz gave Trevanathan a knowing look.

"I heard rumors."

"Remember what I said about reformers becoming martyrs in this country? We will both be lucky if our penance is merely exile."

"I can deal with exile," Trevanathan laughed.

"I, as well. Although I wouldn't object if you could get my million dollars back from the Ministry." Baz grinned.

"I'll submit the usual million-dollar refund forms," joked the colonel.

"I have brought you something as a memory of your tour here," Baz said, handing a tissue wrapped package to Trevanathan.

"That's very kind, sir," said Trevanathan, opening the package. Inside were the green and purple ceremonial robes of an Afghan chief, of the type most memorably worn by Hamid Karzai during his many television appearances while he had been President. "These are beautiful, my friend. Thank you," said Trevanathan, not mentioning the irony of being dressed like the man many believed launched the virus of corruption within the Afghan government.

"Be safe. Salaam, my colonel, and thank you."

"Salaam, Sir. It has been my privilege. Be safe as well."

Chapter 37

Camp Resolute Support, Kabul, October 2016

In his final days in Kabul, Trevanathan tried to get General Baz reinstated as MCTF commander, simply to prove that the ACJC was operating above politics. But the hourglass ran out on Trevanathan's deployment before he could accomplish that final goal. For each soldier, the day comes when your helicopter is waiting at the LZ and it's someone else's turn to be in charge. Trevanathan knew it was the inherent nature of trying to do complex, long-term projects through one-year deployments, but it made it no less difficult to let go.

Trevanathan was, of course, anxious to get back to his family and "normal life" where a night's sleep didn't include the background music of automatic weapons and incoming rockets. But he also wondered what backsliding would occur as soon as he left and his GIRoA counterparts felt they could backtrack on their commitments. Commemorating one meeting with an Afghan official who had called Trevanathan a "bully" when he rejected their lengthy proposed timeline to start the court, the colonel's staff gave him a going away plaque that dubbed him the "The Bully of Afghanistan."

The night before his flight, Trevanathan met one last time with Jodie Upton and Major Brandt at the U.K. Embassy, to celebrate their success and discuss the ACJC's future. Each of them knew that the progress attained so far could easily be undone without daily vigilance by the court's Western advisors. Their meeting place was a pergola by the now-drained embassy pool. Above them, snow was building once again in the mountain passes surrounding Kabul, bringing the fighting season to a welcome end for 2016.

"So, are you ready to go, boss?" asked Brandt, leaning back in one of the faux wicker seats.

"Not a bit. I'll be up until 0300 packing the rest of my gear. The Ops section was badgering me all day to get the COM some new slides to support his latest GOGI[97] of a new multi-agency task force to directly fight corruption here. Bringing back FBI, DEA, Interpol, etc., to investigate corruption."

"They're going to have Western cops fight corruption directly, instead of having the Afghans take the lead?" Brandt asked.

"They didn't ask me if I agreed. I guess I'm old news now. They just asked for slides of how to possibly structure it. General Crist is reassigned in Europe now, and the new CSTC-A commander is just doing what the old man tells him. I warned him last week that if we start chasing the next shiny object, and doing enforcement for the Afghans again, it gives them an excuse to not follow through on the ACJC."

"We hadn't heard about this," Upton commented, wrinkling her brow.

"That's the other point I made to the new guy. We just spent a year cobbling together international support for the ACJC, and now if there's a shift now to a U.S.-centered enforcement effort, it will send conflicting signals. Are we expecting the Afghans to step up and be responsible, or are we going to keep wiping their backsides for them?"

"To say the least. What did he say?" asked Upton.

"He agreed and then pointed out that the COM had four stars and he had two, so he would do his best to influence matters, but couldn't guarantee anything. It was underwhelming."

"Can you speak to the COM?" Upton asked, increasingly concerned.

"Not the way the Army works. I don't get to jump over my chain of command and go knock on the COM's door to tell him I think his idea is shitty. Besides, helicopter tomorrow, remember?"

"This sounds like a rerun of something they tried a few years back," said Brandt. "One of your predecessors, some Army JAG

---

[97] GOGI – General Officer Good Idea. A tongue-in-cheek term employed by subordinates on a general's staff to describe the latest whim passing through the general's mind that will cause them untold hours of work, often leading to little benefit or effect.

general developed a plan for a huge American counter-corruption unit, with its own vehicles, equipment, and hundreds of pax. The org chart got so bloated that it never got off the ground, and the next commander just stuck a fork in it."

"We're masters of following the same gameplan—even if it takes us over a cliff. In some ways I think we're a victim of our own success. No one was paying attention to corruption last fall," said Trevanathan, "and now that the ACJC has gotten some positive attention back in Washington, they're defaulting back to the usual military approach—throw personnel and money at the problem and hope it equals victory. We did this thing on a shoestring budget—a couple million in UK money, really—so now the belief is that *bigger* will make it *better*."

"Except they're not talking about making the ACJC bigger, are they?" asked Upton. "This is an entirely new idea—another complete shift in direction, when what is needed is consistency on what we've built over the past year. Our people investigating or charging Afghan bad actors accomplishes nothing in terms of changing Afghan government culture. It feeds into the Afghan view that we can't focus on anything for more than a year and perpetuates an 'us versus them' mindset that will likely create more GIRoA duplicity. As soon as the Afghans sense we're distracted by some new idea, they will gut the ACJC. They must realize that don't they?"

"What day is it?" joked Trevanathan. "On Mondays we realize that. The rest of the week we chase the squirrel."

"Very concerning, I must say," said Upton.

"How much longer do you have?" Trevanathan asked her.

"Sixty-three days, although there may be the possibility of an extension. Depends on funding, as usual."

"And you?" Trevanathan looked at Brandt.

"Thirty-two and a wake-up, sir."

"The new guys are going to have to hit the ground running," Trevanathan said, shaking his head. "That's a lot of turn over." He paused. "Wait a minute, why are you here longer than me?" he said to Brandt. "You were here when I arrived."

"Better looking," Brandt dropped the line without missing a beat. The three of them were wiping tears from their eyes for the next several minutes.

"Oh my, I almost forgot," announced Upton. "I know you are not permitted to have alcohol under your General Order Number One, Colonel, but I do have something to celebrate the end of your tour." From beneath her chair, she pulled a covered plate, under the dome of which was a glazed Christmas cake. "It's my mum's rum cake," she declared proudly. "Had them whip it up in our kitchen–they owed me."

Plates were passed, and no one mentioned the rocket trails arching across the horizon. Someone else was being shot at, so it wasn't worth remarking upon. "Ahh, this is wonderful. Thanks very much," said Trevanathan, relaxing for the first time he could remember since arriving a lifetime ago. "I'm sure the alcohol burned off in the baking process, so no one can complain."

He took a large bite of cake, and his eyes began to water, as a familiar burning sensation went down his throat. He coughed, "That's some cake," as Upton beamed.

"I didn't say that the rum was added *before* baking," she laughed.

Brandt was finishing his second piece with great enthusiasm, before the colonel had finished his first. "Save some of this for Hawthorne and the boys," the colonel said, "or we're going to have a helluva' time explaining to our security detail why we reek of rum after our *business* meeting here."

"A bribe, sir?" Brandt grinned.

"We've learned from the best!" Trevanathan replied.

◊ ◊ ◊

Colonel Bill Trevanathan left Afghanistan on October 26, 2016. The colonel replacing him had arrived early enough that the two of them had a week together to exchange relevant information and get the new EF3 Director up to speed on why it was important. However, the Pentagon then decided to send a National Guard brigadier general to lead the growing EF3 section instead, but he would not be on the ground for another month after Trevanathan left theater.

Trevanathan and the brigadier spoke twice by phone, but the brigadier was interested in new ideas, including embracing the COM's new counter-corruption task force, so the connection frayed. Once again, most of the insider knowledge gleaned by the incumbent through a year of hard lessons would slip between the cracks and need to be relearned the hard way, as the Afghans slow-rolled the FNG.

Major Charles Brandt and Jodie Upton rotated home shortly after the colonel, leaving a significant void in the leadership that had launched the ACJC. General Crist was already gone, reassigned to an Army staff job in Europe. As soon as the institutional memory at Resolute Support and the UK Embassy was gone, the Afghan Attorney General backed out of his commitment to use polygraph results to remove corrupt prosecutors. "It is insulting to our honor for you to presume that we are corrupt," he piously declared. Bribery within the ACJC prosecutor's staff immediately increased.

The Afghan judges also refused to be polygraphed. "It is insulting to our position as judges for an external power to require we prove our honesty," the Chief Judge insisted. The number of convictions against Ghani allies declined, and Abdullah supporters were increasingly targeted.

With the firing of General Baz, the Major Crimes Task force was no longer the impartial investigation body the ACJC needed. President Ghani replaced its commander annually, ensuring a lack of continuity in the important position, and incumbents thereafter knew they were on a tight leash held by the Palace. Heavy briefcases and parliamentary visitors once again began to appear at MCTF headquarters to "discuss" important cases. The number of investigations of serious military corruption declined, as did prosecutions. Nearly forty percent of MCTF investigators failed their polygraphs in 2017, suggesting ongoing deception, and yet were allowed to continue working, in violation of the founding agreements between Resolute Support, the international community, and GIRoA, as preconditions for establishing the institution. As with so many reforms initially agreed to by GIRoA, the ACJC increasingly became toothless.

Trevanathan, Upton, and Brandt stayed in contact, and tried to be helpful with background context on the ACJC effort when asked, but questions from their successors were few. The lasting lesson GIRoA politicians gleaned from the ACJC was not the importance of corruption reform, but rather how they could exploit it for political and economic benefit. They unwisely continued to ignore the renewed discontent among their citizens and soldiers, who were once again paying for the excesses of Afghan politicians.

In one of their later exchanges in 2020, after the initial positive impact of the ACJC had wilted, Jodie Upton raised an uncomfortable question in an email exchange with her old partners, "Did we help improve things, or did we create a Frankenstein's monster?"

Trevanathan remained convinced GIRoA had been given every chance for success with the ACJC and chose to fail. "We gave the Afghans the chance to succeed after everyone else, including our own Embassy, had written them off in 2015. They chose to squander their chance."

Brandt, in his usual direct manner replied, "Even the best surgeon can't cure greedy and stupid."

Upton, the thoughtful conscience of the group, remained less certain. "I feel the U.S., NATO and the international community still bear some responsibility for this—pouring all that unregulated money in for years and fostering a culture of impunity in the first instance. It's the Afghan people who now bear the cost of those bad policies."

The three of them would continue to discuss where the responsibility lay for years to come. Whoever was right, as the snow began to melt in the high mountain passes of the Hindu Kush in spring 2021, Afghan politicians, distracted by their illicit riches and power, ignored a long recognized military maxim—"The enemy gets a vote."

Chapter 38

Unknown Location, Western Pakistan Border Region, January 2021

The flow of money from Pakistan, China, Iran, and Russia, as well as profits from prior years' poppy harvests, placed the Taliban in an opportune position in 2021. When the Taliban senior jirga[98] met along the Pakistan-Afghanistan border to plan the upcoming fighting season, its leaders were frustrated. Victory had been in their grasp so many times over the past five years, only to be snatched away by superior American technology. Victory would be theirs someday, but would any of them live to see it? Several, including Sirajuddin Haqqani, were on the U.S. terrorist list, which meant their last moments on earth would likely be the sound of an incoming Hellfire missile from an unseen drone. It was only a matter of when, as the leader of the Pakistani Taliban had learned two years before.[99]

The issue facing the jirga over the several days was where they would place their main effort in the upcoming fighting season. In the south? At the northern provincial capital, Kunduz, a perennial target? Or should they focus on removing the infection presented by the growth of Daesh[100] within their borders? The group of twelve sat in a circle of cushions on the floor of a large cave. Platters of roast goat and steaming rice sat before them, next to generous plates of naan bread.

"The Americans have no stomach left to fight," declared Haqqani. "Their fat President signed the papers to withdraw. A man cannot

---

[98] Jirga – a traditional gathering of Afghan elders, often for the purpose of reaching consensus on important decisions.

[99] Pakistani Taliban chief Mullah Fazlullah was killed by a U.S. missile in June 2018 in the border lands between Afghanistan and Pakistan, while riding in a vehicle.

[100] Daesh is the Arab name for the terrorist group ISIS (sometimes referred to as ISIL), which fought both the Taliban and NATO in Afghanistan.

leave and stay at the same time. We should focus on maximizing American casualties to hasten their departure. They have become afraid and cower behind their walls."

Many in the room murmured their agreement.

"That may be true," observed the Commander, Supreme Leader Akhundzada, who had assumed overall control of the Taliban upon the death of Mullah Omar in 2016. "But any such attacks can be accomplished by our special detachments. The question before us is where to focus the large numbers who have recently joined us. We cannot leave them idle, and movements will have to begin as soon as the snows melt." Again, the group murmured approval at the words from their leader.

"Where, but also to what effect?" asked Mullah Akhund. "We occupy district and provincial capitals every year, like migrating birds, but we do not hold them. The soldiers scatter, the police strip off their uniforms and hide, but a month later they are back in the same positions after the crusaders smash us from the skies."

"Perhaps we should not fight this year," said a young man seated to the left of the Supreme Leader. This time there was no murmur of approval.

"Explain," said Commander Akhundzada, turning to stare at Mohammad Yaqoob, the young son of Taliban founder Mullah Omar. A person of his youth would not normally have a role at such a senior jirga, but his renown as a fighter at the age of thirty had led to his promotion as the Taliban's leader of military operations.

"We must always ask the question, 'And then what?' for any proposed military action. Do we fight for the sake of fighting or to accomplish an objective?"

"The answer is obvious," replied Mullah Akhund. "We fight to drive out the foreign infection and return our people to the correct path."

"Agreed," said Yaqoob. "So, what will lead to that end? Does forever trading cities back and forth while our fighters die do so?"

The side conversations had a distinctly deeper tone to them now.

Yaqoob ignored the discontent and continued. "I was visiting Hajji Khan last month and met a former soldier who now treats our wounded. I was advising their doctor to prepare for many casualties this spring. The soldier laughed, which I took as insolence at first. But he apologized and made a comment that has stayed with me. He asked, 'Why do you make the same attacks every year and suffer so many to die, when you can just pay the army not to fight?'"

"I was shocked by the simplicity of his observation. I told him that I do not believe they are so corrupt that they will surrender for money. He replied that I should study my enemy more closely."

The jirga hummed louder with side discussions.

"Commander Haqqani, may I ask, how many men do you need to take a position from a platoon of the ANA?" asked Yaqoob.

"It depends. What they call a platoon often has only twenty-four men. In the east, I need maybe six. Here in the south, probably four or five."

"Three to shoot and two to carry away the dropped rifles, am I correct?" Yaqoob joked. The gathering laughed appreciatively.

"You are not far from the truth. We have all seen this," said Akhundzada, sipping his cup of tea.

"The enemy is tired. The government soldiers are slaves who want to go home. The Americans want to leave. What if that former soldier is right? Should we approach the problem differently and instead of repeating past campaigns, simply pay them not to fight?" asked Yaqoob.

"That is a lot of people to pay, my brother," observed Mullah Akhund.

"We don't need to pay everyone. We embrace the game those in Kabul have taught so well–loyalty has a price, and everything is for sale. We find the right people in the right decision-making positions and ensure that they take our contribution instead of dying for a government that doesn't value them."

"There are many who will fight," observed Haqqani. "Too much blood has been spilt."

"Those who fight will be dwarfed by those who do not. No one wants to be the last to die," said Yaqoob.

"And the Americans?" asked Mullah Akhund.

"The Americans beat us when we concentrate on one or two objectives," replied Yaqoob. "Their army is made for that—to have us mass on a central target and then pound us from the skies. But if there are no pitched battles, no sieges, no large concentrations of our men, but simply a melting away of their allies, then the entire garment comes apart at the seams. Their superiority will be diluted. They cannot bomb a man who is not fighting—they have failed at destroying us for twenty years when we go silent."

The kernel of an idea had been planted. The idea would be argued and debated in the following days, but the audacity of buying their way out of the war, letting their enemy's greed consume them, rather than repeating another year of predictable and unsuccessful combat, had captured the jirga's imagination.

◊ ◊ ◊

When the final Taliban offensive launched in June 2021, there were stalwart ANA commanders who stood their ground and fought back—the Afghan Special Forces among them. Some disparate units had not lost their will to fight due to good leaders who prioritized their troops' welfare. But those units were few in number and defeating them was not the Taliban objective, an error that President Ghani and his military advisers failed to recognize. Those elite units were engaged simply to fix them in place, making them protect irrelevant strongpoints, while the Taliban flood swept around them toward Kabul, as the garment that was GIRoA came apart.

A larger number of officers and senior noncommissioned officers of the Afghan army accepted their Taliban-funded separation packages and laid down arms. The ANA enlisted soldiers quickly picked up on the scent of defeat and headed home by the tens of thousands. There was no one to stop them. Some soldiers even switched sides, tired of watching their comrades die while their superiors became rich. The Americans were already deeply engaged in the military withdrawal negotiated under the prior U.S. President and were not about to reverse course. First one provincial center and then the next fell to the Taliban with little resistance. Afghan military checkpoints were abandoned with vehicles, weapons systems, and ammunition left behind. As predicted, no one wanted to be the last casualty fighting for something no one believed in.

In southern Afghanistan, a medic who had served in both Afghan armies moved slowly north, little surprised by what he saw.

Chapter 39

South of Kabul, August 2021

"Hurry. I am waiting to kill you."

Daniyal smiled at the gruff tone of Muhammad, who was chastising him from the bed of the Toyota pickup they had "liberated" from a municipal compound near Qalat. The daily threat of his demise had become a ritual between Daniyal and Muhammad. Muhammad never openly displayed anything remotely demonstrating friendship. Daniyal learned that Muhammad tolerating his presence—without delivering a cuff upside his head—was the strongest endorsement he might receive.

Daniyal finished relieving himself beside the road. "Oh, most merciful Muhammad, please take pity on your dishonorable servant. My life is yours to forfeit," Daniyal mocked as he climbed into the truck bed.

Muhammad tried to continue his menacing glare, without success. "Always the fool," he observed. "Drink some water," he continued, handing a skin to Daniyal.

They were roughly eighty kilometers south of Kabul. They had been on the road for nine days, walking and driving northward, always expecting to encounter the Afghan army, or a checkpoint of paramilitary forces, but finding nothing. The countryside was littered with discarded ANA uniforms, vehicles, and weapons.

Daniyal had changed in the past five years. He was more muscular. He now wore a beard that he did his best to keep somewhat short, so it did not interfere with his medical duties. "Another of your womanly ways," Mohammad chided.

"Yes, of course," Daniyal countered, "all of the women in my family wear short beards."

Daniyal looked healthier than he had while with the Afghan army. His diet had improved, and his austere life in the Taliban camp had developed a tough shell. But he still looked as if a strong wind might carry him away. His skills as a medic had grown and earned him grudging respect amongst his captors. Daniyal could handle everything from easing gastric illnesses to removing shrapnel. Muhammad had suffered for years with severe pain in his empty eye socket: Daniyal reduced that by administering a mild saline solution every day.

Daniyal's medical education came through a combination of mentoring from Dr. Baseer, learning by necessity amidst the chaos of combat, and by studying medical books he had found in a mobile clinic looted for medical supplies.

Muhammad banged on the roof of the cab. "Let's go," he ordered Baseer, who was driving. "We need to see the Hajji tonight."

A boy of roughly nine years appeared over the berm at that moment, yelling in Dari, "Death to Ghani. Death to the Americans."

"Everyone's a politician," observed Baseer.

"Give me bread," yelled the boy. "Ghani is a donkey." Enjoying the laughter he had earned, the boy ran to the truck.

"We have no bread to spare, halak[101]," said Muhammad. "Be off."

"My name is Tamir, not halak," declared the boy defiantly, sticking out his chin.

Muhammad hesitated at hearing the boy's name.

"Give the boy some bread," suggested Daniyal. "We have plenty since that last compound." He looked down at the boy. "Tamir, where are your parents?"

"Dead. Soldiers."

The two words told the entire story. The men did not bother to ask how or why his parents had died. It did not matter.

"Where is your village?" asked the doctor.

"Zaydabad, near Kabul. I've been walking four days."

"What did you say your name was?" questioned Muhammad.

---

[101] Pashto for "boy."

"Tamir. My mother named me to become rich one day and support her." He paused, looking at the ground. "But none of that matters anymore."

"Can you shoot?" asked Muhammad.

"I can learn," declared Tamir, again lifting his chin. "I fired my grandfather's musket once…but it knocked me down."

Daniyal looked at Muhammad. He was about to speak when Muhammad cut him off. "Get in the truck, boy. You have the honor of joining the forces of the Islamic Emirate of Afghanistan."

"What are we doing?" asked Daniyal, confused, looking from Muhammad to the doctor and back again. Muhammad had never shown the least interest in children, orphans or otherwise. The country was full of them. The doctor waggled his head uncertainly from the front seat but had learned not to second-guess Muhammad.

Muhammad beat on the roof again. "Let's go," he yelled, "before every stray in the countryside is in the back of this truck."

The boy squeezed into a space between Muhammad's knees and several ammunition cannisters. Daniyal tore off a piece of hard bread and handed it to Tamir, who attacked it with enthusiasm.

"Give him some water, too," ordered Muhammad. Daniyal shrugged in reply and passed the boy the water skin.

◊ ◊ ◊

The men spent the remainder of the day driving north. They fell in among other vehicles—HMMWVs, cargo trucks, pickups, and donkey carts—all packed with Taliban fighters. The pull of the capital was strong, and the roads were jammed. The fear that they would be ambushed by the Afghan army was gone, validated as they passed one empty checkpoint after another. There was increased activity as they came near Kabul, but not of the type expected. A stream of planes was in the skies, fleeing south and west. The might of Western airpower paid little attention to the flood of Taliban forces converging on the capital, focusing instead on getting their citizens out of the way before the play's final scene began.

What little remained of the Afghan National Army was now scattered groups of young men tramping along the road in the opposite direction from the capital. No uniforms were visible, but a sure sign these were deserting ANA soldiers was their inability to make eye contact with the triumphant Taliban fighters.

Other than an occasional derisive call, no one accosted the soldiers of the broken army. The orders from Mohammad Yaqoob were clear. "No one is to harm any member of the Afghan security forces who does not fire on them."

When the boy, Tamir, began hurling insults from the bed of the truck at the passing soldiers, Muhammad cuffed him and told him to be silent. "We will not reawaken a defeated foe through stupidity," Muhammad instructed. Hajji Khan's directions had also been clear before the final push on the capital began: "We want to make it easy for them to go home. Don't give them an excuse to fight."

Yaqoob's winter plan had worked masterfully. Corruption had been the grease keeping the gears of the Afghan government turning for twenty years, and now it was the catalyst bringing that regime to an end. The war had been sustained by promoting fear among the people of what the Taliban would take from them if they returned. Over time, suffering presumed future indignities under Taliban rule did not seem appreciatively worse than the actual daily humiliations suffered under Ghani's government. *Death and poverty under Ghani's eternal war versus oppression and poverty under the Taliban?* Not a great choice, but a distinct choice for many.

In the back of the truck, Daniyal was nervous. *This is all too easy,* he worried. *Surely, the Americans are going to come.* While others in the growing column smiled and occasionally let loose with a burst of celebratory fire, he was tense, waiting for the American fighter-bombers and cruise missiles to turn the packed highway into a flaming graveyard. *Allah, whatever my fate, may I see my mother one last time before I die?* he silently prayed.

They reached the outskirts of Kabul as darkness fell. An ancient religious site known as the Guldara Stupa had been chosen for their rendezvous point, as they hoped the Americans would be reluctant to bomb a historic shrine. Thousands of armed men milled about, not sure what to do. The advance on the capital had been so swift that they had outrun their orders. There were fights, as different factions competed for sleeping space and food. *It is easy to know what to do when someone shoots at you—you shoot back,* Muhammad pondered. *But, when only one side shows up to a fight, idleness can consume an army.*

Muhammad settled them into a utility shed near the road, being careful to chain their truck to the outer wall. He did not know many of these other men who were milling about and did not want to walk again if someone took a liking to their truck. Near midnight, a messenger from Hajji Khan found Muhammad, with a summons to their leader's tent.

"It looks like the Americans are leaving," explained the Hajji. "But the news is too good to accept based on news reports alone. They could lure us in and slaughter us with their drones and aircraft. Many planes are going out, but that means many planes are coming in as well. I need to know if those planes are coming in empty, or if they are reinforcing."

"Yes, Hajji," replied Muhammad.

"The airport—their *Karzai* Airport," he laughed, "I think it may soon have a new name. I need you to get on the large hill above it. The one here." He pointed to a steep ridge running parallel to the main runway on a map of the city. "Count the aircraft coming in and going out tomorrow, and track what they are unloading. We do not want to fight the Americans now. We want them to leave. But we need to know their capabilities in case this is a trick."

"Yes, Hajji."

"Maybe you can take Brother Daniyal. He knows Kabul. He might help you get there quicker."

"That is a wise thought, Hajji, but I wish to respect his decision to not act against his old army. He has been with us long and done much of value. But we still need his services as a medic. He is more valuable treating our men if there is a fight than sitting on a hillside with me."

"That is your choice. Pick someone who will not stand out, that can relay messages."

"I have such a person in mind."

"Good," the older man said. He reached behind himself and brought out a brand new American M4 rifle. "This is for you. It belonged to an ANA commander in Logar Province. He was persuaded to not obstruct our advance with a sizeable gift. He provided this rifle as a show of his good faith. You have served with honor. I want you to have it."

"Thank you, my Hajji, I am honored."

"Now you must move. Kabul is a large city, and you must get to the other side before dawn. Be careful. The army and police have largely melted away, and some of our people are already in the city. But those moving at night will be suspected by everyone."

Chapter 40

Kabul, August 31, 2021

Daniyal stood before Bahar Tower, where he had lived with his mother and siblings before being thrown into the back of a truck by an ANA press gang. It looked taller than he remembered, and some of the windows were replaced with plywood, but it was home. The city was quiet. Few people were on the streets. The last American plane had left the day before. Everyone was holding their breath to see what came next from the new, former rulers. Seven years had passed since he had stood on this spot. *It feels like that was someone else's life,* thought Daniyal.

"So, what do you do now?" asked Muhammad, having returned with Tamir from tracking the evacuation flights from the airport.

"I need to see if my mother is still alive. Or where my brother and sisters are, if she isn't."

"And then?"

"I'm not sure. I haven't had a choice about my life in years. Staying alive for this moment has been my goal. Now that it's here…going forward…I have no idea. The Americans are gone, so where will money, food, *anything* come from? What of you?"

"Fortunately for you, I have decided not to kill you today," replied Muhammad, the corners of his mouth twitching.

"That's very good of you," replied Daniyal smiling. "But what are you going to do?"

"I've been offered a job in the new Interior Ministry. Security chief at the airport."

"Sounds impressive."

"It sounds like death. Shall I spend my days looking through people's dirty underwear for alcohol? I'm going home. To my village. This city makes my skin itch."

"And then what?"

"I found this stupid child." He gestured toward Tamir, standing on the opposite street corner kicking a bag he had crumpled into a ball. "I have to teach him to be a man. He doesn't know how to shoot or ride. He has never herded goats or slaughtered a sheep. He may as well be a woman."

"Hmm."

"You should be a doctor," Muhammad declared. "Or with that beard, maybe a nurse."

Daniyal smiled, but noticed Muhammad seemed uneasy, as if waiting for something.

"You are mostly worthless, but you have a gift as a healer. Do not ignore your gifts," said Muhammad, looking at the sky. "You…you have helped many."

"And the country? What happens now?" asked Daniyal, raising his palms in question. "Who is even in charge?"

"What country?" replied Muhammad. "I am Pashto. My home is Ghazni. Shall I worry about lines drawn on a map by infidels a hundred years ago?"

"You know what I mean. There has been so much suffering, and many of those claiming victory today are not fit to run—*whatever this is*—of which Ghazni is a part."

Muhammad ignored the geography lesson. "Fit? What does that mean? Were the last ones fit? They abused you, killed your friend, killed my brother, and orphaned that boy. Were they fit because they could lie with smooth tongues? The world said so, so I do not know this word 'fit.'"

Daniyal heard the passion in Muhammad's voice.

"Those we fought with may not govern well," Muhammad conceded. "I cannot change that. I didn't fight for their philosophy. I fought because the others killed my brother."

Daniyal nodded. He recognized that every man had his own reasons for fighting. The bully Ali, Muhammad, Baseer. None of them cared for the power struggles that had driven this war for a generation.

Muhammad stopped himself, realizing he was revealing too much. "I must go," he said. "I'm already making speeches. If I stay longer someone will make me a governor." He reached into his worn leather bag and pulled out a pair of gloves. "Take these. The next time you desert they'll keep your hands warm."

Daniyal accepted the gloves from Muhammad. They were hand stitched from goat leather, with a thick fleece lining. Daniyal saw that they had been made for him. Nine fingers.

"Thank you, I…"

"I have no time for your nonsense," the Ghazni man interrupted. He grabbed Daniyal roughly by the shoulders, kissing him on both cheeks. "Go…*go*…*live*," he whispered into Daniyal's ear before releasing him.

Muhammad turned and walked away, an American rifle bouncing on his back.

Epilogue

President Ashraf Ghani fled Kabul in early August 2021, mere hours after promising the Afghan people he would fight to the death alongside his countrymen. He abandoned his remaining security forces and left for a new life in the United Arab Emirates. He justified abandoning his people claiming, "I believed it's the only way to keep the guns silent and save Kabul and her six million citizens." Since there were few guns firing at that point, his excuse was received as thin gruel. He denied accusations made by some members of his government that he left the country with over one hundred million dollars in Afghan government funds. That figure remains disputed.

The U.S. Special Inspector General for Afghanistan Reconstruction estimates that Ghani fled with a mere $500,000-$1 million in cash, but that estimate also does not include what government funds, if any, may have been previously moved overseas, *just in case*. It is not subject to serious contention that he left a broken country, without a sustainable economy, and deserted a traumatized nation that had reluctantly placed its trust in his leadership—a nation that was nearly picked clean by its now former leaders.

The dying continued, despite Ghani's claimed selflessness. Afghan children died from unexploded ordnance. Thirteen U.S. Marines and several dozen Afghan civilians died when an ISIS terrorist blew himself up at the Abbey Gate to HKIA airport during the hectic final days of the American evacuation. Three days later, the U.S. military, worried about a repeat attack, preemptively targeted a suspected ISIS car bomb in heavily populated Kabul with a Hellfire missile. There was no car bomb, but there were seven Afghan children and three Afghan civilian adults who were killed for being in the wrong place when American generals got twitchy.

The American evacuation at HKIA airport was a fiasco, with U.S. troops doing the best they could under horrific circumstances, trying to help Afghan allies who would suffer under the Taliban if they remained. A comprehensive discussion of that operation is beyond the scope of this book, but this story would be incomplete without noting it as a final denouement of U.S. inter-agency feuding that undermined the Afghanistan mission for years.

As soon as the Taliban took Kabul, they began going door to door looking for persons, including Afghan translators, who had aided NATO. The State Department announced that its personnel in Kabul would be fully engaged in aiding our Afghan allies evacuate, to avoid another Saigon-like debacle. This was a farce, with the Embassy's primary focus being on getting its people out of the Afghan capital as quickly as possible. Afghan allies were told that they would receive a call from U.S. Embassy personnel when they should come to the airport for emergency visa processing. Those calls could not be made by State Department staffers who were already winging their way to Germany and their next assignment.

What happened, instead, was a modern day cyber-parallel of the WWII Dunkirk evacuation. Private individuals, contractors, Afghan veterans, U.S. military officers now serving elsewhere, and other U.S. Government employees who had worked in Kabul, stepped up to coordinate evacuating as many Afghan allies as they could. Instead of small boats crossing the English Channel, it was phone calls, texts, and emails between U.S. forces holding the HKIA perimeter, Afghan allies (including many with dual U.S. citizenship) hiding in buildings around the airfield, and their personal contacts and advocates around the world that enabled so many to get out. There were still many left behind.

The Taliban demonstrated the future for Afghan women, as Taliban guards surrounding the airport perimeter used whips on women and children trying to reach the safety of the U.S. forces perched on the airport wall. Those U.S. forces were ordered not to intervene outside the walls of the airport and could only witness the spectacle playing out. Regardless of the desire of American troops to help, it still took the courage of individual Afghans to run a cordon of beatings and abuse to reach the safety of the airport, dashing past Taliban sentries and then being physically pulled up and over the walls by U.S. Marines and Soldiers as Taliban sentries glared from mere yards away.

At first, Army and Marine units used vetted evacuation lists to allow only pre-approved Afghan personnel over the wall and onto the airfield to be evacuated. As the days went by, however, and the bedlam outside the walls increased, the process for selecting who was allowed into the airfield became more arbitrary. The lists were incomplete; State Department personnel who could help resolve disconnects had left; the Army did things one way, and the Marines another. The process changed daily, and instructions from Washington did not match up with the reality on the ground.

Escape for Afghan VIPs and translators often depended upon whether they knew someone able to pull strings within the Pentagon. This led to Afghan translators who had loyally served NATO for years, GIRoA officials, and even U.S. citizens with their families, being left behind if they lacked connections, or worse yet, trusted that *the process* would take care of them.

On August 30, 2021, a day before the agreed upon departure deadline negotiated between the U.S. and the Taliban, the last planeload of troops from the U.S. Army's 82nd Airborne Division left Hamid Karzai International Airport.

The Afghanistan War was over.

Afterword

This book is a novel, and its dialogue and storyline are fictional, although inspired by the Afghanistan War and the impact of rampant corruption upon the lives of the Afghan people. The story of Daniyal presents the privation Afghan soldiers endured during twenty years of GIRoA corruption and civil war. The concurrent story of NATO's efforts to build the institutions and will to counter corruption, in coordination with the British Embassy, are based on actions taken seeking to reverse the declining political legitimacy of GIRoA.

The U.S. and its NATO allies recognized that their ability to leave Afghanistan without a political-military disaster was directly linked to the willingness and ability of the Afghan military to take over the fight against the Taliban, supported by the Afghan people. The ANA and MOI leaders showed little interest in doing so, however, leaving the U.S. and NATO trapped in an increasingly toxic relationship with GIRoA, somewhat akin to a marriage where one partner repeatedly promises to change a self-destructive behavior, yet never does.

After twenty years of ruinous behavior, the leaders of the Government of the Islamic Republic of Afghanistan had by 2021 rendered themselves more despised in the eyes of its citizens than the enemy it was sending its young men to fight. In the everyday calculus of war, the soldiers of Afghanistan decided they would no longer take a bullet to defend a system they didn't value. The average Afghan, particularly those in urban centers, did not want Taliban rule. They had seen that movie before—intolerance, poverty, and cruelty. But they wanted the government of President Ashraf Ghani and his minions even less—especially when the price of the GIRoA kleptocracy was their lives, and the lives of their sons, decade after decade.

The Western effort to give the government in Kabul a veneer of legitimacy was perpetually a patchwork quilt of good intentions and stumbling execution. NATO's attempts to establish a stable, reliable regional ally were hobbled by its own lack of continuity in personnel, diminishing political interest by member nations to effect generational reform, and a codependent sense of entitlement by Afghan officials who believed that the Americans and their friends would tolerate their misbehavior regardless of how much aid money they stole.

Afghan government corruption was not collateral to its functioning, nor did it evolve incrementally from a few bad actors: it was a core policy decision by GIRoA leaders to bind disparate tribes and competing political factions together in a loyal patronage network. In a country where decentralized power along tribal lines was historically and culturally preferred, regional power brokers were convinced to support the central government in Kabul by being bought.

The Afghan National Army, an organization built by the U.S. military and marketed to U.S. taxpayers as a modern fighting force able to defeat the types of terrorists who attacked them on 9/11, was therefore, at its core, a for-profit business that existed for the primary purpose of enriching its stakeholders. It was an ongoing criminal conspiracy, dressed in uniform, that evaporated within weeks of being called upon for the first time to defend its nation without American intervention. This was not a reflection on the lack of equipment or training provided by the U.S. and NATO, as much as it reflected disinterest by GIRoA leaders more interested in profit than victory.

The Afghan government embraced a "play for a tie" mindset, so foreign to an American military culture focused on battlefield victory. Perpetual conflict with the Taliban served a valuable purpose for Afghan politicians: keeping billions in aid dollars flowing from NATO, the U.S., and other donor nations. The war kept an otherwise destitute Afghanistan treasury solvent, and its leaders rich. Senior Afghan officials did not want this fiscal smorgasbord to end, as the country had no other income streams of significance. During the timeframe of this story, 80% of the Afghan national budget was funded by its Western patrons, without which the economy could not survive. Conversely, the United States wanted the quickest possible victory so that it could exit and refocus military and fiscal resources on other geopolitical threats. Two sets of allies pulling for opposing outcomes explains much of the lack of success in Afghanistan.

Once corruption takes root, it is never fast nor easy to remove. Committing resources to a sustained strategic plan over a period of years mandating the Afghan elite stop stealing from their own people was the only approach with a chance for GIRoA to regain legitimacy. *Chance* is the key word. Experts can legitimately argue how likely success ever was with counter-corruption initiatives in Kabul, when Afghan politicians never saw reform as a desired goal. Instead, *reform* was just politically convenient theater, necessary to keep Western dollars flowing.

There was legitimate concern that the establishment of the ACJC might give President Ghani another weapon with which to undermine his political opponents. If, for the sake of argument, we accept that criticism, then it's fair to ask, what other course was there at the time, other than allowing GIRoA to keep stealing aid money with impunity? There were no other policy alternatives being presented by the critics, beyond empty statements such as, "It's up to the Afghans to figure this out." In late 2015, the NATO alliance and other international donors, as well as the U.S. Embassy, were in a state of resignation, ready to give up trying to reform GIRoA excesses, and searching for a palatable way out of the Afghanistan quagmire. The ACJC never had a guarantee of success, but it always had a better chance than giving up.

The claim that efforts toward accountability and corruption reform would trigger GIRoA's collapse was a fallacious argument, but a convenient one, often made by those focusing on the exits. This was the political equivalent of watching a train wreck without taking responsibility for having helped lay rotten tracks in the first place. Proponents of this policy did not consider that the smaller evils they had been willing to enable over the years would gradually accumulate, until they mutated into a corrosive force that hollowed out the Afghan military and rendered GIRoA illegitimate.

Afghan politicians and generals were indeed corrupt, but U.S. bureaucrats taught them there were no consequences to being corrupt. For the NATO team, the early focus was on destroying Al Qaeda often to the exclusion of broader concerns, such as promoting rule of law and deterring criminal conduct. By the time NATO began to focus on corruption, with an on-again, off-again approach,

GIRoA's culture of corruption and impunity was too entrenched to remove.

By analogy, if a parent were to catch their child shoplifting and "punish" them by buying them a new bicycle, what future conduct should the parent expect? Reform or a repeat of past misbehavior? GIRoA politicians and generals stole an estimated 25-40% of every aid dollar provided to them[102], with the sanction for their misconduct being that their Western allies continued to give them $8 billion annually in aid. Theft described in percents doesn't sound like much: translated into tens and hundreds of billions in stolen aid over twenty years, it was the theft of the century. There's little room for self-righteousness in telling this story—just frustration that the sacrifice of so many, including nearly half the Afghan population that was not yet born on September 11, 2001, went nowhere but to a circuitous return to Taliban rule.

There was no decisive battle that returned the Taliban to power. No *Tet Offensive* to demonstrate military capability and political will. No *Dien Bien Phu* moment to humiliate the ruling power. Taliban forces were regularly obliterated on the battlefield every time they attempted to stand against NATO forces. But the Taliban did not need military success to gain ultimate victory: they needed only to survive long enough for the Afghan government to rot from within.

Those who served with the U.S. military in Afghanistan know that there wasn't one campaign or even several campaigns over twenty years. There were twenty "one-year campaigns," where the priorities and goals frequently shifted, depending upon changes in who was

---

[102] Those engaged in counter corruption efforts in Kabul during 2015-16 most often cited a figure of 25-40% of Western aid being embezzled. Measuring the actual number is understandably difficult, with various media and Government sources quoting figures between 2010 to 2021 that ranged from 18% to over 50% of Western aid being stolen by Afghan officials. SIGAR 2016 Report: Corruption in Conflict. September 2016, https://www.sigar.mil/pdf/lessonslearned/SIGAR-16-58-LL.pdf, https://www.voanews.com/a/south-central-asia_us-reportedly-lost-19-billion-fraud-abuse-afghanistan/6197383.html, https://www.washingtonpost.com/graphics/2019/investigations/afghanistan-papers/afghanistan-war-corruption-government/

the NATO commander in Afghanistan, the CENTCOM commander overseeing the entire region, the President of the United States, and the nature of his congressional majority/minority. Sometimes Afghanistan was central to our "War on Terror." Often, it was *the forgotten war:* inconvenient and expensive. Al Qaeda, with Taliban hospitality, had coordinated to kill thousands of Americans on 9/11, yet the Afghanistan War soon became secondary as we invaded Iraq for reasons that now seem increasingly foggy with the passage of time. Once Bin Ladin was killed in 2011, American Democrats and Republicans took turns playing politics with why the war was still going on, each blaming the other side. The lesson learned by corrupt Afghan officials from this vacillation was they didn't need to take any reform mandates seriously, as the issue the Americans were passionate about today would likely be forgotten news by next year. And they were right.

The militarization of Afghan life through an economy dependent on war perpetuated a culture where living for today, and ensuring one had the means to get out (again)[103] if the war went badly, become part of the nation's DNA. Peace was an illusion; war was perpetual and profitable. Salaries paid by the Americans were many multiples of what could be made on the local economy. The uncomfortable question no one asked aloud was, "What will happen to the riches when the war ends?" Yet, everyone thought about it, recognizing the status quo was unsustainable and someday Afghanistan would have to stand on its own feet.

The survival instinct is strong. Discussing long-term economic development and the importance of the rule of law with an Afghan bureaucrat who stands a realistic chance of being killed on his way home by a suicide bomber has messaging limits[104]. As an Afghan

---

[103] Many national leaders fled when the Soviets invaded in 1979, and those who returned fled a second time when the Taliban began their draconian rule after the Soviets retreated. Accordingly, keeping an eye on the door and having assets stashed away to ensure a safe escape and comfortable life in exile were ever-present considerations for Afghan officials.

[104] Taliban and ISIS suicide bombers would specifically target GIRoA workers and officials, detonating explosive vests among groups of low-level civilians leaving work, as they exited narrow gates from their government compounds, or aboard shuttle buses known to carry workers outside the

politician expressed to this author, "After forty years of war, we are a nation of traumatized people. It is hard to get us to think past tomorrow." So, they didn't. Ensuring there was enough money to stay in power *today* was the goal. Ensuring there was enough money to be able to flee *today*, if necessary, was real. Long-term political legitimacy, economic development, and military readiness? *That's what the Americans were for.*

Many of those responsible for the collapse of GIRoA are still living—some trying to reach an accommodation within the country, some in hiding, and some living lives of excess abroad on the riches they pilfered from the Afghan people. Several are trying to rewrite history to deflect responsibility, seeking to cast themselves as martyrs of a rapid U.S. withdrawal, rather than recognizing themselves as catalysts for the greed that metastasized and consumed their nation.

To point fingers at any one individual, or a small group within GIRoA, however, is overly simplistic. There was a complex web of actors, who through their avarice, fatalism, and denial of responsibility allowed a government built on the core principle of personal enrichment to bloat and then ultimately collapse from the contempt it engendered within its citizens.

For twenty years, American politicians worried that a failure to deliver victory in Afghanistan would result in a storm of political backlash, with themselves in the center. Their concerns were unwarranted. After a couple weeks of embarrassing news coverage of Americans and Afghan allies evacuating from Hamid Karzai International Airport, the fall of Afghanistan was largely met with a geopolitical shrug. New wars in Eastern Europe and the Middle East elbowed concerns over Afghanistan to the curb. Yet, to those who had served in the conflict, or lost loved ones on foreign soil, the Afghanistan War was a life-defining event. As it was for the international actors who spent years trying to give the Afghan people a better future, and to the thousands of Afghan translators and other individual wartime allies the U.S. abandoned during their

---

Kabul Green Zone. The mere act of going to work could easily cost one their life on any given day.

evacuation. *Again.*[105] These stakeholders, who bought into the Afghanistan conflict with their lives, deserve more of an explanation for why the war ended with a whimper, than the muttered expressions of regret received thus far. The excuses mouthed by U.S. Government officials, explaining away the defeat as an implausible aberration were disingenuous at best. "The truth is, this did unfold more quickly than we had anticipated,"[106] President Biden observed, parroting the obvious.

"The Afghan forces melted away without explanation,"[107] Secretary of Defense Austin thinly rationalized, as if it conveyed some insight that abused, deserting troops tend not to write a "Dear John" letter explaining their departure. Both politicians dodged the core truth. The Afghan security forces indeed melted away, but for reasons that were foreseen, predictable, and fully known. Feigning surprise is a convenient strategy for distracting voters who are not paying attention in the first place, but it is also side-stepping the truth. History deserves better and so do those who sacrificed for a better outcome.

Afghanistan was going to fall the moment the U.S. stopped being its defense insurer, whether that was in 2021 or 2041, due to the recurring, conscious, self-defeating choices made by Afghan politicians. Those who focus upon the speed of the Trump-negotiated and Biden-executed withdrawal of American forces as a causal factor for Kabul's collapse are missing the point. Investing in a corrupt system without mandating change inevitably leads to corrupt outcomes.

When the primary threat to NATO forces in Afghanistan by 2015 - 2016 was not the Taliban, but an Afghan soldier—*an ally*—who would shoot their American, British, and other Western allies in the

---

[105] While the distinctions are many, the similarities of a third world insurgency chasing the United States to the exits in Vietnam in April 1975, after the U.S. backed a corrupt and unpopular regime in Saigon, are difficult to ignore. As is the lack of an organized plan to ensure that locals who had allied themselves with U.S. against the enemy were evacuated in an organized manner.

[106] Statement of President Biden, August 16, 2021.

[107] Testimony of Secretary of Defense Lloyd Austin before Congress, September 21, 2021.

back, the miniscule dividend on twenty years' Western security investment was clear. When each spring fighting season after 2014 brought the routine surrender of district and provincial capitals to smaller units of Taliban forces as apathetic Afghan soldiers dropped their rifles and fled, a quick and bitter end to the Afghan war was not hard to predict. In fact, as soon as the Americans announced their imminent withdrawal, it became the likeliest outcome.

The current iteration of the Afghanistan War ended on August 30, 2021, with the evacuation of U.S. forces from Kabul and the assumption of power by the Taliban. The Interior Ministry was quickly assigned to Sirajuddin Haqqani as its new Minister, placing one of the world's most brutal terrorists at the head of the internal security apparatus. The Afghan people awoke to a nation where half the population is now denied education, the economy is faltering, illicit opium exports are again a major financial engine, and the people are unable to feed themselves. Whether the West will be able to ignore or abide such an inherently unstable international actor remains to be seen. But that is a book yet to be written…

Appendix: U.S. and Afghan Ranks

U.S. Army Enlisted

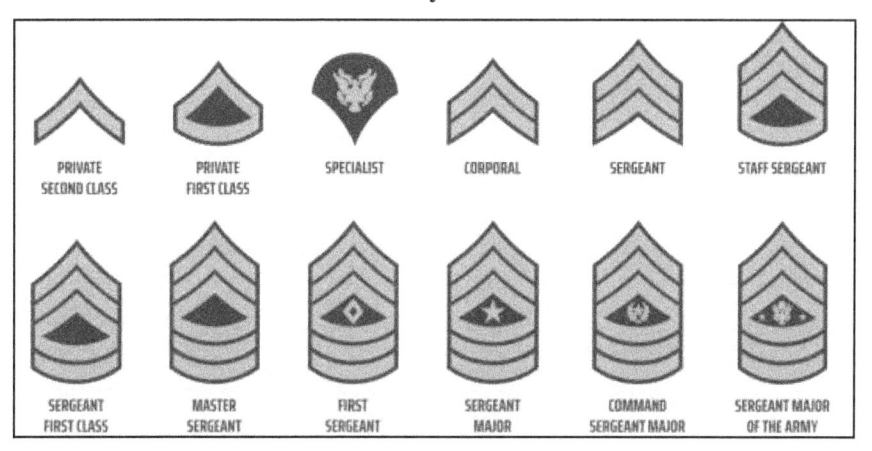

U.S. Army Commissioned Officer

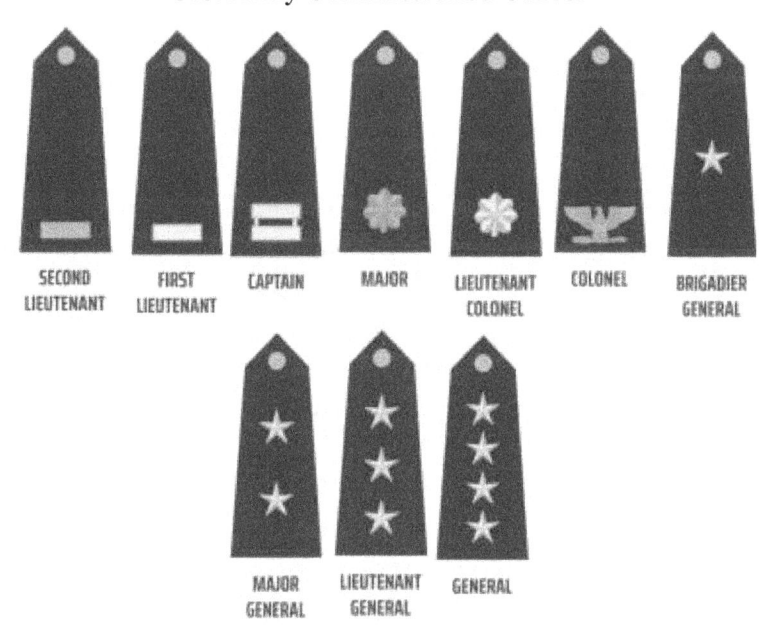

383

In conversation, American generals are addressed as "General _____," with their last name, without distinction to their specific rank. For example, to a major general, one says "Good morning, General Smith," or simply, "Good morning, sir." Similarly, all ranks of sergeant are referred to as Sergeant _____ (last name), except First Sergeants and Sergeants Major, where the complete rank is expressed. E.g., "Good morning, Sergeant Major Smith." This demonstrates why shorthand references to certain ranks are made during the story, but other ranks are fully expressed.

Afghan National Army (ANA) Enlisted Insignia

Rank group	Senior Noncommissioned Officers (NCOs)		NCOs			Enlisted
Afghan National Army	First Sergeant	Staff Sergeant	Sergeant	Corporal	Lance Corporal	Private (No insignia)

Those receiving the rank of Command Sergeant Major in the ANA wore a pin designating the rank, which originated with the U.S. Army (below):